Four Mile Tree
A Jamestown Legacy

By

Ann Belser Asher

Four Mile Tree

A Jamestown Legacy

By Ann Belser Asher

ISBN: 0-9776035-0-4

12 11 10 9 8 7 6 5 4 3 2

Lockwood Heritage Publishing
P.O. Box 15135
Chevy Chase, MD 20825

Library of Congress Cataloging-in-Publication Data

Asher, Ann B.
Four Mile Tree

Chapters

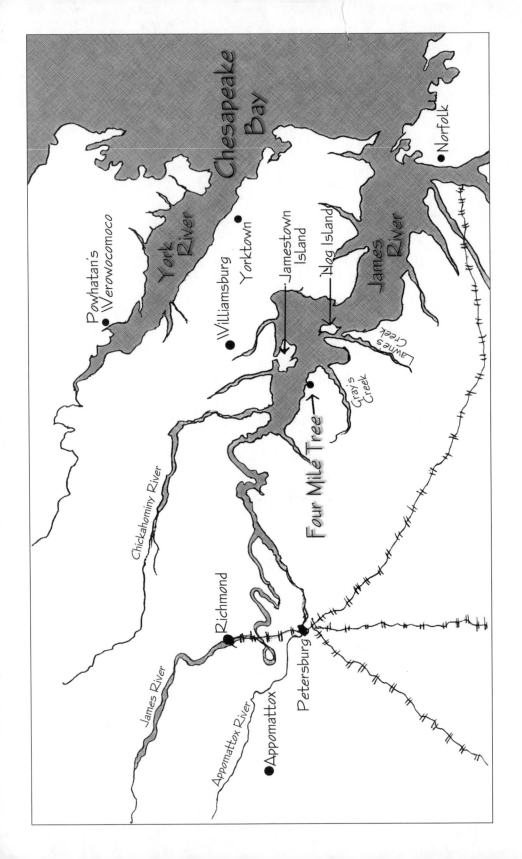

For my husband Norman,
Caroline, Blaine, Norman and John

PROLOGUE
1991

1

The number the Surry County operator gave me rang six times before there was an answer. Only a keen interest in making the connection kept me from hanging up.

"Hello," a female voice said, barely shielding a tone of annoyance.

"Mrs. Young?"

"Ye-es?"

"This is Angela Blount calling from New York. I wrote to the Reverend Young last spring asking if I could tour Four Mile Tree this fall. He sent me a gracious note extending an invitation and suggested that I call a few days before I planned to come." I paused for a response, but there was none. "I- I'd like to drive down from Washington on Monday, October twenty-ninth, if that would be convenient for you."

"I got the message you left yesterday on my answering machine. I haven't had time to discuss it with my husband yet," Mrs. Young said. Her words were sharp and her tone of voice icy.

"Should I call back in a few days?" I asked. Another pause ensued.

"I'm thinking of other things today. Tonight's the opening of the opera season in Richmond. House guests are coming."

"Oh, I'm sorry. My call is ill-timed."

"Never mind, I guess the twenty-ninth would be as good a time as any. He'll be here."

"Great. I've been looking forward to this all summer. Would two o'clock suit?"

"It most certainly would not. I take a nap every day after lunch. You're one of the Browne descendants aren't you?"

"Yes, a direct descendant of Colonel William Browne who put the plantation together in the seventeenth century."

"A Browne descendant came here once demanding to go upstairs. When I told her we weren't prepared to have guests go upstairs, she said she was going up and right that minute."

"How rude. I'd never do such a thing. But the Reverend's letter to me was most cordial. I thought..."

"That woman comes every year."

"But,..."

"There must be a thousand Browne descendants by now."

"Probably."

"They all think this place belongs to them. This isn't my house. I run it for the Browne family and the Historical Association."

"Oh, Mrs. Young. No. No. Of course the house belongs to you. I wanted to see it, because I'm writing a story about the Indian massacre of 1622, and some of the action took place on what was originally part of the Four Mile Tree property. It was called Pace's Paine then. I'm particularly eager to see how the property sits on the water, to figure out where the first shelter might have been and -."

"Pace's Paine is on the Mt. Pleasant property now. Much of the original 3,000 acres of Four Mile Tree has been sold off. You're a writer?"

"Yes, or I should say trying to be. I'm working on a novel of early Virginia. It's centered in Surry County on the south side of the James."

"We're on the wrong side of the James. Anyone will tell you that. However, Williamsburg has become so commercial. It's totally ruined all the lovely homesteads on that side. Now they are threatening to replace the ferry from our side to Jamestown with a bridge. I don't see how they can even consider it with the national deficit so horrendous, but we can't be sure. A bridge would totally destroy our peace and serenity. The government thinks it owes it to the people who live here. They say the people on this side are deprived. The plan calls for the southern end of the bridge to be at the end of our property line. Four Mile Tree would be decimated for sure. You live in New York, Miss Blount, but I don't know anything about your connections or ideas."

"Well," I said swallowing hard.

What does she want to hear. I feel like the Fuller Brush man with only one small toe in the door. Scrambling to think of something meaningful, I blurted out, "I'm a staunch environmentalist if that's of any interest to you. I'm treasurer of our state's chapter of the Nature Conservancy. Do you know about the work of the

Conservancy?"

"Um-m, yes. Very interesting. Friends have told us that's the way to go." There was another pause. "Could you come at three-thirty on the afternoon of the twenty-ninth?" she asked. Her voice sounded lighter in tone and softer.

"Oh, yes."

"I'll look forward to meeting you. And do bring some water-proof boots. It's lovely walking along the beach. We've had very little erosion."

"Is there any evidence of the tree?" I asked.

"What tree?"

"The Four Mile Tree."

"No, none."

"Do you know what kind of tree it was?"

"What kind? No. Probably a cypress. That's the kind that grow along the waterfront. Imagine. Me a lumberman's daughter, and I don't even know what kind of a tree it was. Perhaps, I'll learn something from you, Miss Blount." She laughed. "This might work out rather nicely."

"Thank you, Mrs. Young."

"Till the twenty-ninth."

"Till then."

II

The day was clear and warm as I cruised along the Colonial Highway heading toward Jamestown to catch the three o'clock ferry for Scotland Wharf on the south side of the river. However, the sun, low in the sky, gave evidence that the chill of winter would soon drift in to blanket the countryside.

Good I didn't wait any longer to make this trip. Summer green of the fields has already faded to a pale ocher hue. Why didn't I get to this sooner. What a gamble. Writing much of my novel using the old plantation as the setting for most of it without even seeing the place. Pictures and descriptions from the Historical Association can't tell the whole story. Still I'm nervous about my welcome. They never sent directions. I know what intersection it's near, but with neither road shown on the road map. Lucky I brought their number. I'll call when I get to Surry. Don't want to miss seeing it in the daylight. Where's my peace offering?

Reaching across the seat my fingers encountered the fancy bow of a prettily wrapped box of Godiva chocolates giving a boost to my sinking confidence. Cars ahead began slowing as they came to a small bridge traversing College Creek, a stream that dumped its contents into the larger James River on its way to the Chesapeake before flowing out to sea. A line formed as I approached the Jamestown pier. I checked my watch. Twenty minutes to wait. The old fort at Jamestown and the visitor's center were not visible from the pier, but just ahead on the left, I could see, tied up at an adjacent pier, two of the three replicas of the ships that had brought the original settlers to Jamestown in 1607.

Might as well get another look at those weird, top-heavy crates. Never cease to be astounded at what they managed to accomplish. I released my seat belt and climbed out of the car to get a closer look.

Just two of the three ships were there, the *Discovery* and the *Susan Constance*.

What flimsy little things they are. Hard to believe any level-headed person would voluntarily get into such a contraption for an eight- week crossing of the Atlantic Ocean. Things must have been mighty tough or mighty boring on the other side. One hundred fifty-four people on the three ships. Where did they all stand much less lie down to sleep. No way they could have lured me onto one of those things no matter what I might have been running away from. Bounce, toss, pitch and it's not even a windy day; only a few ripples on the water.

The ferry whistle blew calling me back to the car. From the ferry dock, on the south side, I drove into the town of Surry, found a pay phone and called the Reverend Young.

Returning to my car, I tried to memorize the directions I'd been given, started the engine and headed down a country road that twisted to circumvent Gray's Creek. Turning once, as directed, I traveled a couple of miles further coming dead end into a old plantation. A plaque over the doorway of the house read, Cross Creek 1635. The property was closed; the windows shuttered.

Damn. I did exactly what he said. Did he purposely misdirect me?

My chest gave a heave of disappointment, then a resolute deter-

4

mination came forth taking control of my actions.

I'll go back to the turn. I can't have gone wrong before that.

Several miles back, I made a second turn toward the river, ending at another dead end at a farm facing the water. Fortunately it was an operating farm with the owner standing nearby.

"Hello, there," I called, making a valiant attempt to put a pleasant smile upon my face. "Can you help me? I'm looking for a place called Four Mile Tree."

The farmer ambled over to my car, gave a lengthy appraisal of me, then, perhaps finding me unthreatening in appearance, decided to be helpful.

"You've come a good piece too far. Go back past the burned timber on the right, then through the woods, past the just harvested peanut fields and a little farther on you'll see an unmarked black mailbox on the left with a drive opposite it on the right. That's the entrance to Four Mile Tree. It's almost a mile to the house after you turn in. Good luck," he said turning his eyes away.

Five minutes later, I found the mailbox and the entrance.

That unmarked mailbox and no sign reading Four Mile Tree should tell me something. I'll figure it out later.

The drive from the road to the river seemed long as uncertainty added tension with each turn of the wheels. Suddenly the handsome, four-chimney, antique house, partially hidden by towering trees, came into view, like a princess peeking coyly from a curtained window at an intruder.

Heavens. It's lovely.

The entrance drive took a sudden sharp right then turned back bringing the car up to a previously unseen side of the house.

Gad. What's this.

A disappointing picture emerged. What had looked beautiful from a distance looked run down and unattended to from close up. The side walls of an old cistern lay in a crumbled mass, giving the place a seedy appearance. Stunned with disappointment, I failed to notice a large black Labrador coming round the house until he began barking ferociously. Running straight to my car, he threw his front paws up to the closed window on the driver's side.

Thank heavens the window is closed. I'm not going to budge from this fortress until someone comes out to call that beast off.

What's taking them so long? They have to be expecting me.

After what seemed like an interminable wait, the front door opened and a pleasant looking gentleman with an amused expression on his face appeared, called off the dog and walked toward the car.

"Ah, Miss Blount, you found us," he said with a broad smile and a slight bow. "It took you a bit longer than it should have from Surry. I hope you didn't get lost."

"I did make two wrong turns," I answered, forcing a gracious smile, "but I'm quite delighted to finally be here. I was surprised, though, to find no name at the entrance or on the mailbox."

"Ah, yes," he said, "but that's all part of our plan. You see we live a quiet, retiring life here."

The Reverend was dressed in neat slacks and a rather stylish - looking sweater that appeared to be hand knit. His face had a pleasant, intelligent appearance and an affable look that gave reason for one to think he was fond of people. He didn't look like a man who desired a retiring, quiet life.

"Would you like to see the outside or the inside of the house first?" he asked.

"The outside, please. The sun is already low. Can I see the river view first?"

"By all means. It's the best thing the old place has to offer."

"The Reverend and I strolled out a hundred or so yards, maneuvering ourselves through a labyrinth of ancient boxwoods to the edge of a sharp slope that fell off to the water's edge. The view was breath-taking. Looking across the river and then to the east and west, I could see no sign that man's activities had done anything to despoil its original beauty. My host was aware of my emotional reaction and became immediately cooperative in answering all my questions. We discussed the river's currents, the two hundred and fifty-year-old boxwoods, the architecture of the house behind us and the source of its ancient building materials.

"When do you think the house was built?" I asked.

"Mid 1740's, according to the experts," the Reverend said, "but the house is built on a previously existing foundation, one the same width but shallower in depth. The first house may have burned or just been torn down to make way for the new. We don't know."

"My ancestors must have lived in the first house," I said. "My line moved elsewhere before the 1740's. Still, I find it quite thrilling to stand on this ground knowing that my ancestors lived here nearly four hundred years ago."

"I bet," the Reverend said, nodding his head and giving me a warm, friendly smile.

Talking with the Reverend was easy. Moment by moment he seems friendlier. He finds me to be pleasant company after all. What were they expecting?

"Can you tell me more about the river," I asked. "As I mentioned in my letter, I'm writing of William Pace's nighttime canoe trip to Jamestown to warn the settlers of the impending Indian attack in 1622. How long do you think it took him to paddle from here to Jamestown?"

The Reverend sighed. The question had doubtless touched a sensitive nerve. "That depends on the flow of the current at the time," he said. "I can assure you he had a hard time of it if the current was going the wrong way no matter how pumped up he might have been. Last week I paddled from here to Scotland Wharf without much trouble. I had planned to call my wife to pick me up there, but remembered her sacrosanct afternoon nap so I decided to paddle back against the current."

"How long did it take?"

"The better part of the day. I'm lucky to still be alive."

The thought made me wince.

"Can I see the old cemetery now?" I asked.

"By all means. It's around front, or I should say back. The river side was the front of the house in the early days. Most visitors came by water then."

Walking around the four-chimney, Georgian house, I noticed with surprise that there was not a single flower bed anywhere on the place. The grass looked vigorous and was neatly mowed. The old boxwoods looked stately and handsome. The trees towering above gave a look of grandeur to the house, but nowhere on the grounds was there evidence of a recent effort to enhance the landscape.

What kind of a woman would live in the country and not tend to a single flower bed?

A few hundred feet or so to the right beyond the present front of the house, we approached the Browne family burial grounds. The old cemetery was at least a hundred feet square in size and was enclosed by a beautifully constructed, double brick wall, four feet in height.

"I have a disappointment for you here," the Reverend said. "You must have learned from the Historical Association that this cemetery has the oldest legible tombstone in Virginia. Unfortunately, a preservationist from Winterthur, who shall remain nameless, decided to clean it up by scrubbing it with Brillo. Now it's no longer legible."

"How dreadful. From Winterthur. That's hard to believe."

The Reverend seemed hesitant, deep in thought. "Took a course at Winterthur, I should have said."

As we entered the enclosure, I was shocked to see only two above-ground sepulchers and two tombstones. The rest of the large plot was covered with three-foot-high grass. No other markers of any kind could be seen.

"Here's the tombstone," he said. "You can still read a few words, and the date is here. See. It says 1650."

The Reverend looked at the tombstone with a blank stare. I could perceive a slight shake of his head as if there was something to this with which he could not quite come to grips.

"Where are all the other markers?" I asked. "If the cemetery has been here since 1650 and the Browne's went to all the trouble to enclose such a large area, there must be 50 or 60 people buried here. Where have the markers gone?" There was no answer to the question. A deep silence filled the air.

"I apologize also for the tall grass. The laborers around here are very superstitious and refuse to cut the grass in the cemetery. They are afraid that ghosts and goblins will get them if they do. We'd like to keep it trimmed, but it isn't possible."

Then who trims the grass in all the other cemeteries in Virginia? "I'd hoped to find the graves of several of my ancestors here," I said.

"I know, I know," he answered in a sympathetic tone of voice.

The Lab began barking. I turned to face the commotion and saw a smallish-size woman descending the stairs at the land entrance to the house. She appeared to stumble at the bottom of the steps but quickly regained control of her bearing and walked rapidly toward us. She was dressed in faded denim trousers and a rumpled blouse of the same color. Her sun-drenched skin bore no evidence of make-up. Her shortly bobbed hair was parted on one side and mostly pinned back on the other by a hair barrette that left one strand as though it had been purposely pulled out of place. Her hair seemed to be not so much uncombed as miscombed in a contrived fashion. Still looking at her, it was plain to see that she had once been a beauty. She greeted me graciously with a courteous smile.

"Hello. I'm Lila Young. Wouldn't you like to come inside to see the house now?"

"I'd be delighted," I said, handing Mrs. Young the bow-tied box of Godiva chocolates. "A little something to express my appreciation. I've been admiring the beautiful site. You must love looking at the river."

"We love everything about the place," Lila said. "It has always been the answer to our dreams."

"How long have you lived here?"

"Since 1967," she answered.

"We decided not to work our lives away first and then find a dream house to retire to," the Reverend said, "but instead to find our dream house, move into it and design our lives accordingly. Lila spent months driving all over the area in search of what she wanted. When she found Four Mile Tree she knew it was the perfect spot. Unfortunately, we had to wait several years for Mr. Carter, who owned the place then, to die so that we could buy it."

"You mean it wasn't up for sale?"

"No, but we knew it belonged to an old man in very poor health."

We climbed the front steps to the already opened door and went inside.

The wide entrance hall stretched the full length of the house to large doors at the end that were open to the enchanting river view. The walls of the hall were paneled up to five feet from the floor, the ceiling very high, the furniture and paintings tastefully elegant and the random -width floors covered with antique, oriental carpets.

"The house is Georgian," Lila said. All the rooms are Georgian except for the front parlor. Somewhere along the line, the interior of that room was redone in the Federal style. We thought to put it back to its original form but decided not to."

"I'm glad you left it as it is. It's a lovely room. Houses should reflect the taste of all the families who have lived in them. They grow just as people do. They aren't finished the day the first occupants move in. The color on the walls is superb."

"Over here," Lila said, "is the dining room."

We crossed the hall and entered a charming room furnished with good antiques and handsome portraits of an earlier period. There was much polished silver on display and a large silver chandelier hung from the ceiling. I commented appreciatively on the elegance of the room and headed toward a door at its rear, left slightly ajar, through which I could glimpse a striped sofa and a wing chair. "May we see this back room?" I asked.

"That's a closet," Lila said. "Go sit in the parlor. The Reverend will light a fire for you, and I'll bring some tea."

A closet? But there have to be two more rooms, nearly equal in size to the ones on the front. The house has four chimneys. She's not going to let me see all of this floor, much less the upstairs.

There was a moment of awkward silence, then the Reverend shepherded me into the Federal-style parlor. "We've met dozens of Browne descendants who have come to pay their respects to their ancestors," he said. "I'd regale you with stories of them, but you seem to be chiefly interested in the history of the old place. Plenty took place here. From the time of the first Indian massacre, this place has been a mecca for action. During the Revolution, slaves from Four Mile Tree helped to carry cannons from the ships of the French fleet to Yorktown." He moved the fire screen away, knelt down and struck a match to light the fire. "During the war of 1812, British seamen came ashore and stole the furniture."

"And the civil war?" I asked.

"That's when a cannon ball from a Union gunboat in the river landed in the hall, exploded and did tremendous damage to the structure. You can still see where it hit."

Lila entered the room pushing a tea cart. Evidently the gift of the chocolates pleased her for she had put the tea in a silver pot, brought out English porcelain teacups and handed me a linen napkin. She immediately took over the conversation leaving the Reverend free to sit quietly and scrutinize my face with care.

The conversation turned to topics of general interest, the productions of the Virginia Opera Company, one of Lila's chief interests, the environmental movement, of particular interest to me, and the questionable future of Four Mile Tree.

"I'd hate to see this beautiful home site despoiled by the building of a new river bridge. Jamestown would suffer even more. Now the old ships there have a proper setting for their display. They really would seem out-of-place resting beside the steel girders of a modern bridge. Do you think that any political stratagem might influence the outcome of the controversy?" I asked.

"I don't think so. This just concerns people who care deeply about what they want for themselves," the Reverend answered.

"But hasn't this area recently become the first political district in the state to contain a larger black population than white, enabling a black person to win election to federal office?"

"True, but what would a bridge have to do with that?"

"Well, if a bridge made it easier for whites, who work on the other side, to live here, taking advantage of the cheaper land costs on this side, mightn't the blacks lose their majority? Perhaps you should enlist their help to fight the bridge."

"We're doing everything we can," Lila said.

The conversation came easily and cordiality governed our chatter until quite suddenly Lila gave a startling laugh followed by her saying, "I love to thumb my nose at people as perhaps you can tell."

The inappropriateness of the statement seemed not to occur to her, but it rendered me speechless and ill at ease. I hastened to rise from my chair to take my departure.

"You must come again," Lila said. "Yes, you should come every year."

Night had come. I stepped with care over the scattered rocks and debris of the deteriorated cistern that had stood between the house and my car. Once I was safely belted into the driver's seat and had started the engine, I let out a loud, "Whew."

What a surprising couple. Did they actually begin to like me before I left? She invited me to come back every year. I liked them both, but felt strangely as though I was left out of something important that was going on. It's an enigma, a conundrum, a puzzlement. Why would anyone buy an historic property and then keep it for themselves alone? It's as though they bought a piece of our country's history and put it in their pocket, like a child hiding a piece of candy.

I came to the first turn to be made and studied the road carefully. There were few landmarks to be seen in the dark. The road began a slow rise. Spotting Gray's Creek on the left, I became reassured enough to add pressure to the gas peddle before returning to my thoughts.

I sensed a deep hurt of some sort that has put them on the defensive. Were the Brownes guilty of causing that? Did others harp on them for not being able to restore the old house properly? Were they tired of seeing disappointed looks on their visitors' faces? There's something very peculiar about the whole thing. Like, who took the steel wool to the oldest legible tombstone in Virginia? Could it have been....? No, she'd never have done that. Or would she?

The cemetery has more than three hundred years worth of stories to tell. I don't believe anyone would be scared to cut the grass in it. I'd love to. I'd love to sleep out in the brick enclosure some balmy summer evening in hopes that ghosts might hover around to tell me their stories.

My car arrived at Surry, obviously a very quiet place after sundown. The partially-lit, small brick court house, that had stood guard over the town's center for centuries, looked indomitable and secure, untouched as it was by major fires or the devastation of wars, its records never destroyed.

Lots of heartrending stories are hiding in those old records. I should come down to root them all out. Births, deaths, land battles, wills. It's all in there between the lines. So much about people never changes. On and on they go, living in the world at different times but in the end responding to the trials of their lives in much the same way. Human nature never changes.

The old Four Mile Tree must have seen a bundle. It had to be ancient and venerable even before the white men landed. Did it witness their arrival? What else did it see? I wish I could spend a day sitting in its shadow. If only it were still there and could talk. What tales it surely would tell.

The Messenger
1607-1608

I

A young Indian warrior ran at an even but rapid pace through the wooded forest of his homeland along a trail not far from the Powhatan River. His name was Nemantico, and he was a member of the Paspahegh tribe, a tribe subject to the great Powhatan, overlord and king of a confederation of Algonquian Indians.

The moon was obscured by a covering of clouds making the path dark, very dark. Fortunately he knew the first part of the way by heart as he would see no tree-markings until the break of day. He drew a deep breath. There was a queasy feeling in the pit of his stomach.

Why, oh why was I sent alone? It's eerie being in the woods with unseen things pacing, crawling and slithering about. The dark corners hide bear, panthers and packs of red wolves, hungry wolves. Lazy, lazy sun, why do you oversleep today? It's time for you to wake up and come over the earth's edge. Where are you? I need you. I need you.

Nemantico heard a wolf call. How far away could it be? His ears strained listening for an answer. Looking ahead he saw, in the distance, a dark, round object beside his path. It's the size of a grown bear and I see ears on it. He reached for the short spear strapped to his waist. His breathing quickened. He began to lose the rhythm of his steps but quickly re-set the cadence of his feet to an even pace. Nearing the object, he saw that it was only a dense, round bush growing near to the ground. He started to sigh with relief but found himself threatened again by the sound of another wolf call. Moments later the call was answered.

Oh God Ahone, not again. Sweat prickled out on his upper lip and at the nape of his neck, just below the hair line. The quiet night was rent by another wolf-call. How far? How far are the calls apart? One wolf, I can handle, two could be tricky, a pack could devour me alive.

Nemantico's distress was fierce. The bizarre news he carried in his head was of the utmost importance to the survival of his people. He must not fail. His entire body was charged to full alert as he concentrated his every sense to the awareness of danger. Then, suddenly he heard the first, faint chirpings of birds from their nests in the tree tops high above and knew that his plea had been answered. Somewhere, out of view, the first pale rays of the morning sun had crossed the horizon.

Nemantico came to a small knoll near the trail where he would turn inland to cross the peninsula. He paused for a moment. The eastern sky heralded the coming of the sun, turning the river below a deep violet. He could just make out faint images of the lush, fertile land of the tidewater region and see the shape of the dark river as it nearly encircled the isthmus that was the hunting ground of his people. He could not see the great winged canoes, but he knew they were somewhere in the river. He must hurry.

The sun now rising, gave him the opportunity to enjoy the sights and smells of spring. The earth gave forth the heady aroma of softening soil and new growth. The forest was filled with the sounds of squirrels, raccoons and rabbits quickly scurrying out of sight as they became aware of his approach. A pair of woodpeckers, high on the trunk of a loblolly pine, searched for insects in its hollow cavities. Everywhere the lacy, white blossoms of the woodland dogwood trees stood out in relief against the dark green background of fir trees and hollies. The brooks and creeks cut through the land and bubbled noisily on their way from the inland mountains, down the hills of the piedmont, across the tidewater area, into the rivers and out to sea.

A thrill of excitement mixed with the terror of uncertainty crept through Nemantico's body. He had listened carefully as the message he carried was given to him so that he could repeat it to Powhatan without error. The subtle meanings of particular words were for chieftains to interpret, and he didn't want to change a one of them.

Nemantico's feet made very little sound as they touched the ground with a drumbeat precision. He had learned as a child not to run fast if he had a long journey to make. He could cover more ground with a slow, steady pace. This was of the utmost importance now.

He had seen the odd objects with his own eyes. The size of the largest one was awesome. Its white wings, stretching skyward, had seemed eerie beyond recall. The visitation had surely been sent by the most powerful of Gods, but which one? Was it Okeus, the devil God, or Ahone, the benevolent God? Powhatan would know. He would surely understand it all and know what needed to be done.

Nemantico continued his rhythmic stride out of the forest and across a barren plot of ground, which had previously been planted in maize and beans. Deserted fields, such as this one, could be seen sporadically in the tidewater area. The trees had been banded, the leaves and limbs cut off and burned, then the land around the tree trunks plowed and planted by the native women. This field had served as the garden for about forty or fifty people for perhaps a decade. When the ground, tired from overuse, had stopped producing a hearty crop, the Indians had packed their belongings and moved a few miles further inland to clear and plant another plot of ground. They would return to this site after the ground had lain fallow long enough to replenish itself.

Nemantico's feet tread upon the soft ground of the field, now covered with a volunteer crop of clover and other low-growing grasses. The once tilled ground was soothing to his tired feet, but the softer earth gave a bit with each step causing the loss of valuable time.

Once past the open area, he entered the woods again following an old trail.

Some members of the Paspahegh tribe had balked at the decision of their chief to send so young a messenger. After all, they had reasoned the night before, he was only entering his sixteenth summer. But, the chief had faith in Nemantico and knew him to be the fastest of the young warriors. Besides, the older men would be needed to protect the village should the appearance of the great canoes mean evil for the Paspaheghs.

The sun's arrival allowed Nemantico to smile as he remembered the chief's hand upon his shoulder defending him against the others. He had given Nemantico a great but heavy load. Nemantico would not disappoint him.

The wolf calls had stopped. A cool breeze swept across Nemantico's body, and he breathed deeply of its freshness. His only clothing was a leather belt which had attached to it a vee shaped piece of animal hide which ran between his legs and tied to the belt in back. It was annoying to have to tie himself down but necessary if he was to be able to run for hours without discomfort.

Still, avoiding one discomfort often led to another. Now, after many hours of running, the edge of the hide had begun to cut into the skin of his inner thighs. He hoped it would not start bleeding and cause him delay.

Ahone, Ahone, don't let it bleed. Don't make me stop.

His only other adornment was a distinctive mark upon his shoulder, painted a dark, burnished-red color, to identify him as a member of the Paspahegh tribe.

The young warrior's head was shaved except for a crest of short, stubby, dark hair about two inches wide from his forehead to his neck. This made it easier to pull his bowstring close to his temples without depriving him of a manly display of thick hair.

Nemantico's thoughts turned to the great Powhatan, overlord of the confederacy of Algonquian Indians living between the Chesapeake Bay and the mountains to the west. His mother had told him how her mother and other women of the Algonquian tribe had come together to pick the successor to Powhatan's brother after that chief's death. The Gods had given men superior strength, but they had given women great understanding and wisdom. It was right that the choice should be theirs.

At that time, Powhatan stood over six feet in height, and was in the prime of early manhood with a powerful physique and commanding features. He had easily been selected as their new chief.

Nemantico's father often talked of the way Powhatan had conquered the small village where he had lived when he was a boy. "They came in the night. We were all asleep when the first of the flaming arrows pierced the roofs of our huts. The light of the flames and the suffocating smoke made all of our people rush outside. In the open yard, we heard the first wild screams of Powhatan's warriors as they swept down upon the men of our village, held them to the ground and beat their heads in with heavy clubs. Women and children too were beaten if they tried to interfere. His men moved from village to village, conquering all along the way. Many small villages, hearing of Powhatan's might, capitulated voluntarily. In this manner, Powhatan became the unchallenged ruler of 9,000 Algonquian Indians. The villagers knew that they could not stand alone against Powhatan, and Powhatan knew that none could stand against the Siouan Indians to the west or the

Iroquoians to the south unless all the Algonquians stood together.

"Powhatan is a great ruler," Nemantico's father had said. He was also a demanding one. Tribute from the conquered tribes was set at eight parts out of ten of all the profits of their labors whether derived from agriculture, hunting, fishing or the manufacture of such small items as utensils, tools and pottery. Each year, Powhatan's warriors arrived to count up the blessings of each tribe's labor, seize what they judged to be proper tribute and transport it to their king. This usually involved large amounts of food, furs, pelts, copper and pearls. With little permanent profit from their labor, the tribesmen were not inspired to labor very hard.

All of his subjects knew that Powhatan was not only a powerful man but also a wealthy one. Nemantico's friends talked of the large storehouse, built into the ground at Orapaks, that held his treasures. Many of these, they said, would be buried with him when he died. Other buildings were used to store a large amount of food which was smoked and salted to preserve it for his own villagers and warriors.

In return for the tribute paid by each of the tribes, it was clearly understood by all that they were not only under Powhatan's control but under his protection. This was the reason for the urgent message that Nemantico was carrying.

He had traveled more than twenty miles before sensing that he would soon be at the Pamunkey River. He could smell the salt from its brackish waters. The bay lay only twenty miles to the east, and the salt from the ocean traveled up and down the river with the ocean tides, almost up to the river's falls, fifty miles inland.

Nemantico had been told that a canoe would be in a customary hiding place. He needed it to cross the two-mile wide river to get to Werowocomoco, the present official residence of Powhatan.

He knew where the narrowest part of the river was and had been running along the tree-notched trail that led there. When he reached the spot where the Indians from Powhatan's village usually came ashore and left their canoe while hunting on the south shore, he could find none.

He slumped down beside a large willow tree near the river's edge. With his back resting against the tree's several trunks, he tried to think through this new problem. He yawned. Suddenly he felt his arms and legs grow heavy. Frustration welled up inside of him causing his muscles to weaken and his confidence to grow thin.

"Ahone," he called in pain. "Where are you? You showed me the tree marks and kept the wolves away. Don't turn from me now. I can't do this alone."

The tree felt comfortable against his back. His eyelids began to droop. Quickly he pushed them open with his forefingers, but when these props were removed, his lids slid shut again. In only a few minutes, he fell into a deep and restful sleep.

Several hours later, the rays of the late morning sun, having moved across the outermost branches of the cypress trees near the water, reached into Nemantico's face waking him with their gentle but penetrating warmth. He stretched and yawned. He remembered his mission and with a deep sigh recalled his problem.

Nemantico looked back toward the forest and became aware of the many animals and birds, which unaware of his presence, had appeared in search of food. His eyes shifted with interest from the many small animals and birds to a majestic-looking doe at play with her three fawns in the distance. He leaned forward watching the deer carefully.

Every time a fawn came to a particular piece of ground, covered by leaves and scrub brush, it jumped across the debris. He saw the animals jump over the same ridge of leaves not just once but several times. His heart took a leap. "Ahone," he said aloud. "You have fought off the ill-will of Okeus."

He leapt to his feet and ran across the open ground until he reached the spot where he had seen the fawns jumping. The deer scattered into the woods. Nemantico tore away the cover of leaves, and there lay a small canoe with paddles.

Surely the Gods are with me. Holding his hands together, high above his head, he shouted to the breeze, "Sun God, Moon God, Water God, whoever did this, thank you."

Nemantico laughed and stuffed his short spear into his belt. He picked up the paddles with one hand, hoisted the canoe above his head and rushed toward the river.

The salt water splashed over his legs sending a sharp pain through his upper thigh where his skin had been rubbed raw by the loin cloth. He was too excited to care. He threw himself across the opening of the canoe, maneuvered his body inside and began paddling as fast as he could.

When Nemantico drew near the north shore of the river, still a mile or so from Werowocomoco, several young warriors from the village, painted with the tribal sign of Powhatan, ran into the water to greet him. Shouting their welcome, they pulled the canoe through the shallows of the river's edge and helped to hoist it ashore.

"Powhatan," Nemantico said. "I must see him at once."

II

Nemantico, accompanied by Powhatan's men, ran another mile inland before reaching Werowocomoco. It was strategically situated north of the Pamunkey River about twelve miles south of the confluence of the two large tributaries that carried the Piedmont's flow of water across the tidal flatlands and into the Chesapeake Bay. The village had been placed inland as protection against marauding watermen of unfriendly tribes.

Nemantico's eyes widened when he saw that the village was composed of five long-houses, some one hundred feet in length, placed on either side of a lane that ran down its center. A stockade of tree posts encircled it, blocking off its entrance. The area was guarded at all times by forty or fifty strong warriors.

Outside the stockade area were fields, where the squaws planted and tended their crops of maize, squash, pumpkins, beans and tobacco.

Nemantico was directed to the long-house which served as Powhatan's seat of government as well as his home. He lived there with his present wives, perhaps as many as thirty, and his children, who were so numerous that he could not remember them all. In this society men were permitted to have as many wives as they could afford, and Powhatan could afford as many as he wanted. During his lifetime, it was rumored that he had as many as one hundred.

The walls of the house had been fashioned by planting supple saplings in long rows and when they had grown, bending them toward the center to form an arch when tied together. The outer walls were made of birch bark. Inside the walls were covered with woven matting made of rush, usually the stems of cattails.

In the rear of the official structure was a room set aside as a temple to the Gods. In its center, was a large idol of Okeus, the devil God, who needed to be placated with regularity. The idol was made of four wooden cross pieces, which were padded with moss, then painted a pale tan. It was decorated with all such precious things as could be found, shells, colorful stones, copper and pearls. When it was thought that Okeus was unhappy with the villagers, such as in times of war, pestilence or drought, many precious things were sacrificed to him, including a number of children.

Throughout each night, warriors stood watch at the four corners of Powhatan's home. At given intervals, their leader would turn his head and whistle to the guard at his right, he in turn whistled to the guard on his right until all four had been heard from to insure their vigilance. Nemantico could see that Powhatan had no intention of giving his enemies a chance for revenge.

Within the walls of the long-house, the older members of the tribe slept on raised platforms, covered with pelts that had been sewn together and stuffed with feathers to make an elongated cushion. The houses encompassed corn cribs, drinking troughs, storage areas for other foodstuffs and utensils, such as clay pots, bowls, spoons and plates. There was a fire going throughout the winter months which was moved outside when the winter days were past. Nevertheless, throughout the year, the smell of cooking grease, burning firewood, as well as the permeating smell of dogs clung to the air in a suffocating manner.

III

While Nemantico was approaching Werowocomoco, Powhatan was in his long-house contemplating his many blessings. At this point in time, he had seen more than sixty summers, and now another was approaching. Although unaware of it, he had been mellowing as the years progressed; he was beginning to find much pleasure in simple things.

Today he thanked the God Ahone, a truly kind God, though not one so powerful as Okeus, for the subsidence of the pestilence that had visited his people for the past three years. It had caused much suffering and cost many lives.

Powhatan was thankful that the spring crops had been planted, the woodland animals were busy making their annual increase, the shad were running, the air was balmy and the water comfortable for bathing. He gave thanks that a fresh green growth had covered the barren trees of winter and laid a handsome mat upon much of the ground. He observed that his blessings, like his many wives and children, were too numerous to count.

On this day, Powhatan could think of only one real problem. That was that he was beginning to feel old. His great energy had started to slacken. There were many times when it was necessary to act more powerful than he felt. However, appearances were important. He knew that. Thus, he kept his aches and pains to himself and took his daytime rest when no one other than his current wife could see him. Ostensibly, he went into the private quarters of his long-house, each afternoon, to confer privately with the Gods, to listen to their advice and to seek their blessings. However, much of this ritual was performed while he was asleep with his full girth resting upon a soft, double thickness of tanned hides with a multitude of feathers stuffed between them.

He was in just such a state of reclining communication with the Gods when the warriors, who had greeted Nemantico at the river, came running into his official reception hall with the news of the messenger's arrival. Acting as his cover, Powhatan's wife insisted that the messenger wait until the king's session with the Gods was over.

In time, Powhatan was aroused. He went through a proper grooming by having his thin, gray hair combed into place and his body painted with red powder that had been mixed with walnut oil. He donned a headdress that was a mixture of ornaments and feathers. On his chest he put a long chain made of tortoise shells, which had been artfully shaped into a handsome necklace. Around his waist, he tied a wraparound skirt of soft animal pelts.

Powhatan entered the public reception room of the long-house and moved to the raised platform, covered with raccoon skins, that had been stitched together with thin strips of hide and decorated all around with the dangling tails of small animals. He then called for the warriors to bring forth the messenger.

Nemantico entered the room quietly and for a few moments stood respectfully before Powhatan in silence and fear. Then upon seeing the great ruler lift his hand in permission, he burst forth, uncontrollably, with his news, not repeating the words of his chief, as planned, but spewing out his own thoughts and observations.

"They have come again, great father. The pale men, who cover their bodies with cloth and wear tall hats with brims to shade their faces They have sailed up the big river in three large houses that move not by the work of paddlers but by white wings stretched high into the sky so that the wind can do the work for them.

"There is one vessel much larger than the other two. All carry men, 'though some seem to be only boys. They have come up the Powhatan River, up beyond the place where the great cypress tree on the south shore marks the half way point between the bay and the falls.

"For days they have been sailing back and forth as if they are looking for some place to land. Each day, they lower a small boat over the side of the largest, and a few men work it to shore. They land cautiously, search the area, make loud banging noises with the long sticks they carry and then return to the large vessel as if afraid to stay on land. They seem to fear what might come out of the woods.

"Our chief thinks they will land when they find what they want. He is prepared to fight them and kill them all. He calls for your help, great Powhatan. He told me to say that the strange men have many pieces of metal and all carry the long sticks that make the big noise and kill any thing that gets in their way."

Nemantico saw Powhatan's mouth fall agape. He saw his neck muscles go limp, allowing his head to fall forward in a dispirited nod. Quickly, however, he seemed to gather his wits and remember his position of power. He lifted his head high and stared unblinkingly at Nemantico with a strong majestic expression upon his face. He gathered his thoughts for a few moments and then asked,

"Do they wear sleeves to their elbows?"

"Yes, yes, and leggings that billow out to their knees. They are covered except for their hands and faces. Some of the men climb up the tall poles of their canoes into the wings. Others stand at the railing and look ashore through another long stick that makes no noise."

"They are the same as the last," Powhatan said.

Nemantico remained silent as he watched the king close his eyes and fall off into what seemed to be a prolonged daze. He watched as Powhatan lifted his head skyward and gave out a long, deep, aching wail. Suddenly, Powhatan seemed to be talking and listening to another person, whom Nemantico could neither hear nor see. His ears perked. He cupped a hand around one of them, lowered his head and sat in total silence. Then he began to speak.

"For a hundred years there have been rumors, strange tales of meetings with clothed men who came out of the sea, terrified the people, returned to their floating sea houses and sailed away. I heard of these things from my brother when I was a small boy. I didn't believe them, but the rumors kept coming. Some people thought the viewers were bedazzled by the sun shining on the ocean's surface. Some thought they had seen strangely shaped clouds floating on top of the water which had caused them to imagine objects that were not there. Others thought the rumors had come from troublemakers who found pleasure in making mischief.

"I was interested but not worried about the tales until twenty years ago, when word came from the most savage Croatan tribes, far to the south, that a vessel had landed in their country, and a group of clothed and vile-smelling men had disembarked, set up camp and remained after the others had sailed away. The Croatans claimed to have killed them all. They said such poison should not be allowed to remain in the land."

Quiet moments ensued during which Nemantico watched Powhatan close his eyes and moan as if he was remembering many things.

"Do the pale men have yellow hair?" he asked.

"I don't know," Nemantico said. "Their hair is covered by the hats, and no one has been close enough to see."

"I didn't believe the story. I thought the Croatans were trying to scare me into thinking they were stronger than Powhatan."

"Ten years ago another strange thing happened. Two young women of the Kecoughtan tribe, living near the bay, were in the woods near the mouth of the great river, hunting for spring berries and greens, when three clothed, white men sprang at them from the bushes. The girls screamed, wiggled, bit and scratched but were unable to free themselves from the laughing and teasing men. The men repeatedly raped the girls all the while enjoying themselves immensely. After their lusts had been satisfied, they jumped into a small boat and rowed out to a larger one that was waiting in the channel."

"Later that day when the girls had dragged themselves back to their village, sputtering out their bizarre story, their tale of horror was met with disbelief. By the time the Kecoughtan warriors had reached the spot of the girls' trial, they found the sea to be calm and empty.

"The women clung to their story. After months of misgivings, it became obvious that one of the girls was filled with new life. When the babe was expelled from the womb, crying lustily and wiggling, a loud moan escaped the throat of the attending squaw. The new-born had very white skin. Its head was covered with a light color-less fuzz. Within weeks this fuzz fell away and was replaced by hair of a pale yellow color."

"Chief Opechancanough of the Pamunkeys, my younger broth-er, traveled across the mouth of the large river to see the child. When he saw the yellow hair, he believed the birth to be a direct message from the Gods that all the previous sightings of foreign vessels had been true. He sent a message to me saying that we should begin preparing to fight this seaborne enemy. He was con-vinced that we would need to kill them all. I did not see the child myself or I might have agreed."

"My father heard many people tell of seeing strange objects in the sea," Nemantico said.

"Then three years ago, a foreign vessel sailed into the Pamunkey and traveled up river to Werowocomoco. Seeing the size of the large canoe and realizing the knowledge of its captain, there was nothing I could do but to receive the strangers as guests. The encounter was friendly, but my people were much afraid. We knew that the previous sightings had been real. I knew that in time these people would come again."

"Did they kill?"

"No, but later a messenger came with news from the Rappahanocks that the same captain with his crew had sailed up their river, come ashore, quarreled with their king and killed him. Upon retreating, they seized several young warriors, took them aboard their ship and sailed away."

"Three summers have passed. The white men did not return. I consulted the Gods. I thought they heard me. Now that they're here again, I must ponder the meaning of all this."

The weary chief turned to face Nemantico.

"We will not rush into battle," Powhatan said. "I must plan. This is the land our Gods gave to us. They will show us how to pro-tect it. We know the land; the white men do not. We will move with caution. The Gods may have sent these men to our land to help us. We must give much thought to many things before we do anything that might offend the Gods."

"Father, father," Pocahontas called, "I have heard. More ships have come out of the sea bringing the pale-faced men with their beautiful clothes and their funny, funny hats. I want to see them. Where are they?"

Pocahontas rushed into the long-house, laughing as she came, showing not the least bit of concern for the seriousness of the private meeting that was taking place between her father and Nemantico. Gracefully leaping down the open corridor of the one hundred foot-long house, she rushed to the fur covered platform, upon which Powhatan was seated, charmingly encircled his neck with a loving embrace and then seated her completely nude body upon the throne beside him. Pocahotas then turned her gaze to Nemantico and allowed a broad smile of greeting to cross her face.

She was neither a child nor a woman. Having seen, perhaps, twelve or thirteen summers, she was somewhere in between. She had a tall, lithe body with long, graceful arms and legs and delicate hands and feet. Her thick black hair had been closely shaven for an inch or more away from her forehead and temples. The thick locks of the crown and the back of her head had been neatly tied together in a single, dangling braid which reached to her waist.

The steady, penetrating contact with which her eyes encountered Nemantico's immediately told him that he was in the presence of a true princess. Her face was unique, not in its beauty, but by its undeniable declaration that the mind within was quick, eager, able and daring.

Nemantico could not hold the contact with her eyes. His eyes turned away to those of Powhatan, but before completing this transition, they wavered just long enough for him to notice the small, pale, virginal nipples at her breasts and to see the light fuzz that was just beginning to cover the feminine mound between her legs. This moment of indiscrete awareness was not lost on Powhatan. In only a moment, he too took in the changes that had recently taken place in this favorite of all his children and took immediate action.

"Thank you," Powhatan said to Nemantico. "Leave now and join the men outside. Supper is cooking. Eat and rest. At sunrise, my reply will be ready for you to take back to your chief."

IV

By dawn of the following morning, Nemantico was seated on the ground, outside of Powhatan's reception hall, waiting to receive the message. He was watching the warm glow of light on the eastern horizon when the figure of a bent and crippled old man appeared limping toward him. Without a word to the messenger, the man walked straight by him and into Powhatan's hall where he needed no permission to enter.

From outside the hall, Nemantico heard Powhatan say, "Rawhunt, you will carry a message to both my brother and sister." The woven-matting walls of the long-house did little to muffle Powhatan's deep, penetrating voice.

"You will go to Pamunkey to summon King Opechancanough and then on to Appomattoc to summon Queen Opossunoquonuske. With their lands encircling the headwaters of the big river, they will be an important part of our plans."

How can that old man go any where, much less all the way to the head of the river? Why him?

"You are of great value to me, Rawhunt. You manage my pompous kin without causing our ties to break. See that they waste no time in coming to Werowocomoco. It is my order."

After the departure of Rawhunt, Nemantico was called to Powhatan's presence and given the message for his chief. Later when Nemantico reached the river for his return journey, he saw Rawhunt sitting in the middle of a large ornately decorated canoe being paddled upstream by two powerfully built warriors. He's a man of great privilege. A strong enough mind doesn't need to be in a strong body.

Nemantico was also provided with a warrior to help him reach the south shore of the Pamunkey River. The current was not favorable for this return trip so a warrior was sent to paddle stern while Nemantico paddled from the bow. Even with this doubling of power in the boat, the trip would surely take twice as long as it had taken the afternoon before when the current had been working in his favor.

Upon reaching the south shore of the Pamunkey River at a more easterly spot than the one from which he had departed, Nemantico scrambled up the river bank, raised his hand in a farewell salute to his fellow paddler and continued on his journey.

The qualms and fears of the previous day had been replaced by a growing excitement that seemed to commence in the pit of his stomach, increase in size as it traveled up to his chest until it burst forth in a spurt of energy that caused him inadvertently to increase his speed. Soon, however, he slowed his pace to assure endurance.

Some of the Paspaheghs are bigger and stronger than Nemantico, but Nemantico has always been the fastest. He threw his arms in the air in a gesture of victory without breaking the pace of his run. They joke that my winning all the races means I can run away from the enemy more quickly in time of war. Yesterday, they laughed at me. They ruined my joy. Today, I'm important. They do nothing but pine for such a chance.

Nemantico shook his head as he thought of the message he carried. My chief won't like it. He was strong in his message asking for a fighting force from Powhatan. Our people have paid an enormous tribute for many years, and now it's time for Powhatan to keep his end of the bargain. I must not forget a word of the message. I'll say it over and over to make sure that it will stick. He lifted one finger into the air. "First, all subjects must stay out of sight and neither hinder nor encounter the white men should they decide to land." Two fingers shot up. "Second, kill no intruders." Another finger was extended. "Third, Powhatan will send his own son, Nantaquaus, to make the first contact with these men should they land and stay. Last, we must keep him continually informed."

By mid-afternoon, Nemantico had reached his destination. As he ran into the camp of the Paspaheghs, he was greeted by a phalanx of squaws, children and dogs that descended upon him with a wild and noisy clamor as they shouted with joy at his safe return. The scattering of small huts and tents seemed crude to Nemantico after his trip to Werowocomoco. Living was more comfortable in Powhatan's village.

Before he had time to catch his breath, Nemantico heard shouted at him, "The strange men have landed, Nemantico. They have spent the night on shore and set up their camp on our hunting ground."

"You came very close to them," another tribesman shouted in a loud voice. "The three great boats are at rest in the cove."

Nemantico rushed past the throng without stopping. He went straight to his chieftain's tent.

Several days later, Nemantico reappeared at Werowocomoco. He ran the mile from the river's bank to Powhatan's long-house without pausing. When he was admitted to Powhatan's presence, he burst out with his news.

"The white men have landed. They have gone ashore, unloaded much heavy metal and many provisions on the isthmus of the north shore that is the hunting ground of my people."

"They build covers with long pieces of flat wood that they carry out of their canoes. They take down the large white wings of the canoes, stretch them out on the ground, then sit like women to sew on them. Our warriors have many ways to spy on them. Our men are so enraptured by what they see that they are unwilling to do anything else. The Paspaheghs have counted more than one hundred men and have seen five boys." Upon questioning, he answered, "I have seen no women, but their bodies are completely covered. It's difficult to tell."

Before finishing, Nemantico said, "There was one encounter with the white men in the woods. My brothers shot arrows at them, wounding many and probably killing one. The strangers pointed the long sticks at them and shot something that traveled unseen and then sent a burning fire through the bodies of several of the Paspaheghs. Our warriors had to flee with the wounded. My chief has suffered much outrage at the loss of our hunting ground to these unwelcome intruders and is also distressed at the power of their weapons. He pleads again, great father, that you send many warriors to wipe out the abominable vermin."

V

The following day, Nemantico had reached the Pamunkey River, on the first leg of his return journey to the Paspaheghs, when he saw a long caravan of canoes in the upper reaches of the river heading toward Werowocomoco.

Queen Opossunoquonuske was seated in the lead canoe with one of her female attendants kneeling nearby to fan away any objectionable insects from her face. Two tall and powerfully built warriors were paddling her canoe which was followed by seven others, some carrying warriors and two carrying females to attend to other needed comforts of the queen.

Following the Queen's entourage were twenty additional canoes carrying Opechancanough's sixty prepared warriors and an arsenal of bows, arrows, clubs and stones.

At the shore, Nemantico stood awe-struck at the parade of splendor. He could see that the queen had gone to much trouble to have her hair dressed as befitted her station and to have her body painted in an intricate and colorful design by her attendants.

Around her waist she wore a belt that held knee length aprons to cover front and back. Around her shoulders, she wore a tanned deerskin from which the fur had been removed so that it could be embroidered with shells. Her ears had jewels attached to them, and around her neck, she wore heavy necklaces of copper.

The queen stayed aloof from the other members of her traveling group even when traveling four in one canoe. The expression of superiority upon her face was unmistakable. Her attendants gave the utmost care to provide for her every wish with expressions of concern that implied not so much love for their queen as fear of her temper and power.

In contrast, Nemantico could see that Opechancanough cared little for the appearance of power. What he cared for most was power itself. Though he was wearing only a small loin cloth to cover his hips, had painted only the mark of the Pamunkeys on his shoulder for identification and wore no jewelry, he carried with him sixty of the best trained warriors in the entire kingdom. Opechancanough was a man of conviction and resolve.

When the royal party departed from their canoes to walk the last mile to Werowocomoco, Nemantico could not resist the urge to retrace his steps and follow them.

They arrived in the late afternoon. Nemantico watched all the proceedings. He saw that Queen Opossunoquonuske sat under a mulberry tree, to one side of the open, center circle of the village, with her attendants arranged around her and her warriors standing behind. A large fire was burning in the center. Her two brothers sat side by side across the open circle from her with their body-guards and warriors at the ready.

At twilight, a priest entered their presence. Leaping, jumping and performing a dance step of unregimented movement, he dropped a handful of wheat into the center of the circle. Next came a group of young warriors who, with hollers of undecipherable but eerie sounds, beat their chests, and with screams of passion, proceeded to drop a large circle of corn around the heap of wheat kernels and the fire. Drums began to add their sound to the background noise. Dogs joined the performance by howling in unison. The women and children began to wail and cry.

The priest, covered with a great skin to which the tails of weasels and other small animals had been added as fringe, and crowned with a large display of feathers, fell into wild gyrations. He made many signs with his hands and his head at the end of each song and the laying out of another circle of corn. He then tossed cakes of deer suet, deer flesh and tobacco into the fire. The howling and gyrations continued until dark when the evening meal was ready and hopeful-ly the Gods had been made aware of the assemblage of rulers.

Before eating, the royal members of the party were brought water with which to wash their hands and feathers with which to dry them. These ceremonies completed, all began to eat.

After supper, the royal personages, with a few selected advisers, went into a private conference.

Nemantico followed the royal party to Powhatan's long-house. He sat down outside near the place where he thought the royal conference would take place. He leaned his head back to a crack in the exterior wall and pretended to fall asleep. He could hear clearly.

"The messenger, Nemantico, has returned," Powhatan announced. "He brings news that the three ships have been anchored in the cove of the peninsula, four days up the Powhatan River from the bay and directly across from the great cypress tree that marks the half way spot between the bay and the falls. The land on which they are making their camp is the main hunting ground of our brothers the Paspaheghs. The white men have unloaded much heavy metal and equipment. All of them are armed with the long sticks that kill. No one has seen women."

"Why have they come?" the queen asked. "If there are no women with them, they will not stay. Who would do the daily work? Who would bear the children? Surely, they must be seeking something other than our land. But what?"

"We must kill them all now," Opechancanough said. "If we do not, more will come to join them. In future, there could be more of them than us."

Queen Opossunoquonuske nodded approval.

"We must slaughter them, take all their ships and all their weapons. Then, we will be strong and able to fight off any others that may follow."

"If we kill them now," Powhatan said, "how will we learn to use the large canoes? How will we learn to grow the crops that make the fire for their weapons? How will we learn what they want from us or from our land? How will we know why the Gods have sent them?"

"Could the Gods have sent them to punish us?" the queen asked.

"Perhaps the Gods have sent them to help us," Powhatan said. "If we are clever, perhaps we can get them to help us fight our enemies beyond the mountains."

By the time the pale light of morning had begun to creep across the sky, Powhatan had decided what his course of action would be. "We will continue our waiting game," he declared. "Go back to your kingdoms and wait for further orders from me."

His mind made up, there was nothing the others could do but to obey.

Nemantico left at dawn the next day to return to the Paspaheghs.

VI

A week later Nemantico was running, once again, along the now familiar path between the land of the Paspaheghs and Powhatan's Werowocomoco. He found himself eagerly looking forward to his arrival at the strongman's headquarters. The trip itself was beginning to seem short as familiar landmarks appeared to break the monotony of the long run. There was no longer any concern that he might lose his way, and each recognizable sight allowed him to estimate the length of time left before he could reach his destination.

As he ran, one image kept crossing Nemantico's mind, and then re-crossing it again and again. It was the image of Pocahontas running down the center hall of the long-house, calling to her father, "I've heard. They have come again." He remembered her graceful body as she leapt upon the dais to seat herself beside her father and remembered too, the way she had looked straight into his eyes and given him a warm and friendly smile.

Nemantico was fully aware that Pocahontas was far beyond him in her position as the daughter of Powhatan. He had no delusions that she smiled at him for any reason other than friendship. Still, he could not keep himself from wanting to see her smile again.

When Nemantico entered the village, his eyes scanned the various groups of women and children, but Pocahontas was nowhere to be seen. When he entered the long-house of Powhatan, his eyes traveled to all corners of the building, but still they could not find her.

Nemantico's conference with Powhatan was lengthy as the news he brought was both detailed and disturbing.

"There has been an encounter between the Paspaheghs and the white men at the fort," Nemantico said, "Several of our tribesmen were killed and many white men wounded, whether killed or not, I do not know. Since this trouble, our tribesmen have stayed away from the intruders and spied only from the woods and the under-brush. We know that the white men call themselves Englishmen. They have doubled, even tripled their building efforts since the con-flict. They have erected several buildings of good size, with heavy walls and strong roofs. They have completely enclosed the camp with a wooden palisade. The Englishmen are now well protected as long as they stay within the enclosure of the fort."

"I expected them to remain weak much longer," Powhatan said. His slow speech reflected the sadness he felt at hearing the bad news.

Soon Powhatan's sadness turned to happiness, however, as he heard Nemantico say, "The two largest of the three ships have sailed away. They did not sail up river to search out more land. They sailed down river, into the bay and out to sea."

Nemantico saw Powhatan's eyes brighten, and heard him give a short laugh. "This last piece of news proves my good judgment. There will be fewer Englishmen to fight now. Perhaps they will all turn and run. How many are left?"

"It's hard to tell," Nemantico answered, "but perhaps two out of every three. Those remaining can not possibly leave in the one small ship that is left."

Nemantico felt Powhatan's hands on his head. He heard the great ruler say, "You have given good and faithful service, my son. Watch everything they do. You remember things well and are an able man. When next you see anything of importance, you are to tell no one else about it. Report the information directly to me. Go."

VII

Back in the Paspahegh village, Nemantico took every opportuni-ty he could find to get into the English fort. It was guarded day and night by sentries, but each day, some unarmed Indians were admit-ted for the purpose of trading food for trinkets and baubles.

The Englishmen, during the two months of their settlement, had become dependent on the bare-breasted natives. The Indians were needed as guides when they ventured out, as teachers concerning the edibility of native plants and as the purveyors of such basic needs as corn.

The Englishmen had rushed through the building of Fort James in response to the Indian attack of late May, and by June fifteenth had completed a store house, a common house and a small chapel, all of which had been enclosed by the wooden palisade. With this very necessary project completed, some had begun to spend their days in a more leisurely fashion. Many were even idle.

The July heat was stifling as it settled over the swampy, miasmic peninsula. The white men were unaccustomed to the humidity and unprepared for it. Their clothing was unsuitable for the sweltering conditions and clung heavily about their bodies holding in perspiration, heat and odors. It might have been wiser had they taken a lesson from the Indians and stripped down to a bare nothing, but centuries of living in another culture kept them from even thinking of doing so.

As soon as he had returned from Werowocomoco, mindful of his instructions from Powhatan, Nemantico filled baskets with various food items which he carried to the fort at Jamestown. He then spent the day in trying to tarry as long as possible to prolong his opportunities for surveillance. On the third of July, some three weeks after the completion of the fort, he was in its courtyard with two baskets of fresh crabs and one of oysters, taking his time in making a deal to trade them for the trinkets that were offered to him in exchange.

Captain John Smith, a member of the venture's council, was listening with amusement, as the fort's cook tried, unsuccessfully, to buy the entire lot for a few strings of beads, and finally, could not keep himself from entering into the bargaining process. Captain Smith could seldom resist a challenge.

"Why do you not want these jewels?" Captain Smith asked with a gesture.

"No good," Nemantico answered by slicing the air with his flattened hand. "Need tools," he demonstrated by acting out the hoeing of crops.

"Tools are dear," Captain Smith said by clasping a spade to his bosom and mocking love. "Crabs all gone in one day; tools last many years. Not a good trade."

Nemantico studied Captain Smith as he tried to interpret his meaning. *He is a very important person at the fort. He is, perhaps, the werowance. He wears clothes over all of his body despite the heat. His sleeves are rolled up to show bare arms, and his shirt's open at the throat. He tries to stay cool, but I can smell the sweat of many moons in his clothing. It is no surprise that these men can not get their own food by hunting. The animals smell them before they see the animals. All Paspaheghs know to bathe before hunting in order to creep up, unexpectedly, on their prey, but these smelly men can not be bothered to make such necessary preparations. They deserve to starve.*

Nemantico smiled, trying to cover his revulsion at Smith's stench. *Thieves. They are all thieves trying to rob my people of their given land. They have chased the game from the isthmus with their building, shouting and smell, game that has fed our people from time before memory.*

Nemantico watched as Captain Smith took out a pack of small, thin pieces of metal and put a piece of thread through the tiny opening at one end. He watched Smith's fingers as he pushed the metal and thread through the material of his shirt several times to show its uses.

Someday, I'll cut those fingers off, soak them in brine and sew them to the fringe of a headdress. Fingers of a thief.

While Nemantico and Captain Smith were engaged in these negotiations, a noisy rumble broke through the country air announcing the approach of a number of people. Suddenly, the sound of drums could be heard in the distance.

Fort guards moved into a position of alert and took a stance at the palisades with muskets raised and triggers cocked. The handful of laborers and boys, who had been tending the sparse fields beyond the fort's walls, came rushing into the yard.

The sound grew louder as the still unseen visitors approached. Tensions were aroused. The alert guards watched the surrounding forests with care. Then suddenly, ushered in ceremoniously by the sound of rapid drumbeats, one crooked, bent, old man came walking into the open yard. He was almost naked, carried no weapon and held his two hands, palms together, fingers pointed skyward, in a sign of peace.

Governor Edward Maria Wingfield heard the strange raucous

noise, came out of his private quarters, and exchanged questioning glances with Captain Smith.

"Rawhunt," Nemantico said aloud.

"What? Who?" Captain Smith questioned.

"Rawhunt, Powhatan" Nemantico said.

"Powhatan's man," Wingfield said. "My, my. Go to meet him, John. See what he wants."

Nemantico watched as Captain Smith, without hesitation, walked through the palisade gates and raised his hands in front of his waist to match Rawhunt's sign of peace. The exchange of words between the two could not be heard, but nods of agreement could be seen. Then at a single motion from Rawhunt, Powhatan's son, Nantaquaus, and daughter, Pocahontas, emerged from the thicket behind and were followed by two warriors carrying a freshly killed deer.

Captain Smith motioned for Governor Wingfield to come into the outer yard to receive the guests and the peace offering.

Governor Wingfield hesitated. For a moment, it appeared that he might turn back to his quarters. Then, straightening his stance, he turned, and with a look of unabashed displeasure, walked forward to receive the children of the emperor of the Powhatan nation.

Upon meeting the two English officials, Pocahontas clapped her hands in glee and gave them a heartfelt smile.

Captain Smith invited Nantaquaus, Pocahontas and Rawhunt inside the palisade. Governor Wingfield gave an unenthusiastic nod of approval.

Pocahontas and Nantaquaus spent the next hour touring, observing and marveling at everything they saw in the fort.

Nemantico trailed as closely as he could to give added protection to Pocahontas. He watched admiringly, seeing that the young princess' able mind and deep curiosity led her to ask questions about everything she saw. He saw that she often burst into giggles as she learned how to sit on a bench at a table, how she looked in a mirror and how to turn night into day by lighting a candle. He saw that her greatest surprise came upon being shown the books in the preacher's library. Her mood changed from glee to one of deep thought as the concept of saving thoughts for others to learn of them later was explained to her. She looked at the pages with awe and tried to comprehend the importance of this miraculous invention.

Nemantico saw that the Captain admired the tall, handsome Nantaquaus and his young sister, a child who possessed no fear and occupied herself solely with the thrill of seeing the new and acquiring knowledge. After the tour, he stood by as all settled on the ground to refresh themselves with water to which fresh mint leaves had been added for flavor.

Across the courtyard were four former cabin boys, lounging around a large, circular tree stump which had been sawed flat on top to serve as an outdoor table. At the first sound of drumbeats, the boys had scrambled in from working on the small garden plot beyond the palisade and had watched every detail of the royal tour with interest. Nemantico stood near them and listened.

"Is she really a princess?" Nathaniel asked.

"Captain Smith says that she is the daughter of the emperor of all the tribal kingdoms here and about," James answered. "That surely must make her so. Why do you ask?"

"It's hard to think of a princess walking around naked like an animal in a forest," Nathaniel said.

"She's not naked," Samuel said. "She's wearing a short apron, front and back."

"What do you think she has on under that thing?" Richard asked. "Some panties?"

"I'd say nothing," James said.

"I'd say it's a little piece of cloth to cover," Samuel continued.

"Want to bet?" Nathaniel asked.

"Sure. I'll wager my bag of walnuts," he said, placing the bag on the tree stump. "What have you got to match?"

"I'll put up my box of bait worms," Nathaniel said.

"How are we going to find out?" James asked. "Are you going to peek?"

"Do you think I'm suicidal? She has relatives here. A fellow must be a bit more clever than that. Let me think."

A moment later, he jumped up saying, "Watch me, and do what I do."

Nathaniel shouted in a firm voice, "All right, James. Let's see who the champion is. Winner takes all. Follow me." With that, he moved into the open center of the yard, and throwing his hands onto the ground and his feet into the air, he began to walk on his hands. After only three upside-down steps, he fell to the ground bringing roars of laughter from the other three.

"Now it's your turn, James. See if you can do that."

As James, who had quickly caught on, was making his hand-stand attempt, Pocahontas got up from her resting spot and strolled over to them clapping her hands.

"What's this?" she asked with a gesture.

"A game," Nathaniel replied. "Best hand-walker gets the prizes."

Pocahontas laughed.

"James won," Richard said.

"No he didn't, " Samuel said. "Nathaniel was much better."

"We'll have to do it again," Nathaniel said. "You're first this time, James."

Each boy made his attempt again, and both fell quickly to the ground. The others burst into uninhibited laughter.

Pocahontas was delighted by the fun of it all. Pushing both boys aside, she motioned, "Watch me." Pocahontas then cautiously put her forehead to the ground, placed her hands an even distance from her head and gracefully put her long legs, one after the other, above her head in a perfect headstand. From this position, she pushed herself up into a handstand and with her body under as complete control as that of any professional athlete, she walked slowly across the courtyard on her hands.

The entire assembly of men stopped all activity and was momentarily mesmerized into total silence as they saw that underneath her apron, she wore nothing at all.

When Pocahontas righted herself, the boys were still stunned by the success of their subterfuge and stood motionless with their mouths agape. Then, they applauded vigorously.

Encouraged by this acclaim, Pocahontas turned several cartwheels as she worked her way back to the place where the boys were standing. She looked at them with the broad, pleased smile of a victor.

"You won, princess," Nathaniel called out. "Here. The prizes are yours," he said, stuffing the bag of nuts and the box of worms into her hands.

Nemantico noticed the way Governor Wingfield wrinkled his nose in disapproval and said, "She's wanton."

"No, no," Captain Smith said. "She's not wanton. She's a wood-nymph. She thinks of her body no differently than would a squirrel running out along a tree branch."

Nemantico, who had stood quietly throughout the recent events, understood clearly what lay behind the antics of the boys. He exercised the greatest control of his lifetime in not grabbing each one and beating his brains out. His face turned a furious red. Turning away, he gathered his baskets of untraded seafood and fled through the gates.

Once outside the fort, Nemantico's semblance of civility vanished quickly and was replaced by a burst of savage emotions. He visualized himself torturing the boys to death. He raced through the forest trying to lessen the violence of his feelings but to no avail. Hatred was growing within him. Nemantico let out a wailing, anguished scream.

I'll slaughter them all.

VIII

During the later months of summer and early fall, Nemantico regularly delivered reports of his surveillance at the fort to Powhatan. Pocahontas was also often at the fort, drawn as she was by its more sophisticated way of life, and she too reported all that she saw and heard there to her father. Through these two sets of eyes and ears, Powhatan kept close watch on the Englishmen's activities. He learned that Governor Wingfield was not well respected, that it was Captain Smith, not the official werowance, who got things done.

When the first cold winds of winter blew down from the mountains to the west, Nemantico made another of his customary runs to Werowocomoco. His cheeks were flushed from the biting cold and particles of snow powdered the two-inch-wide tuft of black hair that striped his head from his forehead to the nape of his neck. The news he carried was so uplifting that his bare feet fairly pranced across the frozen ground.

At Werowocomoco, he ran without stopping into Powhatan's hall, and dashed in without waiting to be announced. Coming to a halt before Powhatan, he quickly caught his breath and blurted out his message.

"The white men have fallen prey to sickness and disease," Nemantico said. "Many have died in recent months."

"Aha," Powhatan said. "Praise be to Ahone. I am not surprised. The Englishmen have been scared to leave the fort. They have used the same water to take away the waste and to quench the thirst. They forget the shifting tides. We know not to do such a stupid thing. What form does their sickness take?"

"They bleed and bloat."

"Aha, just as I thought. How many have died?"

"At first it was easy to count, because they shot off guns each time they put a man in the ground. Later, they came to know of their mistake and stopped telling us of their losses. Nevertheless, the Paspahegh chief has been able to count. He estimates that about half of the men left in the fort, after the others sailed away in the two larger ships, have died. That should leave about three or four hands full," he said, flashing his ten fingers as he spoke.

"My plan is working," Powhatan said.

"Captain Smith, with five comrades and two Indian guides, has left the fort on a large barge and traveled up river into the interior," Nemantico said.

"Why?"

"One moon ago, our Paspahegh chief put a stop to trading with the Englishmen. The fort's store of food must be low. My chief thinks the white men have gone inland to seek out another food supply."

"Ah," Powhatan said. "We have got them where we want them. The time is right for action."

Powhatan put his hands on the messenger's head. "You are a valuable man, Nemantico. You will go to Pamunkey. I can not send Rawhunt out in this cold. You will take his place. Tell Opechancanough to search out Captain Smith and his men. Capture them any way he can. Then, bring Captain Smith to me."

Within a week, Nemantico returned to Werowocomoco full of news and once again glowing with pride.

"Opechancanough captured the Captain," he reported. "He encircled him with two hundred warriors to take him alive."

"What of the others," Powhatan asked.

"They were captured first," Nemantico said, "when Captain

Smith went ahead to explore alone. They were tied to a tree. Their hands, ears, feet and other parts of the body were cut off and eaten before their still-seeing eyes." Delight showed on the messenger's face as he spoke. "The rest of their bodies were burned at the stake."

"They deserved as much. Where is Opechancanough?"

"He traveled north with Captain Smith. He was following the needle that wiggles."

"The what?"

"He has taken a longer route to obey your orders in safety," Nemantico said.

More than half a moon passed before Opechancanough arrived at Werowocomoco with his captive. Nemantico waited anxiously. He is too daring. I could feel Powhatan's fury at the delay. Why would Opechancanough risk being disobedient? He feared a clash between the brothers and did the best he could to stay within earshot of their first meeting.

"You mad dog! Where have you been all this time?" Powhatan asked.

"Brother, I have marched Captain Smith around to many of your tribes so that all could see what the Englishman was like and know of your power in conquering him. I took him all the way to Rappahanock to see if he was the sea captain who killed their king three summers ago. They said he was not. The other captain was tall. Captain Smith is short."

"I think there is more to this than you tell. Speak."

"Brother, Captain Smith is not the bad man I had thought he would be. He is a man of wisdom. When captured, even before he was brought to me, he sent me a gift, a box with a precious needle inside. It was a small, bone box that he carried in his pocket. I could see the needle moving as I turned it up and down, but when I tried to touch it, I could not.

"When Captain Smith was brought to me, he showed me how the needle worked. The needle always points to the bright star whether the star is in view or not. It never forgets. With the box, one can never get lost.

"Seeing that Captain Smith knew many things that we do not, I asked him questions about the things that have always puzzled us.

"He has taught me about the earth, that it is round not flat. He has explained the sun and how the earth and other objects travel around it. He has explained why the sun comes up at dawn and why it disappears at dusk. He has told me about the moon, how it travels around the earth and why it changes from a sliver to a half, to a full moon and then back to a sliver again."

"I don't believe this," Powhatan said.

Opechancanough's eyes began to glisten and his voice to waver as he continued. "He has told me of the kingdom beyond the sea, of his king, named James, of other people living in other places, whose skin is yet a different color and who speak a different tongue also.

"He knows other forms of magic besides the needle in the box. He can take a piece of tree bark, make marks on it, then send it to someone far away. When the person looks at the marks, the marks speak to him. They can do the same thing and send the talking bark back. People can talk to each other from far away. He knows other magic as well. Kill the others at the fort if you wish, Powhatan, but I pray you, do not kill this man."

"Aha," Powhatan said with a scowl upon his face. "I see that he has used his magic tricks on you as on Pocahontas. She's been pleading for his life since the time of his capture. Last spring, you wanted to kill them all in great haste. Now, he has turned you into a scared sparrow."

"But, brother, he is a brave man. Our warriors had him surrounded and he was sinking into death-trap sand, but still he showed no fear. My men were awed by his courage."

"It's fortunate that I didn't attack them when they first came," Powhatan said. "The powerful Okeus has already seen to the death of many. They may all die without our losing a single warrior. Bring Captain Smith to me. I will decide whether he is to live or to be sacrificed to Okeus. Prepare the hall for an audience."

IX

Nemantico crept down the dimly-lighted, far side of the longhouse wall. He was fearful that his position as the messenger of another tribe would not entitle him to be present at the audience. From the dark corners, he could see the stage being set and many tribesmen moving quietly into place. The quiet caused an eerie strain among the people.

Nemantico had a good view of Powhatan seated upon a raised platform with one woman at his head and another at his feet. There was a fire burning in an open pit before him. His ten chief advisers and warriors were standing to the side of the fire, and ranged behind them were the same number of women. All of the women had painted their faces, necks and shoulders with red paint and wore long strands of white beads to create a frame for their somber faces.

Powhatan clapped his hands. Captain Smith, with his hands tied securely behind him, was brought into the hall and placed kneeling before the emperor.

Powhatan stared straight into Captain Smith's eyes and studied him with seriousness of purpose for many minutes before speaking. Small beads of perspiration broke out on the captain's upper lip, but his eyes held the stare.

When Powhatan finally spoke, it was to ask a simple question. "Why have you come to my land?"

Captain Smith continued to look straight into Powhatan's eyes. Nemantico marveled that the Captain could remain calm. He is a trapped animal. Why doesn't he tremble? He's stunned by the strength in Powhatan's face. He marvels at the sight of him. Why isn't he shaking? How can he hide his fear? What magic keeps him brave? Doesn't he know he's doomed?"

Nemantico saw Pocahontas, who had stood hidden behind the warriors, come forth. She welcomed Smith with a restrained nod and a nervous smile, then seated herself next to her father. She was to help the two men to understand each other.

Captain Smith began to speak. "Our sh- sh- ships were in a fi-fi- fight with our enemy, the Sp-Spanish," he said.

Nemantico saw his body begin to shake.

"We were overpowered and had to retreat. The weather was extreme. We lost control of our sh-ships."

Nemantico saw beads of salty perspiration run down Captain Smith's upper lip and into his mouth as he spoke.

"We were driven ashore. Some natives shot arrows at us. But the Kecoughtans were kind to us. We asked for fresh water. They told us that up the great river all the water was fresh."

There was a long silence while Captain Smith steadied his voice. "At Paspahegh, they were also kind to us."

"You lie," Nemantico whispered.

"Our smallest boat had a leak. We were forced to stay to mend her. Our father, Captain Newport, has taken the other two ships back to our homeland. He will soon return with the things we need to mend the leaking ship. When it is mended, we will all sa-sail back to our kingdom."

A slow smile of approval broke upon Powhatan's face.

"My brother has told me of all the things you have told him," Powhatan said. "I want to hear more of your kingdom."

Nemantico saw confusion flicker across Captain Smith's face as he tried to grasp a turn in his fortunes. He took a deep breath and with new confidence began, "King James' kingdom is vast." A long silence ensued. "He controls large parts of the world. He has many ships under his control, and he uses the ships to seek revenge on all who harm his subjects."

Smith colored his stories as best he could by demonstrating the sound of trumpets that blared as Englishmen went into battle. He mimicked the roar of his majesty's guns and the inspiring cadence of his battle hymns. Before his story telling was over, he had enchanted Powhatan as he had Pocahontas and Opechancanough before him.

"You will be free," Powhatan said in an aside to Captain Smith. "You will go back with guides and gifts. But first, we must show my people. They must understand."

Powhatan leaned over and said something to Pocahontas. He pounded his club to call attention. In a commanding voice, he said, "Bring in the execution blocks of stone. Lay them by the fire."

Nemantico could see Captain Smith stiffen. What is happening? Will he be set free or executed? I sensed that Powhatan was warming to him. Is this a game? The devil deserves to die. Kill him.

Wild hollering and animal yells erupted from the crowd. Smith was dragged forward and his head placed upon the stones.

Now he'll get it.

The rattle of beans enclosed in large gourds created a cacophony of savage sounds. Two tall and powerfully built warriors, whose bodies were painted in grotesque designs, rushed eagerly to the center of action, each holding a long, heavy, round-ended club. The tempo of drumbeats was added to the wild frenzy of noise within the long-house. Captain Smith with his eyes opened wide was paralyzed by the surge of blood that rushed to his heart.

The two executioners lifted their weapons, held them ready and waited for the final signal from Powhatan. All sound in the room ceased. The hundred or more spectators made not a move. Each face looked frozen as though any expression of thought or flicker of feeling might leave them guilty of what hovered, waiting, only a moment away.

Nemantico saw Captain Smith's lips make the slightest of movements as though in prayer.

No God can save him now.

Sudden movement startled the crowd. Pocahontas rushed forward. She gathered Captain Smith's head in her arms and laid her head upon his. The crowd gasped. Powhatan signaled the executioners to retract their clubs. He then rose, faced the assembled group, and let his strong powerful voice cut through the quiet of the room with a raucous bellicose laugh.

X

The snows returned. The fall was heavy. Nemantico ran barefooted over the frozen, snow-covered ground. At a distance, he was following the guides and warriors as they escorted Captain Smith back to Fort James. An unsettling feeling gnawed at him. He had seen more than he could understand at Werowocomoco. He could not remember ever seeing Powhatan look so old. The chief had appeared to be under a great strain. His mood had not lightened until he heard Captain Smith say that the Englishmen would be leaving as soon as the two larger ships returned with all that was needed to mend the smaller one. Then his eyes glistened as he teased Captain Smith with the execution scene. Did Powhatan believe what he wanted to believe because he was too old to face the truth? This time the great chief seemed more tired than powerful.

Nemantico watched as the guides took Captain Smith back to the open field outside of the fort and then let him go to the gate of the palisade alone. He heard the loud cheering of the Englishmen inside when the gate was opened. He paused for only a moment to witness the action. Walking further, he followed the path as it neared the Powhatan River. Then he turned right toward the village of the Paspaheghs.

The following day, he arose early. Telling his mother that he still had work to do for Powhatan, he set out again for the fort. Upon reaching the small ridge, from which he had a clear view of both the fort and the cove where the Englishmen secured their ships, he was surprised to see that the two larger ships had returned and were in the cove beside the smaller one.

So they have come back. Good. They will get the others and leave within a few days. The adventure is over.

For a moment, he seemed almost sorry at the thought of their leaving. Then he noticed a strange thing. There were many more men down by the ships than there should be, even more than when the ships had first come the spring before. Now, there were at least twice as many men as he could ever remember seeing.

Nemantico ran out onto a spit of land that looked out over the water to the small harbor and saw that the ships were not being loaded but unloaded. He saw fresh supplies, large mounds of tools and racks of guns. There were chickens in crates and pigs and goats on foot being led from the ships.

"Okeus," he wailed. "What have you done? They are not leaving. The canoes with the large wings have returned with more."

Nemantico sat down abruptly and lowered his head into his hands.

We have been tricked. They never meant to leave. Oh my Gods, oh my God, Ahone. How has Okeus won out over you? The wrath of Powhatan will enflame the world. Things will never be quiet again.

The juices of hatred toward the Englishmen began to surge through Nemantico's body anew. He threw his head back and looked up into the morning sky. His heart was about to burst.

"They have lied," he yelled. "Thieves. Vermin. I curse them all."

When his mounting fury could be controlled no longer, he let out a loud, prolonged, wailing cry of agony.

THE ORPHAN
1608-1622

I

While Captain John Smith was in captivity in Virginia, manip-
ulating Opechancanough and charming Powhatan with the
answers to the questions that had puzzled the natives for time
beyond memory, the Flood family in England was preparing to celebrate the holy day of Christmas on their small farm in one of the
out-parishes of London.

In Virginia, Captain Smith knew that he was in imminent danger of death. He faced it boldly, used all his talents to fight it and
came out the victor. In England, the Floods were caught unaware.
They were walking in the sunshine when the shadow of death overtook them.

John Flood was only seven years old that Christmas of 1608.
The memory of the holiday might have faded from his mind with
time, had it not been the last of the days he would spend with his
family or on the farm. His brother Charles, fourteen years old when
their parents died, had been at home for Christmas Day just a few
days before it happened.

The cabinetmaker in London, to whom his brother was apprenticed, gave Charles a day-and-a-half off so that he could celebrate
Christmas with his family. With no horse at his disposal and no
cash with which to hire one, Charles had to walk the thirteen miles
from London to the farm. It took him four hours. There were no
maps or road markings to show him the way, but he had traveled
the path several times before with his father when helping to transport some of their farm produce to the London markets.

Four days before Christmas, a goose was killed for the celebra-
tion. It was not the best time to kill the goose, but the silly bird had
stuck her head out at the wrong moment, just as John's father had
swung through with an axe while chopping firewood for the fami-

ly hearth. John remembered how they had kept it fresh by soaking it in a tub of near-freezing water until time for his mother to cook it for the holiday meal.

Before feasting, the family walked across nearby farm fields to a small, one-room, village church where they worshiped with their neighbors. There, the vicar expounded at length over his interpretation of the Book of St. Matthew from which he read passages to them from the only copy of the printed bible that the people of the parish possessed.

Later in the day, the family sat at a large table before the fire where they devoured the roasted goose and listened for hours to Charles' stories of life in the bustling city of London. The city was growing like a weed patch.

John was too young to remember all the things that were said, but he listened to everything and remembered a great deal. He loved hearing his older brother talk.

Charles amused them all by giving humorous accounts of his master's customers, some grand, bursting with the importance of their positions, and others humbly trying to barter and trade services for the carpentry work they needed to have done. He seemed years older than he had seemed before going to London.

"The grand ones never offer services in exchange for labor," Charles said "probably because they have no intention of paying up in the first place."

"Do rich men steal labor from the poor?" his mother asked.

"Oh, they pay up eventually," Charles said, "But not till they feel like it. Sometimes it takes them years to pay their debts. The government is almost as bad. It's always a year behind."

"They don't understand how tough it is for laboring people," his father said. "The drought four years ago was a disaster in these parts. Then having the bubonic plague on top of it was almost more than we could endure. The rich didn't suffer like we did. They don't understand." He threw up his hands as though in frustration.

"They say London lost one out of four in the epidemic," Charles said. "Glad I was here then instead of there. Country's much safer."

"Our parish was lucky. Even so, we have more widows and orphans than we can feed. Tell Charles about the tavern birth, Mother. That was colorful."

"Should I?"

"Why not?"

"It's not a pretty story." His mother tightened her lips and twitched her nose as if reminded of something unpleasant. "Oh well. I'll try. Last month, when his majesty's troops marched through the village on their way to the fighting in Ireland, followed by the usual straggling group of gypsies, easy women and homeless children, a young girl from the group went into labor and was brought to the tavern by some of the soldiers.'

"What's labor? John asked.

"Having a baby, silly," Charles answered.

"She gave birth to a bawling boy around mid-night, and the word spread immediately to most of the houses in the parish. Before dawn, thirty or more of our women were outside, encircling the tavern. We aimed to see that she didn't escape town leaving the babe for us to rear. We have too many orphans of our own to worry about. We stayed until she and the infant were carried away.

"It was sad to see her all bundled up in the back of one of the service carts with the baby in her arms. She seemed not a day older than you, Charles. Her face was tear-streaked and her eyes very sad."

"Did you have to throw her out the very next day?" Charles asked.

"We didn't throw her out. We just said she couldn't leave without taking the baby. The soldiers were moving on. She had to go."

"Don't you like babies?" John asked.

"Of course, we do, angel," his mother said. "Everyone loves their own babies. It's other people's babies they don't want dumped on them if they can avoid it."

"We were lucky not to be left with both of them," their father said. "We don't like to be so hard, but our parish has been over-run with widows and orphans since the epidemic. We're stretched as far as we can go."

"How did you get the money to pay Master Harold ninety pounds to take me on as his apprentice?"

"Made a compromise. Your future against our security. I borrowed the money from his lordship, gave him a trust on the farm as bond. I can pay the interest on the loan with a share of the crops until you begin your own trade in five or six years. Then we can try to pay off the loan itself.

"It's the only way for us to move ahead, son. Learning to read and write and learning a trade are the only ways to improve one's lot. It's not easy to live now that the rich have taken to enclosing their land." He lowered his eyes and contemplated his words before continuing.

"Time was when a man could fish and hunt anywhere he pleased. Now, there're few places a man can shoot other than his own property. Putting food on the table each day is hard work. That's why I want my sons to learn a good trade."

"Can you harvest enough without my help, to give his lordship a fair return?" Charles asked. He was stunned to learn that he was the cause of a family indebtedness.

"John works with me now," his father said. "He helps me greatly. He works hard for a lad his age. He also studies his letters. I aim to see that both my sons can read and write."

"But, father, John's only seven years old."

"He helps me more each day."

Charles gave a deep sigh. The deed was done now. There really was no way to change it.

"When I become a master builder, I'll build a beautiful house for you to make up for all this."

"I'll help," John said.

John had slept only half the night when he heard the first stirrings of the household the next day. He knew that Charles would have to leave early. He rushed to pull on his trousers and tie the strips of cloth that closed his shirt front. He didn't want to miss a second that he could spend with his brother.

In the main room of the cottage, he found his father rebuilding the fire that had petered out during the night. Charles was gulping down a warm glass of milk that had just come from their cow a few minutes before, and his mother was putting together some of the remains of the previous day's feast so that Charles could snack on it during his return journey.

A deep sadness came over John as he watched Charles wave to them all and start to walk down the front path toward the road. Charles had walked only to the end of the cottage path when their father, grieved at seeing his eldest son leaving after so short a visit, bolted out of the farmhouse and ran down the path behind him. Catching up, he called back to the others, "I'll take the day off and walk Charles back to London. Don't forget to milk Flossy. I'll be back tomorrow."

"I want to go too," John yelled.

"No, no. You must stay and take care of your mother."

John's father came back in the late afternoon of the following day, bringing with him a freshly-caught fish for their dinner. "This proves," he said, "that I walked all the way to the city."

That night after dinner his father had been taken deathly ill with vomiting, diarrhea and a raging fever. John and his mother had nursed him as best they could, but he died before morning.

Next, John became ill with the same malady, and his mother, though stricken by the shock of her husband's death, had nursed him too. She had gone out into the freezing cold to fill the pail with water from the well. She had stayed by his cot and insisted that he drink cupfuls of it. She had used much of the water to wash his face and body to control the fever and the rest to clean up the mess. John's fever peeked before midnight, after which, he fell into a restful sleep. Then his mother was taken ill. Throughout the rest of the night, weakened by his ordeal and moving in and out of consciousness, John could hear his mother call, "Water, water. G- get me some water."

Once he had managed to drag himself out of bed and cross the room to the water pail, but the pail was empty. He staggered back to bed and collapsed in a long uninterrupted sleep. When he opened his eyes the next day, it was to see the vicar and the doctor standing over his mother.

"Was it the plague?" the vicar asked softly.

"No," the doctor answered. "There are no swollen pustules and no black spots under her skin. They all had the same thing. I'm not sure what it was, but the symptoms speak of cholera. She actually died of dehydration."

"Dehydration? A lack of water?"

"Yes. The only way to survive cholera is to drink as much water as the body loses from the diarrhea and the sweating."

"No. No," John cried. He let out a deep groan and burst into uncontrollable sobs. "She's dead. It's all my fault. I didn't get the water."

"There, there, my boy," the vicar said. "We're sending for Charles. He'll surely be here by tomorrow. Don't cry, John. We'll take care of you."

When Charles returned to the farm from London, John was better but still distressingly weak. Charles had permission to stay only one full day so a double burial was held in the morning and the afternoon was spent in the cottage with the vicar and justice of the peace to make arrangements for John's care.

"I'll have to reside in London at Master Harold's house for the next six years," Charles said. "Unfortunately, I can't take John back with me."

"Are there no relatives?" the justice asked.

"No, none we've ever known."

"There's no one to run the farm then," the justice said. "It'll have to be sold. The money it brings should be enough to pay for boarding John out with a local family until he's old enough to be gainfully employed."

John sat silently in the background but listened to every word. He felt a strange knot in his chest. I don't want to leave the farm to live with anyone else. I want to live here with Charles.

As his elders talked on, their voices faded into the distance and John remembered the story his mother had told at Christmas dinner. He could hear her saying, "Everyone loves their own babies, it's other people's children they try to avoid being stuck with." Now someone will be stuck with me. I'm the big problem. It hurts.

The rumble of wheels on the road was heard in the distance. The sound got louder as it approached and then came to an abrupt halt at the end of the cottage path. All those in the cottage looked up, surprised by the sound. It was unusual for anyone to come other than by foot.

Charles peered through the high window at the front of the cottage and exclaimed, "It's his lordship walking down the path toward our house."

Upon entering the cottage his lordship patted John on the head. The lace edge of his shirt-cuff tickled the back of the child's neck causing him to squirm. The richness of the aristocrat's attire made a sharp contrast with the simplicity of the cottage. "I've come to offer my sympathy to these two fine boys." he said. "I want to help."

"How gracious of you," the vicar said. "They have serious problems."

"I know that funds for the support of the youngest one will be needed so I have come to make an offer for the property."

"That's ever so kind of you," the justice said. "We were just now trying to make plans for the sale of the farm. What's your offer, Sir?"

"One hundred twenty pounds for the lot of it." his lordship answered.

"One hundred twenty?" the justice said. "I thought it would bring a bit more." He shifted his eyes around to each of the others trying to perceive their reaction to the offer.

"These are hard times," his lordship said. "Of course, you're free to try to get more from someone else."

"One hundred twenty," the vicar said. "That might be just enough." He looked to the justice for approval. "It might just see to John's care until he is old enough to get proper work."

"Yes," agreed the justice, "That amount might just be enough."

John's spirits began to rise. If his way could be paid for he would be less of a burden.

His lordship dabbed at his nose with his handkerchief and lowered his eyes. He reached into his pocket pulling out a sheet of paper with signatures and a gold seal.

"That offer is conditioned on ninety pounds of the one hundred twenty being paid back to me to cover the lien I already hold on the property."

John's heart sank. Charles let out a short, stifled yelp. The vicar looked with a stony stare at the richly attired aristocrat. The justice shook his head in despair. The remaining thirty pounds would not go far.

There were no other offers for the property. In the end, the vicar and his wife took John to live with them, and out of necessity, accepted the thirty pounds for his keep. Charles made only one demand on his brother's behalf. He agreed to the arrangement on the condition that the vicar take the time to teach John how to read and write.

"What an unusual request from someone your age," the justice said.

"My father cared aplenty about our learning to read and write." Charles answered. "He thought no one would be able to succeed in life in the future without knowing how. He was ambitious for us.

That's why he put the lien on the farm."

By the time John was ten years old, he had learned the rudiments of reading and writing. The money for his board at the vicar's house had run out, and there were other orphans in greater need than he for the vicar's wife to nurture. Charles was called once again from London. He made the long walk to the vicarage with a troubled conscience because of his own inability to care for his brother. In turn, John's conscience bothered him that he had caused so much trouble for everyone by not getting up on that frosty night, more than three years before, to fetch the water from the well for his mother.

The vicar's wife generously welcomed Charles to share a meager dinner on the day he walked from London. After eating and conversing politely for a spell, he asked John to go for a walk with him although after his walk from London, it was the last thing he wanted to do.

"We must talk alone," he whispered as they left the house. "I may have a solution to our problem."

"I hope so," John sighed.

"The vicar told me that the thirty pounds for your care has all been spent."

"No."

"My apprenticeship still has three years to go. It'll be that long before I can earn any money at all, and there's no way I can have you come to live with me. I have two ideas for you to think about. First, you can go to the orphanage. It's not the most pleasant of places. Since the plague, it's been very overcrowded. I heard the food servings are skimpy and that once you're signed into the orphanage, it's almost impossible to get out."

John stiffened. "Not the orphanage," he said.

"I've another idea. Three ships are being loaded in London to go to Virginia. Master Harold says he can get you signed on as a cabin boy. You'd be working to support yourself. The Captain would supply your victuals and clothing. When you got to Virginia, you would be expected to work for the London Company or anyone the company assigned you to for seven years. After that you'd be free and old enough to be on your own."

"Virginia," John said, "Virginia's thousands of miles from anyone I know."

"It'd be a great adventure," Charles said. "The Lord De La Warre will be leading this expedition himself. He's to be the new governor. They say Virginia's a thriving new colony with friendly and helpful natives."

"It's beyond the sea," John said.

"The land sounds like paradise. The climate's mild and the soil fertile. There are birds, fish and animals by the millions. It could be the opportunity of a lifetime. I wish I were free to go."

"I might never see you again. You're all I've got left."

"I promise you, if you go to Virginia, I'll send for you just as soon as I can make enough money to pay for your passage back and to buy out the un-served portion of your indenture. If I were you, I'd rather go to Virginia than to the orphanage."

II

John sailed to Virginia aboard the *Swan*, served as a cabin boy and was indentured upon his arrival at Jamestown. With the exception of his first year, as servant to a drunkard, which he now thought of as his year in purgatory, he was kindly treated.

The propaganda that over a thousand people had immigrated to Virginia by the year 1610, failed to mention that most of the emigrants had died. There were only fifty former colonists still alive when the *Swan* arrived. Most had died of disease or starvation. However, a goodly number had been killed by the so-called friendly Indians. Despite all this, John was not sorry that he had chosen Virginia over going to the orphanage. He only wished that he could stop feeling so blue about it all.

John's first master had been a horror and a terror. Upon his arrival John's indenture was sold to a gentleman who thought himself too good for manual labor, and who as a result, could think of little else to do with his time in Jamestown but to drink. He consumed anything with alcohol in it that he could get his hands on, be it beer, wine or liquor of quality or dubious origin. He had been drunk most of the time. During John's time of waiting on and cleaning up after this inveterate sot, he had suffered periods of hunger, neglect, many fist bashes to the head and a tormenting, all-encompassing loneliness that at times engulfed him both body and soul. Then good fortune turned his way. His first master died on the eve of the arrival of the fleet of Sir Thomas Dale in 1611. His master had been on a prolonged drinking bout and died, while in a stupor, from an assortment of maladies that included liver distress, acute acidity and John thought, just plain meanness. After that, John's indenture had been reassigned to the Reverend Alexander Whitaker, who came to Virginia with Dale.

Luck actually had little to do with the turn of John's fortune in his being assigned to a virtuous man. The day after his first master's death, when Dale's fleet came sailing up the river toward Jamestown, John took fortune into his own hands. He heard the voice of his previous guardian saying to him, "God helps him who helps himself."

Early on the day the new settlers arrived, John ran down to the river, near the approaching vessels, and sprinted along the bank shouting, "Welcome. Welcome."

John called out and waved to the prospective colonists as they hung over the ship's railing for a glimpse of their new homeland and was the first person to meet any of the new arrivals. He thrust his hand out in greeting to numerous men as they disembarked from the vessels, each time studying the faces of those whom he saw until his still small hand was gently shaken by the Reverend Alexander Whitaker, and he looked up to see the face of a saintly man.

"I'm John Flood, Sir. My master died last night, and I want to work for you."

"Goodness, my boy, I don't plan to have a servant. I came here to work myself."

"I've worked for a vicar before," John said. "There are many things I can do for you. I can read and write. I can copy writing in a fair hand."

"Wait, wait. I don't need a servant."

"I've been here a year now and have learned to cook, wash clothes, plant and till vegetables and care for the sick. I can help you with your services too, Sir. I lived at the vicar's house outside London for three years after my parents died."

"An orphan, are you? How old were you when your parents died?"

"Not yet eight, sir."

"I, too, was orphaned young, John. My mother died when I was four and my father when I was ten. How old are you now, son?"

the Reverend asked.

"I'm eleven years old, Sir. Old enough to be a big help to you."

"I'm sure of that. I'll talk to Sir Thomas about it. In the meantime, I'd like you to show me around Jamestown."

Thus John came under the cloak of a kind, learned and godly man. It was the greatest good fortune of his youth.

John left Jamestown with the Reverend Whitaker, traveled inland, up the river, to a spot twenty miles short of the falls, where Sir Thomas Dale was establishing a new town on a peninsula made by the loop of the river forming a natural protection and a ready water supply. Governor Dale thought that it would be healthier and safer than Jamestown and would lend itself more to the development of a few minor industries.

Alexander Whitaker became the first minister to the new region of Henrico. He picked out a one hundred acre plot of land on the south side of the James River, directly across from the new town. After having the church land impaled, he built a fair-sized manse which he named Rocke Hall. From this location, the Reverend thought it would be easier to minister to the new settlers then building a plantation where the Appomattox River flowed into the James, known as Bermuda Hundred. It was at this site that John Flood spent the remaining six years of his servitude.

John performed any task requested of him by the gentle and good-natured churchman. He chopped the wood, laid the fires, tilled and tended the garden, raised, neck-wrenched, plucked and cooked the chickens, milked the cow, fed and curried the horse, washed the clothes, tidied the manse and emptied and cleaned the Reverend's bed-pot.

In exchange, he got a cot to sleep on and as much food to eat as he could help to raise and cook for himself and his new master. He also had opportunities to read and write. The Reverend, after realizing John's abilities, made his small library of a few books available to him. This was the best life that John had known since his parents' death.

On a sunny, mild day in March of 1614, John was turning over the soil in the vegetable garden at the new parsonage. It was an unseasonably warm day even for Virginia. The ground had softened early, and John was taking advantage of it in hopes of getting a head start on the spring planting.

A hungry robin was hopping along some twenty feet behind him as he tilled a straight furrow through the newly thawed earth. The robin held one ear cocked to the ground listening for the movement of any worms that's John's tilling might uncover and kept one eye trained on John to see that he kept a safe distance away.

John knew that he was being followed, and occasionally, to see if his avian friend was properly alert, he would take a step backwards instead of forward. The robin always responded by jumping back an equal distance as if more by instinct than decision.

"What a distrustful little fellow you are," John said aloud. "Here I am working my hands raw to prepare your supper for you, and you think I might do you harm."

John straightened himself up from his spading, looked the robin straight in the eye, rested his folded arm on top of the spade handle and let the gentle breeze blow across his cheeks and through his hair. The southwest wind reminded him of his childhood on his father's farm. As a child, he had loved getting outside in early spring after having been cooped up for most of the winter in their small farmhouse. Putting in the seeds and gently covering them up had been his favorite chore.

On this clear, balmy late winter day, John was enjoying the outdoors again and feeling content with his place in life. He was working the field just outside the Reverend's office window, which had been raised to let the spring breezes blow through the house.

Inside, the Reverend was giving instruction in the Christian faith to Pocahontas, daughter of Powhatan. She was planning to marry an English planter named John Rolfe.

Rolfe had delighted Governor Dale by asking permission to marry the Indian princess. Dale thought that such a liaison would help to insure peace between the Indians and the colonists. Dale had first, however, insisted that Pocahontas be instructed in the tenets of the Christian faith and be converted to Christianity. He sent her to his good friend, the Reverend Whitaker for her instruction.

Pocahontas' rudimentary knowledge of the English language and Whitaker's almost total ignorance of the Algonquian tongue made a difficult subject more difficult to explain or to be understood. Thus, to serve as interpreter, Pocahontas had brought with her an English boy of about John's age, named Henry Spellman.

The same year that John was serving the drunkard in

Jamestown, Henry Spellman had been left at Werowocomoco in a hostage exchange. The idea had been to leave the English boy with Powhatan and to take an Indian boy into Jamestown to safeguard the peace. Unfortunately, a skirmish had occurred in the woodlands that resulted in the killing of several of Powhatan's warriors. Hearing of the killings, Powhatan went into a rampage, vowing to kill Henry.

Pocahontas, who had grown fond of the boy, hid him in a thicket for the night and the next day led him north to the Patawomekes, a subject tribe of Powhatan's. There he lived for several years until he was found by an English sea captain, out of Jamestown. The knowledge he had acquired of the Algonquian tongue made Henry one of the most valuable members of the Jamestown settlement, but because of his youth, he was seldom paid for his services. Of course, he would never have charged Pocahontas anything. She had saved his life single-handedly.

John was planning to plant squash, onions and beans on the land he was tilling. He had carted barrels of decayed leaf-matter from the nearby forest and was vigorously working it into the heavy soil for use as a nutrient and to lighten the soil so that his seeds, when planted, would not be smothered by the clay-like earth.

Blowing toward him through the office window, John heard the steady noises of a lengthy conversation that was taking place between the Reverend, Henry and Pocahontas, but he could not understand anything that they were saying. Every once in a while he could hear a sharp, "no, no," in Henry's voice, and then the slow, quiet voice of the Reverend would continue in its lengthy, sermon-like cadence.

Occasionally, John would detect a note of frustration in the timbre of the voices reaching him, and he wondered what the problem could be.

Abruptly, the sounds reflected a change of mood. There was laughter. The voices took on a cordial, pleasant sound. The front door to the parsonage was opened, the group of three emerged, and the Reverend beckoned to John to join them.

"John, I want you to escort the Princess Pocahontas and Henry Spellman to the river pier. See that they are not molested by any wild animals or domestic hogs along the way, and get them safely launched in their boat," Reverend Whitaker said. Then turning to Pocahontas, he continued, "It has been a great privilege for me to have the honor of instructing you, Princess Pocahontas. We will try again next week when you have had time to think about these matters. You must be certain that you understand all of these things before you offer to accept them."

"Thank you, Reverend Whitaker. We will visit again next week."

The two fourteen-year-old boys and the nineteen-year-old princess eyed each other with interest and set off down the path that led to the river.

"What seemed to be the problem?" John asked Henry. "I could tell from outside that you had run into rough waters."

"We made some progress," Henry said. "She's grasped the idea of there being only one God. She knows that she must stop acknowledging the heathen gods she's been brought up on, but it's hard for her. The real trouble is she can't understand the trinity. One minute the Reverend tells her that there's only one God, the next minute he tells her that God is in three persons. I think she almost understood the part about Jesus, as God's only son, coming to earth to show us the way to Him, but when he tried to explain the Holy Ghost, she sank into complete confusion."

"She's not alone. Lots of Christians don't understand the Holy Ghost," John said. "It's hard to explain."

"I sometimes wonder whether I understand Him myself," Henry said. "I usually think of Him as that part of God that is in each of us, if we are Christians. After all we're all God's children."

"That part of us that's able to love, you mean. I'm not sure that all Christians can."

"The real trouble is her tongue doesn't have words to explain it. She's going to have to learn the meaning of the English words afresh without any translation. She's very smart though. She'll get it."

"You learned her language well, I guess?"

"I learned about all there was to learn. It has a limited number of words. There're words for most things but not many ways to express ideas."

"Maybe we can make lists of the Indian words and their meaning. I'd like to know how to talk with the natives myself."

It took the threesome a quarter of an hour to reach the river. John enjoyed walking beside the princess. There was something very pleasant about being with a woman. He had seen almost none during his three years in Virginia. As he glanced over at Pocahontas, her body now covered with a full, flowing dress of modest fashion in keeping with English tradition, he was acutely aware of her femininity.

With a sense of embarrassment, John realized that he and Henry had been talking over Pocahontas' head rather than with her. He was aware of this rudeness and wondered how he could make amends. He felt awkward but could think of nothing to do or say. Reaching the boat, he helped them both climb in and secure the oars. The boat headed out into the river, and he waved a spontaneous farewell.

Watching as the boat began to appear smaller, he felt a large salty tear run down his cheek. Pocahontas reminded him of his mother. He could barely remember her face now, but as long as he lived he would never forget the last days of her life. A heavy load of sorrow and guilt started to spread through his body. His chest began to fill with an ache that left him feeling as though he might burst into tears. Six years had passed since his mother and father had died, but still he could not get away from the pain of his loss.

III

Several years of peace and prosperity followed the auspicious marriage of Pocahontas and John Rolfe. Feeling more secure in their relationships with the natives, the Englishmen began giving them greater liberties. Every day, the Indians mingled in almost every aspect of the colonists' lives. They could be seen in the streets of Jamestown, at the boat dock, at the trading center, in the tavern, in the churchyard and in the houses of many of the residents.

Sir Thomas Dale served as Governor for over two years, but he was an active, restless sort of man, and by the time he had gotten order restored in Virginia and improved economic conditions so as to encourage the colonists to work, he was in a mood to move on.

In early April of 1616, Governor Dale sent word to his beloved friend, Alexander Whitaker, that he would be paying him a farewell visit the following week. He said he would be leaving Virginia by mid-month to return to England upon Captain Argall's ship and that Pocahontas and her husband, John Rolfe, would accompany him. The Reverend Whitaker called John Flood to tell him of the impending visit, and from that moment until the Governor's arrival, the parsonage was in a frenzy of preparation.

John was at the pier to meet Governor Dale and his party on a brilliant but cold April morning. He escorted the group to the manse where fires were burning in the two principal rooms of the house, the kitchen and the Reverend's study. The Governor's accompanying retinue was ushered into the kitchen for refreshments and a noontime dinner. The Governor and the Reverend settled in the study.

John was back and forth continually trying to serve in both places. His ears perked with interest when he heard the Governor say, "You've made a cozy place of this old abandoned Indian ground. I can see that I've missed much pleasure by not coming here more often. Tell me, how'd you get anything to grow in the worn-out soil you found here when you took over this plot?"

"John gets credit for that," Whitaker said. "He carried cartfuls of top soil and detritus from the decaying leaves of the forest, just to the east of here, and worked it into the garden's soil. He remembered his father doing that when he was only a small boy. It worked beautifully. He's a real farmer's son."

"He's been a Godsend to you hasn't he?" Dale said.

"I can't imagine how I could have survived without him. I had no conception of how primitive things would be over here. I thought we'd all be eating in a mess hall in Jamestown with a cook in the kitchen."

"It's still hard for me to believe what we found when we got here," the Governor said, "men playing at bowling in the streets when their houses were about to fall down upon their heads, not troubling themselves to plant a spring crop even though only a few months supply of food was left in the storehouse."

"Some men do deserve their poor lot in life," Whitaker said, "although many who have it do not. Is Pocahontas happy to be going to England?"

"She's excited at any rate. Nervous, but eager. Hope she's not disappointed. One never knows how she'll be received there."

John arrived at the door carrying a flat wooden platter with two glasses and a bottle of port.

"For your health, Governor," John said. "We were sorry to hear you'd be leaving."

"That's kind of you, my boy. I'll miss my friends here, particularly your master, more than I can say." When John left the room, Dale continued. "You've done wonders with the boy too. He actually smiled at me."

"He smiles often these days." said Whitaker. "He has only one more year of service to give. That may be what is making him smile more now. He should get some land of his own if the London Company ever gets around to doling it out as they promised to do."

"That's one of the things I'll have to work on when I get back to London. The common storehouse principal on which the Company set up the Virginia experiment is a total disaster. No one will do any work that he can squirm out of when the product of his labor goes into a common pool. That policy has bred the laziest group of dullards I've ever encountered. When we built Henrico, I had three acres of tillable land allotted to each man so that he could farm it on his own in his spare time. Immediately, production went up ten fold over what it was in Jamestown. Unfortunately, I didn't have the right to give them the land. It still belongs to the London Company, but with the use of it so that they can keep and sell their crops for their own profit, they have all worked their hands raw to make it produce. Somehow I've got to get the idea across to the policy makers that they should parcel out land for private ownership. Man works for himself and his family, not for the good of the group. Yet as a result of his working for himself, the entire group ends up better off."

Dale was a handsome man and one who enjoyed living life to its fullest. He loved women, wine, good food and almost anything else that could give a man pleasure. His inclinations were such that he could easily have become a ne'er do well had he not possessed a superior intelligence and a great love of tackling any difficult situation and mastering it. He was ruthless to the core. No means were out of bounds for him if it helped him to reach a needed goal. During his tenure in Virginia, he had been accused of the harshest of tactics including violence, torture, even execution of the guilty by the wheel and rack. He had, however, accomplished his mission. He had taken the settlement he found on his arrival, a place of thievery, drunkenness, idleness and anarchy, and he had turned it into a tranquil, law abiding, prosperous place. Somehow, through it all, he and his old friend, the Reverend Whitaker, had remained the most admiring of friends. They were direct opposites of each other in both personality and actions yet each could sincerely appreciate the other.

John Flood reentered to bring the men their mid-day dinner. He set two benches up on either side of the Reverend's writing table and placed wooden plates, and spoons beside them. As he began to serve the meal, the men changed their conversation to more general subjects.

"How is it you haven't planted any tobacco here?" asked Dale. "Are you the only man in Virginia with no need for cash?"

"We only grow what we can use ourselves," answered the Reverend. "Haven't time to become a farmer for profit. I have my flock of souls to tend to. Anyway, every other person in these parts has planted tobacco so it's probably a good thing for one lone parson to grow something digestible. Have you acquired an affection for tobacco during your stay in Virginia?"

"I can use it or not."

"I think it's an abomination," Whitaker said. "I hear King James agrees with me and is trying to get it outlawed."

"It's caught on in England like a rampaging fire," said Dale. "I don't think even he can stop its importation. The people want it."

John finished his serving and left the room, but he could still hear much of the conversation through the thin interior walls.

"You've done a superior job here, my friend. You've brought law and order. Everyone is grateful."

"It hasn't been easy. I had to do a great many unpleasant things before I could get the idea across that we were not going to tolerate anything less than a firm discipline. The men we had to deal with were no angels. And, too, there have been few women about. Men are wild without women to keep them on a straight path. I'm sure that you disapproved of many things that were done."

"I regret some of the means, but like everyone else, I marvel at the results. The marriage of Pocahontas and John Rolfe has been a great blessing. You had a keen foresight in approving the marriage. I must confess to having had some misgivings at the time. How did you know it would work so well and bring peace with her people?"

"Marrying the enemy is an age-old English custom. You surely can think of many royal examples of it. It doesn't always work, but it does no harm."

Sir Thomas moved back on the bench, patted his stomach and said, "Your farm boy's a good cook." Looking around with interest at the Reverend's abode he added, "Why don't you lock this place up for a while and take the ship back to England with us?"

The Reverend sighed. "I can't leave. So few ministers have come out to help with the work. In every church publication, one reads of their railing against surplices and subscriptions, yet, though we use neither of them here, they don't come."

"They're spoiled," Dale said. "They don't want to give up their comforts."

There was a slight pause in the conversation as Alexander Whitaker weighed the idea of broaching a delicate subject. Finally, he said, "So you are actually going back to your lovely wife with a clean conscience despite your effort to acquire an Indian mistress." Whitaker kept a straight face, but there was a teasing twinkle in his eye.

"How'd you know about that?"

"God knows everything, and sometimes He lets a few of His subjects in on some of His secrets."

"It was just a political move. I wouldn't have consorted with her. She was only thirteen. I just thought Pocahontas might be happier with her baby sister in Jamestown, and that another Indian-Englishman alliance might be good for peace."

"You can't squirm out of it that easily. You asked Powhatan for the girl's hand in marriage, and you already have a wife."

"Well, that old bull has had at least a hundred wives. He could-n't blame me for that. Anyway, it didn't work out. He said, 'no', so there was no harm done."

The Reverend got up from his bench and led the way back to the two chairs beside the fire. He tapped the table with his knuckles to call John back for the cleanup. When John returned to clear away the last of the meal, the conversation had shifted again.

"When you get to England, I wish you'd put forth an idea I've been working on. I've written it up so you can present it to the London Company and to the church groups as well. I want to see a school here where we can take young Indian boys as boarders, teach them to be Christians and train them in a useful trade. It's a dream of mine. In it, I see the boys going back and converting their fellow tribesmen to Christianity. That would be my way of secur-ing the peace."

"It's a good idea. I'll present it to anyone you suggest. I have some plans of my own. I want to push the London Company to start giving out the parcels of land they've been promising to grant to the settlers. John here, has been a faithful colonist for six years. He deserves a share of the enterprise. How much longer does your indenture last, John?"

"One year more, Sir."

"Whatever will I do without him when the time comes?" Whitaker asked.

"Buy another one, of course. Orphans are made every day."

John looked at the two men. What a strange friendship. They're so different in every way, and yet, anyone can see that they delight in each other's company. Each sets off the other and makes him seem more appealing. They'll be talking through most of the day. I'll hear the rumble of their voices far into the afternoon.

When the sun began to cast long shadows across the floor of the study, Governor Dale said, "I'll miss you greatly, you know. I'll never find another friend such as you."

Alexander Whitaker, with John a few steps behind, walked the long path to the river dock with Governor Dale and watched as he boarded the small pinnace in which he and his party had come. John stayed patiently on the dock for some time after the ship had cast off watching the Reverend as he in turn watched his friend of many years depart. The Reverend stared sadly at the receding boat as it and its occupants became smaller. He did not turn his glance away until he could no longer see the features on Dale's face. Then with a heavy heart, he walked back with John to the manse.

The two friends were never to see each other again. The following spring, shortly before John's indenture was to be completed, the Reverend Whitaker drowned in a boating accident as he was crossing the river. At the age of thirty-two his life's work was done.

Pocahontas also died that year. After a successful sojourn in England, where she was graciously received by the queen, she died of the aftermath of chicken-pox while aboard ship preparing to return to Virginia. She was twenty-two, or perhaps twenty-three, years old.

Governor Dale never returned. He died in India, of a languishing illness, just two years after the deaths of Whitaker and Pocahontas. Thus, the three people who were the most responsible for the peace in Virginia were lost to the cause.

IV

Two years later on a hot summer day, John was precariously straddling the edge of the roof at Rocke Hall, trying to plug up a leak, when he heard an English voice shout out, "Nemarough, ka ka torawincs yewo." Turning in the direction of the call, he saw Henry Spellman coming across the open field toward the manse.

"You'd never fool an Indian with that sound," shouted back John. "You sound as English as any limey at sea." John quickly dropped his tools and shimmied down the drain pole to greet his friend. He gave Henry a cordial slap on the back with one hand as he extended the other for a handshake.

"Mercy, you've turned into a yellow bird," Henry said. "Your hair's the color of light wheat."

"Been working in the sun. It always bleaches out this time of year. Hope you've come to stay a while. It's lonely out here without the Reverend."

"Just an hour or so, I'm sorry to say. Could you spare some cool water for a chap who's parched?"

"You know I can. Come on in. How's it you've come this way?"

"I wanted to talk with you. There're things need doing."

"You know I'm still waiting here for a new parson to come."

"I heard. I also heard that Governor Argall won't let you leave, that he isn't granting freedom to those who have worked out their indenture."

"It's been a bit sticky," John said. "Let's go inside. It's cooler there. Besides, I'm itching for a long talk."

They entered the manse, fetched themselves each large mugs of water and settled down in the late Reverend's study.

"You bet, I'm still indentured. It seems that Governor Dale declared martial law in Virginia when he was trying to establish order. He forgot to disestablish it before going back to England. Governor Argall decided to keep it. He likes the power."

"Something has to be done about Argall, John. That's why I'm here. We've got to get word back to the London Company as to what's going on here."

"Don't they know?"

"The letters of most of the officials and guards are being scrutinized. People are afraid to write straight to the authorities. The board of the London Company sees Argall as the naval hero who blazed a shorter sea path to Virginia."

"That he did."

"They remember that he brought us horses from Canada and successfully expelled the French from their settlement in Maine. They don't know about his dark side. That's only come out recently."

"It's strange. He started out so well. Then his greed seemed to get control of his good sense."

"You can't know all the things he's done. This year he started selling off the supplies from the common store. Then he had the public cattle slaughtered so he could sell the hides and converted the settlement's grain supply to his own use. You know about his refusal to honor prior contracts. That's why you're still not free."

"What can I do?"

"We want you to write a letter to your brother in London. Use the same paper and pen you always use. Tell him your story. I'll include another sheet of paper telling of Argall's other misdeeds and telling him who he's to show the letters to. It's dangerous. If the letter gets into Argall's hands, it could mean serious trouble for both of us."

"Would a letter from one servant carry any weight?"

"You're not the only one being asked to do this. We hope to get a number of letters through, all saying basically the same thing. That way we might get some action."

"Who is to carry the letters to England?"

"You don't need to know that. We know a Captain we think we can trust. If you'll write the letter, I promise you it won't get into anyone else's hands except the Captain's, and it won't get into his hands until seconds before the ship casts off from Jamestown."

"Let's start writing, "John said.

The two men set upon the task, consulting each other as they wrote. When both approved of the contents, the letters were folded and tucked into a hidden pocket on the inside of Henry's shirt. Then, they relaxed with more water and a morsel of food.

"Have you ever heard of a Paspahegh called Nemantico?" Henry asked.

"Sure have," John said. "He's the Indian who delivered the message that Pocahontas was dead. Very churned up about it, he was. Came to tell the Reverend about her death, but the good man had already drowned by that time. I remember Nemantico saying that the English had killed her. He didn't try to disguise his fury. How did she die?"

"She came down with small pox while in England. They thought she had recovered, and they started to set sail for home. While the ship was making its way down the Thames, she died of some aftermath of the disease. It's as great a loss for us as for the Indians. She was by far the most advanced member of her race. She had qualities of greatness that one rarely sees in members of any race."

"You wouldn't be here if it weren't for her, would you?"

"She saved my life all by herself."

"Why do you ask about Nemantico?"

After Powhatan died and Opechancanough took over as chief werowance, Nemantico left his tribe and joined up permanently with him. He became his chief deputy. Been causing trouble. Peace is shakier than it was a few years ago. Be on your guard."

"Thanks for the news. I'll start bolting the door."

V

Argall's deeds became so notorious that the London Company heard of them from many sources. Governor Argall was recalled to London to explain his actions, and the colony slid further into mismanagement and decay.

One day during the Lenten season of 1619, a traveler from Jamestown stopped at the manse on his way from Jamestown to the plantation at Bermuda Hundred. His news was the most welcome that John had heard during all his days in Virginia.

"The new Governor, Sir George Yardley, has arrived," said the traveler.

"Hallelujah!" said John. "Virginia couldn't have gone on much longer without an overseer. Does he look to be good?"

"People are happy so far. Course anyone would be better than Argall. Yardley brought a parcel of orders from the Company. The indentured, who've worked off their time, are free now."

"Holy Mother of God," John said.

"Do you have trouble with that?" the traveler asked. "I always thought you was free."

"Should have been a year ago."

"All you have to do is travel to Jamestown with proof that your time is up, and the Governor will sign to your freedom. But, there's more good news. The Governor came with instructions to divvy up land to the early settlers."

"That must mean me."

"Sure. Anyone who's been here since 1616 is entitled to one hundred acres of land not only for his lifetime but for his heirs as well."

"A hundred acres," John said. His eyes widened and began to shine.

"You better get out there looking for the plot you want. I'm heading up to the falls to search out mine."

John's spirits soared. He could hardly wait to get started, but before going to Jamestown, he decided to do some scouting around in hopes of finding the perfect piece of land that he could be happy with for a lifetime. He readied his newly purchased horse, bought with the profits of his first Indian trading, and spent the late spring and early summer months roaming the south shore of the James River for a home site.

John felt certain that most of the eligible settlers would be asking for land on the north shore, which had easy access to Jamestown and agreements for peace with the surrounding Indian tribes. The south shore Indians were considered to be less predictable. They had never come to peace terms with the colonists upon the marriage of Pocahontas and John Rolfe. She was not their princess. John surmised that Opechancanough's tribes were probably no more dependable than any of the others now that Pocahontas was dead, and he might get a choicer piece of land on the less settled side of the river.

One day while riding through the heavily forested land with its many small hills, dales and fresh water creeks, he descended the slope to a sandy shore. There, he came upon a giant cypress tree that towered above the others and sent a long sturdy, leaning trunk out across some yards of the brackish river so that it could be seen from a distance by boaters traveling in either direction.

John dismounted in order to have a better look at the ancient tree. Stepping inside its highly raised knees, he stretched his arms trying to encircle its central trunk but could reach only half way around it. The many knees, which the mammoth tree had sent up above ground to breathe fresh air and stabilize its weight in the shifting sandy soil, seemed to enclose him and warmly welcome his presence. It was like climbing back into some long forgotten but comfortable past. He felt that he was in nature's embrace.

John looked up at the towering top branches of the tree and wondered how old the majestic cypress might be. He knew that the tree must have witnessed an unaccountable number of momentous events during its long sentry on this much-traveled Indian waterway.

From the base of the tree, John could look up a gentle incline of land that ascended more than a hundred feet above the water level and then flattened out in the form of a plateau. Some of the plateau land had been cleared and tilled in the past by local Indians, but it appeared to have been deserted for years. There was something so appealing about the layout of the site, with its ancient cypress looking out across the river toward Jamestown, that John decided to put in his claim for it as soon as he could get to the Governor's office.

Primarily because of his horse, it was necessary for John to travel back more than forty miles toward the falls before he could find a place narrow and shallow enough to ford the James River. His trip from the site of the cypress tree to Jamestown, which was separated by only a three-mile-wide river, took him several days by land.

It was a sultry, hot, August day when John rode his horse into Jamestown. His shirt was moist from the exertion of the long ride and was sticking uncomfortably to his back. A swarm of insects played the role of a welcoming party. When he slowed the pace of his horse from a trot to a walk, green flies attacked the animal's rump causing it to switch its tail vigorously and give out a loud snort.

John's eyes wandered to all corners of the settlement, noting the many changes that had taken place since his last visit two years before. His first impression was of tobacco plants growing everywhere. He could not only see the sticky, large-leafed plants in every direction that he looked, but he nearly gagged over their sickly, sweet aroma.

John rode down the center street of the town noticing that the frame and log houses on either side of the road were in a fair state of repair, yet there seemed to be something lax and sloppy about the town's general appearance. There was an undisciplined look which he soon realized was caused by the number of Indians he saw lolling about. They were not only there, they looked as though they lived there.

John tied his horse to a post before the office of the Governor. He walked a few steps to the door and was almost knocked down by a tall red man who rushed through the door carrying a musket in his hand.

"Hey!" John shouted to a trio of settlers nearby, "What's that Indian doing with one of our weapons?"

"Don't worry about him, fella. He won't shoot you," one of the men answered. "He's the Governor's shot, an experienced marksman who hunts birds and game for the Governor's table."

"You mean the Indians are being taught how to use our arms? No wonder the town looks so loose."

Inside the office, John found the Governor's secretary ready to help him. He decided to clear up the matter of his expired indenture first, that being the most important matter at hand.

John gave the secretary his half of the work agreement that had been made in England, on his behalf, by his brother and his guardian, the vicar. After the agreement had been signed by both parties in 1610, the paper had been ripped into two parts. The Captain of the *Swan*, acting for the London Company, had kept one part and John was given the other. If there had been a dispute concerning the terms of the contract, the two pieces would be pieced together to verify that the contestant had a part of the original agreement. The indents had to match.

"You're a lucky man," the secretary said. "The new Governor called an assembly of representatives from each of the hundreds to air the grievances of the settlers. One of the first things they did was to declare that all contracts signed in England had to be honored in Virginia."

"How'd they assemble?" John asked.

"The burghers came here a fortnight ago, all spiffed up in their finest clothes and taking their duty very seriously. They met in the choir stalls of the church on two of the hottest days since

Englishmen set foot in Virginia, and the Governor paid careful attention to all they said."

"Did he give them what they wanted?"

"The assemblymen couldn't make any laws themselves. They could only make recommendations, but the Governor already had instructions about the contracts. That won't be a problem anymore. I'll place your name on the list of free citizens of Virginia and give you a paper to prove it."

After clearing up the matter of his freedom, John said, "If it's true that all colonists who came before 1616 are entitled to one hundred acres of land, I'd like to put in a claim."

"It's true, all right, but you've got to know which acres you want."

"I want a hundred acres on the south shore on the point nearest to Jamestown. The place where the giant cypress grows."

"Funny you should want to settle on the south shore." the secretary said, "Most people are scared of the Indians over there and want to stay on this side. Unfortunately, however, some others have already asked for the land with the Four Mile Tree."

"Four Mile Tree?" John said. "What's that?"

"The ancient cypress tree that you just described to me." the clerk said. "Captain Argall named it that earlier this year. While he was still governor, he laid out the limits of James City. It goes from Hog Island on the east to the great cypress three four miles to the west. It's the boundary landmark so he named it the Four Mile Tree."

"How extraordinary," John said. "How disappointing. Who asked for that site?"

"There's a group of four that filed claims together. Five if you count Pace's wife. All were friends in Middlesex before coming here. Richard Pace and Isobel are both ancient planters so they get two hundred acres between them. They plan to build a house and settle permanently over there, if they get the patent. Then there's Captain William Perry. He'll do the same. Third one is William Powell. He's Captain of the Jamestown militia so he has to live here. He'll pay Pace and Perry to farm his land for him. The forth is John Smith. He's Captain Powell's brother-in-law. I don't know his plans, but they're all in this together. It's a kind of partnership."

"Sounds like a very impressive group."

"Why don't you scout out something else?"

"I think I fell in love with the tree."

"Save yourself for a woman instead. There's lots more beautiful trees than women in these parts, even though the *Margaret* out of Bristol came in a month ago with ninety young beauties that the Captain sold as wives. They were all spoken for before you could open your purse to see if you could afford one. But, they'll be bringing in some more."

"You mean to say they sold English women to anyone who could pay for them?" John asked.

"Sure did," the secretary answered, "and some of the girls were mighty unhappy about it."

"They must have come voluntarily."

"Huh!" the secretary said. "Some may have, but if you ask me, some were as good as kidnapped."

The mental picture of the scared girls made John feel queasy. He knew what it was like, what they were bound to suffer. John made a fist, digging his fingernails into his palm until his hand went numb. His throat went suddenly dry. He tried to push his thirst away.

No. It was the blue mood starting to envelop him again. He couldn't allow it to take control of him.

He saw a pitcher of water on the table. "For anyone?" he asked.

"Help yourself."

John forced down a cupful. He mustn't punish himself, even though he felt he deserved it. He turned to leave. He wanted to get away as quickly as possible.

Waving his hand behind his head he said, "Thanks for your help. I'll be back when I find another plot of land."

Outside, the day was sunny and cheerful despite the frightful heat. John left his horse at the hitching post and walked back through the town looking for the tavern. Searching the door signs for some indication of a public house, he noticed a young boy, no more than ten years of age, running into the enclosure. When he neared, John could hear him yelling, "Dutch Man-o-War coming, full of Nigras. Dutch Man-0-War coming, full of Nigras."

People seemed to emerge, as if by magic, from the twenty odd houses that bordered the street. Almost all were men in different stages of dress, pulling their attire together as they ran toward the river.

John forgot temporarily about finding the tavern and began following the crowd.

A sailing ship flying the Dutch flag was maneuvering its way into the docking area. From the air slits in the main hold, just below the crew's quarters, white eyes, framed by dark faces, could be seen peering through the slim openings.

The Dutch captain came down the newly extended gangplank, bowed his greetings to all present and asked to see the Governor.

Captain William Powell, commander of the Jamestown militia, was the first official to arrive on the scene.

"Captain Powell," the Dutchman acknowledged, "My regards to the Governor. May I have permission to bring some African cargo out of the hold and onto the land? They are in need of some fresh air and mild exercise. We will guard them closely."

With the permission granted, the Dutch captain and his crew slowly brought the first twenty black people up from the hold of the ship, down the gangplank and onto the soil of Virginia. All were tied and manacled. They were a hungry, mal-nourished and terrified-looking group of human beings.

Captain Powell, seeing their condition, immediately sent a soldier to the storehouse for bread and water.

For a lengthy period of time, the Africans, with their eyes smarting from the strong sunlight, stared at the colonists, and the colonists, who knew not what to think of this unusual event, stared back at the Africans.

This is more than I want to see today. How can anyone make a living out of dealing in human cargo and still think of himself as a human being? Look at that Dutch captain, standing with confidence in seemingly excellent health waiting for the Governor to arrive. A sudden urge to smash his face caused John to stiffen his arm and double up his fist. The same queasy feeling that had come over him in the Governor's office was beginning to return.

A young woman, whom John had not noticed, moved up close beside him and without introduction asked, "Will those people be staying here?"

"I don't know," John said, relaxing his fist and turning to see his questioner. "This is the first I've seen or heard of black men in

Virginia."

John looked appraisingly at the young woman. He was almost as surprised to see a female as he had been to see the Negroes. She was a plain enough wench. Her dark hair was parted in the middle and pulled back in a severe bun that was pinned at the nape of her neck. Her skin was fresh and clear revealing her youth, but her eyes had an intense, controlled quality to them that immediately spoke to him of sadness. "I didn't see you when I first got to the dock," he said. "Who are you?"

"I'm Beth Young," she said. "No. I mean to say, Beth Blackthorn. I've just recently been married."

"You're not one of the women who came on the *Margaret* last month are you?"

"Yes," she said, turning her head away in embarrassment.

"Some man was lucky," John said, "My name is John Flood."

"I haven't seen you before either. Have you just arrived?"

"To Jamestown just this morning. Came in from Charles City, but I've been in Virginia since 1610. I came when I was ten years old."

"Came as a child, did you? I heard all the early child-immigrants had died."

"Most of them did."

"I just came to Jamestown this morning myself," Beth continued. "Came to find someone to write a letter for me. I want my sister to know that I'm alive and where I am."

John stared at the young woman remembering that the Governor's secretary had said, "Some were as good as kidnapped." He took a deep breath and said, "I'll write your letter for you. Let's find the tavern and some paper and ink. You must be thirsty, too, on this suffocating day. Anyway, I don't want to watch this scene any longer. It's beginning to make me feel sick."

In the tavern, John was able to buy paper and ink. The tavern keeper lent him a quill. The two new acquaintances sat at a table near the window to get a good light, and a waiter brought them each a cooling drink. John noticed that Beth had become nervous and agitated. He surmised that it would be difficult for her to share the private thoughts she wished to convey to her sister with a stranger. He wished he could put her more at ease, but he didn't know what to do or say so he decided to just get on with it. "First,

I'll have to know where the letter's to go."

"It's to my sister. Her name is Mary Young. She's in the employ of Sir Reginald White at Moor's Haven, Gray's Parish, outside of Bristol. I worked there too before coming to Virginia."

John wrote the address on the upper backside of the paper and waited for the message.

"Dear Sister Mary, I'll say," Beth said in a slow and deliberate manner. "I'm safe in Virginia." There was a long pause before she went on. "I'm married but not to the man you met before I left. I'm married to an older Englishman who has lived here for some years. He paid the captain for my expenses when I arrived. My name is now Beth Blackthorn. The man who asked me to marry him and come to Virginia was not on the ship. He was already married. I was tricked. Mr. Blackthorn and I work at a place called Berkeley Hundred. He farms. I cook and farm. Virginia is a pleasant place, but there are not even a thousand people here. There're many Indians, said to be friendly, but they scare me. Don't pity me. Mr. Blackthorn says he'll soon have land of his own. Your loving sister, Beth."

After John had finished the writing and turned the paper around so that Beth could make her mark under her name, she gave a gasping cry as though she had been attacked by homesickness. "Can you add, oh, how I miss you?"

"To be sure," answered John making the addition. "How was it you were tricked?" he asked quietly.

Beth hesitated for a moment. Then tears and her explanation flowed out as the wall of inhibitions gave way to the pleasure of finding a sympathetic confidant.

Beth's tale was one that could have been repeated many times by others of the ninety women who had arrived on the *Margaret*.

"A very handsome, young sailor asked to be introduced to me when he saw me on the street in Bristol. He said he'd been watching me for months and that he'd loved me from first sight." Beth lowered her head in embarrassment. "He called on me at Moor's Haven every day for a week and wooed me as though his life would be ruined if I refused to go to Virginia with him when his ship sailed. He begged me to join him saying that the captain would marry us on the ship. He told me to pack all my things and come to the ship *Margaret*, in the harbor, on the day it was to sail. He said he would take care of the cost of my passage. I was to give my name to the captain but to say nothing to anyone else until he looked me up after the ship had sailed.

"I told no one but my sister about it. She thought it the most romantic thing ever could happen to a lass. She went with me to Bristol and saw me on to the ship.

"The handsome sailor never showed up. He wasn't on the ship. It wasn't until the ship was far at sea that many of the other women began to share tales with each other. We found out that many had been lured and tricked in the same way.

"When the *Margaret* arrived in Virginia, the captain announced that there would be husbands for us all. We were sold like slaves at the waterfront," Beth said in a whisper.

"Slaves are subjected for their lifetime," John countered.

"Do you know of any marriages that are not for the lifetime of at least one of the partners?"

"True," John said and nodded. "But I'll wager there'll be a few new husbands who find some very colorful mushrooms in their stew."

"I must go now," Beth said picking up the letter. "My husband might not like my being here in the tavern. What should I give you for writing the letter for me?"

"Nothing. You've already paid too much."

"You're nice. If you want a wife, I could ask my sister to come over for you."

"I'm not ready for a wife yet, but thanks just the same."

The encounter with Beth had left John in a strange mood. Woman's lot is a difficult one under the best of circumstances. She'll get used to it all in time. She shouldn't have much trouble finding someone to pay for her sister's passage to Virginia. She's a resourceful one.

John left the tavern and strolled back down the hill to the dock area where the chief action of the day was taking place. He had not walked far when he heard his name called out. Turning to see the possessor of the familiar voice, he saw Henry Spellman loping down the bank behind him.

"Hey, John. How's it you're in Jamestown?"

"Came to get my papers. I'm a free man at last."

"Congratulations. How does it feel?"

"Great. Your pocket full of letters to the big guys must have gotten through."

"Something did anyway. Who knows what?"

"How are things going with the Indians? No one seems the least concerned about them around here."

"Opechancanough has let us know that he holds all the power Powhatan held. He's meaner than a bull in heat, hates all Englishmen, is much younger than Powhatan was, and unfortunately is in perfect physical health. Let's sit down for a minute. We have lots of catching up to do."

The two men sat down extending their legs on the sloping bank for support and began an animated conversation.

"I'm a captain in the guards now," Henry said. "I also keep very busy as an interpreter with the Indians. How about you?"

"I spend a good bit of time trading with the Indians. Just small things that are easy to carry. I learned my first bits of the tongue from you, you know. Then, many Indians came to the parsonage. I learned plenty from them. They trust me more than the other traders, because they think of me as the Reverend's man. They loved him. Anyway, I try not to take advantage of them. I take them needles and nails, not beads and baubles."

"You're a brave man. I'll never be able to trust them. My childhood adventures left me with little taste for dealing with any but a few of them. I stay as much as possible in Jamestown. Things are going much better since Governor Yardley took over. He even allowed an assembly of colonists to be called to speak their minds."

"I heard something of that."

"Not only was it called, it seemed to work. The burghers were here only a fortnight ago. They got quite a few problems out on the table. Then the meeting had to be called short because of the heat. One of the burgers actually died of prostration. What are you planning to do now?"

"I'm trying to find a hundred acres of land to my satisfaction and put my claim in on it. I found a site I wanted, but unfortunately some people named Pace, Perry, Powell and Smith have already asked for it. I'll have to start scouting again."

"They want the land just across the river," Henry said. "I'd have thought you would want land near Charles City since that's where you've been living."

78

"No, I want to be near enough to get into Jamestown. I've been alone as long as I want to be. I like people."

"Captain Powell is down there with the Governor haggling over whether to buy the Dutch captain's cargo or not. We can talk with him when he's free. I hope they don't let the Africans stay. We've got enough trouble with the Indians without adding another problem."

"You can see the Africans don't want to be put back on the ship."

"None of them want that," Henry said. "Can you imagine the horror of that journey? It's a tough decision for the Governor to have to make."

"Well, there are only twenty of them. Twenty people can't cause much trouble."

At the river's edge, John and Henry waited until all negotiations between the Dutchman and the Governor had been completed. The decision was made to purchase the Negroes for work in the tobacco fields. It was uncertain whether they would work for the London Company or be sold to individuals for their own use.

The Africans were somewhat revived by the bread and water they had been given from the common store, and they began to stretch their arms and legs and to babble to each other in muted, eerie tones of voice.

One of the guards approached them and prodded them into a line indicating that they were to march up the hill.

The slow flicker of a smile appeared on the face of the tallest member of the group as he began to perceive that they were not to be returned to the ship. When he was satisfied that such was so, he sang out three base notes in a strong but dolorous voice and waited for the others to repeat the sound. Next, he sang four notes, high, low, high, low, as they marched up the hill. The high notes of hope tempered by the low notes of despair were repeated by his followers. Before they reached the top of the embankment, the notes had melted into a deeply moving rhythm of sounds that seemed to transcend time and space. The sound was one that John would never forget. He would hear the music many times in the years ahead, and it would always remind him of how it had all begun.

Captain Powell was not alone when Henry took John over to meet him. He was talking with William and Margaret Finch, a handsome couple, and their four-year-old daughter, Frances. The Finches were new arrivals from Bristol, who had been recruited by the steward of Berkeley Hundred, a large plantation some miles upriver from Jamestown. Some of the plantations were being managed more efficiently, and carefully thought-out lists of the type of people needed for the proper operation of the enterprises had been given to the veteran sea captain, Tracy, for the recruitment of immigrants with particular skills.

William Finch was a lumberman who had been hired to improve the operation of timber harvesting, one of the few profitable exports of the colony other than tobacco. He and his family were caught up in the thrill of the adventure.

Captain Powell had been in Virginia even longer than John and remembered him as a boy. When he heard that John had wanted the acreage across the river with the great cypress tree, he laughed heartily. "There must be hundreds of trees as old and as large," he said. "Pace will likely get that particular plot, but do look around some more on the south shore. We need all the good men we can get as a bulwark against the frontier."

"You mean against the Indians, don't you?" Finch asked.

"We don't really worry about them. All has been peaceful for the last several years. The London Company has set aside land near Charles City for the building of a college. Some Indian boys will be entered so that we can bring them up as Christians. and teach them a useful trade. They're entering more and more into our lives. With time, they'll become a part of us."

Margaret Finch let out a sigh of relief upon hearing this last declaration. A broad smile flashed across her face, and she turned her glance toward John and Henry in hopes of hearing their agreement that all was peaceful with the natives.

While Henry embarked upon a recitation of his own particular views of the Indians, John stood silently and studied the delicate features of Margaret's face. The dark curls of her hair were mostly hidden by the hat that sat squarely on her head and tied beneath her chin. She was dressed properly in an inconspicuous manner. Nothing about her looks or demeanor suggested that she sought any special attention from those around her, but she had a powerful femininity that could not be disguised. John felt the stirrings of manhood within him. So acute were his feelings that he was certain she must be aware of them.

"We'll be on our way now," William Finch said. "We're moving out tomorrow. I'm eager to get to Berkeley so Margaret can start turning our promised cabin into a home."

John's eyes followed Margaret as the family of three left. What a lucky man. How I'd love to be going to a cabin in the woods to make a home with that woman.

Margaret followed her husband obediently, as appeared to be her custom. Just as she reached the top of the embankment, however, her head turned ever so slightly for a fleeting moment, just long enough to see that John was still watching her.

VI

In the fall of 1620, John once again took up the task of looking for land for his claim and extra land that he might buy in addition. Meandering around the creek area on the south shore, he found a pleasant plot of land that both bordered on the river and also had the advantage of including the headwaters of a pristine creek. He traveled all the way to the trickle of water and felt sure that he could acquire both the river frontage and the watershed if he could accumulate enough assets to buy five hundred acres. He hoped that he had built up enough credit to make the purchase.

Traveling from the newly-found acreage along the south shore, he took a nostalgic journey along the river front until he came upon the original spot he had set his heart on the year before. He saw that two houses had already been hastily erected upon the site. Pace must already be in residence. But why the second house?

The afternoon sun was declining in the west, causing sharp shadows to stretch across the fields near the edge of the western forest, when John rode out of the woods and into the open, tilled area of the farm. He saw a young Indian boy hoeing the soil in a garden patch near the house. The boy seemed to be not more than twelve or thirteen years of age. Approaching him, John called out a few Indian words of greeting and then asked for Mr. Pace, but before the boy could respond, the door to the larger house was thrown open and Richard Pace emerged calling a welcoming greeting to John as he took the reins of his horse in hand and helped him to dismount.

"I've been expecting a call from you, Mr. Flood," he said. "William Powell told me you were reconnoitering the land around these parts. Hope you've found something to your liking. We're in need of good company on this side of the river. My wife particularly gets lonely."

"I've found something I like," John said, "but it may already be spoken for as this place was. I'm eager to see what I can arrange. I'm amazed to see that you've already built two houses. You're a fast worker."

"One of them is not much of a house," Pace said. "It's just one small room. Captain Perry has no wife, and says it will do fine for him for a while. The larger one is mine and Isobel's. It has two rooms, a good fireplace and a loft over the main room where Chanco sleeps. I'm a trained carpenter, Mr. Flood. I was apprenticed for seven years in Middlesex and had been admitted to the guild before pulling up stakes and moving to Virginia."

"My brother's a carpenter in London," John said. "With such credentials, I'm surprised you'd leave England. Please call me John."

"I'd be happy to, if you call me Richard. As to my leaving England, the pull was great. My lifelong friend, William Powell, was already over here. He wrote to entice us. I'm a big man, physically speaking, as you can see, and I felt penned in at Middlesex. I found myself every week taking orders from some pipsqueak of a patrician even if he hadn't paid me for my services to him in months. One day I decided I never wanted to humble myself again. I made up my mind to try a new way of life over here."

"Was Mrs. Pace just as eager to leave?" John asked.

"Oh, no. She had to be coaxed, but she finally came round. She's happy to have this farm, and I'll build her a beautiful house someday."

"Chanco," Pace called. "Take Mr. Flood's horse to the trough for some water."

The two men walked toward the hilltop that overlooked the river. Across its three-mile breadth, one could barely discern the outline of a ship at the dock in Jamestown. The setting sun gave a rosy glow to the western sky and created a glaze across the water's surface. Twilight was only minutes away.

"Mrs. Pace will come to greet you in a few minutes. She's busy cooking something just now."

"Tell me about Chanco," John asked. "I know a great deal

about the Indians and their ways. I've never seen a male domesticated as he seems to be. Indians think of gardening as women's work. How is it you can get him to hoe?"

"Chanco came only two months ago. His brother is under Perry's tutelage. The two boys are part of an effort by the college committee to convert some of the Indian youths to Christianity and teach them how to do useful work in the English tradition. The London Company officers see it as a peace initiative. They're eager for the natives to be assimilated into our way of life. Master Nicholas Farrar, father of the treasurer of the London Company, died early last summer. His will left three hundred pounds to the new college to be built at Henrico, which is to be paid when twelve Indian boys are enrolled there. For the meantime, he left twenty pounds yearly, to be paid out to three God-fearing members of the colony who would be willing to take an uncivilized Indian boy into their home and raise him in the Christian faith and to a useful trade. Perry and I volunteered at once and got two of the three boys."

"I treat Chanco as I would a son. He eats with us and attends our evening prayer every night. I work with him in the field. I teach him a new word or so every day, and I don't ask him to do anything I wouldn't do. So far all seems to be working well. We're even making progress along the lines of religion. He's beginning to understand."

John chuckled. "Wait till you try to teach him about the trinity. It was trying to understand the Holy Ghost that gave Pocahontas the most trouble."

"Chanco is not ready for the Holy Ghost yet. I'm still trying to convince him that there's only one God."

"That'll be a big accomplishment."

John saw Mrs. Pace was walking toward them. She was carrying a wooden plate filled with corn patties and a large jug of fresh water.

"I hope you'll stay the night with us, Mr. Flood," Isobel said "We're always hungry for company. I was just cooking up a large pot of stew made from a rabbit Chanco trapped this morning. Our stews are fairly tasty this time of year when there are plenty of roots and vegetables to add to the pot."

"Thank you, Mrs. Pace. I'd like that. I want to get to know you both better. I'm hoping to become your neighbor."

After spending the night with Isobel and Richard, John returned to Jamestown. He left his horse in the charge of Chanco and borrowed a boat from Pace in order to row himself across the river. When he got to the town to put in his request for the five hundred acre parcel on the south shore, only a short distance from Pace's Paine, as Pace's property was called, he found that it had not been spoken for, but he learned that he did not have enough credit to acquire the whole parcel. His intention to purchase the land was recorded, and he was told to come back for the papers to it when he had enough money.

John spent the next two years intensifying his efforts to trade with the Indians. He packed his saddle bags as best he could, with all the small-sized commodities he thought they needed and traveled alone far into Indian territory in order to make the best trades. He often saw Indians in the distance whom he knew to be tracking his journey. Traveling alone made him feel very vulnerable, but he reasoned it kept him from being a threat to them. They could easily attack and kill him. Then, all the goods in his bag would be theirs. However, he knew they knew that should they kill him, there would be no more tradesmen to bring them the things they needed.

John liked the trading game. He never left an Indian camp without trading something. The things they had to trade were not always appealing, but he let them have something they wanted regardless. He was happiest when he could trade his goods for furs and other pelts. They brought the highest profit.

On numerous occasions John had to travel through the territory near Berkeley Hundred, and he always managed to stop over for a visit with Margaret and William Finch. The Finches had received the promised cabin from the London Company, but it was precariously located in the woods by itself, not in the main group of houses at the plantation center.

Once after John had stayed the night, sleeping in his bedroll just outside their small cabin, he left Margaret three large beaver pelts in appreciation of her hospitality, so that she could sew them into a warm blanket. He worried that William might take exception to the gift as too costly to be appropriate, but if he had been bothered by it, he showed no concern.

The spring of 1621 gave way to a bountiful summer. Tobacco prices were rising weekly. Colonists had planted so many fields of it that they were in danger of not having grown enough foodstuffs for their own consumption. The winter of 1621-22 was rugged for Virginia. Several snows left the ground covered for days, but the season passed quickly. The ground thawed and was ready to be worked by early March.

VII

John was in Jamestown seeing to the sale of hides and pelts from his most recent trading with the Indians. At long last, these transactions gave him enough credit to acquire the five hundred acres he wanted on the south shore. He was in the Governor's office making the final arrangements for the property when word came to him that the new Governor, Sir Francis Wyatt, who had replaced Sir George Yardley in the fall, wished to see him personally.

"That was quick," John said to the clerk. "I became landed gentry only three minutes ago, and already the Governor wants to meet me. Does he congratulate all new proprietors this way?"

"He does not," the clerk said. "It's most unusual."

John was ushered into the Governor's private reception room and introductions were made. There was a warm fire crackling on the oversized hearth that made the room far cozier than John had expected. His uneasiness at meeting such an important person was immediately put to rest by the gracious bow the Governor gave to acknowledge their introduction.

"I hear you've just acquired a fine piece of land," Sir Francis said. He motioned to John to sit down. "Congratulations."

"Thank you, Sir."

"I hope you'll plant something on it besides tobacco. I've been instructed to encourage the production of silk worms, dyes and medicinal herbs. We've got to become more than a one crop colony. The London Company sent the makings of a foundry over with me. It should enable the colony to make its own tools, hinges, locks, utensils and even some weapons. The excavations have already been dug for it up near the falls, and the work of assembling the machinery is in progress."

"Sounds like Virginia is on her way."

"My secretary tells me you acquired most of the funds for your land purchase through Indian trading."

"That's right. I trade mostly with the Appomattocs and the

Weanocs."

"I've also heard that you trade with them alone."

"I do."

"Have you ever heard of an Indian trader named Morgan?"

"Yes, Sir. He was a competitor of mine. He traded more with the Paspaheghs and the Pamunkeys.

"He went out more than a month ago with his servants and did not return," Governor Wyatt said. "He's presumed to be dead."

"I heard, Sir. I think his mistake was in taking servants as protection. It may seem safer, but it can make the Indians wary, even downright scared."

"I've just received a report that an Indian warrior named Nemanttanow_"

"I know him. He's one of the best."

"That's unfortunate," the Governor said. "He appeared before a group of Morgan's friends wearing the hat that Morgan had been wearing when last seen."

"He may know his whereabouts."

"If so we'll never find out. The men were so infuriated at seeing Nemanttanow grinning and prancing around in Morgan's hat that they bludgeoned him to death."

"Oh, no. He may not have killed Morgan."

"They didn't stop long enough to think of that," the Governor said. "I'm sending a message of deepest regret with my apologies to Opechancanough. This is a very serious matter. As I understand that you have a fine grasp of the Indian language and are a man they trust, I would like for you to accompany my emissary so as to act as his interpreter. The party will be well protected."

"I'd rather go alone," John said.

"Not this time," the Governor replied.

When those on the peace mission returned, they reported that Opechancanough had at first been furious, that his eyes had blazed as he listened to them, and that only the number of uniformed guards they had taken with them had prevented their being murdered on the spot.

Everyone in Jamestown was distraught and thought of nothing else. Then a week later an Indian messenger arrived at Jamestown with a surprisingly different message from Opechancanough. The great chief sent word that fury would not solve the Indian's problems with the white men. He declared that he wished to continue the previous policy of peace.

Doors that had been latched the week before were opened and the Indians once again began to roam the streets and loll about the environs of Jamestown.

John was sleeping on the floor of a room at the tavern, preferring that to sharing a bed with a stranger, when he was awakened by the sound of a lone gunshot before dawn on Good Friday. He knew with certainty that a shot at that hour could mean little other than trouble at hand. With amazing speed he rushed to buckle his belt and pull on his boots. He grabbed his musket and within seconds was out the door of the tavern and racing toward the palisade in the direction of the gun shot.

"What's up?" John shouted.

"Can't tell yet," the guard said. "Looks like a lone boatman crossing the river in the dark. The moon has just gone behind a cloud. When it comes back we should be able to see."

"Is he Indian?"

"One of us, I think, but I've got him covered. Only a crazy man or a desperate one would cross the river in the dark. Get the Captain."

"Here he comes."

Captain Powell arrived just as the clouds opened up revealing the boatman who appeared to be traveling at high speed. He, John and others who had arrived on the scene rushed out of the palisade area and down to the waterfront.

"It's Pace," John shouted. "It's Richard Pace. No one else has a frame like that."

"What goes?" Captain Powell called to the boatman.

"Indian attack. Coming this morning," Pace yelled.

Richard Pace reached the shore and was helped from his boat. He dropped to the bank from exhaustion, resting a few moments to catch his breath and find his voice. "Opechancanough ordered all white people in Virginia killed this morning. He has traveled up and down the river, with his deputy, Nemantico, to give the orders to every tribe. The attack's coming when the sun's rays reach the top of the pine trees. About eight o'clock."

"Eight o'clock," Captain Powell said. "That gives us little more than two hours."

Governor Wyatt arrived. He immediately ordered that all local citizens be brought into the fort and the fort put into readiness for the attack. "How did you learn of this?" he asked Pace.

"My Indian boy, Chanco, was told to murder me and my wife in our sleep. His brother was to kill Perry. At prayers last night I told the Maudy Thursday story of Judas' betrayal of Jesus. We saw that Chanco was visibly upset by the story. In the middle of the night, I awoke to see him staring into my eyes from only a few inches away. He was kneeling by my bedside, crying. He shook his head and said. 'I love you, father, I can not kill you.'

"Every settlement's to be hit. By nightfall, Opechancanough expects to have rid his land of all of us."

"We must warn the others," the Governor said. "We need volunteers to go out to every settlement that can possibly be reached."

"Round up all small boats and canoes," Captain Powell shouted. "Water travel will be the safest and the quickest."

"I'll go to Berkeley Hundred," John said.

"That's too far away. You could never get there in time to warn them."

"I don't care. That's where I'm going."

"The full moon is still high in the sky," Richard Pace said. "Before I pushed off from the south shore, I cursed the moon. Its bright light seemed treacherous and made me feel vulnerable and exposed. As I began to row, the moon-struck river began to comfort me. I felt a surge of energy shoot through my body. The boat suddenly dashed toward Jamestown. It was then I knew that God was with me. The current was flowing in the right direction. The moon was working for me after all."

Within minutes boats and canoes were heading out in all directions to alert arising settlers. Other guards and citizens went to nearby settlements calling all local inhabitants into the fort. The neglected palisade was shored up, the main entrance blocked, powder and balls brought from the storehouse and all weapons loaded. Before the sun had reached over the tree tops, Jamestown was ready and waiting.

John could not reach Berkeley Hundred in time to give warning to the settlers there. He was paddling with all the strength he could muster when he heard the first gun shots in the distance. Where, oh where is Margaret? What is happening at the cabin?

When John finally reached the shoreline near Berkeley Hundred, some hours later, and turned the canoe to within arrow-shot distance of the land, he picked up his musket and put it across his lap. The previous noise of gun shots had given way to a deathly silence. John brought the boat ashore and, hunching his body so as not to make too large a target of himself, ran toward the plantation center. A shot rang out as he approached, and he quickly realized that he was being shot at by one of the colonists. Darting behind a large tree and peering around, he could see that there were no Indians in sight. "It's John Flood here," he shouted in a loud voice. "Let me enter."

There was an eerie pause before his call was answered. Then in a weak voice one of the settlers called back, "Come on in, Flood."

When John got into the settlement, he learned that the Indians had approached at eight in the morning bringing food-stuffs to trade and seemingly unarmed. They had dispersed and intermingled with the inhabitants. Then all at once, as if orchestrated by Opechancanough from afar, the Indians had grabbed the colonist's weapons and attacked any and everyone in sight be it man, woman or child. They struck with a rapidity and brutality that was beyond comprehension. Before the settlers were able to retaliate, the savages had slaughtered twenty people including Captain Berkeley.

Not waiting to hear all, John asked, "Where are Margaret and William Finch?"

"At their cabin, I guess. They were alone there. It's likely they're all dead. Things are so horrendous here that we haven't had time to go to them. We're still numb."

"I'm going," John said. He bolted from the scene. "I'll be back to help you later."

John raced over the nearby fields, where he still saw signs of the hatcheting of field workers, and through the woods that led to the cabin, a mile and a half away. His eyes were constantly scanning the area for the sight of any Indians. He saw nothing to suggest that they were still about. Reaching sight of the cabin, he saw to his relief that it looked very much as it always had except that there was no smoke coming from the chimney. Creeping up to the open tilled area, where the Finches grew the crops for their own table, he was stopped in his tracks by the sight of William Finch lying dead in the garden plot. John inched closer. He saw that William had been brutally hacked in the face and then dismembered by many hatchet blows to his body.

John looked anxiously at the cabin. Margaret, Margaret. Where are you? His body was ablaze with pain. His eyes scanned the garden and nearby woods in search of her. He felt choked by the lump in his throat.

Suddenly a gun fired and the shot whizzed by his shoulder sending him scurrying once again to take cover behind a tree. From the place on the tree where the shot had hit and the direction it was going as it passed him, he knew it had come from the cabin. A gagging cry of relief escaped his throat. Thank God. She's alive.

It took a few seconds for John to find his voice. Then he called out his name and waited for a reply. It took so long in coming that he thought he had been mistaken. At last, he heard her voice. The words were so faint that he couldn't make them out, but he knew they were hers. Inching out slowly from behind the tree, he partially exposed himself to her view. No shot came in response. With long strides he ran to the door of the cabin and waited as he heard the door being unbarred.

Margaret opened the door only slightly, pulled John inside and quickly barred it again. She was quivering with fright, her face a mask of deathly emotions. Frances ran to him from across the room, threw her arms around his legs and burst into uncontrollable sobs.

"They killed my papa," Frances cried. "They chopped him down."

Margaret stared at John, wavered as she started toward him and then collapsed in a heap at his feet.

John squatted down on the earth-packed floor beside her. "How did it happen?" he asked.

"Th- they c-came early," she said. "Ju-just as we were about to l-leave the cabin to work in the fields. They were laughing and friendly. I was standing in the doorway with Frances when two of them started attacking him. Another one started for us, b-but I jumped back inside, slammed the door and bolted it just a second before he threw his full weight against it.

"I grabbed Will's gun, which was always loaded, stuck it through the narrow window-opening and fired. I can't hit anything, but it seemed to scare them away. We knew Will was dead. We saw the blows. Since then, I've been almost frozen to the gun fearing that they'd come back."

"You almost got me," John said. "You may be a better shot than you think."

"It was my fault," Frances wailed. "I should have run out to help Papa. I just jumped back and hid."

John grabbed the small child, gave her a shake and said, "Don't you ever let me hear you say that it was your fault again. How could you have helped save your father? You're only a six-year-old child. Why, you're not even big enough to pull a pail of water up from the well. If you'd left the cabin, they'd have killed you too."

John pulled the child to him in a warm embrace. As he stroked her hair and tried to comfort her, he heard repeated in his mind, "You're not even big enough to pull up a pail of water from the well."

Why did I say that?

Gently pushing the child away, he looked at her in wonder, realizing how small and helpless she was. Then it came to him that she was the same age he had been when his mother died.

All the years that followed, I thought it was my fault for not getting up to fetch the water for her. How absurd.

Suddenly, John felt as though a pailful of fresh spring water was running through his entire being, removing all the cloying dregs of guilt that he had carried within himself for fifteen years.

How could I have thought that I could have pulled up a pailfull of water even if I had gone out to fetch it?

John let out a sigh of relief. What was it the Reverend tried to teach Pocahontas about the Holy Ghost? The Holy Ghost is that part of God that is in each and every one of us if we believe in Him. That we may be made one body with Him, that we may dwell in Him and He in us.

John reached over and gently pulled Margaret to him. He patted her back cautiously and then stroked her disheveled hair. She was the first woman he had touched since the death of his mother. He had not known any to touch.

Margaret's sobs began to subside. Her breast gave a last heavy heave, and she became very still. The horrible memory of seeing her husband murdered gave way to thoughts of her own dangerous and helpless position.

"Alone," she sighed. "Frances and I are all alone. How can I go on without him? I only came here because of him, and now he's gone. Frances and I have no one."

"You have me, Margaret," John said. "I'm yours to have or to use in any way you want."

Margaret stayed in John's arms but gave no reply. Frances moved over and crawled under John's other arm. The three remained quiet for a long time.

"I don't think the Indians are still around," John said at last. "I'm going out to bring Will's body in. I'll dig a grave near the cabin door. After we've buried him, we must make a dash for the settlement. We can't stay here much longer. They could return tonight."

An hour later, John wrapped the beaver blanket he had given her around Margaret's shoulders, picked up Frances and said, "Don't be afraid, just run."

VIII

It was days before the toll of the massacre could be tallied. The Reverend Throop, who had worked hard at improving the life of the Indians and who was working toward the building of the college that would instruct them, was murdered while kneeling in prayer. The foundry being built at the falls was destroyed and its construction workers slaughtered. Plantations in most of the outer regions were hard hit, losing not only men but women and children who had trustingly welcomed the Indians into their homes as friends and then been brutally attacked, killed and dismembered.

Jamestown was mercilessly spared any loss due to the Christian faithfulness of Chanco and the responsible, courageous efforts of Richard Pace. When the tally was in, it was found that 347 men, women and children had been killed out of 1,250 colonists. Of those spared in the outer regions, many packed up their belongings and marched into Jamestown for protection. Depression was felt everywhere, as survivors tried to patch together the remnants of their lives.

John took Margaret and Frances to Jamestown where they found some degree of safety. Richard Pace, Isobel and William Perry abandoned their newly-planted grounds and moved temporarily to Jamestown with the rest.

When word reached London of the heinous events, sentiments were so outraged that a great backlash of hate for the Indians, with whom they had tried so hard to be just, burst out like flares from a fireworks display.

Less than three months after the massacre, word came to the settlers from the London Company that all efforts toward instructing the Indians were to cease. The new policy of the Company favored extermination. The colonists were encouraged to waste no time in implementing it.

On the same ship that brought the new directive from the Company came a letter for John from his brother Charles. It held another jolt for John. He read it several times before deciding what he must do. Charles had written, "News of the massacre hit London with a mighty force. I rushed to the palace to scrutinize the posted list of names of all who had been killed. I can not tell you how relieved I was to see that your name was missing. I should have written sooner to tell you that I can now keep the bargain we made years ago when you went to Virginia.

"I have, at last, set up my own business. It is succeeding, and I have the money to pay for your passage home. If you wish to return, I can assure you of employment in my own business."

John's first reaction to the letter was one of disbelief. In earlier years, he had prayed and prayed that just this would happen. Strangely enough, now that his wish had come true, he no longer wanted it. He and Margaret had been married the week before the letter came. During that week he had known the first true happiness since the time of his family's demise.

John was ready to write Charles thanking him but declining his offer. He knew for certain that Virginia was the place for him. Still, gnawing at the back of his mind was the thought that he was not only dealing with his life but Margaret's as well. He feared that she might leap at the chance to return home to England. He began to wish that the letter had never come. It complicated everything. There was only one thing about which he would give no ground. He would not give her up. He had been without anyone to love for fifteen years. Now that he knew what it was like to belong again, he would never, willingly, go back to a solitary life.

John read Charles' letter to Margaret. As he did so, he saw tears start to well up in her eyes. He had a slow sinking feeling. She wants to go home.

When John finished reading, he carefully folded the letter and looked up at her.

"You don't want to go, do you?"

"No," he answered. "I'd rather stay here and be my own man."

"But you read the letter to me anyway."

"I had to be fair."

They looked at each other for some time in silence.

"I saw Isobel Pace today," Margaret said. "She and Richard have gotten permission to go back across the river. They plan to fortify the farming area on the south shore."

A flicker of understanding began to break across John's face. "You mean that you are not afraid to stay and take what comes our way?"

"Are you?"

"With you beside me, there'll be no end to what we can do," he said. "God's will is our only limit."

THE CAVALIERS
1651-1656

I

Richard Blount, second born of the four sons of Sir Thomas Blount, sat straight in the saddle with his head upturned, as he trotted his bay gelding at a moderate pace down the white, stone-edged path that led from the Kidderminster road to the courtyard in front of the family's residence, Clee Manor. The white stones, catching the bright rays of the August moon, acted to illuminate the way. Richard knew that the horse could see the curves of the narrow path ahead as he might see a ribbon with spotted edges laid out before him. So sure was he of the horse's ability to find his way unaided that he turned his eyes skyward to concentrate on the stars and planets visible on this clear summer night.

If only I had a telescope, I could decide for myself whether the earth moves or whether it stays still and all the other heavenly objects move around it.

For months, Richard had been immersed in the writings of Galileo which his father had managed to get hold of for his sons to study. All the boys had been introduced to the radical ideas of the great philosopher and mathematician, but only Richard had been interested enough to let it absorb his thoughts. Sometimes he got so lost in his contemplations that he forgot all else around him.

This night as Richard looked up at the partial moon, he became so mesmerized by the objects above that it was not until he heard the low, throaty, "ba-a, ba-a," of a scared animal that he became aware of a small, wounded lamb lying in the path before him. Reining in his horse with a quick jerk, he acted just in time to avoid trampling the lame critter to death. "Who-a," he called. "What reason has this?"

Dismounting quickly, Richard approached the whining lamb. A shudder of revulsion raced through him as he saw immediately that one of her hind legs had been badly crushed. A flush of pity engulfed him forcing him to turn his eyes away as he leaned over the scared, helpless, doomed animal, encircled her snout with the palm of his hand and gently lifted the soft bundle to a resting spot on the narrow ledge of his manly hip.

The lamb tried to whine but could make no sound. Her eyes darted in a frenzied display of terror as she attempted to squirm loose, but the pain was too great. She yielded to the comfort of Richard's arms, went suddenly limp, and then settled next to his body, giving herself up to her fate.

"You've strayed far more than a field, little one," Richard whispered into the lamb's ear. "I fear your future as a wool producer is in jeopardy. My lord's dinner table is your likelier destination."

Richard managed to remount while still carrying the babe and rode on to the manor's stable, gently stroking the animal's soft coat as he rode. Dismounting again, he saw Reuben, the stable-keeper, coming to take the bay's reins.

"What have we here?" asked Reuben.

"Only a lost lamb, I'd venture, if her wound was mendable," said Richard, " but I fear it's not. Call Silas to take her to cook. Her leg is crushed and broken clear through."

"How could it be?" asked Reuben.

"Hard to tell. Perhaps she was hit by a cart or trampled by a horse. She was far from the flock."

"Roaming's not safe for any critter," said Reuben, "much less a babe. It's a bad omen, she be. Strange things happening always mean trouble."

Reuben was a short, square-built, heavy-set man, his body a direct contrast to Richard's slight, agile frame. It had no grace about it but was unmistakably strong. His shape gave evidence that he was descended from a long line of men who had used strength of body rather than intellect to survive. He was completely illiterate and prone to believe many things that had no place in the world of knowledge.

"Strange things happen all the time," said Richard. "I hope you're not a believer in signs."

"Tis a sign of something," answered Reuben. "Something or someone's badly out of place. Better keep your eyes open. Don't let nothing surprise you."

Richard turned away to walk to the manor house. Ignorance breeds such foolishness. Devils, witches, goblins and omens. Someday they'll probably choke on their own superstitions.

Richard walked into the family supper room just as his father, Sir Thomas Blount, was about to ask the Lord's blessing.

"You're late," his father said. "Your mother was beginning to worry. Sit down so that we can ask the blessing."

Sir Thomas was seated at the head of the table in the low-ceilinged, wood-paneled room that was used for the family supper rather than the large dining hall. A red linen runner stretched from the end of the table, where Sir Thomas presided, to the far end, where Lady Mary was seated. In between, with their pewter bowls and plates resting on the bare table, sat six of their eight children, four young men including Richard, who were ages sixteen through twenty-four and the two youngest of their daughters, ages thirteen and fourteen. The two older daughters had married and moved away.

"We thank Thee for the bounty Thou hast placed before us," said the master of Clee Manor. This ritual completed, the group began to laugh and talk as they raised soup bowls to their mouths to sip a newly simmered broth.

"What did you hear in Worcester, Richard?" his father asked .

"Talk was of King Charles' presence in Scotland and the likelihood of his re-entry into England to regain the throne."

"Who talks of such?"

"My friends, Sir."

"We know the King to be in Scotland. As for his return to England, we may be thinking of such things and hoping for it, but only the foolhardy would be talking of it," Sir Thomas said. Richard's older brother, Thomas, added "Our family is already known for its loyal sympathies. It's most unfortunate. The Roundheads have only to sniff the possibility of active support for the King to seize a man and toss him in prison."

"I'm careful about my companions," Richard said.

"Many conspiracies have undermined old friendships," his father said. "Cromwell's spies are like worms in the garden, everywhere but unseen. His grasp on the country keeps tightening. It's best to keep our political thoughts, as well as our religious hopes, to ourselves."

"Yes, sir."

"Libba, what did you do or learn today?" Sir Thomas asked.

"She did what she pleased and learned nothing," Katie said.

"I did not," Libba said. "I worked with mother on the linens. I did some needed mending and sewed ruffles for dress shirts."

"Well, that was what pleased you, and you learned nothing new. What I said was true."

"That's enough out of you, Katie," Lady Mary said. "If you don't..."

"Father, I hear hoof beats." Thomas gave a pensive look over his shoulder toward the windows on the front of the house. "Who would come at this hour?" He started to rise.

"Stay seated," Sir Thomas ordered. "We're doing exactly what we always do at this hour. Continue the conversation, Katie. If we have visitors, they will be announced."

Richard looked warily at his older brother. Katie was suddenly dumbstruck, but Libba picked up the conversation as instructed.

"The figs are ripe, Father. Today I helped pick some figs for your..." Eyes dilated as they heard the door to the supper room open. "...dinner," she continued. "We'll have them with..."

"Excuse me, Sir," a footman said. "There are three gentlemen in the hall. They say they have urgent reason to see you immediately. They wouldn't give me their names."

"What impudence," Sir Thomas said. "Thomas and Richard, come with me. The rest of you stay in your seats and keep talking."

Thomas and Richard rose and followed their father from the room.

In the dimly-lit, wide hall, lined with gun racks and coat trees for outdoor apparel, that traversed the large manor house from front to back, Sir Thomas received his callers and introduced them to his two eldest sons. There was a moment of awkward silence as the elder of the callers, a tall, nervous, severe-looking man, who had given his name as Mr. Jones, cleared his throat before saying, "We would prefer to talk with you alone."

"Gentlemen, my sons are privy to all my affairs. If you have anything to say to me, they will hear of it here or from me later."

"Er, hem," the caller said. "Yes, yes, I understand." Lowering his voice to a whisper, he continued, "Sir, we are emissaries of the

Duke of Hamilton." Mr. Jones drew a paper with a heavy wax seal from his pocket. "He has sent us to solicit your support and that of your household in rallying to the standard of King Charles."

Sir Thomas' face lit up. Thomas and Richard stiffened their stance and as if by reflex took on the look of loyal soldiers at a dress parade.

"Let's go into my private office, gentlemen. We'll be more at ease there."

In the private chamber, Mr. Jones continued. "King Charles crossed the border from Scotland into England almost a week ago. He'll be in Worcester soon with a large army of both Scots and Englishmen, over a hundred thousand, I am told. We must all rally to his support. Those who do not will be considered traitors when he regains the throne."

A hush fell over the room as the startled listeners absorbed the gravity of their caller's words. Richard and Thomas shifted their stance nervously then turned to their father in anticipation of his reply.

"The King has always had my unflinching support," Sir Thomas said, "and that of my family. We are always ready to serve the King. I can also provide twelve other men, all armed and mounted. The Duke needs only to send word of the date and place of the military gathering."

"Only twelve, Sir Thomas? From such a large estate? We hoped..."

"Twelve trained men, Mr. Jones. Shepherds and housemen aren't soldiers. The king needs men who can gallop with grace, and who will fight when the need arises."

"To be sure, Sir Thomas. Four sons and twelve other soldiers, I'll report."

The callers stayed only long enough to get the promise of assistance. They were present for less than ten minutes before moving on. When the men of the family re-entered the supper room, the soup bowls were just being cleared away.

After supper, Sir Thomas called his four sons into his private quarters. "We will pack our gear in secret," he ordered. "Only the servants we take with us are to know anything of what we are doing. Thomas, you will notify this list of our men that they are to make ready to travel by horseback at a moment's notice and to inform no one, absolutely no one. Richard, you will choose the horses to be used and see that they can be made ready on short notice. All of you will have your essential gear and weapons ready. We mustn't distress the women. When word comes of His Majesty's entrance into Worcester, we'll ride out without a word to anyone."

"Father, do you think there is a real possibility that His Majesty can receive enough support to re-conquer England? Cromwell's men have a solid hold on London and all of the southern shires. Even if he could regain our northwest, where he has the most loyal subjects, it would not assure victory in the rest of the country."

"We'll never know if we don't do our part."

"We're risking everything," Edward said.

"Nothing is secure unless the monarchy is returned,"

"Now that the war is over, our actions would be deemed treason," Richard said.

"Honor compels us to act. How could we do otherwise than to support our rightful king? Everything we have or ever have had came to us through his favor. His Majesty is coming, and I am going to join him," Sir Thomas said.

"I too," Thomas, Edward and William said in unison.

"And you, Richard?" Sir Thomas asked.

Richard hesitated, showing a look of uncertainty. He heard a gasp of disbelief escape from his father, but the sure sound of disapproval was not enough to keep his thoughts from flashing back to the wounded lamb, far from her flock, that had lain helpless on the manor's path so short a time ago. A premonition of loneliness engulfed him. Had Ruben been right? Was some diabolical force about to overpower them? He looked straight into his father's eyes, felt the power of his presence and was surprised to hear himself say, "Yes, of course. I'm your servant, Sir."

Three days later word came by way of an itinerant shoe salesman who announced that he had come to Clee Manor to take orders for shoes to be made by the cobbler in Worcester.

"Tonight," he whispered to Sir Thomas as he rose from tracing the shape of his lordship's bare foot on a blank piece of paper, "His Majesty is in Worcester. News arrived that General Cromwell's forces are marching toward the city from the north to protect England from what they call the Scottish invasion." Aloud he continued, "Your bill, Sir," as he handed Sir Thomas a slip of paper with the familiar seal of the Duke of Hamilton on it.

II

As soon as the sun fell below the western foothills, Richard quietly picked up his gear, strolled out to the stable and disappeared within it knowing that Lady Mary, Libba and Katie would be startled to hear the dull thud of the many horses' hooves as the retinue of mounted men galloped away.

Richard and the others from Clee Manor rode in darkness through the moonless night. While making the ten-mile journey, he had expected to be joined by forces from many of the other manors and estates as they passed them along the road, but no other supporters appeared.

"We may be late," Sir Thomas said to his sons when they remarked on the matter. "Others may have journeyed out before us."

"What should we do if we are separated?" Edward asked..

"If so, each man will be on his own. Each of you must keep two or three of the servants under wing. Remember that your mother and sisters will be in danger if any of us are caught. If the battle goes not our way, return to Clee as stealthily as possible. We must be sure not to involve the others."

The men rode on in silence until they reached the fields outside of Worcester. Then finding a dark spot, they bedded down for the night.

As dawn broke on the fateful September morn, Richard leaned over to his younger brother, Edward, lying beside him, and whispered, "Where are all the local royalists?"

"Where are all the King's troops?" Edward asked. "He should have a hundred thousand men at his side if what Mr. Jones said be true."

"That's beginning to look like a mammoth exaggeration. Did you sleep?"

"No. Too scared. Did you?"

"Not much. I was busy watching Mars. It looked to be on fire. Did you see it?"

"Mars. Of course not. Don't even know which one it is."

"Over there," Richard said pointing. "The one that looks red."

"Are you going to stay in the clouds all day? We've important things to worry about down here. I hope you'll not be looking at the stars when someone starts shooting at you."

Looking out across a field, Richard saw a lone horseman riding at a gallop toward them. "Man your horses," the rider yelled. "We were expecting Cromwell to attack from the north, but the General has circled wide and is approaching from the south despite the river protection there. We must stop them from crossing the bridges."

Richard leapt to his horse. "Reuben, Silas," he yelled. "Follow me."

He was off in an instant waiting for no one. Riding swiftly through the city's gates, Richard headed for the Cathedral's grounds where he knew he could get the best view of the rivers. Once on the Cathedral Close he could hear loud bursts of explosions and knew instinctively that the bridges, which allowed access to the city from the south, were being blown up. King Charles must have ordered it. Worcester sat in the "v" made by the confluence of the Severn and the Teme Rivers. Crossing the rivers would be difficult without the bridges. Riding to the highest spot on the close and turning back to view the rivers, Richard saw to his horror that Cromwell's forces were not trying to cross the rivers on horseback. They were being transported by boats. Richard raced back to find his men. Spotting Reuben and Silas he yelled, "Cromwell has launched boats to bring his men up-river. They won't need the bridges. They'll be upon us in no time."

"They've broken in," a strange voice yelled.

"Where are the others?" Richard asked.

"Don't know," Silas answered. "I only followed you."

For the rest of the day, the three fought valiantly. At one point, Richard, with Reuben and Silas at his heels, rounded a corner of the narrow, city streets near the Cathedral, and saw to his horror the twenty-one-year-old King trying valiantly to rally his troops. Richard rushed to his aid. Within seconds, he found himself face-to-face with a group of mounted Roundheads, who had broken trough the city gates.

Richard unsheathed his sword and began charging the group that threatened the King. He aimed his sword in the direction of the Roundheads, prepared to run its blade through the charging horsemen. "God be with me," he said.

A roundhead picked Richard out of the group and began to charge. Seconds before contact, Richard recognized his enemy. "Oh no," he called out. He lowered his sword, leaned far to the left side of his mount and ducked as the enemy made his thrust. The sword missed him by only a fraction of an inch.

"It's Richard Blount, the traitor. After him."

Richard immediately recognized the voice of one of his oldest and dearest childhood friends causing a gasp of horror and pain to escape his throat. He turned and prepared to stand firm. He could not leave the King. He readied his sword. If they charged he would have to kill no matter who it was. His heart grew sick.

The King's troops reorganized and formed a firm line that encompassed Richard in its ranks.

As the day continued, the fighting became increasingly brutal. The King was seen fighting sometimes on horseback and sometimes even on foot. By the day's end, the Royalists' losses were ten times that of their enemy. The King's hope for a hundred thousand men never materialized. Sixteen thousand was all he had at most. By late afternoon, two thousand of those had been lost. King Charles sent word that those still able to do so should evacuate the city and disperse.

Receiving the word, Richard called out to Reuben and Silas, "To St. Martin's Gate."

At the gate, they almost collided with King Charles himself. Waiting nervously to the side until the royal party exited the city, they followed, hoping to give cover from the rear, but several miles outside the city word came back to them that the King did not wish to be followed.

"What now?" Reuben asked. "Do we head for Clee?"

"No," Richard answered. "We can't go home. It would jeopardize the others. We were recognized in Worcester. We must make them think that we acted alone. Cromwell's soldiers will be at Clee Manor soon to arrest us. We can't let them find us there."

"Where to?" Reuben asked, truly distressed for the first time over not being able to return home.

"Not around here," Richard said. "We're all known in these parts. We'll camp in the hills for a while. The weather's fair."

A fortnight after the Royalists' defeat at Worcester, Richard sent Silas into a neighboring town on market day to purchase food and to listen out for news. He gave him some coins and set him off on foot so as not to attract attention. That evening Silas brought back devastating news.

"A bounty of one thousand pounds has been offered for any news that should lead to the capture of King Charles," Silas reported. "So far, his whereabouts are unknown. I saw the poster myself. Someone read it to me. They read the names of many traitors to the Commonwealth. There's money offered for them too. Your name, Master Richard, was one of them."

Despair gripped the three as they slowly realized that they would not be able to return to Clee under any foreseeable circumstances.

The three men hid out in the fields and thickets of western England for months before finally visiting the home of one of the family's trusted friends and relying on him to travel to Clee Manor for instructions from Richard's father.

On his return the friend found the men waiting anxiously.

"What kept you so long?" Richard asked.

"I thought it prudent to take a circuitous route," the friend answered. "I didn't want to be followed from Clee Manor straight to your hiding place. I went back home first and waited a few days to throw off any watchers."

"What does father suggest?"

"He didn't suggest; he ordered. You are to proceed to Bristol where you will find the ship *Speculator* preparing to set sail for Virginia under Captain Alan Underwood. Ship's passage for the three of you will be arranged by the time you get there. Virginia has remained loyal to the King. You are to go there and try to establish a seat to which other members of the family may flee should the need arise."

"Virginia. All three of us?"

"Yes. There is a bounty out for Reuben and Silas as well. You are to ask Captain Underwood for your locked trunk. Here's the key to it."

"What's happened to King Charles?"

"He managed to reach the continent safely and is in exile in France. Your father's last words were that you were to stay in Virginia until the King has regained his throne."

III

The three men, dutifully following their orders, reached Bristol several days later. They waited until nighttime to search out the *Speculator* on the waterfront and found the ship being loaded with cartons and crates for Virginia. Captain Underwood welcomed them nonchalantly and called a ship's officer to lead away their horses to be sold the next morning. The Captain told Richard that his father's creditor in Bristol had paid for their passage, but that he knew nothing of any trunk.

The following morning when the seamen had almost finished loading the ship, a dilapidated farm cart driven by an old man arrived at the ship's gangplank.

"Here's farm tools you been looking for," the carter called out.

"We're expecting no farm tools," the Captain said. "Who're they for?"

"Mister Richard Freeman at Jamestown," the old man said.

Richard bolted at the sound of the familiar Worcestershire voice. Looking out toward the pier he saw an old man from his father's service that he could barely recognize through his disguise. He nudged the Captain.

"Right you are," the Captain called out to the carter. "My men will help to unload the equipment for you."

"Proof's needed that I delivered," the old man said.

The tools and the trunk, hidden beneath them, were brought aboard ship. The old man came forward to receive a receipt for them. Without sign of recognition he looked straight into Richard's eyes, then turned and left the pier.

The following day, after the ship cast off, Richard opened the trunk. He knew at once that his mother had packed it. Besides pants and jackets for both Reuben and Silas, the trunk contained a wool blanket, heavy duty pants for himself and several shirts, a pair of shoes, a canteen, a knife, a compass and two separately wrapped packages. In the first, he found two small books, one a handwritten book of prayers, the other a printed copy of "Amoretti", a long epic poem by Edmund Spencer.

A lump rose into Richard's throat and his eyes began to smart as he visualized his mother thoughtfully packing not only the necessities of survival but the books for his comfort as well. When he opened the last package, he burst out laughing. It contained a ruffled and be-laced, white linen shirt, a pair of yellow silk britches and a dove-grey waistcoat. Try as he would, he could not hold back two large tears that slipped down his cheeks following his outburst of laughter. "Wherever does she think I could wear these in Virginia?" he muttered. Then his laughter stopped abruptly, and his humor quickly changed to an acute awareness of the finality of the pending ocean flight.

As he began to refold the yellow pants, he felt something hard in one of the pockets. It was a handkerchief which had knotted into it five gold coins.

When the *Speculator* sailed out of view from the English mainland, Richard breathed his first sigh of relief. Tensions had run so high over the past months that he had been unable to relax for a moment. With the sudden disappearance of political danger, he found there was nothing to do but relax, and the change left him edgy and restless.

The nine-week voyage was singularly uneventful. They ran into no hurricanes, major storms, Dutch Man o' Wars or pirate ships. Their fears of capture were changed abruptly to fears of boredom. It was difficult to accustom themselves to their quiet life of passengers on the open sea.

As the days progressed, Richard took to reading the books his mother had packed for him by day and to studying the stars, more brilliant than ever in the clear atmosphere of the open sea, by night.

Captain Underwood frequently had time to talk with him and being a veteran of the Virginia route was able to expand his concept of the political environment of the country to which he was going.

"My father sent word that Virginia sided with the Royalists," Richard said one night as the two men stood at the ship's railing looking into the starlit night.

"That they did," the Captain said, " but it's past history now."

"How so?"

"The Commonwealth took care of that last year."

"Do you mean I'm traveling into a hot pot of Roundheads?"

"No, no. Not that. Almost all the Virginians hold sympathy for the crown. It's just that the Commonwealth forced their declaration of allegiance."

"How?"

"After King Charles was beheaded, the Virginia House of Burgesses declared Virginia to be on the side of the Royalists. They declared the young prince to be Charles II of England and said it would be high treason for anyone to support the Parliamentarians."

"Isn't that still so?"

"No. Things drifted along for a long time. I guess parliament was too busy strengthening its position in England to worry much about Virginia. When it got around to acting, the first thing it did was to threaten to cut off Virginia's market for tobacco. Tobacco is practically all the colony has to sell."

"Was that enough to change their allegiance?"

"That was just the start. When they decided to act, it took very little to bring the self-willed child into compliance with the will of the motherland. Last winter they sent a fleet of gun boats to Virginia. The major part of the fleet blockaded the entrance to the James River while the flagship, carrying four commissioners to deal with the Governor, sailed up-river to Jamestown. With guns on the quarterdeck, a fully armed upper deck and four guns on either side of the lower deck, the Admiral of the fleet announced that Virginia would surrender to the Commonwealth or Fort James would be blown to pieces."

"By Jupiter!"

"Virginia surrendered without firing a shot. The royal Governor stepped down. The commissioners said that the House of Burgesses could continue to rule Virginia as long as they did nothing contrary to English law. Considering all, they were very generous."

"What are we getting ourselves in for?" Richard asked. "Virginia is probably as dangerous as England."

"No, no," the Captain said. "You'll be safe enough as long as you don't stir up trouble."

Nine weeks later, enjoying the sweet scent of land from the forward deck, Richard finally experienced the thrill of spotting the distant shore. He stayed fastened to the railing as he watched the land coming nearer. It seemed to envelop them as the ship first entered the bay, then the wide mouth of the James and finally the confining banks of the river itself.

Silas was as excited as Richard when he saw land. The entire trip had been pure adventure for him. He had no wife or family in

England, and the happenings of the last month had been a welcome break in the monotony of his former life.

Reuben, on the other hand, had a woman in Worcester, whom he had hoped to marry in the near future. Every day of travel on the open sea had made him grouchier and more discontent as he perceived the distance he was putting between himself and his intended bride. He had not understood the distance they would be going when the ship set sail. Now, he was already calculating the shortest length of time he would have to stay and how long it would take for the return voyage.

IV

When the *Speculator* reached Jamestown, Richard and his two men disembarked carrying the trunk, their weapons, the farm tools and three saddles with no accompanying horses. The air was cool and crisp allowing the clear rays of the sun to reveal a land of lush green and a cloudless sky of deep blue.

"Where's the city? Reuben asked.

"I think it's hiding," Richard said. "All I can see is a small fort with palisade and a street of houses outside of it. Surely there must be more."

"Looks like that's about all," Silas said.

The three men walked up the slope from the pier to the fort, and once inside, sought out the capitol building which turned out to be no larger than a small house. Richard wanted to register their arrival and their intention of making a permanent settlement. He found a clerk to assist him and declared himself and his two servants as desirous of becoming colonists. Next, he asked about the prospects of acquiring some land.

"Since you came un-indebted for the price of your passage," the clerk said, "you're entitled to fifty acres of land for yourself and fifty acres more for anyone else whose passage you paid. Since you brought two servants with you, that makes one hundred fifty in all. I suggest you scout out the land around Lawne's Creek on the south shore. That's probably the best available at this time that's not too far from the safety of Jamestown."

"Where is it?"

"The land I'm talking about," the clerk said, "is south of Hog Island, which you passed just before you reached Jamestown.

We've given about twenty-five grants in that area and land has been set aside for a parish church. It's protected from the Indians on three sides by the configuration of the river. It ought to be a right good place for you to seat yourself."

"Are the Indians still a major threat?"

"You bet they are, Sir. It's been eight years since the last massacre. Things have calmed down a good bit since then. But where Indians are concerned, you never know. You should waste no time in settling on a piece of land. It'll take awhile to get your request approved formally, but as long as we know that no one else has put in for it before you, you're not apt to run into ownership problems. Most of the colonists have already finished their spring planting. You men will have to get to work if you expect to reap a crop to see you through the winter. Every man has to look out for himself here in Virginia. I'll draw a map of the land I'm talking about."

Richard saw the clerk draw a crude map of the river with the land on each side. He marked off Jamestown, Hog Island, Lawne's Creek and then shaded in the land area for which grants had already been given. "There's a notched, loblolly pine just around the third bend in the creek with a large "G" burned into it. All the land south of that tree notch is open for new settlement."

The clerk folded the piece of paper and wrote Richard's name on the outside spelling Blount as it sounded Blunt. Richard started to correct his spelling, then quickly changed his mind. It might be better if he were not so specifically identified. He could make corrections later.

The men stayed three more days in Jamestown, sleeping in the open air to conserve funds. They needed the time to get organized. Richard surmised that it would be difficult to manage on foot in the vast reaches of the Virginia territory so he sought out anyone who might have horses to sell. To his surprise he found that the money he had received for the sale of the three horses in Bristol would not even buy two horses of lesser quality in Virginia. He juggled the price by throwing in the third saddle to complete the purchase of two. He felt sure that he had gotten the poor end of the deal, but he was in no position to haggle. The three men would have to take turns, two would ride and one would walk for the time being. Two horses would need less fodder anyway. Richard was not quite sure where the fodder or human victuals would be coming from. The thought made him uneasy.

The last night in Jamestown, Richard left his men and sought out the tavern in hopes of finding anyone he had known in England. He knew that many hundreds of Royalists had fled to Virginia. He was lonely and felt sorely in need of company. It was beginning to sink in on him that he might have to stay longer than he had planned and that loneliness was apt to be his painful reward for loyalty.

The large center room of the tavern was full of smoke and the smell of a gamy stew, simmering in a large iron vat in the fireplace. Laughter and raucous voices filled the air helping to dispel the sounds of clanking mugs and the scratching of benches as they moved across the floor. Night had fallen. A few lanterns gave a glow of light to the room but not enough for good visibility. When Richard's eyes adjusted to the scanty light, he saw that the room was filled with unkempt-looking men, apparently of the lowest class. Some had obviously been drinking too much. His nose twitched with instinctive distaste. He turned to leave without speaking to anyone. As he did so, he noticed a table in the far corner occupied by two men who appeared to be gentlemen. He studied their faces carefully but recognized neither. The sight of them gave some hope. Otherwise, it seemed a motley crew. Turning on his heels, he left the room.

The next day, Richard wrote a letter to his father informing him of his safe arrival in Virginia, of the prospect of acquiring a hundred and fifty acres of land, of the political situation as he could understand it and of his desire to return to England as soon as his father deemed it safe. He closed by saying, "I fear there will be no one in Virginia with whom I can discuss Galileo's theory of the universe."

Before crossing the river, Richard handed the letter to Captain Underwood and entrusted him with its safe delivery.

After stocking up on as many supplies as they were able to carry on the backs of two horses, the men traveled across the river by ferry to begin their quest for an appropriate piece of land that would enable them to subsist until their exile was over.

V

A week later, after riding and tramping over much of the unclaimed land around Lawne's Creek, Richard stepped off and marked what he thought to be one-hundred and fifty acres bordering on the creek. With relief at solving this first large problem, he rode back to Scotland Wharf with Reuben, and leaving Reuben on the south shore to guard the horses, prepared to take the ferry back to Jamestown to put in his claim for the land.

At the wharf, the ferryman told Richard he would have to wait for a party of three who were going to Jamestown for the assembly of the House of Burgesses. It would be the first Assembly to convene since the surrender of Virginia a year before. When the party of three arrived, it was Colonel John Flood, Burgess for Surry County, his son, Thomas, who was going to assist with any Indian matters that might be on the Assembly's agenda, and his daughter, Mary, who was to attend the various social functions that would accompany the session. When the three boarded the raft, the ferryman introduced Richard to them, and the raft pushed off from shore.

"Welcome to Virginia, Mr. Blount," said John Flood. "Glad to hear you plan to settle on the south side. I've made my home here since a short time after the first massacre in 1622. The land's good and the people are good company without being nosy. You've made a good choice."

"I'm a total novice, Colonel Flood," Richard said. "I hope I can raise a roof over our heads and grow a crop to see us through the winter, but I'm not sure I can."

"Just stick to a few things at first. Corn, squash and potatoes are the easiest. Get through the first winter before you worry about the cash crop, tobacco. There are a number of edible greens growing along the creek beds to help see you through the summer, and there's good fishing and hunting along the south shore. You may miss some of the comforts of home, but at your age you should have no trouble surviving. Just remember that wolves are our worst problem. They travel in packs and will devour any live-stock they can get their paws or jaws on. There are bear and panther in the woods too."

"Bear and panther?" Then turning his attention from Colonel Flood to his daughter, whose golden tresses were shining in the afternoon sunlight, Richard added, "And I was just thinking how serene and at ease you looked."

"I seldom go outside after dark," Mary said.

Richard could sense that he made her uneasy. He noticed that she studied his features carefully and did not seem to be put off by his ungentlemanly attire. It wasn't his fault that he was dressed the way he was. He had no intention of apologizing for it.

"These are sad times for England," Colonel Flood said. "Mary, here, was in London, spending a year with my brother's widow, when King Charles was beheaded. After Virginia declared loyalty to Charles II, we were afraid she might not be allowed to return."

"You've been to England? You're a lucky lass," Richard said. "Did you make the trip all by yourself?"

"My sister Jane was with me," Mary said. "It was a splendid trip except for the execution. That left us and everyone we saw in the depths of despair. My sister married while we were there so I had to come home alone. I've good memories of most of the trip, but I'm very glad to be back."

The raft reached the Jamestown pier. In departing, Colonel Flood said, "Get a field cleared and plowed just as soon as you can, Mr. Blount, and when I return after the assembly session, I'll send you some good seeds and instructions to go with them. We need good men on the south shore. If you're not afraid of hard work, you should have no trouble."

"Thank you, Sir. I'd be much indebted to you," Richard said. He then turned his attention to Mary and added, "It was a pleasure to meet you, Miss Flood. I hope to have such a pleasure again." Mary gave only a weak nod of her head and made no reply. *She thinks I'm a low breed.* He looked down at his motley, uncoordinated attire. *She won't see me like this again. Virginia might not be so bad, after all.*

A fortnight later, Silas was busily tilling an open area of ground near Lawne's Creek. The men possessed only one till which was insecurely attached by harness-reins to the back of a riding horse. It was easy to see that the horse was unhappy with his demotion to the rank of a field worker as he snorted and tried to shake off the attached equipment. The work was not easy for either the horse or the farmer.

Richard and Reuben were engaged in trying to build a cabin. Reuben's brawn, which facilitated the sawing and placement of tree logs, and Richard's analytical mind, which enabled him to give meticulous care to the factors needed in the building of a workable fireplace, made them a good team.

The rustle of bushes at the edge of the field caused Richard to look up from his work. He saw a young man approaching with laden saddle bags and a clump of something green resting on the rump of the horse.

"Hello. Looks like you really mean to settle," the visitor said as he dismounted his horse. "I'm William Flood, another son of the Colonel's."

"You're a welcome sight," Richard said. "This spot is lonelier than a graveyard at midnight."

"Brought you some seeds and roots."

"Hallelujah! You make me feel optimistic about our chances."

"Pa also sent you instructions. He knows all about farming so you better do as he says. This paper tells how the ground should be prepared, how to plant the things and how to care for them. The last gift is a large clump of watercress that must be planted immediately in a shady spot beside the creek. The cress is from my sister, Mary. She dug it up this morning down by Gray's Creek on the outskirts of our farm."

Richard's face radiated a fresh glow of delight, which was missed by no one. Reuben threw his eyes up to the sky and said, "Devil's caught him. Now, how are we going to get home?"

William stayed for several hours. It gave him time to water his horse, stretch his legs a bit and give some advice of his own on the proper way to build a fireplace. By the time he decided to leave, he and Richard had become friends.

"Can't you stay for supper?" Richard asked.

"Wish I could, but there're wolves and bear aplenty in these woods. Sometimes panther even come too close for comfort. It's not smart to travel alone after dark. Got to be on my way."

"Thank your father for me. We might all three have perished without his help. I'm overcome by his generosity and concern."

"We all want more colonists on this side of the river," William said. "We need you to scare the Indians away."

"Please tell your father and sister that I'll call in person to thank them just as soon as I can get all these things into the ground."

Richard noticed a strange look on William's face. Seeing that he was looking past him at something behind, he turned to see what it was. To his dismay, he saw that Reuben was scowling at William but quickly changed the expression on his face to one of total innocence. What had it been before? Richard also saw an expression of confusion and uncertainty on William's face and was perplexed as to why the visit had ended in such an unsettling manner.

VI

"Get my horse saddled up early tomorrow," Richard said to Reuben a fortnight after the visit from William. "I'm planning to ride up to Southwark Parish Church for Sunday services and to call on the Flood family afterwards."

The following morning after making himself as presentable as he possibly could under the circumstances, Richard went out to mount his horse only to find that the other horse had been saddled as well.

"I only asked to have one horse saddled," Richard said. "Where's the other one going?"

"Figured I better go too," Reuben said. "Mr. Flood said there's wolves and bear about."

"I don't remember that he had any concern about riding during the daylight hours, but come along. The ten mile ride might do you some good."

At the Southwark Parish Church, Richard sought out a place to sit against a side wall. From there he had an unobstructed view of both the pulpit and the Flood family as well. He tried to keep his eyes on the minister throughout the long and dull sermon, but somehow they kept gravitating toward the front row bench where Mary was seated between two of her brothers. Richard watched the back of her head, and wondered if she could tell that his eyes were on her. Meanwhile, Reuben placed himself standing against the back wall where he had a clear view of both Richard and Mary.

The minister's voice rang out in conviction at the many sins of his communicants. He preached on and on about the need for all to repent and lead a new life of virtue. So enthralled was he at the sound of his own voice and so self-centered was he in his own thoughts that he completely missed the chief drama of the morning service. It happened when Mary at last felt the prickly warmth of Richard's stare on the back of her neck and, turning her head around, found her eyes looking squarely into Richard's penetrating gaze. For a moment their eyes locked, a warm blush rose to Mary's cheeks and a restrained smile forced itself upon her face. She began to feel slightly faint as she slowly turned her attention back to the pulpit. Although the occasion had been totally missed by the preacher, not a smidge of it had been missed by Reuben from his vantage spot at the back of the room.

After the service when Colonel Flood learned that Richard had ridden north to express his thanks for the planting material and instructions, he insisted that Richard return with the family to their home for Sunday dinner.

John Flood, his wife Margaret and the five children they had raised on what had earlier been thought of as the southern frontier, had succeeded in becoming both prosperous and highly respected. John and Margaret had built their home on land bordered by the James River to the north and surrounded by a circling Gray's Creek on its inland side. The house had been continually added on to as the size of the family increased, and it rambled in a functional though un-designed fashion. The original part of the house was a quarter of a century old just the year before when the last room of the structure was added as a working office, with its own outside entrance. The homestead included nine rooms. None were the same size. Few had ceilings of the same height, and the windows each had styles and shapes all their own.

The narrow entrance door to the house was opened by Mrs. Corder, the woman who had served as cook, charwoman, laundress and confidant to Mary's mother, Margaret, for more than twenty years before the latter's demise and who had managed the household on her own since the day Mary and Jane had left for England. She had come to the Floods' as an indentured servant with her husband. He had died before their indenture was completed, and Mrs. Corder, not wishing to marry again despite several suitors, and knowing no place else to go, had stayed on. She was a freely employed servant, but it was assumed by all that she would never leave.

During the first year after her husband's death, Mrs. Corder attracted the interest of several men in the area, but finding no response to their advances, they left her alone. Matrimony had not brought the happiness to Mrs. Corder that she had anticipated, and she had no interest in subjecting herself to the wishes of any man again. Still she did enjoy a bit of company in the house. It had been hard work managing the household on her own while the girls were away. She had known much loneliness as the only white woman on the place.

Inside the house, a warm blaze on the hearth lit up the parlor, and the smell of beech wood burning gave off a pleasant scent. It was late in the season for burning fires in the fireplace, but a cold wind had blown in from the northwest putting an unseasonable chill in the air.

On this first visit, Richard had brought, as a return gift for the family, the only possession he had to offer, the book of poetry by Edmund Spenser that his mother had packed in the trunk for him to lighten the days of the voyage across the sea. On presenting it, Richard said to Mary, "You must ask your father to read verse XXXIV of Amoretti to you if you wish to hear a beautifully expressed version of how I feel as an exile from my homeland."

"You are assuming that I cannot read myself," Mary answered, "How very manly of you."

"Do you mean to say you can? I'm most impressed. There're many ladies from well-educated families in England who won't go to the trouble of learning."

"Pa insisted upon it, and I must say that reading provides me with much pleasure. I also write regularly to my sister in London, and she to me."

"Then you must read the entire poem yourself. Spenser is a master poet."

"How can you part with it," Mary asked.

"Oh, Mary. You're forgetting the tedium of the nine week crossing. I memorized every word of it. What else was there to do?"

"Memorized it? Then we'll have a presentation. You must recite the verse you mentioned so that we all can hear."

"Well, I... I really don't know that I want to do that."

"You memorized it? Don't be bashful. We're eager to hear."

Put on his mettle in such a way, Richard had to comply. The room was hushed. His thoughts raced back to his days on the ocean with nothing to do but read the verse over and over again. He began:

Like as a ship, that through the ocean wide,

By conduct of some star doeth make her way,

Whenas a storm hath dimmed her trusty guide,

Out of her course doeth wander far astray;

So I, whose star, that wont with her bright ray

Me to direct, with clouds is overcast,

Do wander now, in darkness and dismay,

Through hidden perils round about me placed;

Yet hope I well that, when the storm is past,

My Helice, the lodestar of my life,

Will shine again, and look on me at last,

With lovely light to clear my cloudy grief:

Till then I wander care-full, comfortless,

To secret sorrow, and sad pensiveness.

Looking up, Richard saw that Mary had been moved. A deep sadness seemed to have come over her. Seeing her thus, he had a strong urge to put his arms around her but knew that he dare not.

VII

By late summer, some of Richard's crops, which had been faithfully fertilized with detritus from the forest's floor, as instructed by Colonel Flood, had matured. A good deal more had failed to do so. Richard learned that farming was more difficult than he had thought. His building efforts, however, provided tangible results rewarding him with a spring house beside the creek for the storage of smoked meats and salted fish and a small barn for the two horses with partitioned bins for the harvested corn and oats. The bins were not as full as he felt necessary. The horses would have to do a good bit of winter grazing. Still, there was something powerfully satisfying about starting in the springtime with a bare plot of ground and ending the summer season with all the things needed for survival. Although these possessions were meager and simple compared to those he had known on his father's estates in Worcestershire, Richard could never remember a time when he had been more satisfied with his accomplishments. The sadness of his exile was being overcome by the rewards of his work, and his moments of loneliness replaced by thoughts of seeing Mary again.

Richard's Sunday rides to Old Southwark continued, and he was always rewarded for his effort by being invited to dinner at the Floods'.

On one of these occasions, Richard learned from Colonel Flood that Oliver Cromwell had made himself Lord Protector of the Commonwealth, and that he was thought to hold more power than any king had held before him. The news was saddening, but not at all surprising.

From that time on, Richard's conversation changed from talk of his feeling exiled to concern over the welfare of his family. He talked about improving his property so as to be ready should any of them need to join him in Virginia. He began to describe his plans for adding a room to the cabin, for enlarging the barn and for planting more fields. Although he still had it in mind to return to England someday, he began thinking of asking Mary to marry him. Everyone else had been thinking about it for some time.

In the kitchen at the Floods' house, Mrs. Corder and Reuben became more relaxed with each other, and with time, Mrs. Corder began confiding her fears in her regular Sunday visitor.

"He'll be popping the question to her soon, I guess," she said as they dined on the remains of the family dinner. "You can tell that he's hot to make his move."

"What'll she say, yes?" Reuben asked.

"Course she will. We got none fancy as him round these parts. Others what comes round are yokels side of him. I want her to be happy, but I'd hate to have her leave an' go back to England with him."

"I'm more 'fraid he'll marry her and not go back to England," Reuben said. "I'd do most anything to cool him down."

"The ferryman's wife at Scotland Wharf's got all kinds of potions to do just that. She got things to cool men down and things to heat 'em up. I don't know as her potions work though. I tried some on my husband before he got sick and died, but nothing she ever give me cooled him down." She shook her head and laughed bawdily. "If I'd knowed he was 'bout to die, I wouldn't have bothered. She don't give her stuff away for just nothing."

"What's she give it for?"

"Strong drink's what she wants. She don't care whether you bring her wine, liquor, or something else she can trade for wine or liquor. It's all the same to her."

"What'd you give her?"

"I took her some of my Muscadine wine. If I let it ferment long enough, it gets most strong as liquor itself."

"How's she make her potions?"

"She hunts through the woods for certain plants, mushrooms and roots. She knows all about 'em. She grinds 'em up and mixes her own recipe that she says a black woman give her. Then she kills some small animals and puts their organs into the brew, and while she's mixing it all up, she says lots of strange things that only she can understand. She says, 'It's magic.' It may be even more than that."

That evening long after the guests had left the house, Mrs. Corder was still tidying up her kitchen. She had been sewing on the bodice of a blue silk dress for Mary, earlier in the day, and had left it laid out of the way in the corner while fixing the dinner. Now that she was picking up the pieces, she was frustrated by the fact that she could find only one of the sleeves. She searched everywhere for the second sleeve and could not understand how it could have been mislaid. If she had looked more intently as she scanned all corners of the kitchen, she might have noticed that two bottles of her Muscadine wine were missing also.

VIII

A few weeks later in the early afternoon, Richard was measuring off and staking an area of some twenty by twenty feet, on the sunny side of his cabin, where he planned to build an addition. He was eager to begin the construction in order to have an appropriate place for Mary should she agree to marry him. He hadn't asked her yet but felt sure she knew he was planning to do so.

The air was warm and humid. A bevy of gnats seemed drawn to him and persistently swarmed around his head and shoulders despite his slapping and attempts to blow them away. He had just risen from a stooping position and given a swift swat to the back of his neck when he saw, coming out of the woods, a man trudging into the open field carrying two heavily laden satchels. His first reaction was one of curious dismay, but recognizing the man's walk, he suddenly threw down his measurer and dashed out across the field.

"It's Edward," Richard called out to Silas. Then both men were running toward the laden traveler.

Edward dropped his heavy load, ran to meet his brother, and the two embraced with Silas running around them shouting as though a gift had been dropped from heaven. Silas picked up Edward's satchels, and Richard bombarded him with questions.

"I arrived early this morning on the *Speculator,*" Edward said. "Captain Underwood sends his regards. The clerk in the Governor's office told me where I could find you and directed me to the ferry. When that miserable craft finally reached Scotland Wharf, the ferryman told me how to get here." Edward let out a deep sigh of exhaustion then a laugh of delight at accomplishing his destination. "The ferryman said I could leave the satchels with his wife and Reuben could pick them up the next time he was over there, but they contain all my worldly possessions so I decided not to take the risk. I carried them much of the way. A farmer came by in a cart and let me put the bags aboard for a good part of the walk, but he had to take a different road a mile or so back."

"It's good you didn't leave them," Richard said. "We haven't been to Scotland in months."

Richard and Edward settled down in the cabin. Reuben, who had been alerted to Edward's arrival, came running and helped to carry the satchels inside. He then left to prepare some victuals for Edward, who had had nothing to eat during his four-hour walk.

"Tell me everything about the family," Richard asked.

"My news is so dreadful, "Edward said. "I'm distressed to bring it to you, Richard. You better prepare yourself for the worst. Father was arrested. All his estates were confiscated. He was taken to the tower in London and interrogated forcefully."

"You mean tortured?"

"Of course."

Richard let out a gasp of horror.

"Mother packed up a few of her personal possessions and moved into Cousin Mildred's house in London so as to be near him. She was allowed to visit in prison and went daily. But the wounds from the torture never healed. He died in prison."

Richard's mouth trembled and tears began to cloud his vision. "It was probably all because of my being recognized at Worcester."

"That wasn't your fault, Richard. We were all there. Mother seemed to languish after that. She was so heart-broken she couldn't eat or sleep. She died also, just before the New Year."

Richard stared into space without saying a word. Stunned by Edward's news, it was minutes before he could regain his composure sufficiently to continue the conversation.

"Where are Katie and Libba?"

"They're safe with Sister Margaret at Malvern. Even Cromwell's butchers aren't interested in killing innocent girls. There's nothing left for us in England now. The government still has a bounty out for you as well as Silas and Reuben. The rest of us have been in hiding although no notice has been posted against us."

Richard buried his face in his hands and remained silent for some moments. When he was able to continue, he asked the whereabouts of his other two brothers.

"William's hiding in Bristol and will probably join us over here eventually. He says he doesn't want to leave yet. I'm to write him about conditions here, particularly the safety conditions. He thinks things might be as bad here as there. Thomas will not leave England. He still hopes for a victorious return of the King. If such should happen, the estates would most likely be returned. As the eldest he wants to stay and take his chances."

"Do you think the King will ever return?"

"I think it unlikely. Most people are afraid to talk of it. Meanwhile, Oliver Cromwell has made himself Lord Protector of the Commonwealth and has tremendous power both politically and militarily."

Later in the evening when Richard's spirits had been revived somewhat from the depression he felt at hearing Edward's news, he confided his hopes of marrying Mary to his brother. It was decided between them that on the following Sunday they would ride up to Old Southwark for church and to pay a visit. "Fortunately," Richard said, "we have two horses."

Silas and Reuben began sleeping outside after Edward's arrival. The small cabin would have been crowded with four men in it, and the weather was mild.

On Sunday morning when Richard and Edward left, they found the horses saddled and ready for them as requested. Silas was holding the reins and waiting to help them mount.

"Where's Reuben?" Richard asked.

"He walked to Scotland last night," Silas said. "I think He's found a woman there. He don't say nothing 'bout it."

"There's no crime in that," Richard said. "This is his day to do as he pleases. Perhaps you should try to find a woman too, Silas."

On the ride to Old Southwark, Richard said to Edward, "I hope you can find fifty acres adjacent to my property so that we can combine our farming efforts."

"Thanks for the suggestion, but I didn't leave England quite as precipitously as you. I've brought some money with me. I plan to do a lot of scouting before deciding which property to buy. I promise to consider only the south shore though, and to find land that's not too far from yours. Meanwhile, I'll stay to help with the addition so you'll have a place for Mary."

IX

At church, Edward was taken by Mary's beauty and charm. She was wearing the deep blue silk dress that Mrs. Corder had just finished making for her. The color made her hair look even fairer than usual and brought out the color in her cheeks. Even more it matched the deep blue of her eyes and made it difficult for anyone to look beyond them. The effect was tantalizing.

After mid-day dinner at the Floods', Richard asked the Colonel if he might speak with him privately. The two men left the house for an afternoon stroll around the grounds leaving Edward, Mary and her brothers to make conversation with each other. All suspected the reason for the request, and each added his bit to the tensions of the moment. Mary sat silently twitching her thumbs. Edward tried to entertain William and Thomas, but their eyes kept wandering as he spoke to them. After some time had passed, Mary got up to peer out the small, parlor window. She saw that her father and Richard were almost back to the house and that the two were laughing and conversing amiably with each other. She gave a sigh of relief followed by an unexpected giggle. All seemed well. However, just as the men mounted the steps to the entrance, a shattering scream cut through the air behind them. All eyes from both inside and outside of the house turned to see a terrified-looking Negro boy racing from a nearby field. His black face had turned an eerie, ashen-grey, and his short, kinky hair appeared to be standing out straight from its roots as he ran for Colonel Flood. Grabbing his master's coattails, he tried to hide behind them.

"What is it, Sammy?" Colonel Flood asked grabbing the boy and turning him around so that they faced each other.

The boy's teeth began to chatter. He looked up at Mary, who had just come out of the front door, and immediately his whole body began to shake. It took what seemed like an eternity to get a discernible word out of him, but at last he said, "In the field...."

Voodoo."

Colonel Flood took the boy's hand and forced him to show them all what had terrified him so. They walked across the open field at the front of the courtyard to a small field used by the one slave family on the place as their vegetable garden. It took a great deal of friendly encouragement to urge him on, but at last he took them to the edge of the field and with teeth chattering wildly, pointed to a newly dug hole.

William and Thomas walked over and peered into it. Thomas reached down and pulled up an object that was an image at first unrecognizable. The body was made of cleaned animal bones, which had been encased in the skin of a rattlesnake. A frog's head served as a face, and around the head had been attached the flaxen-colored silks of a cornstalk to serve as the creature's hair. But the most disturbing thing of all was that the figure was clothed in a deep blue, silk dress and had two long thorns piercing its heart.

Mary stared at the object; then realizing that the figure's dress was of the same material as the one she wore, fainted dead away.

Sammy, thinking the image had accomplished its purpose, let out a blood-curdling scream. "Demons," he yelled. "They's here. They's gwanna..."

"Hush, Sammy," the Colonel said. "Who could have caused this mischief?"

Mary opened her eyes, and helped by Richard and William, got to her feet. Still feeling woozy, she allowed herself to be led back to the house where she retired to her room.

"This, obviously, is no time for me to address Mary," Richard said to Colonel Flood. "Tell her that I'll return on Thursday afternoon to talk with her. She should have time to recover from this dastardly joke by then. I can't imagine the perverted mind that could have thought this up."

"We'll try to get to the bottom of it. Come back on Thursday, Richard. She'll be happy to see you."

X

On the designated day for Richard to make his call, he asked that his horse be readied for departure by mid-morning. It would be a long ride alone, and he wanted to return before dark. He had not done any nighttime riding in Virginia, warned as he had been about the timber wolves and bear that inhabited the area. He heard about the way the wolves that traveled in packs attacked poultry, sheep, and even cows and horses. He knew that the Assembly had established a bounty of one-hundred pounds of tobacco for the head of any wolf that was brought into Jamestown. Obviously, they were quite dangerous.

When Richard stepped into the stirrup and mounted his horse, Reuben rushed out from the barn with a small package in his hand.

"You'll miss your mid-day meal, Sir. I filled your canteen with fresh water and cooked up some corn cakes for you to eat along the way."

"That was very thoughtful of you Reuben. I've been so engrossed in my plans that I have not thought about food at all. It'll come in very handy." Richard placed the items in his saddle bag.

"Wish me well, Reuben," he said.

"I do. Don't weaken or change your mind. We must all take our happiness where we can find it. Dreaming of things past seldom makes anyone happy."

The ten-mile ride seemed to take an eternity. Trips always seem to last longer when one is alone. He increased his speed by changing the horse's gait from a walk to a trot. The pungent smell of the giant, loblolly pines penetrated his nostrils as he entered the first of several forests along the way. The trees provided a welcome shade, but the decreased light made it necessary to pay more attention to the ground beneath the horse's hooves and thus slowed down his progress. Emerging from the first forest into the sunshine, he allowed his mind to wander. He found himself mulling over and over the words he might say to Mary to elicit the hoped-for response. Thoughts of building the new addition to his cabin occupied his thoughts for a while, and thoughts of Mary as his wife occupied much of the rest. As he neared the plantation, he came out of the woods into an abandoned field that was covered with millions of wild, blue cornflowers in full bloom. He stopped and dismounted to pick a large bouquet. After all, the flowers were almost the same color as her eyes. Surely they would help him find the words to make a charming woman happy.

By the time Richard arrived at the Floods', it was already mid-afternoon. For appearance's sake the family conversed with him for a while before discretely leaving him alone with Mary. Then, despite his long hours of rehearsal, it took him much longer than he could ever have imagined to get around to the matter at hand. He spent a good deal of time talking of trivial things as Mary sat patiently waiting. Finally he took her small hand in his, patted it a few times with the other one and raised it to his lips, gently kissing each finger.

"You must rise and stand near me," he said softly lifting her from the bench where she sat. "I have a strong hold on you now. You'll not be able to escape until I have said my whole piece."

A blush began to creep into Mary's cheeks.

"I couldn't resist stopping to pick the flowers for you. They're so like your eyes. Having never looked into them yourself, you cannot imagine how beautiful they are."

"That's kind of you to say."

"Kindness has nothing to do with it. It's simply the truth." Richard paused as though he could think of nothing more to say. Seconds went by.

"Did you come to tell me that you will return to England soon?" Mary asked looking deeply into his eyes, then dropping her gaze abruptly and lowering her head.

"No-o. Just the opposite. I came to tell you that the overcast sky has cleared. I have seen, anew, the lodestar of my life. Her name is Mary." Richard drew her into a close embrace lifting her head as he did so. Mary's face burst forth with a show of radiance.

"Oh, Richard."

"It's very presumptuous of me. I'm but a poor man. You surely could do better. But...but, I want to marry you. If you agree, I'll promise to be true and to do everything in my power to make you happy. I love you, Mary."

"And I love you,"

"Will you marry me?"

"I will. You've already made me the happiest person in the world. I'll love you always."

Richard slowly lowered his lips to cover her upturned mouth, "No more talking," he said as he sealed the vow.

XI

It was twilight as Richard left the Floods' house and turned his horse onto the woodland path. Looking up through the branches of the tall trees, he could see the thin sliver of the new moon shining between the lacy green arms of the pines. So engrossed was he in the romantic events of the day that he had traveled several miles before feeling the first pangs of hunger in his stomach. He realized to his surprise that he had eaten absolutely nothing since early morning, and suddenly he was ravenously hungry. Opening his saddle bag, he took out the corn cakes Reuben had given him and devoured them all within seconds.

Richard had not reached the half-way point between the Floods' and his cabin when his stomach first knotted into a painful cramp. His throat began contracting in the spasms of retching. He was just able to dismount before the violent vomiting began. He stumbled away from his horse, into the pine woods, which were carpeted with dry needles, and there regurgitated the corn cakes with all their contents in a series of virulent attacks until his body was weak from the loss of fluid and his head splitting with pain.

For some time he was unable to move from his kneeling position because of the lightning-like pangs in his gut. The pale light from the moon made faint shadows across the needled soil. The sun had set and left the forest dark except for the glow of the sliver moon. At last, Richard was able to lift his head, and he wondered how long it would be before he was able to remount and continue his journey. As he watched, a cloud moved across the moon's face and the woods turned completely dark. At that moment, the sound of a lone wolf-call pierced the air. With the eerie sound of the wolf resounding in the woods, the horse rose on his hind legs, whinnied, bared his teeth in fright, and bolted down the path in the direction of home. Richard had barely enough time to assess the precariousness of his situation when the call of the lone wolf was answered by the call of several more from a different direction.

Oh God! How could my fortune have turned so quickly? He pulled himself painfully across the woodland floor. He reached a large tree trunk and propped himself up with the tree at his back. This was more painful than resting on all fours, but he wanted the security of having something to cover his back. Another wolf cry came from the south and seemed to be closer than the one before.

Richard's mouth was dry and he desperately wanted the canteen that he could see on the ground about ten feet away, but he was scared to leave the tree trunk to fetch it. Then he saw that his pistol had fallen from its holster and was lying beside the canteen. His stomach churned but gave forth nothing but painful dry heaves. The call of the wolves rang through the night air again. They were converging. Richard had to retrieve his pistol. Finally, he forced himself to his knees. He could not stand. He crawled as quickly as the pain in his stomach would permit to the place where his gun lay. The thin moon came out from behind the clouds, and just as he picked up the gun, he saw a pair of blue eyes, not thirty feet away, that had caught the beam of a moon-ray. Richard cocked his pistol and fired frantically in the direction of the eyes. Then he grabbed the canteen and made it back to the large tree trunk.

For hours Richard sat with his back to the tree and his pistol pointed forward. At intervals, he took small sips of water. Then he swished a bit of it around in his mouth and spit it out upon the ground. He rationed what he had with care. He wanted desperately to lie down on the ground and sleep, but even through the befuddled cloud of his thoughts, he knew that if he passed out, he would never see another day. The adrenalin of his glands took over command of his body, and he did not sleep.

The horse made it back to the farm before midnight, but it was several hours more before Silas was aroused and in turn awakened Edward to say that Richard's horse had arrived at the barn without his rider.

Before dawn, Edward and Silas were riding back along the lonely, dark trail calling out, "Richard, Richard." When Richard first heard the faint call, not recognizing his name, he thought that the wolves had returned. Great charges of electricity shot through his body. He cocked his weapon and waited. Then as the calls came nearer, he knew it was Edward and that he had been saved. He tried to answer the call, but when he opened his mouth, no sound came forth.

As the first rays of dawn began to lighten the sky, Edward and Silas came around a bend in the path and saw him. He was so dehydrated that he had not the power to move or speak. His eyes had a death-like glaze over them, but they were wide open and alert. Not thirty feet away was the corpse of a dead timber wolf, shot through the chest at close range.

Reuben greeted Silas and Edward when they arrived at the cabin with Richard tied to the neck of one of the mounts.

"Is he all right?" Reuben asked.

"He's asleep," Edward said. "We'll let him be. We'll just have to wait to find out what happened. Vomiting, a run-away horse and a dead timber wolf are not enough clues for me to figure this out. Help us get him inside."

Reuben carried Richard inside and laid him on a cot. He looked nervously at his master. His eyes began to smart and his mouth to twitch. It's lucky I be that he's asleep. When he talks, I'm finished. That old hack told me the brew would cool him down. Instead, it 'bout killed him. Guess she was right. Dead men don't want for nothing.

Before Richard awakened, Reuben had bundled up his few possessions and taken off on foot. He first walked back along the trail some five miles to the spot where Richard had been stricken. Finding the wolf where it had lain since being shot, he quickly decapitated the animal with one swift slice of his hunting knife. He found a strong vine and managed to push it through the eye socket of the wolf so he could tie the head to his belt. The head was worth a hundred pounds of tobacco. That might come in very handy. Reuben placed the blood-stained knife in his belt and turned east toward Scotland Wharf.

Arriving at the ferry landing, he saw that the river raft was not there. He surmised that it was in Jamestown, and Mrs. Blackthorn must be alone. He entered her house quietly, without giving notice, and found her in her back-room apothecary in a drunken stupor. He looked at her with disgust.

You bitch. You aren't a witch at all. You only know how to kill people. It's bitch not witch, and a very drunk bitch at that.

Reuben's disgust turned abruptly to fury, and with the sharp knife that still held traces of the wolf's blood, he quickly slashed across her neck and throat. She gave out one gasp, opened her eyes wide and fell from her chair.

Reuben let himself out as he had entered, apparently without being seen. He walked in a daze along the north shore. He hadn't planned to harm Richard, and he hadn't planned to kill Mrs. Blackthorn, but he'd done both. He had the eerie feeling that he no longer controlled any part of his life. Some demon, surely, had taken hold. The potions had worked more against him than Richard.

Reuben started north. He had to walk inland to get across the mouth of Gray's Creek, but once across, his wanderings drew him back to the river. A bit more than a mile up the river's edge from the creek, he came upon a sandy beach. Tied to a tree nearby, he found a rowboat, but there were no oars with which to row it. He moved over to the large cypress tree at the water's edge and climbed over the ridge of knees that supported the ancient tree. He sat down within its raised roots to contemplate his options, made note of the direction of the tidal current, and wondered how long it would continue to run in it's easterly direction. He decided that he had no choice but to risk a river crossing. The partial moon, resting low near the horizon appeared to be huge as it began to rise in the darkening sky. He moved out over the knees of the cypress, untied the boat, tossed his bag into it and climbed into the craft himself. He was turning the last remnants of the control of his life over to another force. The ancient tree stood by as the boat traveled out into the water. With no oars, Reuben would have to go where ever the river carried him.

XII

The next morning when Richard had regained enough strength to converse, he told Edward the entire series of events of the previous day. He felt certain that he had been poisoned by the corn cakes, but he could not fathom the reason for it. On hearing this, Edward called to Silas, who was just outside the cabin door, and asked him to fetch Reuben.

"Reuben's gone," Silas said.

"Gone! What do you mean gone? Where could he go?"

"Scotland, I think. Probably went to see the old woman again. The witch."

"Whatever are you talking about, Silas? There's no such thing as a witch," Edward said.

"Some thinks there is. Reuben must of thought so. Come see what's in the barn." Silas started out the door. Edward and Richard followed.

In a corner of the barn, Silas turned back a covering of dried grass. Underneath were two small bottles and a jar. Under the bottles was a layer of dried and cleaned animal bones, the head of a dead snake, some corn silk and bits of cornflower blue silk material.

Richard was dumbstruck by the thought that Reuben had been responsible for the buried image of Mary. He opened the bottles and saw that they contained dried, cut-up items of no recognizable things. The jar held part of a dead toad. The evidence against Reuben was overwhelming.

Richard's stomach was still painfully sore. Nevertheless, he insisted upon riding, with Edward, to Four Mile Tree plantation, a large property of some three thousand acres that abutted the Flood's holding on the river's edge, to see its owner, William Browne, Justice of the Peace for the newly-created Surry County.

When Richard told his story to the Justice, he had the strange impression that the Justice had already heard most of it. He showed no sign of surprise, but listened attentively. Then Justice Browne took over the story telling and rendered them not only surprised but flabbergasted.

"The ferryman's wife was murdered last night while her husband was on the river," he began. "She was brutally slashed while drunk, as she often is known to be. Footprints were found leading from her house to the place where an old rowboat is left on the beach here in front of Four Mile Tree. The boat and the footprints went into the water. As oars were never left with the boat, it's presumed that a desperate man cast off in it last night. Most likely that man was Reuben. He could be almost anywhere now, on the eastern part of the north shore, in the bay or even floating in the open sea."

"We found an extraordinary apothecary shop in the back room at the Blackthorn's house. The sheriff will investigate the contents of all her bottles and boxes. She may be lucky to have had her life finished off as painlessly as it was," stated the Justice. "It would have been a witch trial for sure, had she lived. I never could have controlled the fury of the people to keep it from happening. I doubt that you'll ever hear from Reuben again."

"Silas says Reuben wanted desperately to go back to England," Richard said. "He may get there, who knows? I don't think he was capable of understanding how far Virginia was from England when we left. Then he had no means of return. He wasn't a bad man. He was just too ignorant for his own welfare."

XIII

Richard's health began to improve, but the poisoning he had endured left him weak and enervated. His stomach would improve, and then go sour again. There was little food that appealed, and without proper nourishment, his recovery was slow. Even with Edward and Silas doing most of the heavy work, he was held up in getting the new room for Mary ready for their planned wedding.

At last, the addition to the cabin was finished, and the wedding plans completed. The day before the ceremony, Richard and Edward rode north traveling along the same path where Richard had suffered his ordeal. Somehow, riding in the fresh air of an October morning in 1654, the journey seemed so pleasant and tranquil that Richard found it difficult to recall the terror he had felt when left alone and ill along the way.

The wedding was set for noon. Upon arriving at the Floods', Richard and Edward were shown to a spare room for dressing and waiting.

Mrs. Corder had come to realize that love had won out over her own selfish desire to keep Mary at home. In penance, she had spent the week cooking from dawn until dusk to provide a joyous feast for the small group of friends who would be served refreshments after the wedding ceremony. The Brownes were coming and the Jordans, the Grays, the Rivers and the Harrisons.

Mrs. Corder felt badly about being the one who had told Reuben of Mrs. Blackthorn's potions. She never meant to cause harm. Mrs. Blackthorn's murder was a great loss for her, she being one of the few women Mrs. Corder saw regularly at church.

Before Mary entered the parlor, Richard, dressed in the yellow silk britches and the dove-grey waistcoat that his mother had packed in his trunk more than two years before, stationed himself on one side of the minister, who was standing in front of the fireplace. Edward was at his side.

Mary entered the room with her father. She was dressed completely in white except for a halo of bright, orange-colored berries that she had tied with ribbon to the bandeau that held back her long, blond tresses. The orange of the berries made her eyes appear bluer than ever. Richard felt giddy with pleasure.

The vows said, the repast served, the bottles of wine passed around to refresh all those who were celebrating, the afternoon was spent in joyous revelry. The couple were toasted, kissed, hugged, and walked to the river's edge where a large sailboat, with a crewman, was packed with all Mary's possessions. It waited to transport the newly-wedded couple to a spot as close as possible to their new home. The sail would take them past the old cypress tree on the beach in front of Four Mile Tree, past Scotland Wharf, where Gray's Creek entered the James, past Hog Island and a short distance up Lawne's Creek. Silas was to meet them there, with a cart, where the creek became un-navigable.

The guests stayed at the river's edge until the boat had passed the protrusion of land that held the ancient cypress tree, with its long branches reaching out as if to embrace them. Then the vessel moved out of sight

The guests, who had gone to the river front to see the newlyweds off, were climbing back up the hill to the house when they heard the sound of hoof beats along the entrance path. Colonel Flood was surprised to see the sheriff and two deputies ride up to the front of the house.

"Good afternoon, sheriff," the Colonel called out. "This is Mary's wedding day. We've just sent the happy couple off to the groom's home. Come in and rejoice with us."

"We knew it was Miss Mary's big day," the sheriff said. "We waited all day before coming here. Didn't want to do anything to spoil things for her. This is a most unfortunate, official visit. We want to see Mrs. Corder."

Mrs. Corder, who was standing in the doorway, gasped.

"We've come to take her with us," the sheriff continued. "We've gone through every item in Mrs. Blackthorn's apothecary in Scotland. None of us knew she could read and write. Found out she could keep accounts as well. She had meticulous records of everyone who'd ever been her customer, what they bought, and what they paid for it. She must have reasoned that the records would come in handy for blackmail if she ever had to stoop to that. Anyway, Mrs. Corder was listed with the date and the payment she made for Mrs. Blackthorn's goods. She's under arrest."

Colonel Flood stepped in front of Mrs. Corder as if instinctively to protect her. Justice Browne stepped forward to continue in her defense. "Sheriff," the Justice said. "We don't arrest people in Surry County for witchcraft. I'll not hear of it."

"We're not arresting her for witchcraft," the sheriff said. "We've come to arrest her for the murder of her husband."

THE PIRATES
1717-1719

I

Mingo, a fifteen-year-old, house-trained slave on the Four Mile Tree plantation, was sitting on a moss-covered mound in the shade of a large rhododendron bush. The slope on which he sat descended to a narrow beach, the plantation pier and the river beyond. The sun was falling in the western sky, casting long streaks of glittering light across the moving tidal waters, streaks that were divided by the shadows cast from the rippling of the river's surface. For miles, looking up river, one could see waving lines of dark, light, dark, light .

It's like the feeling I have inside me, sad, happy, sad, happy.

The dark shiny-skinned youth was a third generation Virginia slave. His grandfather, also named Mingo, had arrived in one of the earliest boatloads of African cargo brought to the colony. Colonel William Browne, the father of the present owner of Four Mile Tree, had bought him on credit along with several others from the same ship. By the time the Colonel had paid off his debt from the purchase, the group had planted and harvested several crops of tobacco and sired progeny that would insure a future labor force for the plantation. The early investment would pay off handsomely for nearly two centuries before turning sour and ultimately ruining the family's livelihood, way-of-life and very survival.

The younger Mingo, now sitting at the top of the bank, far above the river, to get a bird's-eye view of any vessels that might come into sight, was dreaming of distant places that he had never seen. While serving the dinner table each day, he had often heard discussions of places such as London, Bristol, Montserrat, St. Kitts and Bermuda. The names meant nothing to him except that they represented other places, where other people lived and did other things than to plant and harvest tobacco. He knew that these places were far away, and he knew that the only way to get to any of them was to follow the river out into the sea.

As Mingo sat looking at the water, a small sloop sailed out into the late afternoon sunshine. Tacking against the northern breeze, it moved across the river toward Jamestown. The sail, when it first came into view, appeared to be almost as tall as the highest branches of the ancient cypress tree down on the shore. Mingo watched the sail, continuously diminishing in size, as it moved farther and farther across the river and finally disappeared from sight.

Mingo loved to watch the boats. He had gone many times with Captain Browne on the Gray's Creek ferry to Jamestown to purchase supplies in that town's outdoor market and to help cart home shipments of goods that had arrived from England. It was always a welcome break in the monotony of plantation life. The ferry was, however, an awkward craft. It was nothing like the sleek sailboats he saw racing with the wind. Every time he saw a trim vessel moving speedily across the water, he longed to swim out to it, hoist himself aboard and sail down the river. He spent many a night dreaming of such things. It was his way of moving into the wide, wide world of his future.

As Mingo sat looking longingly at the river, his reverie was suddenly interrupted by a familiar call. "Mingo, Mingo, where is you at?" came the shrill voice of his mother, who was the Browne family's cook.

Mingo looked up the bank to see the stout, middle-aged woman standing at its top, silhouetted against the twilight sky. "Oh, turtle dung," he cursed. "It's time to scrub up to serve another supper."

Before getting up to climb the steep slope to the kitchen house, Mingo took one more longing look at the river.

Some day. Some day I'm going to do it.

II

The Browne family of Four Mile Tree and the Negroes on the place, including Mingo, were preparing for a wedding to be held the following day. The ceremony was to take place on the upper terrace of the plantation house, the home of William Browne, II. William had inherited all of the family's landed property when his father died twelve years before and thus felt it to be his duty to host most of the family occasions of importance. Besides, no finer spot could be found for a summer, garden ceremony than the tiered terraces of Four Mile Tree with their several levels of formal, boxwood gardens descending to the river.

The bride-to-be was William's niece, Ann Flood, who lived on the adjacent plantation to the west of Four Mile Tree. The groom-to-be was William Cocke, who lived at Mt. Pleasant, the adjacent plantation to the east. The bride's mother was William's sister. Another sister, Priscilla, had married Thomas Blount, the only child of Richard and Mary Flood Blount. Thomas had established a large and prosperous plantation on the Blackwater River east and inland from Benjamin Harrison's Wakefield. He had died a few years before and Priscilla was now a widow.

Priscilla and her two oldest sons had arrived at her brother's home the evening before and were occupying the guest bedroom on the second floor. The room looked out upon the garden, the river and the faint silhouette of the ruins of Jamestown across the river.

The plantations along this stretch of the south shore of the river had largely remained in the hands of the families that had established them nearly a century before. Heads of the various households had served the colony well as members of the Governor's Council, or the House of Burgesses, as justices, sheriffs and as vestrymen of the Southwark Parish Church.

Intermarriage between these prosperous families was so prevalent that it was difficult to keep the cousins straight. The Brownes of Four Mile Tree, the Floods of the house by the same name, the Blounts of Blackwater, the Grays, the Washingtons, the Cockes of Mt. Pleasant and the Benjamin Harrisons of Wakefield lived in near proximity to each other. By 1717, they were almost all related in some manner or other.

The colony had survived most of the earlier growing pains that had often struck like a flash of lightning and threatened the very continuation of Virginia. The population had grown steadily during the previous half century and was approaching a hundred thousand people. Approximately one quarter of these were Negros, mostly slaves. Indians could be seen in and around the settled areas from time to time but caused few problems. Indians on the frontier, however, were quite a different matter. The tribes along the outskirts of the settled areas were seething. Tribes to the south and west were ready to fight anyone who infringed upon their territory whether white men or other natives from distant tribes.

There were few towns in Virginia, and those that did exist were small and sparsely populated. Most craftsmen lived on an established plantation and were traded around to others as the need arose. The county seats, where courts convened every two or three months, were usually deserted in between.

Sunday church services were almost the only regularly organized meeting places where colonists could convene and exchange ideas. The very isolated life of the colonists was an impediment to progress. Towns were sorely needed.

The Reverend James Blair, a Scotsman, who had married the daughter of Benjamin Harrison and become Commissary of the Church of England in the colony, saw the need to remedy this situation. In 1693, he established the College of William and Mary, the second institution of higher learning in America and the first one in the south. By 1699, the college and its preparatory school were flourishing in a place called Middle Plantation, some six miles from Jamestown, when that original capital of Virginia burned down for the second time. Rather than rebuild again on the miasmic, swampy peninsula, the Assembly decided to move the capital inland next to the college and to rename the town Williamsburg.

By 1717 the college, founded and presided over by the Reverend Blair, was thriving at one end of a wide boulevard named Duke of Gloucester Street, and a handsome new capitol building had been completed at the other. In between there was a new and larger Bruton Parish Church, where the Reverend Blair was also the minister. There were numerous craft shops, taverns and private homes along the boulevard. A handsome Governor's residence was being built, largely designed and supervised by Governor Alexander Spotswood. Although Williamsburg had become the social center of the colony, it was never a busy commercial town. It existed to house the college and the government. Its permanent, colonial population would never exceed eighteen hundred residents.

On this balmy but clear prenuptial day, the deep ultramarine tone of the sky promised that no rain was in sight. This condition was usually considered bad news to farmers, but on this day it was welcome as it meant that the tables and benches for the outdoor party could be placed and decorated the day before the wedding.

Mingo was standing near the door on the outdoor terrace of the house that faced the river waiting to respond to any request that his master might make of him. He had caught the excitement of the moment. He loved visitors. He loved parties. He loved action of almost any kind. To satisfy this acute interest in others, Mingo spent much of his time seeing that he was close enough to hear all that was going on of importance without making himself a visible intruder.

Mingo was watching his master and saw that he was nervously

fidgeting with his spectacles. This he took as a sign that something important was about to happen so he moved closer but kept himself hidden behind a bush. A moment later he saw Priscilla come out onto the terrace and stretch her arms to embrace the fresh morning air.

Priscilla was not a large woman, but she created a large and arresting presence. Physically, her body was well-shaped. Her back was straight and her bosom high. She had unusually thick hair of a rich brown tone that occasionally showed strands of red when caught by the midday sun. She wore it brushed straight back from her forehead, tied at the nape of the neck and then rolled into a figure eight and pinned securely to the back of her head. The hairdo made her profile her most prominent feature and caused her to stand out in almost any group.

"Ah, wonderful," she announced. "I can smell the distant sea. You've no idea how much I've missed the feeling of contact with the outside world that I always get when I can smell the path to faraway places."

"Gracious, but you have arisen in a poetic mood," William said. "To what may I credit this romantic outburst?"

"Oh, Will, I'm just so happy to be at home. You've no idea how much I've always loved Four Mile Tree. It was a beautiful place to grow up."

"So it was."

"You've improved the place as well. Everything looks better than ever."

"Everything but the books. We had a catastrophe last fall that I didn't have the heart to write you about."

"The whole place looks managed to perfection. What happened?"

"The problem wasn't here; it was in the bay. We had a bumper crop of more than a hundred hogsheads of premium tobacco."

"So?"

"I decided to ship it directly to London rather than selling it to a middleman in Jamestown to eliminate the extra take."

"Seems prudent."

"It was all loaded on one ship."

"Uh oh."

"The Captain said he was almost to the bay when he saw the Pearl, our one and only guard ship, limping upriver to port. He later admitted he knew it was risky to take the loaded ship into the pirate-infested waters without the guard ship to escort it out of the confines of the bay into the open sea, but the alternative was to return and wait until the guard ship could be reactivated to duty. He elected to take his chances and continued his journey in the unprotected ship."

"Was the ship armed in any way?"

"Not really. It had no cannons or even light artillery."

"Keep talking."

"The cargo ship was taken by pirates as it rounded the peninsula at the southern tip of the James. Some of the crew were slain. Others managed to escape, including the Captain, and returned to tell the tale."

"How dreadful. Has this happened often?"

"It's becoming more prevalent. Trade has suffered badly. The loss affects all the producers up the line."

"So you lost everything?"

"We lost the profit from one whole year's work."

"I'm surprised that you're giving this wedding."

"We had enough wine, brandy and ale in the cellar for this affair and enough sugar for Celia to do her baking, but when it's over the cellar and sugar bags might not get refilled as quickly as usual. Where's Mingo? He must bring us some coffee before I get into the wedding plans with you. Mingo," he hollered. "That boy is always off on a drifting cloud all of his own. If he ever spent as much time working as he does daydreaming you'd notice a marked difference around this place. Mingo," he hollered again.

"Here I is, Master," Mingo answered. He seemed to appear from nowhere.

"Fetch us some coffee please, and don't forget to bring the sugar."

"Now it's time for you to help me with the plans for the reception. The two most important men in Virginia will be here tomorrow. It could be our finest moment, but not unless we take care."

Mingo rushed to fulfill his mission. He hated to miss a word. He arrived with the coffee just in time to hear Priscilla say, "The

Reverend Blair has always been severe. I'd hate to find myself on the wrong side of him. I've missed a great deal. I've been deep in the woods and hardly ever out of the nursery these past few years. Tell me about Governor Spotswood, Will. Do you like him?"

"I do," her brother said. "He's handsome, elegant, amusing, stubborn, authoritarian, ambitious and, ...and he's a bachelor."

"Even I knew he was a bachelor," Priscilla said. "How has he managed to remain so?"

"I said he was stubborn."

"Now you've gotten me interested. What can I do to help with these two gigantic problems?"

"I want you to see that these two men are kept on opposite sides of the garden after the ceremony. Not obviously so, you understand. There'll be refreshments served on both sides. I want you to take the Governor to the east side of the garden, and I'll have Jane escort the Reverend to the west side, unless of course, you would rather that I assigned you to the Reverend.

"No, no, you old goat. I'll take the Governor. You can't give him to anyone else now. He's mine for the day."

Mingo served Priscilla and William a second cup of coffee. "I sure am going to be happy to meet the Governor," he said.

"Just as I suspected," William said. "He was eavesdropping."

III

The Reverend James Blair arrived at Wakefield, the home of his wife's deceased father, Benjamin Harrison, the day before the wedding, in order to make certain that no snag would cause him to be late for the wedding ceremony which he had been asked to perform. Wakefield was only a few miles from Four Mile Tree, and a good hard-packed road connected the two. There was far less chance of a mishap by road than by making a last-hour river crossing. The ceremony was scheduled for noon, and he had been seated in the parlor of Four Mile Tree for over half an hour when the moment approached. The Reverend made a practice of never being late.

When noon arrived the bride and groom were both ready and waiting in their respective quarters of the house, and the guests were in the garden awaiting the commencement of the ceremony.

Unfortunately, Governor Spotswood had not yet arrived. His ketch could be seen in mid-river traveling toward the Four Mile Tree pier. It would be unthinkable to proceed without him. The wedding party would wait until he arrived.

The nuptials were delayed for more than half an hour when the ketch finally docked, and the Governor, resplendent in green, silk-cord britches, with pale gray topcoat and stockings, climbed the sloping ground from the pier to the upper terrace of the manse. The guests politely applauded his dramatic entrance, and the hired fiddler gave forth with a flourish of melody.

The Reverend took his place to begin the ceremony. Mingo was standing near and heard his master whisper, "The Governor apologizes for being late."

"Late. What do you mean late?" the Reverend responded. "He was not a minute late. By my calculations, his arrival was punctiliously timed for his own purposes."

Oh my. I do hope Priscilla and Jane remember their duties today.

As soon as the vows had been exchanged, the groom congratulated and the bride kissed by all, both of the women rushed into position as though taking their place for some chivalric pageant.

"Governor," Priscilla said to the tall, affable-looking man who had kept them all waiting, "you must be parched after your river crossing. Please follow me to the refreshment table so that I can serve you. I'm Priscilla Blount, your host's sister, and I have been asked to look out for you."

"Your brother is a most gracious host," Governor Spotswood said, "I can think of nothing more pleasant."

"Did you have trouble crossing the river?" Priscilla asked.

"None whatsoever, but I always look both ways to make sure that no unidentified sails are in sight before setting out on the water. One never knows these days when it might turn out to be a pirate ship. They can be lurking in the least likely places."

"Surely they do not sail this far inland," Priscilla said. She ladled out a cup of brandy-laced punch and handed it to Mingo to serve to her charge.

"They could be anywhere," Alexander Spotswood continued. "With all the effort I have made to capture them and destroy their plunderous trade, I mean to make sure that they have no chance to capture me. I shudder to think of the fun they might have in torturingly disposing of my body," he said with a wink and a smile.

"William says that his entire tobacco crop was taken by the pirates last fall when the ship transporting it was captured in the Chesapeake," Priscilla said. "Why are there so many more pirates now than there used to be?"

"The answer is very simple," the Governor said, warming to Priscilla's charm in seeking his knowledge. "Her majesty built the royal navy into a 49,000 man force during the recent War of the Spanish Succession. The sailors were trained in the art of privateering, to take the vessels of France and Spain wherever they were encountered. Many of the sailors had plied that trade for years and knew no other work. When peace came four years ago, the people were tired of war and taxes. Our new monarch, George, demobilized the navy to save funds. Over two-thirds of the seamen were thrown out of work. Many were bitter that they had fought hard to win the war and were rewarded for doing so by being laid off. A number of the disgruntled ones set out pirating to get revenge for what they saw as their abuse. They are a violent and hateful lot who would love nothing better than to get their hands on a person of authority."

"Here you are, Governor," William said. "I've several guests who are eager to meet you." William nodded to Priscilla that she had done her duty for the time being and was free to mingle. He then returned his attention to the Governor saying, "May I present my brother-in-law, John Flood, the father of the bride. He's very interested in hearing about your expedition across the Blue Ridge Mountains into the Shenandoah.

"I'm delighted to meet you, Mr. Flood," the Governor said. "The journey to the Shenandoah was one of the happiest adventures of my lifetime. It was just this time last year that a scout claimed to have found a pass across the Blue Ridge Mountains. During the summer months, I became determined to investigate the claim personally, and I set about organizing an expedition to repeat the discovery."

"What a lucky group. How'd you choose them?"

"They were mostly entertaining fellows to my liking. We set out from Williamsburg on August 20th, with rangers, Indian guides, servants and pack horses. We picked up additions to the party as we moved westward. It seems laughable to think of it now, but I began that trip riding in my chaise but ended it by wearing out both my shoes and feet, leading my horse and walking much of the way. We were a party of sixty-three men, seventy-four horses and at least a dozen following dogs."

"Did the size of the group cause problems?"

"No. We had a grand time dining off of venison and bear that we shot along the way, but unfortunately we had to deal with hornet attacks, rattlesnakes, measles and other problems too indelicate to mention. My friend Beverley and his horse rolled down a hillside together, and Clouder had to be fished out of a creek. There was never a dull moment. We had taken a good supply of liquors and wines with us to comfort us after these mishaps, and a jolly time was had by all. Last Christmas, we held a reunion, and I gave each of my gentlemen companions a miniature golden horseshoe to commemorate the journey. We now call ourselves the "Knights of the Golden Horseshoe.""

Mingo had been serving Governor Spotswood some small cakes from a food platter when the Shenandoah was first mentioned, and he lingered as long as he could, serving each member of the group as many cakes as he could, in order to hear the description of the land across the mountains. Mingo loved nothing better than serving guests, especially talkative ones. Although he never spoke a word, he stored away everything that he heard and turned it over and over in his mind.

"I'd be more than delighted to assist in any future excursions across the forbidding mountains," John Flood said. "Hope you'll keep me in mind if you plan another trip."

"I don't know when my 'Knights of the Golden Horseshoe' will be assembled again," Governor Spotswood said. "The breakthrough was made in finding our way across the Blue Ridge. It is a major accomplishment for the colony, but there has been much criticism of it from members of the House of Burgesses concerned about the expense of the journey to our taxpayers. Some, such as the Reverend Blair's brother Archibald, feel that it was a great extravagance to pay so much to find our way into land that we are forbidden to settle because of previous treaties with the Indians. But laws and treaties have a way of changing. Now that we know the cut through the mountains, the future prospects are enormous."

"Mingo. See that the guest across the garden are served," his master said. Mingo sighed but did as he was told.

On the other side of the garden, Mingo heard one of the guests say, "I hear you're doing a splendid job with the college, James." I'm proud of you. Young Benjamin is nearly ready for your attention. His tutor has taught him just about all he can. By fall, he'll be in need of more advanced instruction. I feel very responsible for the boy since his father's death."

"You had better write me an official letter concerning his desire to matriculate, Sir. The spaces are almost full for next year. I wouldn't want to cast out another for him at the last moment. We only have room for twenty five at the most, and our enrollment is apt to be full. Please send me something in writing to confirm your intentions on his behalf."

"Will you be expanding the college anytime soon?"

"Not if the burgesses keep allowing the Governor a free hand in building his residence at taxpayers' expense. In Williamsburg, it is already being referred to as the Governor's Palace," the Reverend said, raising one of his eyebrows. "Recently, he submitted a bill for gold-gilt to cover some ceiling decorations in the large receiving room. There seems to be no end to his needs. Sometimes, it is difficult to believe that he's a bachelor. There's almost a woman's need for the superfluous behind many of his requests."

Priscilla, who was standing close behind Jane, pulled her aside to ask, "What does he mean by that?"

"He's referring to the Governor's housekeeper, Mrs. Russell," Jane said in a whisper. "He's being naughty to infer that she has undue influence over him. She was part of his entourage, including his private physician and fifteen servants when he arrived from England. All that's really known is that her quarters are in the Governor's residence, but of course, they would have to be for her to properly run his household. No one was concerned about her until it was noticed that he didn't pursue any of the daughters of the gentry here. He pays them only enough attention to be charming and polite. In seven year's time, even the most comely of our ladies have failed to arouse his continuing interest."

Priscilla's eye's glistened with delight. "This party's getting better and better. Do you mean to say that the Governor has a mistress?"

"Hush," Jane answered. "No one knows."

Just as Jane and Priscilla stopped their chatter, Mingo pulled at Priscilla's sleeve saying, "Governor say he want to speak to you."

Mingo saw a spark of delight cross Priscilla's face. He followed her back across the lawn to the side of the garden where the Governor stood.

"Is there something that I can get for you, sir?" Priscilla asked.

"Mrs. Blount," Governor Spotswood said. "I'm told those two rambunctious boys over there are your sons, and that they haven't seen the new capital. While you are up this far, you must travel with them across the river and on to Williamsburg. The new town is only six miles from Jamestown. I and others have been working diligently to provide it with fine architecture. The capitol is the finest building in Virginia. I feel certain that it would be an educational advantage for your sons to see it."

"How very kind of you to think of them," Priscilla said. "I'm sure they would find the trip to be quite thrilling."

"The college is also in Williamsburg," the Governor continued. "Seeing it might encourage them to pay close attention to their studies. My own residence is not yet completed, but it's in use. I'll inform my housekeeper, Mrs. Russell, that you may be paying a visit with your sons. If I'm detained elsewhere, she will show you through."

With the last remark, Priscilla's chest seemed to fall. "Thank you, Governor Spotswood. We'll try to make the trip as soon as it can be arranged."

The Governor's departure had to be awaited before anyone else could leave, including the bride and groom. Being aware of this, he dutifully said his goodbyes within a reasonable time, and the other guests waved cheerfully as his private ketch moved out into the river. The newlyweds followed by making their departure in a heavily decorated sloop that would transport them to the groom's home, Mt. Pleasant, a short distance to the east. By late afternoon, all of the traveling guests had left. In Virginia, it was still considered foolish to travel after dark.

IV

In the kitchen house at Four Mile Tree, Mingo was helping his mother in cleaning up the serving pieces and putting away the leftover food. He tried to share all of the things he had seen and heard about at the wedding with her. His eyes sparkled with delight as he described the color of the Governor's britches. "They was just 'bout the color of fresh spring grass," Mingo said, laughing as he talked. "I ain't never seen no britches that color before. He be a great, tall man with a big round chest. Look to me like he be a man can do 'bout anything he wants." The admiring tone in the young Negro's voice was unmistakable. "The Governor talked 'bout a place called Shenandoah," he continued. "There's where the land is flat and green, the water clear and fresh, the animals fat and happy and the sky blue all day. I sure does want to see that Shenandoah."

Celia looked at her son with a mother's concern. She knew that Mingo was always thinking of far-off places that were beyond his reach. As he grew older and the dream-talk became more frequent, she became truly alarmed. "You better get that wanderbug out of your head," his mother said with some degree of both scorn and fear. "Wanderin' ain't for niggers, 'less they's hunting for big trouble."

V

The day after the wedding, Mingo was passing biscuits at the mid-day dinner in the sun-lit, dining room at Four Mile Tree. As always, he was going about his duties quietly but listening to every word spoken.

"Governor Spotswood suggested that I take the boys to see the new capital at Williamsburg," Priscilla said.

"To Williamsburg. Why?" William asked.

"To see what a real city looks like," Priscilla said. "And also to see the college. He said it might motivate them to strive. I'm afraid they are becoming a bit lackadaisical and woodsy."

"Williamsburg is far from being a real city," William said. "There're not even two thousand people there. Still, it's true, the boys' educations have been limited."

"Priscilla, you charmer you! I've never heard of the Governor extending such an invitation before. He only spoke with the boys for a moment. What could be behind all this?" Jane asked with a suggestive twinkle in her eyes as she looked at Priscilla.

"I think I know part of it," William said. "He was interested in the Blount name. He knew the story of Thomas' grandfather, being imprisoned and tortured to death for his support of King Charles. He told me his own grandfather had been hanged for supporting the King. That was the end of the Spotswood family's fortunes. His father became an army physician but was never able to do more than provide basic care for his family. He sees your sons as the descendants of an old aristocratic family just as he might see his own sons if he had any, and he wants to be cordial to them."

"That probably is what it's all about," Priscilla said. "At any rate, I'm delighted to have the opportunity it provides. Can the traveling be arranged without too much trouble?"

"I'm very busy myself just now," William answered. "I can't leave, and you can't go without some protection."

"I'll protect the Missus," Mingo said in a loud voice. The room was suddenly charged with electricity like a flash of lightning across a cloudless sky. The diners were brought suddenly around to the fact that big ears were taking in all that they said.

"Mingo, you're not supposed to participate in our talk," Jane said.

"Yes, Missus. But I could do it."

"Why not?" Priscilla said, giving a small chuckle. "That might solve the whole problem. After all, the chief hazard of my traveling alone is that it might cause gossip. Having Mingo with us should signify your approval, and he could help tend to the boys."

"Mingo, more hot biscuits please," Jane said.

"Best thing probably would be for us to take you to the Gray's Creek ferry and arrange coach passage for you from Jamestown to Williamsburg. Mingo can ride on the outside box with the coachman. Perhaps Sarah Blair will be able to put you all up for a few days in the residence at the college. Yes, I think the trip might be arranged rather easily."

"Yow ee," Mingo shouted. He jumped up and down.

Priscilla's face showed immediate alarm. Mingo saw her look and quieted at once.

I almost done thrown away my chance. I's got to be serious from now on.

By the following week, William had made all the arrangements for his sister's excursion, and Priscilla had received a note of hospitality from Sarah Blair. The trip went smoothly, as planned, and the group found themselves in Williamsburg.

Will, Henry and Mingo were spellbound at the sight of Duke of Gloucester Street with its wide boulevard extending from the buildings of William and Mary College to the stately capitol building at the other end. Approaching the capitol, Mingo looked upward and was enthralled, "How they make that roof round like that?" he asked.

"I don't know. I've never seen one like it before."

"How does it stay up with all that weight over the large open space?" Will asked.

In the Assembly room, where the House of Burgesses met when they were in session, the boys ran around laughing as they touched the heavy, carved, wooden chairs and polished tables. "How could they build it so large?" they asked. "Where did all the chairs come from? What holds it all together?"

At the Bruton Parish Church, they learned that Governor Spotswood himself had designed the beautiful, newly-built church, he being a talented although untutored architect. "The Reverend Blair is the minister of this church," Priscilla said.

"You said he was president of the college," Will said.

"He's that too," Priscilla answered.

"He be a hard working man," Mingo said. "Why he work all the time?"

"Some men like to work," Priscilla answered.

"I liked the college, Momma." Henry said. "It would be easier to study with friends around. I'd like to live and study away from home some day with other fellows doing the same thing."

The afternoon before their departure, Priscilla and her brood made their formal call upon the Governor at his unfinished residence. Ambling up the broad walkway from the iron entrance gate to the steps at its doorway, they felt themselves walking in a wonderland. The four-sided, flat-topped roof, enhanced by a balustrade and topped with two open-windowed steeples, one atop the other, gave them their first look at true splendor. A doorman, in colorful livery greeted them on the steps to the front vestibule. Mrs. Russell, the Governor's housekeeper appeared saying, "Governor Spotswood regrets that he can not receive you personally at this time. He is occupied with visiting clergymen and expects to be so for the rest of the afternoon."

Priscilla made every effort to hide her disappointment. "It's kind of you to receive us, Mrs. Russell," she said. "The boys have been looking forward to seeing the Governor's home. May I present my sons, Will and Henry, and this is Mingo, who is traveling as our protector."

"Good afternoon, Will and Henry," she said. Her face showed no reflection of pleasure at meeting them. She eyed them both with suspicion as though she felt instinctively that boys of their age would be too unruly for so refined a dwelling.

"Your servant must remain outside," Mrs. Russell said. "Go around to the garden in back, boy. Your people will meet you there when they've seen the palace." She threw her arm out to show direction to Mingo. She then turned to the visitors to usher them into the house. Mingo heard her say, "The entrance hall is filled with an ornamental display of weapons that represent the royal authority by which.." Then, the liveried doorman closed the door in his face.

Mingo's lips quivered with both disappointment and resentment. He had been included everywhere else they had been. He walked around to the garden and waited.

Half an hour later, he saw the group leave the palace by a back door and descend some steps into the ornate garden. He watched as Mrs. Russell directed his missus to a garden bench. He watched as glasses of some chilled refreshment was served from a silver tray by another colorfully, attired servant. He was thirsty too. His mouth watered. Nothing was sent over to him.

Mingo listened, as he always did, and heard the ladies talking about the garden's design and the various flowers in it, many of which had been sent from England. He saw Will and Henry running wildly through a labyrinth of boxwood bushes, hiding from each other, calling out, "Here I am," and then finding each other in gleeful play. He wanted to join in the fun but stood dutifully in the corner of the garden instead. He watched Mrs. Russell carefully. He could sense a chill between her and his missus.

Governor Spotswood deserves a better woman. Why he settle for her?

At long last, the interview was over and Priscilla showed relief at leaving Mrs. Russell's company. It was obvious to Mingo that the visit to the palace had been the only sour episode of an otherwise joyful trip.

The following morning, the group began the trip home. Almost overnight the air had become hot and excessively humid. Mingo was happily riding high above ground beside the coach driver on his elevated box. From there he could look down on the world below. He tried not to miss a thing that came into sight. The coach made a clackity-clack sound as it bumped across uneven ground that was laced with sawed-low tree stumps and rocks. Small birds flapped their wings to get out of the way as the coach bore down on them. High in the sky, he could see a pair of Red-tailed Hawks gliding in a circular pattern around some prospective victim below.

Mingo loved being off the plantation and out into the world beyond it. Any new sights made him dizzy with pleasure. His all-consuming appreciation of the events of the moment continued until they had almost reached Jamestown where they were to board the ferry once again for their return across the river to the south shore. Then his happiness began to disappear and a heavy feeling of loss seemed to creep into his heart. He knew that it might be years before he could go traveling again, and the thought of returning to the tedium of his daily chores made him unbearably sad.

At the ferry pier, Priscilla noticed that Mingo's broad grin, which had been almost constantly present since the moment he was told that he could go on the journey, had disappeared. His mood had changed from joyous to sullen. It was impossible not to feel his sadness.

"What's the matter, Mingo?" Priscilla asked. "Didn't you enjoy our trip to Williamsburg?"

"I liked all but that last woman we met," he answered. "She give me the feeling of goose bumps in summer time."

"I found her to be pleasant enough," Priscilla answered.

"Missus, why you say that? She look at you just like she thought you aimed to steal her chickens."

Priscilla burst out laughing. "You saw things better than I did, Mingo," she said. "And you know, she may have been right."

The ferry pushed off in mid-afternoon. Priscilla, like a goose caring for her goslings, counted the three boys before the large flat-bottomed sailboat pushed off into the river. Then she sat down, closed her eyes and tried to rest until the boat should reach the other side.

VI

Mingo was watching the river bank recede from view when the ferry entered the river's current. As the people on the shore began to get smaller, the ache in his heart began to grow larger. Then suddenly, as though in a dream, without planning his action, he walked to the stern of the ship, turned to the shady side of the vessel, moved behind a large coil of heavy rope, squatted beside it for a few minutes, removed his shoes, then quickly climbed up the railing and lowered himself silently into the water.

Mingo swam under the water until he thought his lungs would burst. When he could endure no more, he slowly made his way to the surface, restraining his body as much as possible so that only his nose and mouth broke into the open air. He inhaled deeply and then submerged himself again. When he finally allowed his head to surface above the water, he saw that the ferry was far out into the river, and that he was treading water near a ship being loaded by Negroes with large barrels of cargo.

Mingo hoisted himself up onto the river bank and stretched himself out in the afternoon sun to allow his clothes a partial drying. He watched the Negroes loading the ship. They rolled the barrels along the ground, up the steep ramp and then disappeared into the vessel. A few minutes later they reappeared and walked back to the pile of barrels to start another trip. When Mingo noticed that almost all the barrels had been loaded, he got up, walked over to the diminishing pile, selected one of them and rolled it toward the ship's ramp. He followed behind another Negro until he had settled the barrel in its proper storage spot. Then he lay down behind it hoping that no one would notice that he had not gotten off the ship.

VII

Mingo sensed the first movement of the ship as it started its journey down-river. He knew that he had to stay hidden until the ship was out to sea or the Captain would call ashore to someone who would row out and take him back. His stomach began to growl, and he realized for the first time that he had foolishly struck out without bringing along anything to eat or drink. Too late to think of that now. What's done is done.

Mingo could tell from the gentle movement of the ship that it was still in the confines of the river. He lay still, waiting for the movement to change. He could see almost nothing except the outline of the barrels. Above, he could hear the tread of feet across the planking. It continued for hours, then ceased. The hold was completely black. Mingo's eyelids were growing heavy when he felt the motion of the ship change from its gentle movement to one of to and fro pitch. We're in the bay. He sighed with relief. Then slumber overtook him.

Mingo stayed in his hiding place for another full day. He listened attentively to all that went on above and slept another night without incident. On the third day, he awoke with his mouth so dry and his head so dizzy that he could no longer go without nourishment. He staggered up from his resting place and searched for some way to make his presence known. He spotted a long stick of wood in the corner. Mustering all his strength, he lifted it above his head and pounded on the hatch door above.

"Hey. Somebody's down there," he heard from above. "Get the Captain."

Mingo heard wild scurrying. A few minutes later, the hatch door opened and a stream of bright light flooded the hold. His eyes smarted. He felt so dizzy that he feared he might faint.

"It's a runaway. What you doing down there, fellow?"

Mingo slowly climbed up to the hatch door and crawled out. It was a clear, sunny day. No land was in sight.

"A stow away?" the Captain said.

"Yes, sir. I is," Mingo answered.

"Get him some water." the Captain ordered. "We're too far out now to take him back. The Captain studied Mingo's face, then his body from head to foot. "Everyone on this ship follows orders," he said.

"Yes, sir."

"We'll find plenty of work for you so as to pay your way. No one rides free."

"Yes, sir. I's going to do what you tells me to do. That's for sure," Mingo said with a smile. He thought he had made it.

Mingo took deep breaths of the fresh sea air and wallowed in the comfort of the balmy breezes. He loved the sea. Nothing that was asked of him by the Captain or the crew was too much trouble for him.

The *James and Allen* headed south far out from land, some distance east of the barrier islands. Several days later, the ship neared its first port of call, Charleston.

When not working, Mingo stood by the railing for long periods of time looking out to sea, and with his face turned windward, enjoyed the strong breezes that rushed past his head. As they neared the Charleston harbor, he was looking down into the ocean's deep waters, thinking of all the creatures that might be down there, little fish, big fish, sharks and maybe even whales, when he was startled by the sudden, loud clanging of the ship's gong.

"Four ships ahead," the watch yelled from the riggings of the foresail.

The Captain picked up his binoculars and focused them on the approaching ships. "Pirate ships," he yelled. "Man all stations."

Pirate ships? I ain't bargained for no pirate ships. Mingo's eyes opened wide in fear. The larger of the approaching vessels was flying the black and white, death-head flag of terror. Lord of Mercy. Look at the cannon sticking out the sides of those ships. They could blow this here one to pieces. I's got to get out of here. Where I go? Overboard and I drowns.

Mingo quickly moved behind a large wheel of heavy rope and squatted down behind it. Leastways, I's out of the way.

From his partial hiding spot, Mingo could hear the largest of the four ships come abreast of the *James and Allen,* could hear a gangplank placed noisily between the two ships and hear the rapid footsteps of the crew from the pirate ship. Looking around the side of his cover, he saw the pirate Captain board the *James and Allen* accompanied by a group of men each armed with swords, pistols, and daggers. The Captain was a wild looking man. His eyes, nearly covered by thick, bushy brows, seemed ablaze. He wore a long, thick beard that started high on his face, just beneath his brows and would have reached to his waist but for its being twisted into numerous braids, each tied on its end with blue ribbon.

"Blackbeard," Mingo heard a sailor whisper.

Ooo ee. Mingo's eyes grew bigger as he crouched down further behind the rope wheel.

Captain Thatch, the pirate leader, maintained a business-like manner. Ascertaining the type of cargo being carried by the *James and Allen,* he ordered that a large number of the whiskey barrels be transferred to his ship. "I accepted the King's amnesty by turning myself in to the Governor of North Carolina," Captain Thatch said. "We're pirates no more. We'll pay for what we take. Bring over two barrels of molasses," he called to one of his crew still on his ship, *Queen Anne's Revenge*. He and his crew burst into loud, raucous laughter. Turning to the crew of the *James and Allen*, he asked, "Is your Captain good to his crew or cruel?"

"Good," came the answer.

"Lucky for him. We deal harshly with Captains who are cruel." He laughed again.

The transfer of the many barrels of whiskey was a lengthy process. Mingo's legs began to cramp from his squatting position and his feet to prickle from lack of circulation. Just as Captain Thatch stepped upon the gangplank to make his departure, one of Mingo's legs gave way, and he toppled over with a loud thud.

"What's this?" demanded Captain Thatch, turning back and seeing Mingo.

"Runaway."

"We'll take him, too. How much?"

"Not mine to sell."

"Then we'll take him free."

Mingo, his skin ashen and his eyes huge, looked at his Captain. "I aint n-no p-pirate," he said.

"You are now," Captain Thatch said, "Get a move on it."

VIII

From his first encounter with the pirates, Mingo learned that class and rank played no part in their lives. He was treated no differently from the rest for being a Negro. It was something he had trouble getting used to and left him feeling oddly insecure. When he sought out a person to share his thoughts with, it was another Negro, a runaway slave named Sam.

The two men were seated on whiskey barrels in the ship's galley, the ship being laden to its limit with loot. The constant creaking of the wooden vessel allowed them to talk in low voices without fear of being overheard.

"How'd they catch you, Sam?" Mingo asked.

"Didn't catch me," he said. "I run away to them. Got beat bad by my master's overseer."

"That's bad. How come?"

"Cause I killed my wife. Never aimed to kill her. She be a good woman."

"Why'd you do it?"

"She wouldn't let me have no whiskey when I done gone to lots of trouble to get hold of it. Said it made me mean."

"Did it?"

"Guess it did. I killed her."

"When you do that?"

" 'bout five, six years now. I always did hear tell of the pirates. They talk 'bout them all the time in Topsail."

"Topsail?"

"Where the Carolina government be. Pirates go in there and visit at the Governor's house. They all thick as over-cooked gravy. They gives the Governor part of the steal. He do anything Blackbeard want."

"Like what?"

"Like one time, Blackbeard say he want a wife. The Governor gets him a pretty young girl that done growed up in a good house. Blackbeard done gone to Topsail and the Governor, he married them. Then Blackbeard, he fetch her back to the *Revenge* and stayed locked up in he cabin with her for days. Course he done that before. He got lots of wives."

"Where's she now," Mingo asked?

"Send her back, but not 'fore he let all the crew what wants her to have they time with her. He pride heself on sharing everything with he crew. Poor thing. She just about dead when he send her back."

Mingo felt a thick lump swell in his throat. He tried to swallow but couldn't. How come white folks act like that? Course Blackbeard, he crazy, but the governor, how come he send that girl to him? Some white folks is just bad clear through. He didn't want to hear any more. He stood up to go down to quarters. "Night, Sam," he said.

The *Queen Anne's Revenge* and the other three ships in her flotilla spent May and June pirating along the Carolina and Virginia coasts. They overtook eight or nine ships at sea and cruelly imprisoned crew and passengers in the hold of the flagship. The prisoners' lives were then ransomed after which Blackbeard would release them in some God-forsaken spot, usually stripped naked.

The pirates invaded and robbed houses near the water, taking anything they wanted and killing anyone who got in their way. Blackbeard led all the attacks, swashbuckling ahead of his men, with a raised sword in his hand and three brace of pistols hanging around his hips.

Mingo tried to stay as far away from the fighting and killing as he could. With each death, he became more and more confirmed in his desire to make an escape.

The *Revenge*, accompanied by the other three pirate ships, sailed up the Atlantic coast retracing the sea lane that Mingo had traveled down in the *James and Allen*. Mingo prayed that it would go all the way back to the James. If he could just get to the river, he figured, he could drop overboard, swim ashore and somehow manage to get home. He never had bargained on such a trip as this. All his thoughts were aimed at getting back to Four Mile Tree.

Mingo's eyes followed the long bar of sand to the west. It stretched for miles without a break. When a break did appear, it was too shallow for the large ships to enter. At last, the *Revenge* found a gap large enough for entrance, and the ships left the ocean waters for the safety of the sound.

Once the *Revenge* was moored, a barrel of whiskey was brought up to the mess. Captain Thatch, Blackbeard, ceremoniously took the first mug of its contents and gulped it all down without removing his lips from the rim of his cup, then reached for more.

Oh, my God. Now we's in for it.

"Music," Blackbeard ordered in a loud voice, and a fifer began to play.

Mingo sat silently in a corner, as far out of sight as he could get. He watched the men get sloppy; he listened to them laugh and cackle; he watched Sam as he gulped down mug after mug of something that made him laugh and holler with the rest; he wondered how long it would be before Sam turned mean; he guessed that the drinking would go on until all of them passed out; he could think of nothing else that would stop it.

The night wore on. A second barrel was brought up. The mugs were filled and filled again.

Suddenly Blackbeard slammed his fist loudly on the table. Instantly the rabble stopped. A hush came over the men.

"We need some fun," Blackbeard said. All eyes were on the

drunken leader. They watched quietly as he took out a pair of pistols, loaded and cocked them. He placed his hands holding the pistols under the table. Not a sound could be heard. Blackbeard's eyes were afire with excitement. Suddenly, with no further warning, he pulled the triggers. The blast was deafening. Israel Hand, seated across from Blackbeard, gave forth with a sorrowful but quiet whine of pain. He was hit twice. One bullet pierced his kneecap leaving him crippled for life. Blackbeard burst into raucous laughter. "Anyone else want to play?" he asked.

The men were at once sobered. No one spoke.

Mingo saw Blackbeard bend his head down as though to crawl remorsefully into himself. He said nothing. In the background a few men began to murmur. The wounded man gave three moans of misery that eerily kept time with the creaking sound of the ship's hull. Blackbeard jumped up.

"You're all yellow-bellied cowards," he screamed at the top of his lungs. His wind exhausted, he fell to the floor, dead drunk.

The next day, when the crew came to and looked about, they found that the *Revenge* had gone aground on a bar of sand. It could not be budged. Blackbeard, awake and sober, ordered that all the flagship's possessions be transferred to a smaller ship, the *Adventure*. That accomplished, they sailed to a more strategic location in the sound near the island of Ocracoke.

Mingo was thoroughly shaken by the drunken doings of the night before and sought out Sam.

"How far is it to Topsail?" he asked his new friend.

"It ain't how far," Sam said. "It's how bad. There's lots of trouble 'tween here and Topsail. Don't go there noways. They'll send you back to Blackbeard."

Mingo knew that Blackbeard was not only mean but crazy as well. "He do anything to dare the devil," he said to Sam. "Look like he's stronger than the devil too. Devil can't get him."

Mingo thought about his problem long and hard. There'd be danger in going and danger aplenty in staying. The choice was not an easy one, but he aimed, nevertheless, to figure out some way to escape.

On returning to the waters near Ocracoke, the *Adventure* went aground, also. "It don't matter," Blackbeard said. "We need a rest. Fetch me some whiskey."

Before Mingo was able to make his escape, some men, dressed as gentlemen, rowed out to the *Adventure* and came aboard. They went into a private session with Blackbeard, then returned quickly to their boat and rowed away.

"What's that?" Mingo asked Sam.

"Crewman say the gentlemen come from Topsail to warn Blackbeard. Some Virginia ships is coming to get him."

Mingo felt a charge of energy shoot through his body. "What he say?"

"He laugh and say the Virginia ships can't get him 'cause they is too big to move through the shoals. He call for more whiskey."

That day, Mingo never left the rail of the ship. As night was coming on, he saw two boats sailing up the Ocracoke inlet. It's got to be the Virginy ships. I can't fight against no men from my home.

Blackbeard saw the boats too. He ordered his men to fire the *Adventure's* eight guns at the approaching vessels as soon as they came into range, but the Virginia boats anticipated the problem and dropped anchor outside of firing range.

Blackbeard stared contemptuously at them. He gave out a loud, raucous laugh. Then he set himself up to drink and laugh all night. Shortly before he had consumed enough to pass out, two worried members of his crew bent their heads near to his and one asked, "In case anything should happen to you tomorrow, does your wife know where you've buried your treasures?"

"No one knows but me and the devil," Blackbeard screamed. "The longest liver will take all."

The next day, the wind was down, the weather clear and the water low. Mingo was on deck before dawn. Making his final decision to abandon ship, he moved to the far side of the vessel, lowered himself into the water and swam to the nearby grasses. He found a spot in them where he could keep his body submerged and his head hidden by the tall, green blades of grass.

When the sun rose, Mingo saw that the Virginia boats had begun to move forward. They had trouble getting near the pirate ships, but still they kept coming. Mingo could see the names on the boats. J A N E, he saw on one and R O G E R, on the other. He couldn't read the names, but he determined to remember the shapes of the letters. He could see that the Jane had no cannons. He also could see that the Roger stayed out in the narrows apparently to see that no other pirate ships could come to the aid of the *Adventure.*

As the boats approached, the *Adventure* put up a barrage of continual cannon fire. The air was full of smoke. For a time Mingo could see nothing. When the smoke cleared, he saw only two or three men on the deck of the *Jane*. Ooo ee. Has the devil killed off all the other men?

Mingo could see that Blackbeard had decided to make his move. With a dozen or more of his crew, he leapt aboard the on-coming vessel. At that moment, the sailors of the *Jane* who had been hiding below deck rushed up to the upper deck and, with screams and hollers, attacked Blackbeard and his crew.

Mingo watched as Blackbeard and the Virginia Lieutenant faced each other. He saw them draw their pistols and fire at close range. Blackbeard took a direct hit but strangely it seemed to cause him no harm. He is the devil. Ain't nobody going to get him.

Mingo watched full of terror as Blackbeard and the Lieutenant unsheathed their swords. Blackbeard lunged, but the Lieutenant moved just in time. The fighting amongst the crews was deadly causing the water around the ship to turn a bright, bloody red. Blackbeard cocked his pistol again. Mingo gasped, then let out a sigh of relief as he saw Blackbeard drop the gun and fall over dead.

The remaining pirates jumped into the water and called for mercy, but the sailors in their death-fight struggle kept firing at them and killed many more.

Mingo felt his muscles tighten with fear. He stayed motionless for many minutes. When finally he relaxed enough to move, he picked a dry reed from the grasses, put one end tightly into his lips, then lay down on his back in the water leaving only the top of the reed in the open air.

Please, dear God. Don't let 'em kill me.

IX

Some weeks after Mingo began plotting his escape, William Browne stood on the front steps of his home, Four Mile Tree, watching his brother-in-law, Nicolas Meriwether, slowly walk his horse down the entrance path toward the plantation house. He knew that Nicolas was on his way home after attending a meeting of the House of Burgesses in Williamsburg, and he could tell from the slump of his visitor's chest and the sag of his shoulders that the session had been a difficult one.

A quarter of a hour later, the two men were seated before a crackling fire in the parlor of the snug farm house. They had let their bodies ease into the comfort of two deeply-cushioned, leather chairs. A highly polished mahogany table, placed near William's chair, held a decanter of fine Madeira wine and two crystal glasses. The flickering light from the fire danced across the polished surface of the table and illuminated the deep red color of the wine. William poured out two full glasses of the richly-flavored drink and handed one to Nicolas. They were ready for an evening of shared confidences.

"Were you able to get recognition of William Byrd as an official representative of the House of Burgesses in London?" William asked.

"No," Nicholas said. "That's the one thing we were unable to do. The House put in a claim of three hundred pounds, as reimbursement for our having sent Byrd to London to lay our grievances before the crown, and Governor Spotswood refused to approve of the expense. He said all contact with the king had to be made through him, and that we had no right to send Byrd as our agent. Of course, we knew he wouldn't agree to the expenditure of money for the purpose of criticizing him to the king, but the exercise was helpful. It adds one more grievance to our list. After all we haven't many. We did empower him to build the Governor's residence. We just didn't foresee his being so extravagant in doing so. The Reverend is still frothing over that mistake."

"Were the Blairs into the fray as usual?" William asked. "They seldom are far from the action."

"Were they!" Nicholas answered. "At one point in the session, the Governor asked us to approve a fund to supply bonuses for anyone who captures a pirate, dead or alive. He wanted a one hundred pound bonus for the capture of Edward Thatch, Blackbeard, and a scaled down amount for pirates of less importance. That was the one thing the Governor asked for that I heartily agreed with. The damn pirates are costing us a fortune. If we don't do something soon, they might destroy our entire ability to trade. If that happens you might as well dig a grave for Virginia."

"You're not telling me Blair fought that idea, are you?" William asked.

"Blair just has to be his usual righteous self," Nicholas

answered. "He said we had been menaced by a swarming hoard of pirates for over twelve years now, and he wanted to know why the Governor was only now getting around to doing something about it. He said it looked like a diversionary action to him. Blair thinks we have the Governor in a corner, and that he needs something to heighten his appeal to the people."

"I can't object to his having a program to rid the bay of pirates," William said "even if he has been late in getting to it."

"He has to do something now," Nicholas said. "William Byrd is in England trying to get himself appointed acting Governor to replace Spotswood. We have to recognize that there is a great deal of self-serving ambition behind much of this."

"I've never really understood what James Blair wants," William said. Surely he can't be thinking of becoming Governor himself. No member of the clergy could expect that."

"He told me he wants to to see Virginia rid of all cursers, swearers, blasphemers, whore mongers, fornicators, adulterers, drunkards, ranters and profaners of the Lord's day."

William laughed. "Well that should take care of just about every Virginian,"

"I've heard him say that he got rid of Governors Nicholson and Andros for setting poor examples of behavior, and that he would get rid of Spotswood too."

"He must be thinking of Mrs. Russell," William said with a naughty twinkle in his eye and a biting of one side of his lower lip. "I think we should stop concerning ourselves with the Governor's personal life. He's not hurting anyone. I think he has done a great many good things for Virginia. One of the best things he did for the colony was to regulate the tobacco trade. It never helped honest tobacco growers when hogsheads were opened up abroad and found to be leaves wrapped around a bundle of stones. Still, our unappreciative farmers and merchants managed to undo that good deed by getting his Tobacco Bill repealed."

"I have to agree. He hasn't been all bad," Nicholas said. "As a matter of fact, I think he's the best governor we've ever had."

"You'd think he'd stolen a king's ransom just because he ordered leather chairs for all the burgesses and had a few leaves wrapped in gold gilt. And remember how they carried on when he led the expedition to find the cut through the mountains to the Shenandoah?

That was a very difficult and dangerous trip. Even so, the burgesses hollered at the expense of his taking so many friends with him. I'm convinced that his critics were mad because he had fun making the trek even if he did have to sleep on the ground and be constantly on the lookout for vicious Indians and wild animals of every sort."

"Most of our citizens are very happy with the Governor. It's those with ambitions of their own who are stirring up all the trouble."

"It's strange, isn't it?" William said, "the way Blair and Spotswood have become such fearful enemies? Both are Scotsmen by birth. Both are gentlemen who deplore the crude and untutored. Both want to lead Virginia into a greater state of prosperity, and yet they hamper each other's efforts at every turn."

"Well let's forget about them for the time being," Nicholas said, his spirits somewhat revived by the Madeira. "I know you'll be eager to hear what Spotswood is doing about the pirates. I don't want to spend the entire evening wallowing in despair. Let me tell you the good news. Spotswood was able to get hold of two small sloops that can follow the pirate ships into the shallow waters of their hiding places along the North Carolina coast. The *Jane* and the *Roger* will be able to maneuver in the coves and inlets behind the barrier islands. Spotswood had both ships refitted with small arms. Unfortunately, they can't carry any cannon. He sent them out over a month ago under Lt. Robert Maynard, who has been in charge of guarding the Chesapeake. They have explicit instructions to go after Blackbeard and to bring him back dead or alive. Fortunately, Spotswood got the Assembly to agree to the bonuses for capturing pirates just before the ships went out on their hunt."

"Thank God!" William said in a low, heartfelt tone of voice. "It's about time." William reached over for the bottle of Madeira and refilled both glasses. "To Lt. Maynard," he said, lifting his glass in a toast to the Royal Navy officer.

"To Maynard and his crew," Nicolas Meriwether said. The glasses touching gave out a lovely ring.

X

The day after William and Nicolas drank their toast to Lieutenant Maynard, more than a month after the Lieutenant had set out to capture the pirates, they arose to see that the rose and then pale yellow of the distant sky forecast the approach of a pleasant, early winter day. The year was past the winter solstice and the days were beginning to lengthen. During the night, the wind had shifted markedly and by dawn was bringing in warmed breezes from the southeast that promised an unusually warm day for winter.

Nicolas Meriwether was enjoying a hearty breakfast with Jane and William in the dining room. It was their farewell gathering before he mounted his horse again to continue his journey home. Celia had gone to the extra trouble of cooking up all the things she knew would please this special guest, and Nicholas was feeling decidedly stuffed from eating some of each item provided to show his appreciation of her efforts.

"I miss Mingo," Nicolas said, thinking of the happy-faced, black youth who had served the table on prior occasions. "Is there still no news of him?"

"Not a word," William said. "Celia has been heartbroken. We all miss him, and I fear he has run into foul play somewhere along the line. We should have heard something about him by now. It has been a year and a half."

"You think he could have drowned?" Nicolas asked.

"No," William answered. "He was a fine swimmer. He regularly set out our crab traps and worked the river for oysters and shad. He knew all about the currents. He could have made it to shore from any place in the river."

After breakfast the threesome walked out onto the boxwood-bordered terrace so that Nicolas could have a last look at the river before continuing his journey inland. They were standing at the edge of the top terrace looking down the slope to the beloved, ancient, cypress tree below when they were startled to see a slow-moving boat traveling up the river near the shore line. One man was standing at the bow of the small vessel with a large megaphone in his hand waiting until he spotted people along the shore to hear his joyful message. When he spotted the Brownes on the upper terrace, he waved excitedly to them then placed the horn to his lips and called out, "Blackbeard is dead, hallelujah!" When he was sure that the message had been received he added, "The *Adventure*, captured from the pirates, is at Point Comfort heading up river. Come join the throng to welcome her."

Jane and William whooped with delight at the news. William raised his hands, palms together, in thanksgiving and then grabbed Jane around the waist to twirl her around in a sort of jig without accompanying music. They waved enthusiastically to the bearer of the news and shouted, "Thank you, thank you," until their voices were strained and the news bearer had moved out of sight.

"You can't leave now," William said to Nicolas, his voice crackling with excitement. "We must man the skiff and sail to Jamestown to celebrate and hear all the details."

"I'd like to," Nicolas said, "but that would be traveling backwards. I just came from there. I'd better get home to my lady. If I stay any longer, she will begin to worry. I'll be off at once so as not to delay you in crossing the river. I think your streak of bad luck has turned around, William. Bless you."

Jane took little pleasure in sailing on small craft, especially during the winter months, and said she would watch the excitement by setting up the telescope on the upper terrace. William, however, could not rein in his excitement, and by mid-morning he and one of his field workers, named Luke, whom he had been training to work the river and the boat as Mingo's replacement, set off to cross the river in a two-man sailboat. The tide was coming in. It was necessary to tack frequently on the journey to the north-shore, but unless the wind should shift markedly, it promised a speedy return home.

William could see other small craft coming into the river from adjoining plantations, all headed for the same destination. By the time they reached mid-river, they could see the tall mainsail of the *Adventure*, the captured ship of Blackbeard, which had sailed up the river from Point Comfort. Before they reached the shores of Jamestown, they saw the multi-colored pennants of the ship which now bore the royal standards. The *Adventure* was dressed in full naval, victory regalia.

Near the approaching frigate, there were dozens of small craft in the water which at first clogged the waters and prevented the large ship from docking. The pier and the bank of the river were packed with colonists trying to get a good view of the victorious vessel. The people cheered and waved to the sailors.

William and Luke were maneuvering the skiff into a near-shore position when they looked up at the approaching three-masted ship and saw dangling from its bowsprit the de-bodied, gory head of the famed pirate, Blackbeard. The head was bloodied, the death-struck eyes open, the mouth agape with tongue protruding, and the long black beard, for which he was famous, still neatly braided into numerous small tails, each tied with a small blue ribbon.

"Ey-ee," Luke said, "Don't you know that was the devil heself. God done caught up with him. Hallelujah."

The two men managed, despite heavy competition, to berth the skiff along the shore and to disembark from it. They sped down to the central pier in order to join the crowds in welcoming Lieutenant Maynard and his crew. When the ship was safely docked, the Captain of the Jamestown militia came forward to greet the seamen and give his congratulations.

Lieutenant Maynard thanked the Captain and then addressing the nearby assemblage of people said, "We encountered the pirates at Ocracoke off the North Carolina coast on November 22nd. After successfully taking Blackbeard's ship, the *Adventure*, we were counterattacked by the pirates. It was necessary to fight Blackbeard with pistols, then swords and finally at close range with knives before the indomitable pirate could be mastered."

The crowd roared its approval.

Lieutenant Maynard continued, "Many pirates had to be left dead in the Ocracoke waters. We've brought back fifteen shackled prisoners to turn over to the authorities."

The crowd again responded with loud roars of approval. Members of the militia fell into place rapidly, standing at attention with guns at the ready in a make-shift line that resembled a gauntlet in order for the prisoners to walk between them. Lieutenant Maynard raised his hand to signal to his aide aboard ship that he wished for the prisoners to disembark.

A hush came over the crowd as the ragged, scared dregs of mankind began their slow, stiff-legged, shackled descent. So filthy were all the prisoners that at first it was hard to see who or what they were. Suddenly awareness led to gasps of disbelief as the crowd realized that some of the captured prisoners were runaway Negro slaves. Through the solemn silence that followed came a low wailing cry.

"Eye-oh-eye- ee," Luke called out. "Looky there Captain Browne. There's our Mingo."

On seeing Mingo at the end of the line of shackled pirates,

William felt his face grow hot with fury. It had been bad enough that Mingo had shown his ingratitude to his master, who had never laid a strap to the boy, by running away, but for Mingo to have joined the pirates, who were his number- one enemy, was infuriating beyond measure. William's usually kind-looking eyes seemed suddenly to reflect sparks like a flaming fire. He was momentarily paralyzed by his anger and unable to speak. Luke, standing next to him, could feel the passion of his master's thoughts and said in a whisper, "I sure is glad I ain't Mingo this day."

When Mingo reached the bottom of the gangplank of the *Adventure*, he looked up and into the blazing eyes of Capt. Browne. "Master," he cried. "I ain't no pirate, Master. I explain everything. I sure is glad to see you, Master. I's glad in all my heart to be home."

Mingo tried to grab his master's hand to kiss it, but William grabbed his hand away.

"How could you do this, Mingo?" William asked when he finally retrieved his voice.

"All I did was run away, Master. I didn't do the rest. The rest just did itself. I got to tell all that's happen, Master. You got to hear me out."

Luke followed behind his master as William walked beside Mingo who had no choice but to keep walking with the pirates to whom he was shackled. Luke kept his eyes on Mingo and shook his head in despair. William heard him say, "This nigger done found he finish. There ain't nothing left for him but the rope."

William walked ahead to have words with the Captain of the militia. He identified Mingo as one of his run-away slaves who had been missing for a year and a half. He asked the Captain to arrange for him to meet with Mingo so that he could hear what he had to say. His rage was still burning, but he knew that he owed it to Celia to hear her son's side of the story. The militia Captain agreed to the meeting so long as another militiaman was present and told William to follow them to the jailhouse. He could talk with Mingo as soon as it could be arranged.

By the time the three men met in private, William's wrath was beginning to cool down, and he even felt a twinge of sorrow for Mingo although not enough to forgive him. He left Luke outside of the small room where the meeting was to take place, quite sure that his ear would be to the keyhole to hear as much as he possibly could.

"Tell us what happened, Mingo," William said.

"Master, I ain't never meant to hurt nobody. I just wanted to see more than the plantation. I saw my chance to go down the river and something told me to take it. I sure is sorry I did. I jumped off the ferry boat and swum to the shore. Then I got on the ship, there at Jamestown, that was getting ready to go out, and I hid out in the hold with the cargo. Nobody saw me."

William saw that Mingo raised his arm to wipe his sweating brow with the sleeve of his shirt. He was perspiring profusely even though the weather did not call for it. The boy was scared as he had every cause to be. His voice was becoming more tired, but after a short pause he began to tell the whole story.

William was full of grief for Mingo by the time he had finished. He saw tears in Mingo's eyes and could barely manage to avoid shedding some of his own.

"I never meant you no harm, Master," Mingo said. "You got to believe that."

"I believe you, Mingo," Captain Browne said. "I'll see what I can do to help, but you must know that you are in very serious trouble. The people of Virginia hate the pirates with all their being."

"I ain't no pirate, Master. I's just Mingo."

Captain Browne touched Mingo's shoulder before leaving the room. He found Luke outside the door with tears streaming down his cheeks. The two men, master and slave, walked rapidly back to the water where their boat was anchored and set sail as quickly as possible. During the three mile return journey across the river, neither of them spoke a word.

XI

With the death of Blackbeard, the flushing out of the pirate's haven at Ocracoke Inlet and the capture of the fifteen pirates who were brought back by Lt. Maynard and incarcerated at the Williamsburg goal, Governor Alexander Spotswood's popularity rose sharply. When it was later learned by the populace that Spotswood had not only masterminded the entire operation but had funded the purchase and re-fitting of the sloops to be used from his own purse in order to guard the secrecy of the endeavor, his popularity soared.

Piracy had taken a heavy toll on the estates that bordered the Chesapeake Bay and on all the trade of the Mid-Atlantic coastal region. The colonists of the area were generally able to feed themselves by their own agriculture, fishing and hunting, but almost all of their non-nutritional needs came into the area by the waterways, and all of the credit by which they could afford to make needed purchases was derived from the tobacco, whiskey, pelts, and medicinal herbs which they shipped abroad. Without foreign trade, the colonial experience would be finished, and piracy was the greatest hindrance to that business.

William had a difficult time telling Jane about Mingo and an even harder time telling Celia.

In February, William was informed by the Governor's secretary that the accused pirates were to be tried by the Court of Vice Admiralty to be held in March in Williamsburg. He told Celia the news and promised to take her there to see Mingo before his trial. True to his word, William made the arrangements, and the two traveled by the Gray's Creek ferry to Jamestown and then on to Williamsburg by coach as Mingo had traveled with Priscilla and her sons a year and a half before.

The meeting between Celia and Mingo was racked with emotion. So touched was Captain Browne by the scene between the loving mother and her son, that he hired a lawyer to defend Mingo. Fortuitously, Captain Browne did not allow Celia to remain in Williamsburg for the trial. He sent her back to Four Mile Tree in the custody of a neighbor, but he stayed himself.

"What are the boy's chances?" William asked the lawyer.

"It's hard to tell. So much emotion is involved in the whole affair. The trial occupies the thoughts of everyone in Virginia. There's a tremendous hatred for anyone or anything connected with the pirates. Almost everyone has lost because of them in one way or another."

"Governor Spotswood has made himself a hero."

"They think he's done more than he has. Capturing Blackbeard was a sensational accomplishment, but there still must be fifty or more pirate ships out there. The problem's far from solved. The trial will be mostly for show. It's really a very one-sided affair."

"Won't it be fair?"

"Nothing's ever fair when the minds of the people have been made up before the evidence is presented. We'll have Mingo tell his story. He still claims that he only meant to run away, not to become a pirate. He's convinced me. We'll have to see how well he can convince the others."

When the trial was over, thirteen of the fifteen were condemned, and two were set free. The thirteen condemned men were hung from gibbets along the Capitol Landing Road in Williamsburg. The bodies stayed suspended for many days, even after the buzzards began to peck flesh from their stiffened bones. Mingo's young body hung amongst them.

THE DEBTORS
1774-1783

I

"Mrs. Brewster," the young coachman said, "the carriage to Williamsburg is waiting. The other passengers are already seated."

"I'll just be a moment," Sophie said. "Have you got all my baggage?"

"Your two satchels are tied on the roof. You'll have to hold the hat box. The two trunks have been placed in the warehouse. There's not room for them with the full load. I'll pick them up tomorrow."

"Is that safe?"

"Captain's honor," the coachman said. "Yorktown Harbor's too."

"There's the Captain," Sophie said. "I'll only be a few minutes more."

Before stepping into the carriage, Sophie looked around again at the charming village called Yorktown. She was surprised to see that the town had several very handsome houses as well as a number of smaller ones that looked welcoming and pleasant. She tried to absorb the reason for the town's appeal and realized that it was the light reflecting from the brick and clapboard walls of its buildings. Sophie had traveled far south of England. The sun in the April sky in Virginia was at an angle reminiscent of its place in a summer sky over London. The air was pleasantly warm, lending the feeling that she was being coddled by soft breezes. She took a deep breath of fresh air and knew instinctively that something bearing white blossoms was in bloom. She felt her spirits rising.

She needed only a few minutes more to gain confidence and composure. From the moment she stepped into the coach, she would have to face the world on her own. Before marriage, her father had ruled over her; during marriage her husband had managed their lives completely; with his death her eldest son had stepped into the family shoes of authority and even during the six week ocean crossing the captain had steered and protected her. From this point on, however, she would have to do everything for herself. For a fleeting moment, she was tempted to go back to the ship to tell the captain that she wished to return to England, but the moment passed. She couldn't do that. The ocean crossing had been expensive, and her sons were counting on her to solve the family's problem.

"I'm sorry to have kept you waiting," she said, seating herself beside a portly gentleman in the only space remaining in the carriage. She was happy that she would not have to ride in the middle between the portly one and the skinny man seated to his left. Across the aisle sat a family of three including mother, father and young boy who would have to ride seated backwards. They appeared to be of servant class. She remembered seeing them on the ship but had not met them, their having been confined to a lower deck throughout the long voyage.

Sophie arranged herself as best she could and placed the large hat box on her lap. Unfortunately, it rested not only upon her knees but extended across one of the gentleman's knees as well. He turned to her with a frown and opening his mouth to speak, revealed a mouthful of decaying teeth. "You traveling alone, M'am?" he asked, releasing a displeasing odor as he spoke.

"Just from Yorktown to Williamsburg," Sophie answered. "How far is it?"

"Ten or eleven miles. Shouldn't take more than two hours."

"Sophie turned away to look out the window of the cabin as the coach began to move. She noticed that the land was flat but luxuriously green. The coach moved onto a woodland road. There were tall pines between the road and the river, but the bareness of their lower trunks allowed her a good view of the York as both the coach and the tidal water of the river traveled inland.

"Strange to see an Englishwoman arriving in Virginia at this time," the man said. "Most think we're going to war. I presume you've come to stay considering the delicacy of the situation."

Keeping her head averted, Sophie replied. "I'm meeting relatives,"

"Oh," he said and that was all.

In the forests that enveloped the road, Sophie saw the beautiful white blossoms of the woodland trees that grew wild in the shade of the much taller pines. Birds were everywhere. On the branch of one of the trees, she saw a bright red song bird silhouetted against the white blossoms of the tree. She marveled at its beauty. She was just about to turn back to speak to the portly gentleman when she felt him move his knee beneath the hat box so that his thigh was resting against her own.

"Oh, no," she said under her breath. "Not that." Trying to act as though she hadn't noticed the advance, Sophie moved as close to the side of the carriage as she could and tried, quite unsuccessfully, to get all of the hat box onto her own lap. The effort was futile. Within seconds, she felt his thigh again, this time putting more pressure upon her own. Being unable to move further, she said to the couple seated across from her, "Excuse me. I should have thought of this before, but I was engrossed in the scenery. Wouldn't your son prefer sitting on this side of the carriage so that he can see where he's going? I'd be delighted to change seats with him."

The boy beamed. He looked to his father, jumping up as soon as the father nodded his approval. Sophie and the boy changed seats. She again tried to hold the hat box on her lap alone. She felt satisfied with the manner in which she had handled the unpleasant problem until she looked up and saw the amused expression on the portly man's face. The sight of his amusement told Sophie that he had gotten exactly what he wanted - more leg room and riddance of the hat box. He burst into a loud, crude snicker. She had been outmaneuvered in her first attempt at independence. Only the look of sheer delight on the face of the boy, as he looked out the coach window, kept her spirits from tumbling.

In Williamsburg, the coach stopped first at a tavern facing a wide green. There, the two men and the family of three disembarked.

"I apologize for the hat box," Sophie said to the woman who had sat beside her.

"No matter," the woman answered.

Sophie watched as the family picked up their few parcels of belongings and walked down the side of the tavern to the rear door. She was sure that she had been right. They were arriving to be servants.

"Mrs. Hays' Guest House is next," the coachman called out as he remounted the driver's box. The coach pulled away with only Sophie remaining inside.

Despite her thirty-four years, Sophie retained an appearance of youth and vigor. Her hair was a rich, dark brown that fell in ringlets around her face no matter how she tried to pin it down. Her complexion was unusually fair for one whose hair was dark, and her eyes were surprisingly blue. Her face was long and narrow. Her cheekbones seemed to disappear in the arrangement of her features caused by the forward protrusion of her large brow. Her forehead, which was both high and wide, hinted of her superior intelligence. This might have been a serious handicap for a woman of her time were it not for the forehead being deliciously surrounded by the twirling wisps of her dark brown hair. The softening effect of the locks somehow turned the threatening feature into one of appeal. As a result, men were usually drawn to her in a way that left other women feeling disturbed.

The coachman turned the horses and coach around to retrace his steps down Duke of Gloucester Street. Once onto Nicholson Street he stopped in front of a very large, handsome residence. He alit from the driver's seat to open the door for Sophie.

"Is this it?" Sophie asked, her face aglow with delight.

"No, ma'am, that's the Randolph House, best one in town. Mrs. Hays' is the one across the street. Is she expecting you?"

"Who?"

"Mrs. Hays"

"I hope so. I've paid for a year's lodging."

"She'll be ready."

"This is a handsome house too."

"Mrs. Hays' husband died a few year's ago. He was the apothecary. She couldn't bear to lose her house so she turned it into a guest house. You'll like it here."

Sophie walked up the path to the guest house carrying her hat box. The coachman followed with her two satchels. Before knocking on the door, Sophie turned around for another view of the handsome house across the street and saw someone in an upstairs window quickly release the curtain they had been holding back. She felt certain that her arrival was being watched. How strange. She knew no one.

Once inside, she was greeted by Mrs. Hays who led the way to the second floor. "I hope these arrangements will be satisfactory," Mrs. Hays said. "There are two rooms in all. The bedroom is small, but it has good air circulation. The sitting room is cozy and has the best view in the house."

"It will do very well," Sophie answered.

"I don't usually rent sight unseen," Mrs. Hays said, "but Mr. William Browne came to select the rooms himself. You come highly recommended. Will your husband be joining you?"

"I'm a widow," Sophie answered. "I've come to get re-acquainted with some of my relatives, most of whom live in Surry County on the south side of the James."

"I know where it is," Mrs. Hays answered.

"The driver will be bringing my two trunks tomorrow. There wasn't room for them today on the coach. When I've unpacked my things, will there be a place to store them?"

"Two trunks you say," Mrs. Hays said emphasizing the word two. "I'll have to search out a spot for them."

Sophie saw that Mrs. Hays was looking her over. She felt sure that the cut of her frock and cloak must seem very new and stylish to the older woman.

"My relations here are the Brownes, the Floods and the Blounts," Sophie said. "Perhaps you have known some of them?"

"Heard of them. Those families have been here since early times. How's it you're related?"

"My great grandfather was John Flood. One of his daughters married an Englishman and returned to live in England. That was my grandmother. The rest of the family stayed here."

"Four generations is a long time for keeping up."

"The families have been in contact through business ever since," Sophie said. "My late husband's firm, Cary and Brewster Ltd., was the London merchant for some of the Surry County planters."

"I don't understand," the proprietress said.

"The planters ship their tobacco to England. Their agents there sell it for them and give them credit for its value. In turn, the planters send long lists of things that they want to have purchased for them and sent to Virginia, things like clothing, furniture, carriages and slaves. The English merchant makes the purchases and sends them to Virginia."

"That's what I've heard all the men arguing about," Mrs. Hays said. "They say they have no control over the price they get for their tobacco or the price they pay for their purchases."

"That's why they need a trustworthy agent," Sophie said.

"From what I hear, there's lots who think their agents are far from that. This is a business visit then."

"No, no. I'm not a businesswoman. My sons run the family business now. I've come to Virginia for a change of scene and to get re-acquainted with my relatives. I may have to look up some land holdings though. Do you know where those records are kept?"

"A good many of the old ones burned in the Jamestown fires. What's left should be in the courthouse. Funny your coming over just now. There's a heap of talk about war with England."

"Surely things won't come to that," Sophie said. "If you don't mind, I'll just unpack my things and rest a bit now."

Mrs. Hays' eyes continued to size up the handsome new arrival. "I keep a very strict house here," she said. "I won't tolerate any foolishness. If anyone bothers you, you report it to me. Dinner will be at one o'clock. Supper's at six. Everyone eats what they're served or goes elsewhere."

"Thank you," Sophie said.

Mrs. Hays walked briskly out of the room. When Sophie heard the door close and the latch click, she collapsed onto the bed. She let out a deep sigh of exhaustion. She looked around the room then gasped and said aloud, "I do believe the old biddie was warning me that I had better watch my own behavior in her house."

II

Sophie gave a sigh of relief when the young coachman, who had driven her from Yorktown to Williamsburg, arrived with her two trunks.

"I wasn't sure I'd ever see my things again," Sophie said.

"Sea captains are quite reliable," Mrs. Hays answered from the doorway to Sophie's room where she was standing, hoping to get a glimpse of what was in the two trunks.

Sophie opened the first trunk and began removing a series of lovely gowns. Mrs. Hays stood spellbound.

"What are you going to do with all those clothes?" she asked.

"Wear them," Sophie said.

They're my ammunition. Looking prosperous is a large part of the charade.

Sophie unpacked gowns, shawls and accessories. She placed her toilet articles carefully on the wash stand and removed a small picture hanging above to place a mirror in its stead. Next, she unpacked her writing portfolio with ink stand and quills. She placed them on a small table to the left of the fireplace. Several books were put on the windowsill beside the one comfortable chair that had been placed near the window for light. From the bottom of the trunk, she took out twenty small tins of her favorite tea which she had brought to Virginia to give as gifts to any and all that might show her kindness in some way or other during her visit. She had heard about the hubbub over tea being tossed into the Boston harbor because of the colonists' dislike of the taxes placed upon it. She reasoned that with all the to do about tea it would be a welcome gift.

Removing the tins from her trunk, she decided to put them in the hat box which would remain in her room after the trunks were stored. She left one tin and a tea cup which she had brought with her, out on the table. Now if she could only figure out a way to get hot water so that she could enjoy it.

Sophie went to the window and looked out toward the handsome house across the street. As she did so, she saw the front door of the house open and a lady of near her own age leave the house, walk down its path, cross the street and come to the front door of the guest house. She heard a knock at the door in the entrance hall below. She watched the lady retrace her steps to the house she had left and at the same time heard Mrs. Hays scurrying back up the stairs to the upper hall.

"Mercy," Mrs. Hays said when Sophie responded to the knock on her own door. "Mrs. Randolph, herself, delivered this note for you. The Randolph's are the most important people in Williamsburg," she said with a confirming nod of her head as she said it, "probably in all Virginia." Holding herself stiffly erect, she handed the letter to Sophie in a formal manner.

"Thank you, Mrs. Hays," Sophie said putting the letter on the table. "I shall read it later when I've finished unpacking."

"Later," Mrs. Hays said. "Upon my word. I have never." She turned and left the room abruptly.

As soon as Mrs. Hays had left, Sophie rushed to open the letter. It read,

"My dear Mrs. Brewster,

Your cousin, William Browne, advised me of your impending visit to Williamsburg. I've been on the lookout for you and was delighted to see your arrival yesterday. We have old family connections.

My husband, Peyton, is in Philadelphia at the moment, presiding over the meetings of the Continental Congress. He will wish to meet you when he returns. In the meantime, would you honor me by coming for dinner tomorrow at one o'clock? I look forward to a favorable reply.

With respect, I am,

Betty Randolph"

Promptly at one o'clock the next day, Sophie raised the highly-polished, brass door knocker of the Randolph mansion. She fidgeted with the bodice of her dress and smoothed the skin under her eyebrow which had given forth with an unexpected, fitful twitch. She was welcomed into the residence by a friendly-faced Negro who ushered her into a handsomely appointed room that had been lovingly decorated with many pots of early blooming flowers.

"You're here. What fun!" Betty Randolph said as she came forward to greet her guest. "I've been watching for you ever since Will Browne stopped by to say he had arranged rooms for you at Hays'. I'm glad you'll be so close."

"I'm glad too," Sophie said, "and overwhelmed at your kindness in asking me for dinner. This is the perfect start for my visit to Virginia."

"Are the rooms to your liking?"

"They suit very well."

"Sit here. I'm expecting another guest, Lady Dunmore, wife of the Governor, but I asked her for one fifteen so we'd have a few minutes to get acquainted before she arrives."

"How kind."

"Will says that you lost your husband recently. You have my sincerest sympathy. I hope that the trip to Virginia will help you recover from your great loss."

"It's been almost a year now," Sophie said, "and it gets easier every day."

"I hope you're not too concerned over the current political problems with England. We expected things to be settled down by now. Last year, we had similar fears and it all blew over."

"How was that?"

"The House of Burgesses arranged for a spring ball in honor of Lady Dunmore. She is much admired by everyone here. Such a charming, beautiful woman. Three days before the ball, while the Governor was in the country, the Burgesses set aside a day of prayer and fasting in support of Boston's colonists whose harbor was blocked by the British.

"When the Governor returned, he was furious. He dissolved the Assembly. Everyone was distressed. I'd spent days tucking silk and sewing ribbons on my gown. We thought the ball would be canceled and all our stitching for nothing. But it wasn't. They gave the ball anyway."

"Did the Governor and Lady Dunmore attend?"

"Oh, yes. She was the star of the evening. She's immensely popular here. There's the knock. She's here. You'll see what fun she can be."

Lady Dunmore made a sweeping entrance. Her beauty had not been overrated. Sophie found it difficult to keep her eyes off the young woman's face. She glowed with youth and health. It was reassuring to see how well she and Betty Randolph appeared to enjoy each other's company. The war talk must be only a game.

During the dinner, Lady Dunmore told Sophie of the fine welcome she had received when she arrived in Williamsburg more than a year before. "When my carriage entered the Duke of Gloucester Street, hoards of people ran beside it shouting their blessings as we moved toward the palace. All the windows of the houses along the way were illuminated by candles. Later that night the sky was filled with the most spectacular display of fireworks."

"They adore you," Betty said.

"It was thrilling beyond words. No greater hospitality could exist than one finds here in Virginia."

"I told Sophie about last year's ball," Betty said.

"The best I've ever attended," Lady Dunmore said with a laugh. "I danced the night away."

Sophie went back to the rooms she had leased, feeling much more at ease than she had upon her arrival. The twitch of her brow had disappeared. This whole disturbance will probably be resolved soon. Political games are always in the works. I'll just stop worrying about it.

Several days after the dinner, Sophie made an afternoon call on Betty Randolph to thank her for her kindness in including her on the very special occasion. As she walked across the street to the Randolphs' house, she rehearsed in her mind all that she would talk about with Betty. It would be a perfect opportunity for her to start gathering information about Cary and Brewster's debtors. She knew she had to be careful and decided to ask about only one family at a time in order to avoid suspicion. A half hour later when Sophie and Betty were sitting in the Randolph parlor sipping cider and munching on ginger cookies, Sophie worked the conversation around to the subject of Surry County where the Harrisons, Betty's family, had once lived at Wakefield.

Betty said, "The men in my family got deeply involved in politics. It became a hardship for them to live on the other side of the river so they left Wakefield and moved to the north shore. We still have ties with the Surry families, however, and see many of them when the House of Burgesses is in session."

"My family in England kept up with many of the Surry families, such as the Brownes of Four Mile Tree, whom I plan to visit soon, and the Blounts, but we have wondered what happened to the Joshua Bensons. Are they still living down in Southampton County, or have they, too, moved to the north shore?"

"They are very much at home in their old place near Blackwater Creek," Betty said, "but they have had a series of great misfortunes."

Sophie stifled a gasp of horror. The Bensons owed Cary and Brewster more money than any of the other planters by far. "How sad," Sophie said trying to hide her distress. "What kind of misfortunes?"

"They've had a series of deaths among their children. Rachel Benson seems able to bear children well enough, but they have lost at least a handful of them before they were two years old. It's been a heartbreaking experience. They have the most beautiful plantation. It's so well cared for. The gardens are lovely. You really must see their place if you travel that far south. It's one of the choice seats in Southampton. Despite their good fortunes, however, happiness has eluded them. There really is nothing sadder than watching one's own children die."

"I'm sure that is so," Sophie said. She marveled to herself that she had been able to find out so much, so easily and from such a reliable source.

That evening after an early supper, Sophie sat at a small round table that she used as her desk and began writing a report to her son, John, in England. She was still nervous enough about the political situation in Virginia to write with care. She thought it highly possible that any letter from a newly-arrived English person, writing home to England, might be opened and read by zealous patriots. For that reason she took special care to take no sides, to refer to nothing political, but somehow to get the information across that the Bensons were living very well while owing them huge sums of money.

Sophie started her letter by reporting on the beauty of the Virginia countryside, and the mildness of the climate. She refrained from mentioning the flies, the mosquitoes or the humidity. Next she told about the dinner at the Randolphs' and of the great cordiality Betty Randolph had shown her. That should satisfy any snooping Americans. Next, to satisfy any snooping royalists, she wrote about meeting Lady Dunmore and reported on her great popularity with the citizens of Williamsburg. Before she had finished the letter, she had tucked in the sad story of the Bensons' loss of many of their children. "Even the rich and prosperous can not buy happiness," she wrote. "We should be thankful for all our blessings."

There. She folded the letter. That should give him clue enough that it would not be a waste of money to put lawyers on the collection trail.

The feeling of security, which Sophie had received from her happy encounter with Betty Randolph and Lady Dunmore, encouraged her to settle into her leased rooms and attempt to branch out socially. She called at the Governor's Palace to offer her assistance to Lady Dunmore and paid another call on Betty.

As the month of April progressed, the Virginia countryside burst into bloom. The barren branches of the many oak, sycamore and dogwood trees that had laced the horizon when she arrived, had opened to display the light green leaves of spring. The deeper green of the evergreens, loblolly pines and junipers gave a rich backdrop to the newly-dressed deciduous trees, and the delicate white-blooming dogwoods gave a dramatic accent to the picturesque setting. Now is the time to go to the country. What more beautiful time of year could there possibly be? Besides, it's not too soon to start working on the main purpose of my trip.

III

By May Day, Sophie found herself and her large, well-packed trunk of clothes deposited in a handsome, enclosed coach, drawn by four well-groomed horses, being transported from the ferry landing at Gray's Creek to Four Mile Tree.

Colonel William Browne had come to the river dock to meet her himself. Her trunk had been hoisted to the rack at the top of the coach by Buelly, the Browne's slave of many uses, before William had seated his glamorous guest inside.

On the ride to Four Mile Tree, William told Sophie how he had inherited the property with most of the slaves from his grandfather. Shortly before, the original old house had been torn down to be replaced by a larger and more modern one. At the time of his grandfather's death, the rebuilding of the house had been only partially completed.

"Did the first one burn down?" Sophie asked with interest.

"It burned," William said, "but it didn't actually burn down. I think the fire was just an excuse for building a newer, more comfortable house. The real reason for replacing what surely could have been repaired more easily was prosperity. Following the completion of the Governor's Palace in Williamsburg, a number of successful planters in these parts began building more graceful and comfortable houses to replace the helter-skelter buildings of the past. William Byrd built Westover, a handsome, beautifully designed, Georgian mansion on the north shore. Benjamin Harrison built Berkeley and King Carter built Carter's Grove. The bug was catching and just about everyone started thinking of at least improving on what they already had. My grandparents, who lived here at that time, had already raised their children and were getting on in years when they decided to rebuild at Four Mile Tree. That fact helped to restrain them in the scale of their endeavor, for which I am very grateful. They built only a slightly larger house but a decidedly more comfortable and picturesque one."

Sophie's eyes scanned the forested, low, tidewater countryside. "What caused the fire in the first place?" she asked.

"Some mortar had fallen out of a brick chimney on the inside of the flue. It caused some bricks to come loose where they were not observed. When a fire was lit on the first crisp day of fall, the flames crawled through the opening and ignited a support beam in the adjacent wall. Only the one room on the first floor and the room directly above it were destroyed. They could easily have been rebuilt, but the old house was small and had grown by happenstance. When more space was needed, a new room was added. It had no real design. Separate structures were built for the kitchen work, the school room, the office and the laundry, not to mention, of course the smoke house and ice house. The new residence was designed first and built second. There's quite a difference in the finished product. This structure was built entirely of brick on the double-pile plan. The second story is tucked under an unusual hip-on-gambrel roof, which is pierced by two chimneys on each side of the house allowing fireplaces in each of the eight, corner rooms. We can heat the house much more uniformly in winter. There is also a wide hall that bisects the ground floor running from the front door to the terrace at the rear, permitting the river-cooled air to blow through and cool each room during the sultry summer months. It's a very modern concept to control the temperature of the house by the design of it, don't you think? I hope you will find it comfortable." William slyly allowed himself an appraising look at this newly-met, worldly cousin.

"I'm sure of it," Sophie replied. "I'm already overwhelmed by your hospitality. Tell me, did you always plan to be a planter? I'm interested in how you found your calling."

"There really was no other option for me," William said. "I was only five years old when I became the owner of Four Mile Tree. My father predeceased my grandfather so the property skipped a generation and came to me. I grew up with my future already arranged. I've just been playing out my role."

As the coach skirted the meandering Gray's Creek, approaching the long entrance drive to Four Mile Tree, William told Sophie that all her distant cousins were eager to meet her and that she could expect a stream of callers. "There are a few families in Surry County that have intermarried over and over again. You may have difficulty figuring out all the connections. Just think of them all as cousins and you will be on fairly safe ground," her host continued.

"There're also others who have done business with Cary and Brewster over the years, who want to meet you. Joshua Benson, who has a magnificent property on the Blackwater near our cousin Thomas Blount's home, is eager to call on you at once. He heard you were in Williamsburg some time ago and has been hounding me to arrange an interview with you ever since."

Sophie was just ready to make a response to this last statement when the coach turned into a long avenue, bordered by giant oak trees that focused the eye of the beholder on the charming house a mile from the country road. She took a deep breath and let out a gasp of delight as they traveled down the well-cleared path that led to the gem of a house, proportioned to perfection, which stood sedately at the end of the lane.

"Oh yes, yes, yes," Sophie cried out. All thoughts of Mr. Benson vanished from her mind as she stared in rapt delight at the artistic symmetry of the Georgian-style house that was unlike anything she had ever seen in England, a house that was uniquely American in all its form and beauty.

Sophie had enjoyed several days of peace and happiness at Four Mile Tree, getting to know both Sally and William, before the day arrived for her to receive Joshua Benson. She had no fixed idea in her mind as to what he might be like but assumed that he would come dressed in modest attire trying to put forward the idea that hard times were keeping him from making any payment on his debts to her family's business. Regardless of the way she expected him to appear, she decided that she must make a quietly elegant appearance so as to establish the fact that she neither lacked the means to dress well nor had any reason to impress him with opulent attire. She chose a light wool challis dress of a deep blue color from her wardrobe. Around her shoulders she tied a white linen neck scarf to act as a frame to dramatize her face, and she secured the scarf with a small buckle-shaped pin.

Sophie was about to leave the guest room assigned to her on the front of the house when she heard the heavy wheels of a large carriage grinding its way along the entrance lane. She moved to the side of the window so as not to be visible and, glancing out cautiously, saw to her surprise a cream-colored, gold embossed coach that was drawn by six well-matched horses. I don't believe this. What can it mean?

In the parlor to the left of the entrance hall, William introduced

Sophie to Joshua Benson. He was a tall, well-built, healthy-looking man of about fifty years. His appearance might have been altogether pleasing were it not for a defiant look from his eyes and a slight curling of the left side of his upper lip that gave a suggestion of arrogance and distain that both shocked and repelled Sophie. Only a few pleasantries had been exchanged when William announced that he would leave them to their affairs and courteously left the room.

"Mrs. Brewster,"Joshua Benson said. "I should like to speak frankly with you and get straight to the point."

"By all means," Sophie agreed.

"As I am sure you must know I have a large outstanding debt to your late husband's company, and I feel certain that hope of obtaining repayment of the debt is in part responsible for your coming to Virginia." He ran a finger around the inside of the stiff collar of his shirt and pushing his chin out defiantly, stretched his neck in hopes of lessening the collar's grip upon it. "I have made this call today to explain my reasons for not paying off the debt and to tell you what you can do to help get it paid off in the future."

"Really, Mr. Benson," Sophie answered, "I am neither a trained nor an acting businesswoman. My son, John, has taken over the operation of his father's share of Cary and Brewster, not I."

"Then I suggest that you communicate my sentiments to him," Mr. Benson continued. "When I took on the debt I have with Cary and Brewster, which was primarily for the purpose of buying land and slaves, I had worked out a sure plan for repaying it. Like many other Virginia gentlemen, including the majority of the members of the House of Burgesses, I invested heavily in land on the other side of the Appalachian Mountains. I made plans to divide the land into small parcels and sell it off to the hoards of immigrants arriving each month who can only afford the cheaper land on the frontier. With the profits that should have been mine from those transactions, I had planned to pay off my debts."

"That sounds appropriate to me, Mr. Benson," Sophie said in as calm a voice as she could muster.

"It was thoroughly appropriate, Mrs. Brewster, but your government chose to change the rules in the middle of the game."

"My government, Mr. Benson?" Sophie said, "Are we not both subjects of the same king?"

"I am British-American, Mrs. Brewster. The difference between being British and being British-American may soon become more obvious."

"What rules have been changed, Mr. Benson?" Sophie asked, not wishing to continue with the dangerous subject of American independence.

"Since I made my investment in land across the mountains, your government has signed treaties with the Indians which prohibit the settlement of white men past the crest of the Appalachian Mountains. This law was enacted by the crown without the consent of our Assembly. The law is said to have been passed out of sympathy for the plight of the savages whose land is being infiltrated. In actuality, it has done nothing to stop the flow of settlers across the mountains. It has only enabled them to settle the land without purchasing it from its rightful owners. Many of the owners acquired the land in payment for their services to the crown during the French and Indian Wars. Others, like myself, acquired the land by paying legal tender or its equivalent to the crown. Now we are forbidden to sell what is legally ours, so the new settlers, who will not be stopped, are crossing the mountains and simply taking what they want. The Indians lose either way, but despite strong entreaties, the crown refuses to repeal its action."

"I can't see what this could possibly have to do with me or my son's company," Sophie said.

"Just this. It would behoove you to write to your son informing him of all the things I have told you. He should work diligently to put the idea forth to all his contacts in high positions that the settlement restrictions must be repealed. If he is ever to receive a farthing of the money owed to him, he must take some action. The Council on Commerce seems to have a particular fondness for English merchants. They listen to them more than they do to us."

"Really, Mr. Benson, you think us to be more highly connected than we are," Sophie answered in a frosty tone of voice.

"Think on it, Mrs. Brewster. You may be able to remember some contacts that you have momentarily forgotten. If a large number of prominent Virginians are threatened with bankruptcy as a result of mismanagement and indifference toward us on the part of the crown, it is likely to lead to very unpleasant times."

"I shall write to my son of your visit, Mr. Benson," Sophie said. "Good day to you, sir."

"I meant no personal affront to you, Mrs. Brewster," Benson said, perceiving that he had perhaps taken too large a step with her.

"I'll show you to the door, Mr. Benson," Sophie responded. "My regrets to Mrs. Benson," she said looking him straight in the eye, "that is, my regrets that she was unable to accompany you on this call."

Sophie had spent the intervening hours since Joshua Benson's visit trying to regain her composure.

I can't remember when I've ever met such an intentionally rude man before. The thought of his calling to lay the blame for his unpaid debts on the policies of the British government makes my skin crawl. I've gotten my picture of the Virginia gentry from a few exceptionally well-mannered and pleasant people, like William Browne and Peyton Randolph. They've been as cordial and courteous as any of the men I've known in England. Mr. Benson represented another type of Virginian, one who acquired property without acquiring the manners to go with it. He's the debtor who instinctively hates the people to whom he's indebted. That's an old story. I'll write to John at once encouraging him to file papers for the repayment of Benson's debt or for a suit that might lead Benson to debtor's prison. He shouldn't be allowed to get away with his insolence.

Later that afternoon, Sally and William called for Sophie to come join them for a walk before supper. "Put on your heavy, lace-up shoes," William instructed. "You'll have to do some climbing."

"Did you hear us, Sophie?" Sally called from the bottom of the staircase.

"Yes, yes," Sophie answered from her room upstairs. "Where're we going?" she asked when she got to the front hall attired in her lace-up shoes and carrying a light woolen shawl to protect her from the coolness of the twilight air.

"Going down to the river so you can see the tree," answered William. "The Four Mile Tree, of course. You didn't think this place got its name by chance, did you?"

"Wonderful." Sophie sighed. "This is just what I need to blow all thoughts of that horrid man out of my mind."

When they reached the river and Sophie saw the magnificent old cypress tree with its knees pointing skyward from its spot on the land's edge and one of its large limbs reaching out across the water, she stood awestruck with delight.

"How old is it?" she asked.

"No one knows," William said, "but we think four or five hundred years old at the least. The Indians used it as a landmark before the white men came to Virginia. Governor Argall used it to designate one of the boundaries of the city of Jamestown during the earliest days of the colony, and named it the Four Mile Tree. This old fellow has seen plenty of action. If only it could talk, just think what it might tell us."

Sophie followed William as he climbed up from the sand of the narrow beach into the lap of the tree. Inside the circle of knees, she felt the most incredible calm and sense of peace. For a moment, it seemed almost as though she had come into contact with her creator.

On the way back to the house, Sophie was able to talk about her call from Mr. Benson without feeling any rancor or distress. She told Sally and William what had happened.

"He certainly has many rough edges," William said, "but he is known to be a very intelligent man. He has a great knowledge of horticulture. Knows more about growing things, including the many uses of plants and herbs, than almost anyone in Virginia, certainly more than anyone else on the south shore. His plantation is quite a beauty. The gardens are the best in Southampton. It's down along the Blackwater very near the home of our cousins Thomas and Ann Blount."

After supper that evening Sophie went immediately to her room. She took out a clean sheet of paper, lit the candle on her large bedside table and began writing everything that had taken place, and all that she had heard about Joshua Benson, to her son in London. She would ask Will how to get it posted the next day.

IV

"Let's get Buelly to hitch up a pair of horses and drive us to Scotland Wharf," Sally said. "We can give your letter to the ferry man to hand deliver to a Captain in Jamestown who will be leaving soon for London. That's the quickest method of getting it on its way."

"Good idea," Sophie said. "When I landed there, I was so busy talking to Will that I missed most of the scenery."

"Scotland's not much to see. It's just a ferry wharf, a country store, and a couple of small houses. The most important thing about it is that it's our closest link to the north shore. It's where we get our post and our news."

"Let's go," Sophie said. "I'll get my bonnet."

The rural road was pitted with pot holes from the spring rains making the trip slower and bouncier than usual. "These holes even out a bit in summer time," Sally said. "This is about the worst time for traveling on them. Still, I always have thought the countryside was its most beautiful during the first week of May."

"When the leaves on the trees are still fresh but are finally all out," Sophie said. "I know what you mean."

The carriage carrying the two women followed the narrow road that wound around the meandering path of Gray's Creek. The distance by road was five or six times the crow-flight distance, but the creek's control of the route of the carriage was unchallengeable. Nature ruled the countryside.

"There's the ferry's Captain," Sally said. "I'll call him over."

"Yes, Mrs. Browne."

"My guest, Mrs. Brewster, has a letter she wishes to have posted as soon as possible. Could you take it for her to the captain of the next London-bound ship out of Jamestown?"

"My pleasure, Mrs. Browne," the Captain said. Turning to Sophie he added, "That'll be two shillings for the ship's Captain and two pence for me."

Sophie's smile disappeared. "But, of course," she said.

"Put it on our account," Sally said. "Is there anything for Four Mile Tree?"

"Wife's got it all including your Gazette. Guess you heard about the latest trouble."

"No, what?"

"Americans up north fired on the British soldiers."

"What?" Sophie shouted. "But that's treason."

"Some don't see it that way."

"Where up north?" Sally asked.

"Up near Boston. Lexington and Concord it was. The Gazette should have the story. Wife's got yours. Just came over this morning."

"Buelly, get our post. This sounds terrible," Sally said to Sophie noticing that her guest seemed to be in a state of shock.

Buelly returned with two letters and the Williamsburg Gazette. Sally opened the paper hastily and began to read.

"What does it say?" Sophie asked softly.

Sally read to herself for several minutes and then answered. "Evidently the big news is about Lord Dunmore. The editor must not have heard about Lexington or Concord when this went to press."

"What happened to him?"

"He wrote a letter to Lord Dartmouth in England advocating a crackdown on the colonies. He suggested that all our ports be blockaded, all trade halted and that the colonies be starved into submission to the crown. Someone got hold of the letter and had it printed in the London paper, causing a sensation. The Gazette got hold of it and reprinted it here. The patriots are furious."

"That plus the news from Boston is horrendous," Sophie said. "This means war. I must pack my things and try to get back to London as soon as possible."

"Sophie. You make too much of things. Lord Dunmore and his family are still in Virginia."

"But what happens if there's a war?"

"Then you wait till it's over. You were planning to stay a year anyway. You've only been here two months. Even if war comes, it will surely be over by this time next year."

"One can't be sure of that. I only have funds for one year. I must get back to Williamsburg. Perhaps I can get help in leaving from Lady Dunmore."

"Buelly, take us home. This news can't wait."

V

A year and a half later, Sophie was sitting in the chair before the window in her rooms at Mrs. Hays' Guest House. She had grown thinner during the recent months as tensions and a more Spartan diet took their toll. Her wardrobe was showing wear as well. She was still a handsome woman. The features of her face were well-shaped, but like the once elegant clothes, the expression upon it was beginning to show the signs of strain.

Upon her writing table nearby, were the three remaining coins from her purse. They were two shilling pieces and a small five dollar piece of Carolina gold. She had obtained the gold piece by selling one of her favorite dresses to a shopkeeper in town. She had expected it to fetch more, but the buyer reminded her that silks and satins were out of style. The ladies of Virginia were wearing only homespun to show their support of the cause. "Drats!" Sophie said. "These pieces won't last long. What then?"

Sophie had first run out of money the year before when her paid-up year's lease had expired. Mrs. Hays had been quick to demand a deposit on future occupancy of the rooms, and Sophie had had no funds or credit with which to pay. Will Browne had come to her rescue. He had loaned her enough for another year's rent which both hoped would see her through the war.

As Sophie sat in solitude in her room, a vision of Joshua Benson broke into her mind.

That bastard. He's living in princely splendor while I'm about to be thrown out on the street.

Sophie could feel the fury beginning to rise in her chest. Her temples began to pulsate. She could not keep the scamp from intruding on her thoughts. She had a vision of Joshua, seated in a high-ceilinged room, being served tea with rich cream and cookies. She closed her eyes. She saw him pucker up his handsome lips and laugh at her as he sipped the delectable brew.

If I could only get my hands on him, I'd pluck out his arrogant eyes and smash those lips straight down his throat.

Sophie felt her heart pounding. She tried to calm herself but to little avail. Her thoughts were going round and round in circles. Suddenly she sat up straight. "The tea," she said aloud. "Of course, the tea!"

She jumped to her feet and rushed to the trunk which had been stored in the far corner of her room. She threw back the lid, and there resting on the bottom of her trunk were her remaining tins of tea. She had started out with twenty. There were fourteen left.

I'll sell the tea. That'll provide some ready coin.

Sophie's face took on an enlivened appearance. Her eyes began to glisten.

I'll try the tavern owner. Surely he must need some good English blend tea.

Within minutes Sophie was walking at a brisk pace down Nicholson to the Duke of Gloucester Street. She had tossed her cloak over her shoulders against the chill of the late December breezes. A sample tin of her stock of tea was held firmly at her side with the cloak covering it. She hurried. It was already twilight. Darkness came early at this time of year.

Sophie entered the tavern and looked around. She was in a hall that seemed to run down the center of the building with several doors opening onto it. As she stood wondering what to do next, she heard a door creak as it slowly opened. There was a moment's pause, then the door gently closed again. Someone had seen but not spoken to her. She entered one of the rooms to the right of the hall. Her eyes took in the dark paneling and a number of tables with chairs grouped around them. There seemed to be only a few customers. Several men were seated around one table smoking pipes of tobacco. The darkness and the tobacco smoke that hung in drifts around the room made it difficult for her to see. Someone came up to speak to her. She realized that it was the woman who had been in the coach with her from Yorktown to Williamsburg two years before.

"Good afternoon, Madame. May I help you?"

"Hello," Sophie said with a smile. "Yes. I'd like to see the tavern owner if he's not too busy." Sophie saw the men at the table look up as she spoke. They eyed her and exchanged knowing looks with each other. She wondered if they were annoyed by her accent. She began to wish that she hadn't come.

"You want to see me?" one of the men said without rising from his seat.

"If you're the proprietor, I do."

"Come here then," the man said. "My gout won't let me leave my chair."

"I'm sorry," Sophie said. She slowly walked toward him. She noticed that his foot was propped up and that he held a cane.

"What do you want?" he asked.

"It's a business matter," Sophie said. "I'd hoped to speak with you in private."

The owner nodded to the men. They got up and moved to a table in the far corner to continue their smoking and conversation.

"Sit if you like," the owner said.

"I'll stand, thank you," Sophie said. "I've come to offer to sell you some tea."

"You what?" the proprietor roared.

"I have fourteen tins of tea like this." She pulled out the one tin she had brought with her.

"And you plan to sell them to me?"

"If you'll pay a fair price for them."

"Young woman," the man shouted. "In Virginia, we tar and feather people we catch drinking tea."

Sophie turned in alarm.

"If we catch people trying to sell it, we string 'em up on the spot."

Sophie had reached the door before she heard the proprietor call to the men in the corner. "Get her. She's a British whore trying to sell me some tea."

Sophie reached the hall and started running down it to the back of the building when a door along the way opened abruptly, and a slender arm pulled her into a small serving room. Her breath was heavy with alarm as she heard the men from the tavern room race to the hall and down and out the back of the tavern as she had planned to do.

"It's me, Ludie, M'am."

"Ludie?"

"The boy you gave the good seat to on the coach."

Sophie exhaled a sigh of relief. "Hello, Ludie," she whispered. She paused to catch her breath. She could hear her heart pumping. "Can you get me out of here?"

"Yes, M'am. The back stairs go up here. Just climb a little way and wait. When the men are back in the front room, you can come down and go out the back way."

Sophie climbed a few stairs, just enough to put herself around a curve and out of sight. She heard the men re-enter the back door.

"How the devil did she get away?"

"Maybe she's a witch as well as a Tory."

"Would you have hurt that lady, Chuck?"

"Hell, no. I'd have given her something she might have liked." The men burst into raucous laughter.

"Let's get another mug of ale. She's wasted too much of our drinking time already."

Sophie heard the men tramp down the hall. Ludie looked out. The hall was empty. He nodded to Sophie. She patted the boy on the head as she quietly left the small alcove, tiptoed down the hall and went out the back door.

Back in her rooms, Sophie sank into the chair by the window. She shook her head in despair. She tried to conjure up the image of her deceased husband for comfort.

John, John, where are you? I need you. I can't go it alone.

Sophie stayed in the chair for hours. Her candle burned low. In her mind she sifted her options. Tomorrow, I'll tell Mrs. Hays that I'm out of money. A tear trickled down her face. I'll ask her to hire me to help in the kitchen or to work as a seamstress. I'll have to vacate these rooms no matter what. Perhaps there's space for a cot somewhere behind the scullery.

Sophie pinched out the candle's flame. She was too exhausted to undress and go to bed. She put her arms under her legs and drew them up into the seat of the chair. With her knees against her bosom and her head on her knees, she fell asleep.

The next morning late, Sophie was awakened by the familiar voice of Mrs. Hays. "Letter for you, Sophie. I'll just slip it under your door."

A letter! Sophie sat bolt upright in the chair. Could it be from London and full of money? Of course not. Nothing has changed. There's still the war. Her spirits, newly aroused, fell again.

Sophie fetched the letter, returned to the chair and ripped the envelope open. She read,

My dear Cousin Sophie,

Thomas and I were disappointed that your planned stay with us year before last was canceled by fears of the war. We had been looking forward to a lengthy, social visit from you.

Yesterday, we received a letter from Will Browne informing us of your predicament in not being able to return to England or to receive funds for your continued stay in Virginia. It is our hope that you will come to our home on the Blackwater to reside with us for the duration.

Thomas thinks that you could be in danger in

Williamsburg because of the strong anti-British feelings there. He and my brother Edwin are both members of the Committee of Safety in Southampton County and know that the Committees everywhere are constantly watching the actions of anyone whom they suspect of disloyalty to the patriot cause. The punishments for disloyalty are most unpleasant. We feel that you would be safer with us in the country.

Since last winter, Thomas' health has been somewhat fragile. I have spent much time nursing him. With nine children and the many activities of the plantation to run, I have found myself unable to do all that needs to be done. I am in great need of a sister to help me and to keep us company.

Enclosed is Thomas' note of obligation to his creditor in Williamsburg to pay for your trip from there to Scotland Wharf. Our surrey and driver, Walley, will meet you at the dock to bring you to us. We need one week's notice as to when you will be at Scotland Wharf.

Please honor us by accepting this offer.

I am respectfully,

Ann Gray Blount

VI

With the onset of summer, Sophie packed her trunk, took the coach from Williamsburg to the Jamestown ferry and crossed the river to the south shore where she was picked up by the Blount's house servant, Walley, in a small carriage drawn by two horses.

The path to the plantation on the Blackwater Creek was lightly traveled by vehicles. The packed earth of the old Indian trail still held the trunks of trees that had been sawed off near the ground level to widen the way for the passage of farm wagons and small passenger vehicles. It was necessary to steer a cautious route to straddle them, making the trip very slow.

As they traveled south and inland, Sophie was aware that the air was becoming more humid and the insects more numerous. She wondered why the Blounts and the Bensons would have decided to settle on inland property instead of settling nearer the river. Then as she viewed the terrain closely, she saw that the soil had become a richer, darker color and the vegetation more dense. The inland properties must produce more abundantly. The quality of the land is key, of course.

Sophie's thoughts moved to Joshua Benson. She knew that his home was near the Blounts', which was far from a comforting thought to her. She had been told of his experiments with plant growth, of his interest in agricultural diversity. The richer soil would be an advantage for that. Tobacco will grow with little provocation, I suspect, but other plants may be a bit choosier about their habitation.

Thinking of Joshua Benson sent a queasy feeling through Sophie's chest and stomach. For the first time she began to doubt the wisdom of the move she was making. Then she assessed the ridiculousness of her situation. She was attempting to flee from danger, yet here she was driving alone, through a dense black forest that was most likely home to black bear, black panthers and black snakes, with a black man, whom she had never seen before in control of the coach, riding down a road she had never traveled to an unknown destination. In imaginary self defense, she crouched down in the corner of the passenger cabin as though to make herself smaller. The palms of her hands began to sweat, and she realized that she had become very nervous. She looked up at the driver seated above her as he patiently followed the road. My life is in that black man's hands. It would not be the last time that such would be the case.

After hours of being on the road, the carriage turned into a long drive that approached a low-lying white house of comfortable size but of no specific design or style. The roof was high pitched in some places, low in others. Parts of the house were two-storied and parts just one. There were three chimneys, not placed symmetrically, and the windows were of varying sizes. It appeared to be a house that had just grown with the years. Still, it had a measure of charm. There was something very personal about its look as though each addition had a story of its own to tell.

Ann Blount rushed from the house at the sound of wheels on the drive. She welcomed Sophie with unabashed enthusiasm. Thomas had stopped in the doorway in order to let the women have this moment of greeting to themselves before offering his opened arms to his cousin in a familial embrace.

Sophie was struck anew by the distinguished appearance of the couple. They hospitably ushered her into their home and into their lives as well. There were lines on the faces of Ann and Thomas that etched in the years of hard work and toil on the plantation, but despite the signs of age, they radiated a warmth that Sophie found instantly appealing. She knew that Thomas was considered wealthy by most any measure, but she also knew that his riches were primarily in the form of land, slaves and animals. These things alone would not produce a gracious life-style without keen management and hard work by the owners.

Ann was the mother of nine children. That took a toll on any woman's health. Nevertheless, she retained a pleasant, comfortable appearance which declared that the life she had led had been most agreeable to her. Ann's father, Joseph Gray, had been the leading citizen of Southampton from the moment it had been lopped off of Surry and become a county in its own right. He had served as Justice, as Sheriff, and as the county's representative in the House of Burgesses almost continually from the county's founding until his death a few years before. After his death, Ann's brother Edwin Gray had taken over most of his father's positions and had been instrumental in forming the Committee of Safety for Southampton County when Virginia declared her independence.

Thomas was a more retiring, less flamboyant man than Ann's father had been. Politics was a field that he avoided whenever his conscience would permit him to do so. He always listened carefully to the fiery talk of his cohorts and friends but kept most of his own views to himself unless he became riled by some injustice or breach of good principal. Then he could unleash his fury and any who had tried him had best beware. Although he was quiet a great deal of the time in the company of the county's leaders, he had no difficulty expressing himself articulately when his good reasoning told him he must.

Before dinner on the night of Sophie's arrival, Ann told her of the difficult health problems Thomas had suffered. It had all started more than four months before when he had over-indulged at a men's dinner in the neighborhood. He had eaten heartily and been encouraged by the toastmaster to drink a goodly quantity of wine. Before reaching home after the affair, he had become violently ill. Surprisingly, he had not improved much in the days that followed. He had been watching his food and drink carefully ever since and had only recently been able to return to eating anything other than soft foods.

Sophie appraised Thomas' handsome face as he presided at the dinner table. His features were neatly chiseled as though his maker had tried to put together the best assemblage he could fashion. The lines of middle-age seemed only to enhance his appearance, adding character to a pleasant face.

Dinner at the family table was lively. The six boys, five of whom slept in a schoolroom dormitory under the surveillance of their tutor rather than in the house, all came to dinner and brought with them hearty appetites. The three daughters and the youngest son resided in the house and were present for all meals. With the tutor, this meant that there were usually thirteen for dinner every day even without any guests.

The children were excused from the table before their elders, leaving some time for adult conversation, and it was not long before Joshua Benson's name was mentioned. Sophie stiffened with displeasure at the mention of him. Her obvious dislike of the man could be observed by the others.

"Benson's property is very near," Thomas said. "It actually abuts ours at a few locations. Joshua is a rough character who needs a bit of polish, but he has done a fine job of helping the local farmers improve their crops. Also, Ann is very fond of his wife, Rachel. She has been deeply saddened by the death of each of her children."

"So I have been told," Sophie said.

The next day Sophie set about trying to learn all that she could about the management of the household so as to be as helpful as possible to her generous host and hostess in return for their giving her shelter. She did the household rounds with Ann, as a beginning, making a special effort to learn which of the servants was responsible for each of the many tasks that needed to be done. She wanted to be able to manage the house and children on her own should Thomas be taken ill again. She learned where all the foodstuffs were stored, how they were kept fresh, which things needed to be kept under lock and key, fire protection measures, food preparations, and the country style of food service which was less formal than that which she had known in either London or Williamsburg. Throughout Sophie's period of service to Ann, it never occurred to her that what she did in household service or to help with the children should be paid for in any way. At that time, not only did slaves work for room and board alone, the women of all households did the same. Little money changed hands in any community. It was taken for granted that the traditional duties of women were always offered free of charge. By the standards of later times, Sophie was more than earning her keep, but at that time, she felt truly embarrassed over what she considered her indebtedness to her Blount cousins.

Not all meals were taken by the entire family at one time. In the interest of enjoying some privacy, Ann and Thomas frequently had their meals put on a crude dumbwaiter that was built into the wall between the dining room and the hall. The food trays were then lifted to a second story outlet that opened both into the upstairs hall and into the guest room which Sophie occupied. The Blounts often dined alone on a round table in the upstairs hall where they were out of earshot of the servants, and where they could have some reprieve from the rigors of family life. With the dumbwaiter opening into her room, it was not long before Sophie had arranged to have a pitcher of hot water sent to her room in mid-afternoon so that, ostensibly, she could soak her ever-painful toe to relieve the symptoms of gout that attacked her every afternoon around four o'clock.

Not many days had passed before Ann caught on to the ploy of the pitcher of hot water and arranged for a tray to be sent up with sugar, cream and cookies as well. Just as she heard the dumbwaiter door being opened, she pounced in on Sophie carrying her own teacup with her.

"My, my," Sophie said. "I heard that the Committee of Safety would tar and feather anyone they caught drinking tea. I've been imbibing secretly ever since I learned of it, but it's much more fun with company. I have some tins of tea I brought from England to give as gifts only to learn that the drinking of it in Virginia was strongly forbidden."

"We won't publicize our actions," Ann said. "After all we aren't buying it from English merchants. We're just drinking up what we already have."

"Has the Committee of Safety actually punished people for drinking it?" Sophie asked.

"I'm sure they must have. In some of the northern colonies the Committees have been quite brutal. Thomas told me of a man in New England who drank a toast to King George in a public tavern. A Committee member heard him and insisted that he recant his loyal allegiance or he and his cohorts would bury him alive. When the foolish man stood up and drank a second toast to the king, they followed up by doing exactly as they said they would. They buried him alive."

Ann picked up the cookie plate and offered Sophie another one. "I've heard of nothing that brutal in Virginia, but then there's always tomorrow. Thomas is very upset over the zealousness of some of the Southampton members of the Committee. My brother, Edwin, is president of it. He and Thomas struggle all the time to keep law and order here. Since Lord Dunmore dissolved the last Assembly of the House of Burgesses, there has been no official system of justice. The court can't sit, legally. Justices have no authority. The Committees of Safety are all that the counties have, and some of the members have let power drive them beyond what Thomas believes to be just."

"I can see we had best keep our tea drinking to ourselves."

As the days went by Sophie often found herself wondering what she was doing in this lonely, inland homestead so far away from all the things she had always loved, society, entertainments, music. Then she would join Ann and Thomas for some plantation activity and realize that she had never known any two people with whom she had been happier.

There must be something about the solitude of their lives that makes them unusually appreciative of others. I can't think of anyone with whom I've ever been more compatible or felt more secure. If only I could pick them both up and sail with them to London. How glorious that would be. Funny, London is being pushed further and further back into the recesses of my mind. It's becoming more difficult to remember. I see my boys the way they looked the last time I saw them, but the heartache that used to accompany these visions has lessened considerably.

Sophie began to feel that she was getting the hang of country life and to feel more at ease with her duties. Then one morning Thomas announced "There will be an emergency meeting of the Committee of Safety here on Monday. You ladies may expect nineteen gentlemen for mid-day dinner."

"An emergency? Whatever kind? Things seem peaceful enough around here," Ann said.

"Things never are quite what they seem," Thomas said. "I'd like to have dinner served by one o'clock. The committee will meet following the meal and its members will need daylight for their trip home afterwards."

On Monday, both Ann and Sophie stood in the hall to welcome the guests as they arrived.

"Welcome, Mr. Benson," Ann said. "I believe you have met our cousin, Mrs. Brewster."

Joshua Benson gave a stiff bow in Sophie's direction but said nothing. Sophie looked straight into his eyes and was surprised to feel something in her chest seem to flip over as a reaction to the encounter.

"Your displeasure is showing," whispered Ann. "Remember these are our guests."

"I'm sorry. I see that he arrived on horseback, not in his handsome cream-colored carriage. Can Mr. Benson be on restricted funds?"

"Hardly," Ann said. "He just bought fifty blankets for the militia with his own money. Remember that he lives nearby."

Sophie and Ann disappeared into the pantry from which they directed the serving of the elaborate meal. Numerous courses were served which required a constant replacement of dishes, many of which had to be washed, dried and reused.

When the sweets had been finished and the last of the dishes cleared away, a number of the men present reached into their pockets for their pipes, filled them with tobacco and lit up. They pushed their chairs back from the table to listen to and contemplate the news of the day.

Relieved that their duties were over and exhausted from their work, Ann and Sophie went to their respective rooms for a late afternoon rest. Once in her room above the dining room, Sophie regretted that she had not ordered a pitcher of hot water be sent up for her afternoon tea. By force of habit she walked over to the dumbwaiter, opened the door and was startled to hear clearly the voices of the men in the room below. Edwin Gray was talking. The conversation was about Saratoga, General Washington and the defeat of the British General Burgoyne's forces by the American Continentals.

The Committee was discussing how they could best use the fifty or more members of the county's militia in support of General Washington. Sophie could hear the rise of voices as the men began to disagree. She could hear Edwin saying, "The enlistments of many of General Washington's troops will soon be up. These men will be returning home just at the time when pursuit of the enemy is necessary. Although the victory at Saratoga is important, it is in no way decisive."

Joshua Benson said, "Southampton should send forth its militia to assist General Washington at once. Victory must be pursued." Others raised their voices in support. Then a gentleman, whose voice Sophie did not recognize, gave a counter opinion. "I feel strongly that sending the militia out of the state could lead to a slave uprising. The militia was organized for local protection. It should be kept for that purpose. What General Washington needs most is money to enable him to re-enlist his retiring troops. I suggest that we all subscribe funds and try to raise money from the neighboring counties as well. Then," he said, "keep the Southampton County militia in the county where it belongs."

Sophie's attention moved to and from the words she heard coming up the dumbwaiter shaft. She was not informed enough on the subjects being discussed to have any opinion on the matter, although she still felt a desire to have Virginia remain a British colony. As the afternoon wore on she heard them discussing the better equipping of the Continental army, the shipment of food and wearing apparel. There was a call for every citizen who owned two overcoats to donate one to the army. It all seemed rather routine until suddenly Sophie heard the strident voices of conflict. The question that arose was over support for an alliance with the French. Sophie could not make out all of the comments because several of the men began talking at once. Above all, though, she could clearly hear the commanding voice of Joshua Benson as he declared that only an alliance with the French would enable the Americans to win victory over the British. The rancor increased and the orations became louder. Suddenly there was a hush that came over the group as Thomas in a quiet but purposeful voice began to talk and all present began to listen.

A lump of distress rose in Sophie's throat. Careful, Careful. She turned her complete attention to the words that followed.

"Gentlemen," Thomas said, "if you do not think it possible for the American patriots to win without the assistance of France, then we should be pursuing a compromise to end the conflict with Britain. The French have been our enemy from the earliest of colonial days. What is to prevent them from coming to the aid of the colonists, with our help ridding the continent of the British, and then continuing their effort by conquering us. Would you be happier being a colony of France than being a colony of Great Britain? If we can not beat the British without the French, then I think we should be working toward a peaceful solution of our difficulties with the crown."

"Oh, Thomas," Sophie moaned under her breath in the room above, "please say no more. Your thoughts are too dangerous for an aroused group of warmongers."

Sophie felt the pangs of fear spread through her chest. Suddenly she could stand to hear no more. With weak knees she tiptoed to the dumbwaiter door and gently closed it. Then she flung herself onto the bed and let her emotions find a needed release. Tears ran down her face as she buried her head in a pillow to stifle the sound of her sobs. Thomas, Thomas. I had no idea that I cared for you so much.

Sophie stayed stretched out on the bed's counterpane until she heard the last of the wheels crackling against the stones of the entrance drive. Her emotional release had drained every ounce of energy from her body, leaving her physically limp. She knew that she would have to do a great deal of pretending to cover up all that she had heard and to keep both Ann and Thomas from learning of her feelings. This was a misery that she had never expected.

When Sophie and Ann came downstairs for breakfast several weeks later, they found Walley waiting for them at the foot of the stairs.

"Mrs. Benson died last night," he said. "I been over there visiting my Judy. Mrs. Benson, she died in her sleep."

"Oh, Walley. How sad," Ann turned to Sophie and said, "I must go over to help immediately after breakfast. Rachel was my closest friend until you arrived. I'm afraid I have neglected her rather badly since then."

"Was she sick?" Sophie asked.

"Not that I knew of. But, of course, losing all those children took a terrible toll on her."

Ann immediately dropped all her chores and rode over to the Bensons' home to see what she could do to be of assistance. She had always loved Rachel even though the latter was a timid and reclusive woman. On returning to her own home, she declared, "Rachel died of a broken heart. Losing all those children would be too much for any woman to bear."

A few days after Rachel Benson's funeral, Joshua called on the Blounts to express his appreciation for Ann's kindness. He stayed for supper. It was all that Sophie could do to be pleasant to him despite his great loss. She knew it would be a dreadful embarrassment to Ann if she were ungracious in any way so she did her best to make light conversation. Still her thoughts were far removed from the words she spoke.

I can't stand to see him look at Ann, and his own wife buried only a few days ago.

Sophie asked to be excused as soon as she felt it was polite to do so. Ann followed her upstairs leaving the two men to discuss subjects of their own interest. Upstairs, Sophie occupied herself with the Blount children until bedtime, which came none too soon for her mood. At long last all went to their rooms, the doors were closed, the candles blown out and the family retired for the night.

Sophie was in that state of deep slumber that embraces the body as sleep first arrives, when she was abruptly awakened by the sound of a loud crash. The entire household was aroused. The girls rushed out of their bedrooms. Sophie met them in the hall, and they all rushed to follow Ann down the hall stairs to the library below. There they found Thomas sprawled on the floor where he had landed from a standing position. There was no sign of Joshua nor the sound of horse's hooves on the drive outside. He had probably been gone for sometime. There was a deathly quiet in the room. Sophie watched in horror as Ann gently turned Thomas over onto his back. His face was beautiful as his features were caught by the light of the candles' glow. He moved not a muscle nor made the slightest sound. He was completely still with his eyes wide open in the blank, expressionless stare of death.

Joshua Benson took command in making all the arrangements for Thomas' funeral. Ann leaned heavily on him for support. Sophie eyed him with distrust. It occurred to her that the Benson property plus the Blount property, if joined by marriage, would make Joshua the richest man in Southampton County. Sophie vowed to see that it would never happen. Returning to the house after the burial in the apple orchard, Ann went straight to her room leaving Sophie alone to cope with Mr. Benson.

"Are you not also in need of solitude to assuage your deep grief, Mrs. Brewster?"

"Whatever do you mean?" Sophie asked.

"I mean, Mrs. Brewster, it was easy to discern the depth of your affection for your benefactress' husband."

"Your words are most unfair, Mr. Benson," Sophie said. "I might remind you that I would not be here at all if you had made the proper payments on your debt to us. I am completely without funds, and you seem to have no intention of doing anything to remedy that situation."

Joshua stood over Sophie. He was a full head taller than she. His standing so near to her made her feel weak and vulnerable. Her knees began to shake.

"Of course not, Mrs. Brewster. If I made any payment to you at all, you would return to Williamsburg at once leaving Ann to fend for herself. I can't see that you are being harmed by making yourself useful while waiting out the duration of your internment. Ann needs you."

"How clever of you to defend your misuse of my late husband's generosity."

"Generosity had nothing to do with your husband's funding of my business enterprises. He lent the money in hopes of making a larger profit for himself. He knew the risks and was prepared to take them."

"You could pay something, I feel sure."

"I could, but whatever I paid to you would be that much less that I could give to the cause. I don't see that you are suffering, my dear. You look very well fed to me."

"Good day, Mr. Benson. I do feel the need for a bit of solitude."

Joshua made no move to leave. There was an awkward moment of silence between them. Then Sophie turned away. With her head held high, she was surprised to feel her knees wobble as she left the room.

VII

"I could never have managed this week without you," Ann said.

"Course you could. I've done very little," Sophie said.

"You've been a true friend."

The two women were seated on the steps that led up to the porch on the front of the house. It was early November, but the sunshine made it feel like a day in late summer. Ann turned her face to let the warmth of the sun's rays soothe the dull ache behind her eyes. "I'm lucky to have the children, too," she said. "Just think of poor Joshua. He lost Rachel and now he has absolutely no one."

Poor Joshua, my foot.

"I can't get over the way the boys have taken over management of the farms. We probably should have given them more responsibility before. Since Thomas' death they've been in the fields constantly seeing to everything."

"Most people rise to what needs to be done."

"I hear horses turning off the road. Can you see anything?"

"Not yet, but it sounds like a whole team."

Sophie stood and pulled Ann to her feet. A group of five men on horseback came into view and quickly approached the house. Sophie realized, immediately, that all five had been at the meeting of the Committee of Safety.

"Mrs. Blount." One of the men rode forward of the others stopping near the foot of the steps. "My respects to you, M'am. Mr. Blount was a fine man."

"Thank you," Ann said. "It's kind of you to call."

"Unfortunately, it's not a social call. We've come for the Englishwoman."

"You've what?"

"The Englishwoman, Ma'am. We're concerned for your safety with her here. We want to try her for the murder of Mr. Blount."

Sophie gasped and began instinctively to edge her way back toward the door of the house.

"My husband wasn't murdered," Ann said.

"Maybe he was. There's some who think she may be a British spy coming like she did just as the war started."

Sophie reached the door, but as she turned to enter it, she was almost knocked down by Walley who came out of the house carrying Thomas' shotgun. For a moment in her confusion, she thought that Walley planned to help the men arrest her. Terror raced through her body. How could these things keep happening?

Ann reached for the gun as Walley handed it to her. "Get off my property," she ordered raising the gun to her shoulder.

"Now, Mrs. Blount. No need to act like that. We come mostly

to protect you."

Ann cocked the trigger and lifted the sight to her eye.

"We're going, m'am, but we'll be back. This British intruder won't last long in these parts." He turned his horse, and with the others rode away.

Sophie was so stunned that it took minutes before she could gather her poise to speak. Finally she asked "How could you be so trusting of me?"

Ann put her arms around Sophie's shoulder. "You couldn't possibly have killed Thomas," she said. "I know that you loved him."

Sophie tried to answer but couldn't. She opened her mouth but was seized by a convulsion of sobs. Ann led her into the house. "Where's Walley?" she asked the black cook who was standing inside the door.

"Gone to fetch Mr. Benson," the cook said.

They waited all day in a state of fear, afraid that the men would return with more accomplices to take Sophie away. In late afternoon, Joshua Benson arrived by way of a back, woodland path. He brought two of his own saddled horses.

"Pack your most need possessions," he ordered Sophie. "Not more than will fit in a saddle bag. Put your boots and riding clothes on immediately."

"I don't ride well."

"You'll learn."

Sophie thought he might be planning to arrest her himself, but for some reason she could not understand, she did exactly what he told her to do.

"The men will be back," Joshua said. "They're itching for some action."

"How can they claim to be Thomas' friends, and do this to us?" Ann asked.

"Wars bring out the worst in some," Joshua said. They stood nervously waiting for Sophie. "Here she comes. Say your goodbyes quickly."

Ann rushed to give Sophie a farewell embrace. She could say nothing. Her throat was swollen and clogged from emotion. Sophie choked back tears of her own, but managed to mount one of the horses. "Aren't you coming with me?" she asked Joshua.

"No, we must create the illusion that you have not left. I brought the horses so that none of the Blount stock would be found missing should the men return. They'll think you're in hiding nearby. I've told Walley what to do. You're not to question his judgment. Do exactly as he tells you."

Sophie felt her heart choke with fear.

"Off with you now," Joshua said clapping his hands to reaffirm the command.

Sophie followed Walley back along the woodland path toward Joshua's plantation. She wondered if this was just a trick to get her away from Ann so that the men could arrest her there instead of at Blount's.

"We's going to Judy's cabin," Walley said. "We's to spend the night there."

"Judy's?"

"Judy's my woman. She does clothes and things at Master Benson's. Her cabin's at the end of the row of slave cabins near the woods. She'll take us in."

That night Sophie slept on the corn cob and feather mattress that served as Judy's bed. The mattress was torn and faded. The scent of the dried corn cobs permeated the air, blocking out all other smells, for which Sophie was thankful, but the few feathers did little to soften the rough angles of the cobs. She felt as though she was stretched out on a bag of bones.

Sophie was trying to sleep when she heard a faint knock at the cabin door. Her heart quickened its beat while her muscles became rigid with terror. They've come. They'll take me away. I'll soon be dead.

Judy opened the door a crack. She spoke in a low voice. She opened the door wider and laughed.

Oh God, it's all been a charade.

Sophie heard the door close. She saw Judy walking over to the bed. "Master sent this down for you," she said as she handed Sophie a wrapped package.

"Open it, please."

Judy did so and handed Sophie the content. It was a small, soft down-pillow enclosed in a freshly ironed linen case.

"Thank you, Judy," Sophie said. She lifted her head, placing the pillow beneath it, and turned her face to the cabin wall. She didn't want Judy or Walley to see the tears that were streaming down her face.

The next morning before daybreak, she and Walley were off, riding toward Surry County and hoping to find a safe haven at Four Mile Tree.

The long circuitous route they took doubled the usual length of the journey. There were long periods of silence as Sophie followed Walley's slow-moving horse through the forests. She had hours of uninterrupted thought, much of which was directed toward trying to understand the cause of all her problems. In the process, she came to realize that much of the cause of an indebted person's hate of the lender was indeed the lender's fault. Lenders think of themselves as generous and of the indebted as ingrates. In truth, many a lender is only using the borrower to get control over him. She thought of all the Jews of the Diaspora, of how many had lent absurd amounts of money to kings and emperors only to have the latter turn on them and brutally expel them from their country when they found themselves trapped and helpless to repay. She calculated that the indebtedness of many American planters might be one of the chief causes of the present war for independence. Whatever the truth of the matter might be, she knew she loathed her own indebtedness to others. She vowed that she would somehow get out of debt and never put herself there again.

VIII

Three years later, as the fighting between the British and the American patriots was nearing its climax at a small village on the York River, just twelve miles north of the James, Colonel William Browne, IV, and Lieutenant William Browne, V, left Four Mile Tree with their two strapping, strong Negro slaves, Buelly and Big Boy, as well as their own team of oxen to be used in helping to transport French heavy artillery from the mouth of College Creek to the outskirts of Yorktown. The job of getting the cannons off the ships was a major engineering feat in itself. Managing to have the heavy guns successfully dragged over twelve miles of sandy soil that tried to swallow the narrow rims with each revolution of the wheels, was a major accomplishment.

Within a week of the departure of the men from Four Mile Tree, Sophie and Sally were able to faintly hear the first, low, muffled booms of the cannonade. They sat on the stone benches of the upper terrace, their needlework clutched nervously in their hands, and listened to the steady thud of the powerful guns as treacherous volleys were being sent into the enemy lines. From the terrace it was, of course, impossible to know which side the cannons belonged to and which line was being hit. This uncertainty gave an eerie feeling to their appraisal of the situation. From time to time the sound would stop; then it would start again.

"I don't think it really starts and stops," Sophie said to Sally. "The wind shifts, causing us sometimes to hear and sometimes not. It's such a strange thing to think that the battle is being waged within earshot even though we can barely make out the sounds."

"I'm daffy from worrying about them all," Sally declared. "How long can this go on?"

"Until one side gives up."

"I wish we'd just kept on as we were," Sally said. "One never thinks that their own men will be in the thick of it when it starts."

"Wars are dangerous even when the battlefield is far away," Sophie said. "Remember what happened to Thomas?"

"Yes," Sally said with a deep sigh. "There are many hidden dangers. What do you think really happened to Thomas, Sophie?"

"I think he was poisoned."

"But why?"

"Thomas told the Committee of Safety that he thought America should bargain for peace with the British rather than risk an alliance with the French. He was afraid that America might end up a colony of France. Someone may have begun to see Thomas as a Tory, a man amongst them who was on the other side. The strange thing is that no one had suggested the possibility of Thomas' having been murdered before the Committee men came to get me. They declared that the Blounts had been harboring an Englishwoman which, of course, was true. They also said that the reason for my coming to Virginia was to serve the British government as a spy."

"Why haven't you told us this before?"

"Joshua told me not to tell anyone what happened. He said it would only place me in greater danger. At the time, I was frightened beyond measure and did exactly as I was told."

"You can't stop telling me now that you've begun," encouraged Sally, somewhat diverted from the revelation by the deep, almost inaudible sound of the distant fusillade. "How did you manage to save yourself?"

"It was Ann who did that," Sophie said. "She showed a strength and resolve that I shall never forget. I just burst into tears and turned into a jellyfish. I remember Walley saying, 'Don't cry like that Miss Sophie. We's going to take care of you.'"

"It's ironic to think how scared I was of Walley when he picked me up at Scotland Wharf to take me to the Blackwater the first time. I had never known much about Black people and felt thoroughly insecure around them. In the end, Walley was the one who saved my life. I asked him once, while we were in flight, why he was risking so much to save me. His answer was, 'Why you ask that, Missus? Ain't we all the same family?'"

"I'd never thought of a black person as being my family before, but I will in the future. That's when I came back to you, Sally, and you took me in again."

"Do you really think Thomas was murdered?" Sally asked. She gave a shudder.

"Yes," Sophie said. "My father often said, 'If you want to know what a man's faults are, listen and hear what he criticizes other people for.' "

After a long pause, Sally said, "The sound of the cannon fire has stopped. Could it all be over?"

"No, they have probably just quit for the night. It's become windy and colder while we've been talking. Those clouds look like a change of some kind. We may be in for a big storm. Let's go in."

Each night, inside the house, the women found themselves to be more distressed than they had been outside in the daytime listening to the soft sound of the far-off fighting. In the candle's glow, Sophie was aware of strange shapes and shadows cast against the walls that reminded her of days long ago when her sons had been only children playing in the parlor of their London home. They had loved making animal heads and birds with their fists and fingers put into the air between the candle's light and the parlor wall. Sophie's memories of her sons had become dimmer with the years. When she thought of them now, she often had pictures in her mind of them when they had been boys rather than the young men that they were when she had last seen them. Sometimes she would stop to count the years.

Edward was seventeen when I left. He must be twenty-three now. And John should be twenty-five. I wonder if either of the boys has married. Has either been ill? It's even possible that one might be dead. When that thought came her way, she would break her solitude with a bit of silly conversation to rid her mind of it. There was no need to be unnecessarily morbid even though the wait for the war to end had been a painfully long and tedious one.

Sophie was becoming more and more a Virginian as she waited out her exile even though she would never have recognized the fact herself. As the images of her life in England continued to fade and the images of her sons regressed more and more into their child-hoods, those whom she had come to care for in Virginia, Ann, Sally, William, all their children, Buelly and Walley had come to occupy more and more of her thoughts. She even found herself fearing that the British might kill some of the young men she had met in Virginia and wishing that the crown would call it quits in America and give the colonists their independence.

When the firelight flickered across the polished hardwood floor in the square, front parlor at Four Mile Tree, Sophie worried not only about her sons, she worried about Ann living so near to the plantation of Joshua Benson. Her reasoning told her that Ann's brother, Edwin, lived nearby, and that he would see that no harm came to her. Still, she could not forget the sight of Benson casting his admiring eyes on Ann at the dinner table only a short time after his wife's death. She shivered at the memory. Bringing her thoughts back to the war she said aloud to Sally, "Waiting, waiting. If only there was something we could do to speed things along."

"I know. Waiting is always the hardest part."

Several days later, Buelly and Big Boy returned to Four Mile Tree with the team of oxen they had driven to help transport the siege-artillery across the peninsula. They traveled though a heavy storm enduring horrendous winds and drenched fields. "I sure was glad it be oxen we's bringing back and not horses," Buelly said when he entered the house to inform Sally of their return. "Horses would a gone wild in that storm."

"We hauled the heavy guns from the creek on the other side," Buelly said. "The trenches, they was mostly dug by the militia sol-diers. The enemy had they backs to the water. Then there was the angels."

"Angels?" Sally questioned. "Whatever do you mean?"

"Angels, Missus. I saw them. The river was full of ships that some of the angels come in. The rest of the angels come marching just like the other soldiers, but the angels was dressed all in white, trimmed in gold. They was 'bout as beautiful as any white men I ever has seen. They all talk in some funny way that I can't understand. God knows what they was saying though. I knows that."

"He must be referring to the French soldiers," Sophie said. "That is the first time I have ever heard them called angels."

"Did Colonel Browne send any special message for me, Buelly?' Sally asked.

"Yessum, he say he ain't got no paper to write, but he tell me to say that our soldiers with the angels is twice as many as the British soldiers and that the angel's ships has got the British ships in a bottle. He says we is going to win for sure."

"Thank you, Buelly. You and Big Boy have done a fine job."

"It ain't no trouble to do the Lord's work, Missus. I done seen His ships and His angels. I know it going to come out His way."

Two days later, the news reached Four Mile Tree that Lord Cornwallis had asked for a cease fire as a preliminary to the surrender of his British forces. The good news spread quickly.

That night Sophie and Sally went out onto the terrace, their shoulders wrapped in woolen shawls against the chill of the October night. They stared out toward Yorktown, only fifteen miles away, where all their futures now lay in the making. The magnitude of the events that were taking place left them feeling like powerless creatures in a gigantic universe. They looked out across the water. Suddenly a brilliant show of meteors streaked across the star-filled sky. A profound silence embraced the women. So awestruck were they that they did not hear Buelly move up behind them. "I told you," he said in a firm confident voice. "I told you that God be there."

The Browne men, father and son, returned to Four Mile Tree almost immediately after the formal surrender at Yorktown. "The artillery fire was fierce," Will said. "Lord Cornwallis tried to retreat across the York River. His escape was foiled by the torrential storm of the sixteenth which made it impossible for the British sailing vessels to transport the troops across the narrow river. That forced the British to surrender." William's delight in the victory was unmistakable, yet still, his voice became heavy with emotion as he described the scene of the British soldiers marching out of their fortifications to surrender their weapons. "I felt great pity for the young men to be marched west to wait out the rest of the war in prison camp."

That night, Sally had Buelly dig up a bottle of port that they had buried years before to hide and save for the day of victory. As the rich, mellow-tasting liquid tickled their throats and lightened their spirits, William explained to them that the war was not over. "General Clinton still holds the bulk of the British forces in New York," he said. "However, the British strength has been dealt a mighty blow. It is unlikely that there will be any further fighting in Virginia."

Sophie listened carefully. Much to her surprise, she found herself deeply satisfied with the turn of events. She was glad that the Americans had won. How little we really know of ourselves.

IX

Before Christmas of 1781, Walley arrived at Four Mile Tree from the Blackwater bringing the possessions that Sophie had left behind three years before. He reported that things were going fairly well at home. Mr. Henry was running the plantation in place of his father, and all the younger boys were helping him. The girls were helping their mother run the house. "The Missus is getting on pretty good," he said, "but I sure do think she misses you, Miss Sophie. She says she'd of sent this stuff before, but she hoped you'd come back for it. Truth is, there was British soldiers 'tween here and the Blackwater most of the time. Weren't really safe to travel till after General Washington sent them a running."

"You can't imagine how I yearn to see her," Sophie said. "But I must think of getting back to England. Tell me, Walley, did your Judy get in trouble for letting us stay in her cabin the night we ran away? I've worried about that."

No, M'am. She didn't get found out. She and I is married now so she lives with us at Blounts. I wants 'specially to thank you for the beautiful shirt you sent me, Miss Sophie. All the ruffles and tucks make it 'bout the finest shirt I ever seen on a black man. I wore it the day Judy stood up with me in the parlor in front of the preacher, and it made me mighty proud. My Judy says she never has seen so many little, tiny stitches. She takes good care of it for me so's I can wear it to church on Sundays."

"I wish I could have done better by you, Walley, but two yards of white linen and a few buttons was about all I had to share with you. I'll always be indebted to you for saving my life. When this war is over, I'll try to find a better way to show my gratitude."

"Why don't you go back there with me? It sure would make the Missus and Master Benson happy."

"The Missus and Master Benson?" Sophie said. "You're not t-telling me that they're m-married are you?"

"No, M'am. What make you think that?"

"Your putting their names together like that."

"Missus talks 'bout you all the time. She don't think 'bout marrying again. She just think about you and her children. Master Benson, he mighty lonely. He come to the house every now and again, but seem to me like he just come to ask about you."

Sophie swallowed hard. "Be sure to get a hearty meal and a good night's rest before you head back. I'll write to your missus tonight, and you can take the letter back with you tomorrow."

X

In early spring, with another loan from William, Sophie packed all that was left of her possessions, expressed her heartfelt, lifelong indebtedness to Sally and William for their generous sheltering of her throughout the years of active warfare in Virginia and returned to Williamsburg. She was in hopes of finding someone there who could make contact with her sons in some way. She had heard that some correspondence was getting through now that the authorities were no longer concerned about the safety of Virginia. Commissioners were in Paris trying to work out the peace settlement and many of the restrictions caused by the war were being slackened.

Arriving in Williamsburg, Sophie found the town to be a shabby remnant of its former self. The government had been moved to Richmond during the middle of the war for reasons of security. The handsome Governor's Palace had been turned into a hospital for the wounded during the battle of Yorktown. The college, with a great scarcity of students during the war years, had begun to fall into decay. Without those involved in government, and with the college in decline, Williamsburg was rapidly becoming scantily occupied and seedy.

Sophie found her former rooms unoccupied, as was most of the town, but lacking some of the furnishings they once had possessed. Still, she moved back into them. Mrs. Hays had saved her stored trunk. Settling in, she started reorganizing her life.

In March of 1783, eight years less one month after Sophie's arrival in Virginia, she received her first post war communication from her son, John. Seated in the one large chair in her quarters at Mrs. Hays' house, she cautiously opened the long-awaited letter. Trying to picture John as he wrote the letter, she found, to her surprise, that she had difficulty seeing him. She tried to remember old friends in England as well, but had trouble remembering them as clearly as she wished she could.

The letter was a long one. She read it slowly, unable to truly believe that it had finally arrived. "I have made payment on this side of the ocean so that you can board any British vessel on which you can obtain passage," it said.

Sophie lowered the letter to her lap. Her long struggle would soon be over. She would soon be sailing back to England.

"Our peace negotiators are in Paris meeting with the American and French representatives. It is only a matter of time until the Americans are recognized as independent. You may be surprised to learn that about half of those here who care about such things favored the American cause. Many English soldiers refused to fight against the colonists."

How extraordinary. And to think that my conscience bothered me so when I began seeing things as the colonists did.

"I have been married for three years now to a beautiful creature from Yorkshire, named Constance Gray. We have a son, named Jonathan, who wants to meet his grandmother."

"A grandson," Sophie whispered, trying to think back to the time when John was an infant.

"Through the Dutch sea captain to whom I am entrusting this letter to you, I am establishing some credit for you in Richmond. You should soon receive a message from our creditor there. I hope the sum will enable you to pay off any debts that you have accumulated before you leave Virginia."

It was all too much. Sophie had to take time to think of all these things. She realized that she was actually afraid to go home. She could think of no friends in England whom she cared to see as much as she wanted to see Ann, Sally and William or even Walley. Then too, there was Betty Randolph whose company she enjoyed as much as that of anyone, anywhere. Something else was disturbing her too, but she couldn't grasp just what it was.

Could I live in my son's home? His home belongs to another woman now. I left Four Mile Tree and returned to Williamsburg, because I was uncomfortable being a perpetual guest in someone else's home. Would I be able to go back to another such arrangement?

Sophie thought back over the years she had spent surviving on her own. Her cousins had come to her rescue, but she had given service in return, helping to manage the plantation houses, sewing and teaching the Negro women how to cut and sew garments of quality. It had been quite satisfying in many ways. She had learned to be useful. It gave her a sense of pride in herself.

Sophie rose from her chair and went to the window. She could see Betty Randolph in her garden across the street. She was inspecting the spring plants that were just showing their sprouts above ground. Betty, too, had been a widow since almost the beginning of the war. The two women had much in common. Sophie went to her mirror, combed her hair, powered her nose, tied a bonnet into place and picked up her shawl. Talking with Betty would help her to see things more clearly.

Betty Randolph set the teapot down to allow the tea leaves to steep a bit before pouring the pot's contents into delicate porcelain cups.

"It's fun to be able to serve tea openly again without worrying about being tarred and feathered," Betty said. "I can't tell you how much I missed it when the ban first came out."

"It was the men who thought the idea up," Sophie said. "It gave them an excuse to drink something stronger. If women had been in charge, they'd have put the ban on something else."

"Probably so," Betty said. "We don't have to worry about those things anymore. You have something on your mind today. I see the look in your eyes. What is it?"

"I could never hide my thoughts," Sophie said. She paused a moment, then mustering her courage continued, "I don't mean to pry, but I've wondered. When Peyton died in Philadelphia, did you ever think that he might have been poisoned?"

"The thought crossed most everyone's mind," Betty answered. "You remember that the crown had published a hit list of colonists whom they said were the enemies of Britain. Peyton's name was on the top of the list."

"Dying so suddenly as he did, you must have thought of foul play."

"At first, yes. But not for long. He was dining in a restaurant with friends. Tom was with him."

"Who?"

"Tom Jefferson. No one else there was harmed. They were all patriots. Why would a murderer have killed only Peyton when he could easily have gotten them all?"

"He was top of the list."

"True, but he was also grossly overweight. He always indulged himself in anything he wanted to eat or drink. Tom told me all the particulars of how it happened. I feel certain that he had a stroke. It could have happened anywhere."

"I keep wondering about Thomas Blount," Sophie said. "I've told you the story. I still worry that he may have been poisoned."

"Poison works rather quickly," Betty said. "Wasn't he alone when he fell?"

"Yes, but…"

"I thought he'd been sick for sometime."

"All winter."

"It was probably just a coincidence that he died after the meeting of the Committee at his house."

"Actually, several weeks later."

"Forget about it."

Sophie allowed her eyes to wander around the spacious parlor of her friend's home. She had come to love the elegance of simplicity that was found in many Virginia houses. It looked as though the Virginians had taken everything good and sturdy from the English styles and rid them of all their superfluous and overly ornate qualities. The furnishings, like the people, were devoid of the useless. There was a solidity about them that gave comfort.

"I've finally heard from my son, John," Sophie said. "He has arranged for me to return to England."

"Don't go, Sophie. I'd miss you so."

"But I've a grandson I've never meet. I didn't even know that John had married. I must go."

"I can't picture you a grandmother. You're much too glamorous."

"Fa de dah. I feel older than Methuselah. John also established some credit for me so that I could pay my debts before leaving. The first thing I want to do is buy a present for you. What would you like?"

"How nice. Do make it something for the garden. Something living."

"Then there's Walley. He saved my life, you know."

"Not really, Sophie. He did what he was told. Joshua Benson is the one who stuck his neck out for you. If he'd been caught helping you escape, there's no telling what might have happened to him."

"I never thought of it that way. He was a Committee member himself."

Committees don't like members who act out of accordance with the group.

"Umph," Sophie said.

"Have you seen him?"

"Who?"

"Joshua."

"Here, you mean?"

"He's been here on business of some sort, but I heard he left for Richmond. Not much business goes on here in Williamsburg now that Richmond's the capital. When do you think you will be leaving Virginia?"

"Soon as I can arrange passage. It'll probably take a few weeks."

XI

Sophie took a last look out the window that faced toward the Randolph's house and garden. The dogwoods were in bloom as well as the Judas and the Quince. She watched a lady cardinal fly by her window and land in one of the dogwoods across the street. "My lady's love will be following soon," she said. "It never fails."

Just as she finished speaking the red, male cardinal appeared and followed his mate to sit beside her on the branch of the white-blossomed tree. "I told you so."

"Is there anything more I can do for you?" Mrs. Hays asked.

"I think not. All the luggage has gone down except for the hat box. I'll carry that myself. Let me know when the coach arrives, and thank you for all you've done."

"I'm sorry to see you leaving, Sophie," said the older woman. "I've become right fond of you."

"Thank you, Mrs. Hays. I know I'll miss you. I'll just sit down in my chair to rest a bit until the coach arrives."

Sophie had not been resting long when she heard the clatter of hoof beats coming down the road and heard the coach stop before the house. As the time of her departure neared, she was becoming apprehensive. The long sea voyage loomed as a large obstacle now that she knew how tedious it could be. She could feel herself getting nervous over the idea of actually leaving. It all seemed so final.

It will take the driver a while to secure all the baggage to the roof of the coach. I have a few minutes more.

A knock came at her door. She picked up her handbag and the hat box to leave.

"Sophie," Mrs. Hays said, "There's a gentleman to see you."

"Really?" Sophie said. "Show him up." She waited thinking it must be Will Browne coming to say goodbye. The door to her quarters opened, and she was stunned to see Joshua Benson standing before her. She let out a little gasp of shock.

"Don't be frightened," he said moving into the room and closing the door behind him. "I heard that you were leaving. I'd thought I would have at least until the final peace treaty was signed. You're off to a fast start."

"I found a Dutch sea captain who would take me," Sophie said.

"Are you eager to go?"

"Well, I... That is..."

"You should have waited for me to have a chance to square things with you."

"I don't understand."

"The debt," Joshua said. "You must have known that I'd square things when I could."

218

"I... I..." The hat box fell from Sophie's hands.

"I'll get it," Joshua said moving to her side. "I was in Richmond attending to the sale of some of my land across the mountains. It will be opened to new settlements soon," Joshua said. He looked Sophie straight in the eye. "When the final peace treaty is signed, new immigrants will flood in here from all over Europe. The price of my acreage across the mountains is already trading at vastly increased prices."

"You're bragging, Sir."

"To be sure. I'm trying to impress you. I've come to tell you that I have sold enough of the land rights in the Ohio country to pay off my obligations to Cary and Brewster. The credit is already in the process of being transferred. It will be in London before you are."

Sophie was aware that Joshua was standing very close to her. She could feel his eyes on her face. Her breath shortened. She looked at him as though she had never seen him before. She could feel her heart pounding. "I thought you hated me for your debts," Sophie said.

"Hated you?" Joshua said, moving a step closer without taking his eyes from her. "I haven't stopped thinking of you for a day since you rode off four years ago, but hate never entered my thoughts."

Sophie started to speak. Her mouth moved, but no words came out. She looked at Joshua again and could feel her eyes start to water. A tear began to trickle down her cheek. Their eyes were locked in an embrace. Joshua moved his face closer to hers. Slowly he moved his lips down toward hers and waited.

Sophie didn't move. She could feel her knees begin to buckle. His arms moved around her waist, and his lips touched her own. She stiffened for a moment, then let loose the flood of emotion that had been building within her. Feeling him crushing her body to his, she softened her lips, relaxed them and began to kiss him in return.

XII

"This coach can't wait all day," the driver said. "I've had her things stored for half an hour now. How much longer's she going to be?"

"I don't know what could have happened," Mrs. Hays said. "I'll just go and see."

The old lady climbed the stairs and knocked loudly on Sophie's door. At first there was no response. Mrs. Hays knocked again. "Sophie," she said. "The driver wants to go."

The door opened only a crack. Mrs. Hays could see that Sophie's bonnet was off, her hairdo askew and her dress buttoned up the wrong way. "Well, I never," Mrs. Hays said. "Such goings on in my own house."

"Mrs. Hays," Sophie said. "Tell the driver to unload my things and have them put in Mr. Benson's carriage. Here's something for the driver's trouble."

"Well, I never," Mrs. Hays said.

Sophie closed the door. She could hear Mrs. Hays stomping down the stairs. Joshua put his arms around her waist again. They heard Mrs. Hays say, "All them clothes. I should of known." They both burst out laughing.

THE IMPRESSED
1813-1815

I

Sally Browne was sitting on a large, burlap-covered cushion with her long, linen skirt tucked discretely around her knees and ankles, staring forlornly at the multi-colored primroses she had just been tending in her aunt's Williamsburg garden. So discouraged was she with her work that she was unaware of the tall, neatly-dressed, young man, of about her same age, who had let himself in the white, picket gate and walked around a boxwood-edged, rose bed to visit with her.

"Why so unhappy on this beautiful spring day, Sally?" he questioned.

Startled, Sally turned to see John Bowdoin, whom she had known since the year she arrived in Williamsburg to live with her aunt and uncle, the Cockes. They had gathered her up and taken her to live with them after the death of her parents, both of whom had died when she was only five years old.

"Oh, John," she said smiling. "You scared me. It's a beautiful day alright. Come sit with me. I ought not to be sad on such a gorgeous day. It's wrong of me."

"Maybe I can help," John said as the two fell into the familiar way of conversation that they had enjoyed with each other since childhood.

"It's just that my flower bed never looks as well as the others. Auntie has the entire garden parceled out to various members of the family. This bed is the one I'm responsible for, and it looks the worst of all. I never seem to do things right. I ought to be able to do things as well as the others, but somehow I never can. Everything I try turns out wrong."

John seated himself on the grass opposite Sally and gave her face an approving study. "What else have you been trying to do?" he asked. "These flowers couldn't cause such a down mood."

"Probably not," she answered, turning her face away from him.

"Fess up."

"You're getting mighty bossy."

He stared at her without answering for a moment until she nervously continued. "Well it's everything, cooking and sewing, drawing and singing. I ought to be able to learn everything that Auntie labors to teach me, but...... but."

"But I think there is something more," he pressed on.

"Well, it's."

"It's what?"

A long pause followed before she was able to let out her confession. "It's that now they think I ought to get married and move back to Four Mile Tree."

"Heavens, you'd have no trouble accomplishing that," he laughed. "I thought you had a serious problem."

"But you don't understand. No one ever does. I know I ought to move back to my own home, and of course, I couldn't go alone. But I feel certain that the reason they are so eager for me to go is that I never do anything right."

"Did they tell you that?"

"No. Of course not. But I'm sure it's so. They say that Four Mile Tree can't go on much longer without an owner present. How could I put Four Mile Tree to rights? I can't even grow primroses much less tobacco and wheat. I'm sure I'd fail at that too."

"That would be your husband's responsibility."

"But I don't want to get married, and I don't want to leave Williamsburg to live with a colony of Negroes in the country. I much prefer to live right here in town. I like to have friends around. I like pretty houses with nice flower gardens and tame pets, not fields of smelly tobacco and thickets full of snakes. Why would anyone want to live in the country when they could live in a pleasant town like this?"

"The country can be pleasant too," John said, "once you get used to it. You have a fine house there and a number of slaves."

"The slaves. The slaves. You sound like Uncle. He says I have obligations. He says I must put Four Mile Tree to rights so that it will be there for my children. He says I have an obligation to the slaves too. I know I ought to feel something for them, but I can't even remember them. I don't want to get married, and I don't want to leave Williamsburg to live with a mess of Africans in the country. I ought to care about them, but I don't."

"My stars! Have you any idea how many times you said 'ought' in the past few minutes. I think you ought to be forbidden to use that word."

"There!" she said bursting into spontaneous laughter. "You said it too."

John kept his eyes intently on her face as a large lump rose up into his throat. "You have no idea how beautiful you are when you laugh," he said. "You ought to do it all the time."

II

Buelly, still buttoning his trousers, opened the door of his cabin. He ran his fingers through his graying hair and beard, rolled the sleeves of his shirt higher and stretched apart the sides of his collar so it would rest out on his shoulders. The air was heavy with humidity even though summer had just begun. A swarm of gnats danced around his head, particularly his ears, causing annoyance. He tried to shake them loose as he walked up the path from the slave cabins toward the big house.

Buelly reached the circle in front of the land-entrance to the house, and turning to look down the lane, saw the sheriff approaching on his bay gelding.

Now what he coming here for? Ain't I doing everything I's suppose to do?

Buelly watched quietly as he saw the sheriff look appraisingly at the handsome, Georgian-style house that stood at the end of the road with its back to the gardened slope that descended to the river. The house was shuttered and locked, giving it the air of being a deserted manor house in some old fairy tale. Long vines had grown into some of the boxwoods that graced the front of the house giving the usually neat-looking plants a tangled and tired look.

The gelding's stride had caused a pale, colored dust to rise from the path, providing evidence that the plantation's soil had grown thin. Many of its nutrients had been drained out by over-production in the last century and in recent years little had been done to replenish it. The entire place looked seedy. Absentee ownership did not enhance its charm.

"Hello, Buelly," the sheriff called out. "That you?"

"'Low, Mister Sheriff. Course it's me."

"This place sure was better looking when the Brownes were here. Looks like it has kind of died out along with the male heirs. Was a sad day when the last of them died leaving this place and all you Nigras to a five-year-old girl. Been years of waste, I'd say, waiting for her to grow up and come back."

The sheriff pulled his horse, Governor, to a halt and surveyed the long line of slave cabins, many now uninhabited and falling into decay. They stretched down to the woods dividing Four Mile Tree from Mt. Pleasant. "Used to be fifty or sixty Nigras living in those cabins. How many are here now?"

"'Tween twenty and thirthy. Most of them old folks or else they's Bea's and my children. What's you got you wants me to do, Mister Sheriff?"

"Two dozen Nigras on the place and you're the only one in sight. Governor scratched one of his hooves in the dry dirt while the sheriff pushed his wide-brimmed straw hat to the back of his head. The flies and mosquitoes that had kept their distance while he was moving, swarmed around him when he came to rest. A regal-looking pheasant marched saucily out of the bushes as though to parade his elegance before the world, then seeing the intruders, quickly turned back toward his cover.

"Sorry if I got you up, Buelly."

"I was just taking a snooze. Not much else to do 'round here these days."

A group of children came from the cabin. Buelly walked toward them. The slowness of his movements gave evidence that age had brought misery to many parts of his body.

"It's kind of sad seeing this place all shut up, Buelly."

"Ain't looked nothing but sad since the Master and Missus died," Buelly said. "That's been 'bout fourteen years, I reckon. What year is this here one, Mister Sheriff?"

"It's 1813, Buelly. End of June, start of summer, 1813."

"I knows the month. I just forgets the year."

"How's Bea? She had any more children since the last time I was here?"

"Bea's good. Just had a beautiful baby girl 'bout a month ago."

"How many's that?"

"Thirteen," Buelly answered, with a wide grin that displayed large gaps where teeth had previously been.

"Seems to me like it would be good to have some of your boys out working the fields." the sheriff said.

"Ain't much reason for it since the embargo," Buelly answered. "The crops can't go nowhere so we just tends our greens and takes care of the chickens and sheep. Overseer from Mt. Pleasant comes to tell us what to do. He the boss of Four Mile Tree as well as the Cocke place. Says he can't even sell the crops from Mt. Pleasant so ain't no need to grow no more."

"The Embargo has been over for four years, Buelly."

"Oh yeah. I remember now. What that other thing they talk about?"

"You mean the blockade? The British blockade?"

"That's what I mean."

"That's still in place for sure," the sheriff said with a deep sigh. "That's kind of what I came to tell you about. Some of my news is good and some of it's bad, but I've got to tell it all."

"I's obliged, Mister Sheriff."

"To start, there has been some nasty fighting down by the bay. You know that we are fighting the British again and that their ships are all over the bay and up and down the rivers too."

"I know 'bout that. How come we have to fight again? I thought we whooped them that time me and Big Boy helped tote the cannons over to Yorktown."

"It was over, Buelly, but now it's flared up again. We've been at war for over a year. They say it's because the British were impressing "

"They what?"

"They were stealing the sailors off our ships at sea, but actually it's about a lot of things."

"Will the angels come to help again?"

"The who?"

"The soldiers in the white uniforms."

"You mean the French?" The sheriff chuckled. "No, the British

225

and some others are keeping them busy fighting in Europe. Besides, they don't like us any more than the British do these days." There was a pause while the sheriff thought about how to continue. "What I came to tell you is that last week the British sailors came ashore at Norfolk and did terrible damage there. After stealing just about everything they could take away, they burned the city. Then they crossed over to Hampton where the British sailors and some French prisoners they had on their ships went wild. There were about a thousand people living in Hampton and hardly any family survived unscathed. The British burned, pillaged, murdered and raped not only the women but the children too. It was a horror scene. I don't like to talk about it, but it's my duty to warn everyone on the river front in this county. Some of the British ships have been seen nearly this far inland. It's possible that one might send some boats ashore here for food and water. I come to tell you two things, Buelly. If that should happen here, you have got to get the women and girls hid somewhere. Better hide the little boys too. These men are gorillas."

"They's what?"

"They're wild animals. Been cooped up in the hold of ships for months. They got no control. The second thing is that you're not to fight them. Just give them the food they want and get rid of them as soon as you can. I don't mean to alarm you unduly. They haven't been seen this far inland yet. Still, if you do see the ships here, remember what I said. Send the women and children far into the woods. Don't resist them. Give them all your chickens, your food stuff, whatever they want,"

"Then, what my family going to eat?"

"We'll take care of that if they come, Buelly. I don't think they will."

"I hopes that was the bad news, Mister Sheriff. Can't be nothing much worse than that."

"Right, Buelly. You'll like the rest. I been asked to tell you that Miss Sally is getting married in Williamsburg in two weeks time. Afterwards, she and her husband will be coming back to live at Four Mile Tree. The old house will come alive again, and there will be lots of company to keep you busy."

For a moment the sheriff thought that Buelly had not heard him as he showed no discernible reaction. Then without changing his facial expression, Buelly began slowly shaking his head as though denying acceptance. Silence continued as the full impact of the sheriff's message began to sink more deeply into his consciousness.

"You are happy to hear the news, aren't you, Buelly?" the sheriff asked.

" 'Course I be glad if she be happy, Mister Sheriff." Buelly said without lightening the tone of his voice.

"That's better," the sheriff said as he continued studying Buelly's face. "Don't forget the rest of the things I told you. Someone's life could depend on it."

"Yes, sir."

"Well that's all I have to say. My duty's done here. Someone will be coming over from Mt. Pleasant in a day or so to tell you what to do to get the house opened up. Miss Sally will probably be here by mid-July."

"Mister Sheriff, don't you want to give us some rifles so's we can fight off the sailors? We ain't got nothing but some old guns what uses buck shot to kill rabbits and birds. Won't kill no person least they be 'bout close enough to kill with your hands anyhow."

"Buelly, you know I can't give you any rifles. The law forbids it."

"Ain't right, Mister Sheriff."

"I know, Buelly, but that's the way it is. Take care of things, old fellow. You can do it." Turning his horse to leave, the sheriff called back, "My best wishes to Bea. Take care of her."

"I always has," Buelly said, shaking his head in frustration.

III

It was late afternoon before Buelly got around to telling Bea the news that the sheriff had brought. Just before sunset, as the clouds in the western sky began taking on the tinge of apricot color that often preceded the day's end, he asked her to walk over to the box-wood terrace of the big house where they could get the best view of the river. With the long shadows of twilight adding eerie shapes to the familiar scene, he told her about the disgusting and violent things that the British soldiers had done at Hampton and what the sheriff said they must do if any seamen tried to come ashore at Four Mile Tree.

Bea was quiet for a long while. Then Buelly saw her whole body shiver as she contemplated all he had said. After some thought, her practical mind began to work. "Can't you have the boys to tear down the pier?" she asked.

"I ain't got no right to tear down Miss Sally's pier," Buelly answered. "And she be planning to come home to it in a few weeks."

"Miss Sally coming here?" Bea questioned. "But she ain't done that since we buried her ma and pa years ago."

"She getting married, Bea, and coming back here to live. Things'll be mighty different from now on."

"Coming back?"

"We has had this place to ourselves what with the overseer being at Mt. Pleasant most all the time."

"Seems so strange."

"Miss Sally's husband be running things here soon."

"You don't sound so good 'bout her coming back."

"I knows. But somehow it don't seem right to me to be owned by a little girl. It was different when Master Browne was here. He was a big man. I been the boss 'round here for a long time now. I won't like being told again, 'specially by a little girl."

"She can't be a little girl if she's getting married," Bea said. "You is still remembering her the way she was when her ma and pa died. You ain't seen her since Mrs. Cocke came and took her off to live in the city. She got to be grown up by now."

"It going to be a big change, Bea. I's getting too old for change."

"Look at that sun go down," Bea said pointing to the colorful spectacle.. It takes all day long to move across the sky, then it slips down behind the mountains in 'bout a minute. When it makes up its mind to go down, it just does it in a hurry. We better get back to the baby. She'll be crying for me soon. Buelly, I been thinking. There must be something we can do to keep the sailors away. It's hard to fight without no rifles. What if they comes in the night and catches the women and girls here?"

"Be bad," Buelly answered putting his arm around Bea's shoulders as they started back to the cabin. "Maybe just a few boards could come off the pier. That'd slow them down if they tries to come in the dark. Tomorrow, I'll get the boys to help me."

IV

Several miles east on the James River, as the large, orange sun descended toward the horizon in the western sky, the *H M S Channel Dragon* was slowly maneuvering into a cove behind the western part of Hog Island on the south shore of the river.

The *Dragon* was a two-masted, square-rigged brig, a middle-sized war vessel that carried 10 guns and required a crew of thirty-six. Currently the captain was managing with only twenty-five. Seamen were hard to get and even harder to keep. Then, to add to the shortage, there had been the messy fracas at Norfolk and Hampton where several of the crew members had been killed. The reduced number of men meant that there would be hammock space for all during the night, a great luxury on the tight ship, but it also meant fewer hands to man the cannons in time of danger. Most of the men would be needed just to sail the vessel should quick maneuvering become necessary.

The lower hold of the brig could accommodate twenty-four hammocks, but with the sailors on the night watch eliminated and the reduced size of the crew, the number of hammocks swinging was only fourteen. Flick placed his hammock as near to Scotty's as he could, leaving a wider empty space between the two of them and the others. He removed both his shirt and britches and with little effort swung his body into the knot-laced sack. Once all the men were aloft and gently swinging to the rhythm of the tidal waters, Flick turned his head to Scotty and placing his fingers to stretch his eyelids up indicated that Scotty was not to fall asleep. The two, neither more than seventeen years old, waited, often exchanging glances with each other, until they could hear the deep breathing of slumber from those nearby. At last, it seemed safe to speak.

"We going tonight?" Scotty asked in a soft whisper.

"No," Flick said using only his lips. "They're watching the piece of land to the woods. Too dangerous."

"How'd you know?"

"Heard the Captain say so. He told Lieutenant Cheatham to put an extra watch on that strip of land that connects the island to the mainland. He don't want to lose no more crew."

"Might not get another chance."

"Have to wait. Captain said this island was used for pigs. Kept the settlers from having to build fences."

"How'd they know whose pigs was whose?"

"Who cares?"

"Why're we going up-river tomorrow?"

"There's a heap of militia boats in these creeks. They're laying in wait to catch us."

"Then why?"

"Captain needs more crew. He too short handed to fight and sail at the same time."

"You mean the *Dragon's* hunting to capture men?"

"Please, Scotty, the term is press."

"Don't care what you call it."

"Captain would say he had a duty to his crew."

"Hah!"

"They got us swinging early tonight 'cause we're heaving anchor before dawn."

"We're missing our chance."

"Don't worry, Scotty. Have to wait," Flick said. He took command in all matters involving the two. "Got loose before."

"They got you back"

"Won't this time."

"How'll I know when?"

"I'll call you by your real name. What is it?"

"Oliver."

"No!"

"Your's any better?"

"Don't got any name but Flick."

"How come?"

"None of your beeswax."

Scotty didn't reply. For a moment he looked fixedly at Flick who was his only hope of salvation. Then he turned his bare torso to the wall. Swollen welts from the one hundred lashes of a cat's tail to his back shone angrily in the near dark. Flick stared at the markings.

One hundred lashes for stealing some food. Flick shook his head. And not a soul got punished for the beastly happenings at Hampton. Serving on a British ship is like no other torture. Any risk is worth trying if it's the only chance, but no need to be fool-ish. Time will come.

V

By the time the morning sun had mounted the tree tops and sent its piercing hot rays across the glistening water, Buelly and his two oldest teenage sons were on the pier at Four Mile Tree prying up several yards of planking that served to connect the river's shallow edge with deeper water. The wood was strong and the nails that held it in place had rusted in the salty air, making it difficult to loosen their hold.

The bare shoulders of the black youths working on the pier were covered with sweat as they toiled in the humid, July heat. Their bodies glistened as the sun deflected from the particles of water that ran down their backs. This was the hardest work they had done all year, and they were in a hurry.

"You think they's coming, Pa?" Tom asked.

"Naw."

"Why not?"

"Nobody comes here no more."

"Sheriff come yesterday."

"Ain't been nothing 'cept watermen after bass and shad 'round these parts. They never comes ashore."

"Sheriff came."

"War's down at the bay."

"What you working so hard for then?"

"Working 'cause your Ma wants me to. She's scared. Want to finish 'fore breakfast. I's hungry."

"Me too."

At eight o'clock, Bea's breakfast gong sounded. Buelly and the boys stood to follow their yearning for food. Tom, looking at the river to the east, caught the first glimpse of the British brig round-ing the curve. It was partially hidden by the high knees of the ancient cypress tree. "Pa," Tom screamed . "They's coming."

Buelly took one look at the river and began a painful rush up the steep slope that led to the terrace above. Before he could reach the top, Tom passed him and was running to the cabin, calling out to

Bea, "Ma, they's here. Get the girls and run."

VI

On the bridge of the *Channel Dragon*, Flick, with a mixture of salt and vinegar in one hand and a polishing cloth in the other, was working his way along the ship's brass railing to a spot where he could hear what the officers were saying.

Captain Harris was leaning with both his elbows resting on the railing. His right hand was raised to cradle a pipe that he held firmly between his teeth. It was early to begin smoking, but he had been addicted to the taste and sweet aroma of tobacco for many years.

"This is where they grow our tobacco, Lieutenant," Captain Harris said to his companion. "Guess I shouldn't be mad as I am at those who provide us with such pleasure, but somehow I can't cool my fury at the American bastards for declaring war on us while we were fighting Napoleon."

"It was a bit unsporting," Lieutenant Cheatham said. "They should be helping us, not causing another diversion."

"They're greedy bastards through and through," the Captain said. "Thought we would be too busy to fight back. We'll show them. They won't seek war with us again when this is over."

"You think this was caused by our impressing a few of their sailors?" the younger man asked.

"Hell, no. This war's over Canada. They thought our hands were so tied fighting the crazy general, that they could rip off our land. First thing they did after putting together a skimpy army, was invade Canada."

"They miscalculated there," the Lieutenant said.

"They miscalculated everywhere, but we'll show them, the bastards."

Lieutenant Cheatham thumped his fingers against the railing. "There're some mighty fine looking houses on this river," he said.

"Yes, siree! All worked by Negro slaves. It's easy living for the owners. They just sit back on their soft asses and watch the niggers do all the work. They got nothing to do with their time but to think up ways to grow richer, and one way they thought up was to try to steal Canada while we were out risking our necks to save Europe." Captain Harris' voice rose with emotion. "I'd go in and raid one of those places if I thought they had any men there strong enough to learn seafaring, but the landowners around here are soft as rotten peaches. I'm looking for an American vessel with seamen on it."

The *Dragon* was traveling up river about a half mile from shore when she rounded the bend near Four Mile Tree. Flick looked out in the direction of land. He saw Lieutenant Cheatham put his binoculars to his eyes. "What's going on over there?" the lieutenant asked, handing the binoculars to the Captain.

"Looks like the darkies are in a dither," the Captain said after raising the glasses to his eyes.

"Were they fishing? Must have caught a big one."

"Looks like they were repairing the pier," the Captain said.

"House at the top of the bank looks closed up," the Lieutenant said. "All the windows are shuttered."

"Owners must be gone."

"Do you think some of those darkies would like to learn how to sail? They don't look like soft peaches to me."

"No harm in asking them, Lieutenant," the Captain said slapping his junior officer gleefully on the back. "Prepare the barges. We'll send some hands to find out."

Flick continued his polishing until the officers departed. Then he rushed to find Scotty.

VII

There was no one in sight near the pier when the *Dragon* dropped anchor in the early morning and launched barges to carry members of the crew from ship to shore. Even Sam, the last of the Negroes to quit tearing up the boards, had vanished. Fifteen sailors, including both the Captain and the first mate made their way by barge to land and then started to climb the steep slope to the manor house with pistols drawn and swords at the ready. From the ship, it appeared that there would be no resistance.

Flick and Scotty had not been allowed to go with the invading party. As their loyalty was questionable, they were routinely kept prisoner when the others went ashore. Today was no exception. They stayed at the rail of the *Dragon* much of the day under guard of Lieutenant Cheatham, watching for signs of activity and listening, always listening. Unfortunately, little could be heard.

"How come you got no other name than Flick?" Scotty asked after a long silence.

"'Cause I don't," Flick said.

"Flick's no real name."

"It's mine."

"How come?"

"'Cause I's a pickpocket."

"You're ribbing."

"Don't believe me?"

"No way."

"Where's your pocket knife?"

"Here in my..."

"No it's not." Flick said taking it from his own pocket and tossing it to Scotty.

"How'd you do that?" Scotty asked.

"I flicked it away." Flick laughed.

"You really was a pickpocket. Son of a gun."

"Told you."

"How'd you learn?"

"Had to learn some way to live. Ran away from the orphanage as soon as I was a man. Wanted to find enough to eat so I just left."

"Your parents dead?"

"Never had no parents. Just came to life in the orphanage. Never had nobody."

"How'd you get by?"

"Just lived around the streets. Picked up food where I could find it. Stole whatever else I needed."

"Where'd you sleep?"

"Anywhere. Winters was bad, but it stays warmer near the sea. I hung around the docks, 'cause the sailors is loose with their money when they get ashore. They're drunk most of the time. Makes it easier."

"When you first go to sea?"

"When they picked me up. Press gangs is always on the prowl where sailors hang out. They got no time to find out if you know anything about sailing when they throw a blanket over your head and tie you up. They always hope to get an experienced sailor, but they take what they get. With me they just got an experienced pickpocket."

The sun was directly overhead sending scorching rays through the cloudless, July sky when Flick and Scotty heard the first gunshots. "They been up there for hours, Flick. You think they're raping women and children again?"

"Can't tell, Scotty."

Just as Flick spoke the air was rent with the sound of rapidly repeating gunfire that sounded like the popping of Chinese fireworks.

"Oh, God! I hate this."

"The gunfire seems to have stopped, but they're still up there."

"Was it Captain Harris' ship that nabbed you?"

"No, another. I thought we was going to fight the French, but the ship sailed to Boston. Wasn't all that bad till after I ran away in Boston."

"What'd you do there?" Scotty asked.

"Picked some more pockets. But it started getting cold. Gets a lot colder in Boston. I needed shelter for the winter so I signed up to be an American citizen. They take most anybody, 'specially sailors. There are not enough sailors anywhere. After I got my papers, I signed on a Quaker whaling ship headed for the South Pacific."

"Then what?"

"Then the whaler was stopped by Captain Harris' *Dragon* outside of Boston harbor. Captain came aboard to inspect the crew, and the next thing, I was a Brit again, sailing on the *Dragon*."

"We still going to jump ship, Flick?"

"When we get the chance? Ran away before, and I'll keep doing it till I get away."

Gunfire erupted again from the top of the long slope. Soon Flick and Scotty could see some sailors carrying a large, heavy table down the slope. They seemed unsteady. One end was dropped several times as the sailors stumbled down the path. "They're skunk drunk," Flick said.

When the sailors got to the pier, they managed to carry the load more easily until they reached the gap where the planking had been removed. Forgetting the absence of the flooring, the sailor who was walking backwards fell in, dropping his end of the table. The two at the other end fell also and the table toppled into the water. The sailors left to manage the barges dove in and by turning the table so that its top was perpendicular to the water's surface were able to raise it and get it onto one of the barges.

When the barge reached ship, Lieutenant Cheatham exploded. He could see that the table was badly scratched. "Captain won't like that," he yelled. "How'd you get so drunk?"

"Cellar was full of bottles," one of the sailors said.

"Any women up there?" the Lieutenant asked.

"Nobody up there but that huge, old Negro," the sailor said. "House was all closed up, but we opened it, opened more than the doors."

"What was the shooting about?"

"Shooting the pigs and the horses, the dogs too."

"What for?" Flick asked.

"For fun," the sailor said with a smile. "Captain has more things he wants brought down."

"Hell, you can't bring them," the mate said.

"We're the soberest ones," the sailors answered.

"Get below, all of you. Flick, you and Scotty go back on the barge to help with the rest. And mind, I'll have a gun on you all the way."

"Aye, Aye, sir," Flick said, finding it hard to suppress his excitement. "Come on, Oliver. It's our time for shore leave."

By the time Flick and Scotty had reached shore and begun climbing the slope, they encountered a stream of sailors carrying furniture, smoked pig flanks, freshly killed chickens and the few remaining bottles of port and brandy. A small herd of sheep was also being led down to the barges for transportation to the ship.

"What a blast," a red-faced tar yelled.

At the house, Flick and Scotty found devastating wreckage. Evidently, Captain Harris had become quickly inebriated and lost control. The first mate and the boatswain were helping him.

"Lieutenant Cheatham sent us," Flick said to the first mate.

"Guess he had no choice. Captain wants that desk," he said. "Bring it fast as you can. We've got to get out of here."

"Aye, Aye, sir," Flick said.

"We going now?" Scotty asked in a whisper.

"Not yet, Scotty, hold on."

Flick took the drawers out of the desk and motioned to Scotty to pick up one end.

"Why don't we make a run for it?"

"Not yet, Scotty. Got to wait. The two men followed the sailors down the slope to the barges and waited till all had boarded. They then placed the beautifully carved desk at the end of the pier and started to re-climb the slope.

"Where're you going?" the first mate called reaching for his gun.

"To get the drawers," Flick called out.

"Mind, I got you covered," the mate said.

Before they reached the top, Flick and Scotty heard the thunderous sound of a large number of galloping animals. It sounded as though twenty or thirty horses were approaching at a mad pace. Appraising the situation quickly, Flick yelled to Scotty, "Now! Oliver. Run for your life." Flick took off at breakneck speed heading for the nearest cover.

Scotty, somewhat confused by the sudden change of orders, hesitated before grasping the situation. Just as Flick made it safely to a concealing copse of trees, the Surry County militia rounded a bend in the road. Spotting Scotty running alone, they fired several shots. One of the bullets caught Scotty in the neck. There was a sudden burst of blood that squirted out like the water from a whale's spout. Then he fell dead.

Deep in the thicket and unseen by the militia, Flick lowered his head in pain and tears.

Poor Scotty. The only friend I ever had. Never knew no luck. Wasn't smart enough. Looks like he always was destined for a sticky end.

Flick lay prone in the thicket trying not to make a move or a sound. He was far from the house, but looking across an empty field. He could make out figures in the distance. He saw the militia rush by Scotty's body to the top of the embankment where they reined in their horses and stopped.

The barges must be well out into the river. They aren't chasing them.

Flick watched as the guardsmen rode back to the front of the house and dismounted. They seemed dismayed by the senseless damage they found. The carcasses of horses, dogs and pigs littered the premises. The doors to the manor had been torn off and many windows pushed out. Amid all the ruin, Buelly stood talking to the horsemen, holding a large kerchief to his face and from time to time blowing into it.

Lucky they killed all the animals. Can't hide from dogs.

Within an hour, Flick saw the men remount their horses. One of them touched the huge black man on the shoulder, and then they rode away.

Flick didn't move from his hiding place. It was too soon. He could hear his heart pounding. The militia might return.

In late afternoon, he saw a scraggly line of about twenty Negroes, mostly women and children, creep out of the woods on the other side of the house and enter several of the slave cabins.

Flick had eaten nothing since early morning rations aboard ship. By the time twilight was obscuring his vision of both the cabins and the road, he had become ravenously hungry. Looking out at the dead animals in the field, he wondered how he could get something to eat. Then he saw the twisted contortions of smoke coming from the stone chimney of the first cabin. A fire in early July could mean only one thing; food was cooking.

Hungry as he was, Flick stayed put. He knew he needed decisive plans. Two young Negroes came out of the cabin with shovels in their hands. Flick watched as they went down near the apple orchard and began digging. About a half hour later they walked back to Scotty's body, still lying where it had fallen, picked up his feet and dragged him to the hole they had just dug.

"Scotty, Scotty," Flick said. His eyes grew moist. He watched the Negroes put the body into the grave and cover it up. He saw them bow their heads as though in prayer. "Jesus Christ!," Flick muttered, "Those slaves is Christians."

Flick put his hand into his pocket and pulled out several gold coins and a small hard object, a little larger in size, that turned out to be a small, oval, leather case. Releasing the clasp that held it together, he saw that the case contained miniature portraits of two handsome and gentle-looking people.

Be damned. They don't look nothing like the Captain. Why would he be carrying.....? Suddenly he understood, and his plans were made.

Flick saw the Negroes return to the first cabin, where smoke was coming from the chimney. He got up from the ground and stretched. His bones ached from lying so long on the hard ground. His stomach growled. "Hush," he said.

Flick quickly moved across the open field. He expected to have a bullet catch him at any moment, but all remained silent. He reached the cabin and hesitated. He heard voices inside and knew that some were the voices of small children. He could smell meat cooking. His mouth began to water. He moved around the corner of the cabin to the side with the door. The door was wide open. He inched closer in the dark. The fire below the heavy pot in the fireplace enabled him to see into the cabin. He could feel the fear pulsing through his body. He stepped backwards and looked behind him.

There must be a safer way. He was about to run when he felt his arms grabbed, one on one side and one on the other. He was thrown to the ground and pinned down by two heavy-set Negro boys. He was completely helpless.

"Where you come from?" Tom demanded.

"The ship," Flick said.

"Lord above," Bea wailed.

"I'm alone," Flick said.

"What you doing here, boy?" Buelly asked.

"Jumped ship," Flick answered. "I'm American."

"Don't sound like one," Buelly said.

"Lawdy, Lawdy," Bea wailed.

"Need your help to find an American ship." Flick could smell the heavy odors of the pork. His stomach growled again.

"You got a gun?" Buelly asked.

"Just a pocket knife," Flick said.

"Leave him be, Tom," Buelly said. Look outside and make sure there ain't no more. I'll take the knife."

Flick obediently reached into his pocket and tossed the knife to the ground.

"I brought you something else too," Flick said. He reached into his pocket again and pulled out the leather-cased miniatures.

"Land sakes," Buelly said. "These be two little pictures of Miss Sally's ma and pa. You was one of those who tore up the house and stole everything,"

"No," Flick hollered. "They made me stay on the ship most all day"

"How'd you get this then?" Buelly asked.

"I picked the Captain's pocket when they were bringing him down the hill drunk. Those were in it. I want you to put them back."

Buelly opened the clasp of the leather case again, his fury subsiding by the moment, and looked at the miniature pictures of William and Elizabeth Browne, the deceased owners of Four Mile Tree. "Miss Sally'll be happy to get these back," he said with a note of thanks in his voice. "You sure you is an American?"

"Yes," Flick said his voice still wracked with tension.

"You hungry?"

"Starving."

"Get some stew there, Mister Sailor, and start telling us why you's here."

Flick took the wooden bowl that Bea offered him, ladled a large helping of stew for himself and sat down on the dirt floor of the cabin facing Buelly. He noticed that the two youths, who had buried Scotty, were seated with their backs resting against the door jams. He knew that his story had to be good or he'd never get out of the cabin alive. He thought for a moment and then decided that the best story of all was the real one so he began telling them the story of his life.

By the time Flick had finished, his listeners had changed their feelings toward him from suspicion to true sympathy.

"You just stretch yourself out over there, honey," Bea said to Flick. "I knows you needs a good rest."

"We'll think out the rest tomorrow," Buelly added. "You just get yourself a good sleep."

The next morning Buelly, Bea and their children saw Flick on his way. They traded a shirt of Sam's and a pair of pants of Tom's for

Flick's uniform, and Bea affectionately packed him some corn cakes and dried bacon for his journey. It wouldn't be enough to last him until he got to the sea, which perhaps he never would, but at least it would be a start.

Buelly returned Flick's pocket knife and gave directions as best he could, having never been further from Four Mile Tree than Yorktown, the time he had driven the oxen to tote the cannons from College Creek, some thirty years before. "There's only one road going east," he said. "Least ways, I think so, and it ends up in Norfolk. When you find it, just keep walking till you get there. You'll be safe if you just don't talk," he said. "You don't sound like no American 'round here."

VIII

After Flick's departure, a fresh mood gripped Buelly and Bea. They never had thought that white folks could have so much trouble. "He never did have no family at all," Bea said, shaking her head in disbelief after the sailor's departure. "Keep thinking 'bout his being no older than Sam or Tom."

"We's got a better life than some," Buelly said. "But, I still does think it ain't fair."

"Gimme those pictures," Bea said, "I'm going to the house to clean it up. Not any big things can get done till Miss Sally gets here, but I can clean up the blood they tracked in after killing the animals. You better get Tom and Sam busy on those carcasses."

"You know Bea," Buelly said, "might not be so bad for Miss Sally to come home. Least I knows she won't be whipping us with no cat tails for stealing food. We always had what we wanted to eat 'round here."

"Might be kind of nice having her home," Bea said. "Think he'll make it?"

"Who?"

"Flick."

"Don't know. Long way to Norfolk. He do seem to know how to take care of heself though. Guess it depends on what God wants."

"God got him this far. I think he'll make it."

IX

The rattling and crunching of heavy wheels on the entrance lane to Four Mile Tree alerted Bea and Buelly to the fact that Miss Sally had at last returned. They had spent the days since the British plundering of the old homestead doing all they could to clean it up, but the ransacked house was still in disarray.

A closed-cabin carriage, piled high with trunks and boxes on its flat-topped, racked roof, carried Sally and John in the cabin with Bessy and Solomon riding on the outside driver's seat. The slave couple had belonged to Sally's mother and father and had gone with Sally to Williamsburg after their death. They had been dreaming of returning to the country and their extended family for years but had not been able to do so until Sally married and returned herself. Just as Solomon held the reins of the horses trotting before him so Sally held the reins to Bessy and Solomon's lives.

Sally and John, dressed in new finery purchased in Richmond on their recent wedding trip, made a handsome, although disturbingly young-looking, couple as the carriage drew up to the south entrance of the old house. The trunks and boxes, some secured by heavy straps to the roof of the carriage and others being hauled by a cart behind, carried not only their clothing but the family silver and china that had been stored in Williamsburg since the death of Sally's parents, and the wedding presents recently received from their friends. The honeymoon trip to Richmond had provided opportunity for making more purchases and these too were in the attached cart. Altogether, as the carriage approached the house, it gave the impression of unabashed opulence, which contrasted sharply with the home they were nearing.

Sally's heart became fluttery when she first saw the symmetrical lines of the handsomely designed, Georgian residence outlined against the clear blue of the summer sky. She and John were holding hands and laughing gaily as she leaned out of the carriage to wave to Buelly and Bea, standing in welcome on the mansion steps. Then suddenly Sally gripped John's hand with a force he had not known she possessed. Holding her hand firmly and following her eyes, he saw what had caused Sally to stiffen in terror. Her home was in shambles.

Buelly rushed to the carriage and before even saying a word of welcome, blurted out, "The British sailors been here, Miss Sally. They done this to the house. Bea and me, we took good care of the place till little over a week ago when the British sailors come. They tore it all up, broke up the furniture, and carried your pa's desk away, all but the drawers, stole twenty-six head of sheep and all the fowl. Then shot most of the others. We been trying to clean it up for you. I'm Buelly, Miss Sally, and this here's Bea. Welcome home, Miss Sally," he said dropping his head in a bow as he finished.

"Hello, Buelly and Bea," Sally said, giving each of the slaves a handshake as she got out of the carriage. "This is your new master, my husband, Mr. Bowdoin."

"Howdy do, Master," Buelly and Bea said in unison.

"Was there no way to stop them?" John asked.

"We could've stopped them for sure if we'd had guns, Master. There ain't but the one narrow way up from the pier to the house. Me, Tom and Sam at the top of the bank could've stopped them, but Sheriff wouldn't give us no guns. The British what come only had some pistols and swords, but all we had was buckshot. Man can't fight bullets with buckshot."

"Of course not, Buelly," Sally said, now standing beside her husband. "I'm sure you did all you could. Here's Bessy and Solomon. You remember them. They have been eager to return to Four Mile Tree." Her voice cracked as she spoke, and warm tears began to run down her cheeks.

John put his arm around Sally's shoulder and tried to comfort her. "There, there," he said. "We can't let this ruin our happiness. We'll have it all fixed up."

"Oh, John," Sally cried, "I wish we had never left town."

"No, no, my love. It's good that we came," John said steering her away from the others. "We've arrived just in time. We'll not only fix it up, we'll start afresh making the house exactly what you want."

Sally knew that John had been instrumental in bringing about her return. Even her uncle would not have championed the idea so strongly had John not brought great pressure to bear. She sensed he was feeling guilty. He must think it his duty to do all in his power to make the decision turn out to be right.

"We ought to fix it back the way it was," Sally said. "It ought to be like Ma and Pa left it."

"Ought, ought, ought," John said. "I think you ought to have what you want. The house is yours now, not your mother's or father's. You loved the new houses in Richmond. We could..."

"I did," Sally agreed, her spirits making their first improvement. "I loved the Greek columns and the houses with the smooth, plaster walls."

"We'll take your things inside, Miss Sally," Buelly said from the carriage. "Here you niggers, help me cart this stuff."

"Who that callin' me nigger?" Solomon demanded

"I does," Buelly said. "I's the slave boss around here."

"We'll see 'bout that," Solomon shouted. "Field hands don't tell house hands what to do."

"I does," Buelly said, raising his chest and shoulders to display his full size.

Sally and John entered the house through the drooping unhinged doors and stood staring at the wreckage before them. The handsome paneling in the wide, central hall had been pitted and scored as with a sword or perhaps even an axe. They walked through the hall and out the door at the far end of it, stepping out onto the boxwood terrace that remained unharmed above the river.

"This is a glorious spot for a home, Sally," John said. "We'll make the house grand again. We'll put columns wherever you like and stucco the brick to look like ashlar."

"John," Sally said crying and laughing at the same time. "We ought not to spend all our money. We ought to save some for a rainy day."

"This is a rainy day, my love. We need to bring back the sunshine."

Sally smiled, quietly thinking a bit. "If we're really going to do it over," she said, "we ought to have the kitchen moved up to connect to the house. Food always gets cold when it's moved from one building to another."

"That's a very practical idea," John said. "Now, how about a frivolous one?" If you could have any one new thing for the house that you never thought you could have, what would it be?"

"One thing?" Sally said, her thoughts beginning to race. "I don't know. I suppose... Well. Let's see. Oh, I do know," she said beginning to laugh. "It would be an orangery."

"An orangery?" John laughed. "You're always a surprise. I thought you didn't even like to grow primroses."

"I never said I didn't like to grow them." Sally said. "I just never seem to do it right. Anyway, an orangery would be a frightful extravagance. We really ought not to think of it."

X

John hired carpenters and masons from Richmond to put the house in order. When the hammering, sanding, pointing up, stuccoing and painting had all been done, Sally adorned the residence with her fine china, silver and a few newly purchased pieces of furniture. The kitchen was moved up and attached to the main house, much to the delight of Bessy. New columned porticoes were added to the center of the north and south facades of the house, and the brick exterior walls were covered with stucco to resemble the Greek revival buildings and residences they had seen in Richmond. Even a handsome, though largely useless, orangery had been added to fulfill Sally's wishes.

On a clear, warm afternoon in late August of 1814, a day that followed a week of violent storms and high winds, Sally took refuge from the heat of the day by having a canvas lounge chair and several pillows placed in the orangery. There she could stretch out in the cool, stone-walled, flagstone-floored addition to the house. The large, glass windows of the structure let in the morning and mid-day light, but by afternoon the room was shaded from the sun by the house on its western side. The floor and walls had been built of stone to allow for frequent watering of the exotic plants which Sally anticipated planting after her baby was born. So far, the room was adorned with only a few pots of large ferns and some teak-bordered squares of soil that held planted herbs. The room was largely empty but pleasantly cool.

Sally propped herself up enough so that she could work at embroidering a linen baby dress, on which she had been working for some months.

Sakes alive. She held up the small garment. By the time this is finished, it will probably have taken me more time to make it than the baby will have to wear it. I doubt if it will fit for more than a few months.

Every few minutes, Sally had to stop working in order to fan her neck and shoulders with a woven straw fan. Even in the orangery, she found herself frequently perspiring. Although there was another month before the baby was due, she was already uncomfortably large and felt as though the baby had displaced most of her organs, pushing them up to the bottom of her throat.

How could Bea have gone through this fourteen times?

The orangery had another advantage besides coolness. The large windows afforded a perfect view of anything or anyone who might venture down the entrance lane. At the moment, Sally could see John on his horse walking slowly toward the house. She knew that he had ridden over to Mt. Pleasant to see her visiting Cocke relatives.

He'll be full of news. Why, oh why is he dallying?

"You're full to the bursting point," Sally said as John came into the orangery. "I can tell."

"So are you," John said giving her an affectionate kiss and seating himself on a bench beside her. "Baby not here yet?"

"You know it's not due for a month."

"Well, I can always hope, can't I?"

"Oh, you. What's the news?"

"There was lots of it actually. Everyone asked about you and sent their love. That St. George is a rascal if ever there was one. He came in, all dressed up in a little soldier suit, carrying a toy sword. Evidently someone had told him that the sailors who plundered Four Mile Tree had come off of a ship called the Dragon. He asked me to tell you that you should have called for him. 'St. George would have slain the dragon,' he said, demonstrating by slashing the air with his sword."

"Five-year olds are endearing," Sally said, laughing as she did so.

"Then the General spent some time chastising us for spending so much money on the house instead of investing it in things that would eventually pay off, such as the replenishment of the land and rebuilding the livestock."

"They do like what we've done, don't they?"

"But with the war prohibiting foreign trade," John said without seeming to hear her question, "I don't see why."

"They like to be bossy."

"He says it takes a long time to replenish land and build up livestock, and that I ought to be doing it now so that we'll be ready when the war is over."

"Perhaps we ought to follow his advice. He has always done well. His other plantations are even more prosperous."

"The land around here has grown thin with time. Some think that it never will produce again the way it did. There's news from the Blackwater that two of your Blount cousins are planning to leave Virginia to take up fresh land in Georgia."

"Georgia!" exclaimed Sally. "Why not go to the moon?"

"Georgia's trying to encourage people to settle there now that the Indian problem has been solved. They're giving away large chunks of land to anyone who'll move there and work it. A man and his wife can get two hundred acres for themselves and an additional fifty acres for each child, servant or slave they take with them. Then there are large land bonuses for anyone who will build a grist mill, saw mill or a foundry."

"But they would have to start from the very bottom," Sally said, appalled at the thought of the work involved.

"They say there's big money to be made out of growing cotton now that the cotton gin has been found to work. Cotton needs a long growing season. Georgia's perfect for it."

"I can't believe they would give up all they have and start over again. Which ones are going?"

"Joseph and Thomas."

Sally sighed. "Joe was always my favorite of all the Blounts. Was that all?"

"All what?"

"The news, Silly."

"No, but the rest was really bad. Are you sure you want to hear it?"

"Of course, I do."

"Well, do you remember my telling you a fortnight ago that a fleet of some twenty British warships and several transports had been spotted traveling up the Chesapeake Bay?"

"How could I forget? You're not going to tell me they're headed this way. I'll die on the spot."

"Heavens no, we're no longer important enough for that. It was a large fleet commanded by Admiral Cockburn, who was in charge when they burned Norfolk and plundered Hampton last year. Seems they met up with some other ships in the bay, landed troops at Patuxent River and marched on Washington. It was the same day we had that violent storm last week. No one had expected them to come at all, much less that way. They occupied the city with little resistance."

"They didn't capture President Madison, did they?"

"No. The President and his cabinet fled. They didn't capture anyone important, but they occupied the White House and burned it down."

"Our White House?"

"They also burned the Treasury, the Capitol and the War and State buildings. The flames illuminated the sky all night. The next day, the storm that leveled our old oak tree, moved in and put out the fires."

"This war has been nothing but disaster," Sally said. "I've never understood why it had to be."

"Honor demanded it, Sally."

"Honor? Honor? What's so honorable about losing everything you've got?"

Sally saw that John was studying her face. He looked perplexed, as though he feared he had said too much for her good.

"Dr. Warren has gone up to Washington to help with the wounded," he said, thinking it best to change the subject. "He left a message for you that he will be back in ten days."

"He what?" Sally cried out in distress. "But what if... what if?" Just at that moment she felt a sudden rush of warm fluid flow unexpectedly down between her inner thighs. She was so appalled at the doctor's departure that it took more than a moment for her to realize what was happening. Then with quiet resolution she said, "The baby won't wait ten days. It's on its way now. We ought never to have come here."

Twenty-four hours later after a prolonged, dry labor, Sally was delivered of a baby girl. No trained physician had been present, and no painkiller, stronger than brandy, had been available. Bea had done all she could to help, but Bea knew of no way to keep Sally's body from being ripped and torn. Sally lost a great deal more blood than was customary before they were able to staunch the flow.

Sally moved in and out of consciousness for more than a week before the lusty cry of her daughter, also named Sally, brought her around.

"My baby," she said, trying to sit up.

"You just rest your head back on that pillow, sugar. I'll take care of our little girl," Bea said.

"But she needs me."

"She's just fine as she can be. Doctor came yesterday and he says you is to do nothing but rest. You're not to trouble yourself about our little angel. Bea going to do that."

Throughout the fall and winter, Bea nursed Sally Edwards Bowdoin along with her own newborn child. Both babies thrived. However, Sally's health started a slow and steady decline. The color of her cheeks became pale and her body weak.

John spent as much time with her as he could, always remembering that it had been he who had wanted to live the life they were living in the country, not she.

In April, Sally was brought down to the orangery. Pillows were placed again on the canvas chair where she had sat waiting the fall before to hear John's news of his visit to Mt. Pleasant. The large glass windows gave her a perfect view of the activities going on outside. She was happy to be downstairs again but still felt distressingly weak.

She watched John riding around the fields giving instructions to Negroes who were working there. She saw the overseer from Mt. Pleasant arrive and converse with John for some minutes, then move on.

Bea came in and brought Sally, her child. "I's just finished feeding her," she said. "She's just 'bout to sleep. You hold her a while. If she gets too heavy put her down here in the cradle. If she cry, I'll come get her."

"Thank you, Bea. I'll try."

John came into the orangery and sat down near Sally. "The overseer came over from Mt. Pleasant to spread the latest news," he said. "The war's officially over, Sally. We knew it would be, but it's good to hear that it really is just the same."

"I don't feel much like cheering, do you?"

"No."

"What are the men planting?"

"Grass and things. General Cocke's idea. We should have done it last year."

"Why?"

"When the grass, mostly clover, grows, I'm to have it turned back into the soil to enrich it. The general says it works like magic."

"Is there something like that you could do for me?"

"What? I don't understand."

"I need a bit of magic to nourish me too."

"If love could do it, you'd be well in no time," John said.

"I know. I ought to be well by now. I ought to be nursing my child myself and playing with her. I ought to be tending to my garden. I ought to be sharing my love with you, but somehow I never seem to be able to do even the simplest things right."

"Maybe we asked you to do things that weren't right for you," John said. "You never wanted to come back to Four Mile Tree."

"I ought to have wanted to."

"Ought, ought, ought. The men in your life ought to have let you live a life of your own."

In November of that year, Sally died. She was only twenty-one years old. She had been allowed to make no important decisions in her life. The choices were made by the men who loved her, her father, her uncle and John. They felt sure that they knew what was best. She was buried in a large, above ground sepulcher in the brick-enclosed cemetery to the south of the house.

With Sally's death, because of entailment, Four Mile Tree passed on to her baby daughter. The house, the land and all the slaves became the property of a one-year-old child, who in time, like her mother, like Buelly and Bea, and like many young men of the sea, would be impressed into living a life that was pre-planned for her.

THE FAITHFUL
1864-1865

I

The train made a frightful racket as it chugged along the track from Goldsboro north toward Petersburg. This was the main, southern line and had been continually utilized to bring in supplies and troops from the south throughout the three years of war. Petersburg was the hub of the southside lines. It was the crossroads for supplies from the east, the west and the south. Its protection was vital, its vulnerability well-known. For the north, it stood as the brass ring on the merry-go-round toward victory; for the South, it was the last dike before the deluge.

The 38th Artillery Battalion, along with other parts of Hoke's Division, was on the move from Kingston to Petersburg on the urgent orders of General Robert E. Lee. "Return to Petersburg at once," the order had read.

The artillery pieces, the caissons and all their other equipment were loaded on railroad cars at Goldsboro as were all the men not needed to bring the horses. Colonel James Dearing, former commander of the 38th, was leading the cavalry north. Captain Joseph Gray Blount, commander of the Lynchburg Artillery, a battery of the 38th, was on the train with the battalion's equipment and most of the 345 men of his battery.

The train let out a billow of dark smoke. All the railroad equipment was getting old. The engines needed overhaul badly, but there was no time for that. All the trains had to be kept moving.

Inside the lead car, just behind the locomotive, the boxes and crates of the battery's equipment were stacked high. Men stood between the cartons, leaning against the crates for support. The passenger seats, of days gone by, had been stripped away to provide more room. Officers were occupying the four benches attached to the front and rear walls of the car which had been left in place.

Captain Blount and Lieutenant Potts were sitting at one end of the car, Lieutenants Folkes and Blackwell at the other. Andy Green, the bugler, with his instrument strapped against his chest, papoose style, and Jimmy Chenault, the drummer boy, with his tall snare drum resting on his lap, sat on boxes not far from Captain Blount. Their voices traveled backward, allowing their conversation to be heard by their Captain despite the fact that they were speaking low.

"Guess you're happy to be going home. Petersburg's your home, ain't it?" Jimmy said.

"Yeah, but they've all left, my family that is. Guess the house is still there. I don't know."

"Notice you've found a spot for us down near Captain Blount, as usual. You sure do like to stick to him."

"He's the one makes things go right," Andy said. "When the war's over, I'm going to get a job working for him."

"Doing what?"

"Don't know, doing whatever he asks me to do, same as here."

"You sure have got him sitting up high in your mind. You can't see doodley for him."

"Don't tell me Colonel Dearing's a better man," Andy whispered.

"Naw, he's too much of a showoff for me. Always on stage looking for applause."

"Right. Way he pranced around on that white horse at Gettysburg when he should have been getting us more ammunition was the bottom. How come he's a Colonel and Blount's only a Captain anyway?"

"I asked Captain Blount about that after Gettysburg. He said Colonel Dearing is a fine soldier. They were both in the same class at West Point when the war started. Captain said Dearing stood higher in the class than he did and deserved the higher rank. Just between us, Dearing's a Virginian. Blount's from Georgia. Everybody knows Lee's partial to Virginians."

"It ain't fair."

"What is?"

Captain Blount saw Andy look over toward him. He was struggling to suppress showing any reaction to the boys' conversation. Turning his head he found himself looking out at the yellow jasmine that was in full bloom in the swamps. It made a pretty picture from the train. The gold of the jasmine's blossoms covered the distant countryside like gold lace woven in and out amongst the evergreen pines. But he hated the swamps. He was thankful that they were leaving Carolina. He loathed that mosquito-filled terrain. The tall covering trees had made it often seem dark even at high noon, and he had had to be on the lookout for snakes and scorpions as well as the enemy's bullets. He had hated trudging through the swampy area where the wheels of the heavy caissons had constantly mired in the soft, sandy soil.

At least at Gettysburg the ground beneath us was firm. Gettysburg. The thought of it caused his whole body to shutter. Almost a year had gone by since that fateful battle, but he had not gotten over the shock of it. The artillery had been on the ridge bombarding the enemy line when he reported to Dearing, then commander of the 38th, that the ammunition was almost gone. Major Dearing had presumably called for a re-supply and then grabbed the battalion battle flag. Followed by some junior officers, he rode from right to left, backward and forward on his large white stallion, exposing himself to enemy fire and calling attention to the battery's position. He could have gotten us all killed showing off like that. He should have been getting our ammunition chests refilled. Blount would never forget calling out, "ammunition's all spent," just as he saw General Pickett's five thousand men emerge from the woods and charge across the open field toward the enemy, knowing that the artillery Pickett was expecting to support the charge no longer had the power to do so. Thoughts of Gettysburg caused him to let out a low, painful groan.

" You all right, Captain?" Andy asked from where he stood.

"Yes. Sorry. Dreaming, I guess. Didn't mean to bother anyone." He wondered if Andy stayed near him out of fear or to take care of him. The boy was good for him, at any rate. The Captain's stomach growled. It had been empty all day.

The two boys, Andy and Jimmy, were still in their teens despite three years of service. Their parents had given permission for them to enlist on the assurance that they would have light duties and no actual fighting. In reality, they had shot no bullets at the enemy, but had both been in frequent danger, and because of their youth, been given every piddling, niggardly job in the battery that any officer, commissioned or non-commissioned, could push off on them.

"We're in Virginia now, Captain," Andy called out. "I recognized the Roanoke about ten miles back. This must be the Meherrin. The Nottoway can't be far."

"Thank God," Captain Blount said. "We're in..."

All at once the train gave out a loud screech and began to shake and shutter as the engineer pulled the emergency brake in a frantic attempt to stop the train as quickly as possible. Captain Blount and the other officer by his side were thrown forward by inertia and both would have been hurled down the train car had it not been heavily packed with boxes and crates of supplies. Andy reached out to grab Captain Blount as he went hurling forward and helped to break the impact of his motion.

"What the hell?" said the other officer who had been sleeping and luckily was still relaxed when his body was thrown against a forward crate.

"I'll go see what happened," Jimmy said.

"We've stopped," Captain Blount said. "Andy, can you see any of the cavalry alongside?"

"No, sir. The road they were on veered off about ten miles back. They should be getting here soon though. The bridge across the Nottoway should be just ahead. They'd have to come back here to get across the river."

"The bridge," Captain Blount said. "Something's happened to the bridge."

"Bridge is gone," Jimmy called out as he ran back down toward the car he had left. "Yankee cavalry blew up the bridge. Train can't go no further."

By the time Jimmy had returned with the news, Captain Blount had pulled himself together and dropped down to ground from the railroad car. "What now, Captain?"

"Be on the lookout for our cavalry," Captain Blount said to Lieutenant Potts who had followed him off the train. "Colonel Dearing is riding. We'll need our horses and his orders."

"Dust to the right, sir. Must be our men."

When the cavalry arrived with its riding horses and draft animals used to pull the heavy artillery pieces, they were being led by a junior officer.

"Where's Colonel Dearing?" Captain Blount asked.

"Took off a good ways back," the officer said. "Left me in charge of the horses from here on. I think he wanted to go by Mr. Birtchett's farm, sir."

Mr. Birtchett's farm. The beautiful Roxanna, of course. Captain Blount said, "Petersburg is another twenty miles, and the bridge ahead has been destroyed."

"Looks like you're in charge, sir."

"Looks that way," Blount answered.

Most of the soldiers had jumped train and were milling around waiting for orders. "What'll we do, Captain?" Lieutenant Potts asked.

"General Lee ordered this battery returned to Petersburg at once. Order the men to unload all our possessions, Lieutenant. That includes all the boxes and crates of ammunition and food, all the artillery including the two, thirty pounders."

"Lord, Captain! What good will it do here?"

"It won't be staying here, Lieutenant. It'll be going to Petersburg. Blow an assembly call, Andy. I need everyone's attention."

Andy unharnessed the bugle from his chest, put it to his lips and blew the call. The sharp staccato notes pierced the air and brought the men, over three hundred in all, into close formation.

"In the absence of Colonel Dearing, who's on a scouting mission, I'm in command," Captain Blount began. "We're going to get the equipment over the river. First, the train must be completely unloaded. Get our wagons out and load them up. Harness the artillery horses to pull the caissons. Be sure that the strongest draft horses are harnessed to the thirty pounders. We'll have to march up-river until we find a place to cross. Have your weapons ready. The Feds aren't far away. We'll march and haul. Once over the Nottoway we'll head back to the track. I doubt that we'll have to march all the way to Petersburg."

The weary and hungry men followed the orders of their commander. By late afternoon, the battery had succeeded in moving all their gear including the twelve-pound Napoleons and the thirty pounders, across the river and back to the train track on the other side. Captain Blount congratulated the quartermaster. "Admirable job, Lieutenant, you'll have no difficulty finding gainful employment when the war is over. There're more than three hundred men here who'd write a recommendation for you."

"Thanks, but one recommendation from you will be all I'll need. When there's a job needs doing you're the man to get it done."

"Look there, Captain." Andy called out. "There must be five trains waiting on this side of the river to pick us all up."

"Get them loaded, Lieutenant. We may be in Petersburg for dinner. I could use a real meal tonight."

II

A lone candle lit a corner of the large officers' tent that had been erected inside the outer trenches near Petersburg. Poor air circulation made the room excessively hot. Captain Blount sat on a three-legged stool pulled up to a camp table in one corner of the tent where he was trying to write a letter. On a cot, at the other end, Colonel Dearing was stretched out in his stocking feet as he waited for Andy to scrub and polish his boots. It was still early. The sky was not yet dark.

Joe Blount and James Dearing were close friends. They had studied artillery together at West Point and enjoyed a rivalry for rank within their class. When the South seceded from the union, they had resigned from the U. S. Army, traveled south and volunteered their services as soon as they reached Virginia. They had served together during much of the war.

"Are you writing to Maggie?" Dearing asked.

"Yes, I'm trying to catch her up on things. Been no time to write for the last month. There's so much to tell. I'll probably be at this all night."

"She agreed to marry you yet?"

"Not yet, but I'm sure she wants to. Her father still disapproves."

"He's crazy."

"No. He has his reasons. I performed rather badly the first time I met him. Guess he hasn't forgotten about it yet."

"I want to thank you for covering for me on the bridge incident. I should have been there to take charge, but I didn't foresee any problems. You know what it's like to love someone without being able to see them."

"I know."

"The Birtchett farm wasn't that far away. I thought I could slip by there to see Roxanna and get to Petersburg at the same time as the rest of the battalion."

"Well, you did," Blount said. "No harm done. Forget it."

"You going to file a report about the bridge?"

"You're the ranking officer. Why don't you write the report? I'm busy with this letter to Maggie."

"Thanks, Joe. Andy, where're my boots?"

"Here, sir. Just finished them. Can you take yours off, Captain. Might as well polish them as well."

"I can polish them," Blount said. "It's almost time for you to blow."

"I got the time, Captain. Just stay put and stick your foot out. I'll polish them on you."

Joseph Blount obliged by extending his foot to the side. "Have you seen your family, Andy?"

"No, sir. None of them's here. I went by the house today. It's been badly damaged. The people who live next door said my family had gone to Richmond,"

"They'll be safer there. Sorry to hear about the house."

"The whole town's been shot up."

"I saw."

Andy waited until he saw Colonel Dearing put on his boots and leave the tent before saying what was on his mind.

"Aren't you going to report that you was the one who got the equipment 'cross the Nottoway?"

"Colonel Dearing will report what happened," Blount answered. "You're not supposed to hear our conversations."

"Can't help seeing and hearing," Andy said.

Captain Blount studied the boy's face carefully and then turned back to his writing. He had only one piece of paper and so much to put on it. After filling both sides with his small controlled hand, he looked back at the start of the letter.

"Camp near Petersburg, May 15, 1864

My Darling Maggie,

You can't conceive of the amount of hardship, marching and starving we have undergone since last I wrote. The railroad is now cut between Richmond and this place as well as from here south."

He continued reading the two full pages. He was not nearly through, but he had run out of paper. He folded the letter and put it in his pocket. He would have to finish it later. He turned back to Andy who was still polishing. "Isn't it time for you to blow?"

"Yeah, got to get a move on it now."

Minutes later the sound of Andy's bugle pierced the cool, night air, calling the men to quarters. There were tents for the officers, but many of the men would have to sleep in the open. Half an hour later, Joseph Blount was stretched out on a cot in the officers' tent. Quiet had fallen on the room. He was thoroughly exhausted but still wide awake. He wondered what it was that General Lee had called them back to do. He felt certain that the next day would be a difficult one. He listened attentively to each note as Andy played his bugle. The sweet sound of taps gave comfort to the end of the day. He hoped he would be able to sleep through the night.

The following evening, Joseph continued his letter. He had not found more paper, but had so much to tell that he took out the covered sheet, turned it sideways and continued by writing across his own script.

"Camp near Petersburg, May 16

Since writing the above I have been engaged with the enemy. We drove them back with slight loss. General Beauregard defeated them at Drury's Bluff. I am to move in a few minutes on the road to Richmond. We will have to fight our way. We are fighting stubborn and will fight with desperation if it comes to the worst.

Don't you or Mother think that I am killed until you hear from me. I shall take the precaution to let you know if anything occurs. You know I think only of you. Even in the thickest of the fight your face constantly rises to cheer and nerve me to strike with more vigor. I must close. I am moving on the road to Richmond. Write to me often, Maggie, darling. With much love, yours, B."

III

Two days later, Blount's artillery, along with Dearing's cavalry, as part of Hoke's division, received five days' rations and took to the road to position themselves to halt Grant's wide sweep around Richmond. General Lee was fearful that Grant, moving to the east of Richmond on the north shore of the James would hook up with General Butler, east of Petersburg on the southside, to get control of the James River. The river was still the most vital artery to the health or even the survival of the Confederacy.

Nearly a fortnight later, Captain Blount, who had moved forward of the artillery in order to ride with his old friend, and Colonel Dearing were traveling at a slow pace toward their destination, another railroad crossing called Cold Harbor. Moving the artillery pieces was slow work, and the cavalry was moving at an equally slow pace in order for them to stay together. The pace allowed for easy conversation.

"I've been thinking about something you said the other night," Dearing said.

"What's that?"

"You said Maggie's father had good reason to oppose your marriage."

"He has."

"What did you do?"

"Misbehaved."

"I've never seen you do that."

"It's a sad story," Blount said. "I doubt you'd like hearing it."

"I'm wild to hear it. You always seem the picture of propriety to me."

"Five years ago," Blount said, "the first time I met Maggie or her father, they came to call at my home in Talbotton. My older brother, George, was there, my mother and father and the youngest member of our family, my four-year-old brother Bart. You sure you want to hear this?"

"Do I. Go on."

"It was a beautiful spring day, so mother had benches moved outside onto the lawn, and we were being served lemonade there when it happened. George saw that I was taken with Maggie the minute I met her, so he went out of his way to flirt with her just to rile me. I was quite wrought up before anything happened. You must remember that I ran into a few problems at West Point over my hot temper. Guess that's why Papa arranged for me to go there in the first place."

"I remember. No signs of it any more though."

"Three years of war can mellow a man. I think I have my temper under control now."

"What happened?"

"One of our Negroes, Lazarus, was chopping up a downed tree on the front field when we went outside. My brother, Bart, was running around, laughing and jumping about like any four-year-old, happy to be out on such a day. He kept running over to Lazarus trying to distract him from the job he was doing. No one paid much attention. I was just trying to control my irritation at George for monopolizing Maggie. I knew he wasn't really interested in her. Just wanted to get my goat."

"He knows how to do that."

"While we were sipping lemonade, and George was putting on this all-out performance for Maggie's attention, Bart was teasing Lazarus by sticking his finger out over the log to be chopped. Every time Lazarus lifted his axe, he would have to stop. My mother called out to Bart to stop pestering Lazarus, but it didn't do any good. He just kept sticking his finger out and laughing when Lazarus had to stop. I guess it gave him a tremendous sense of power over the black man."

"I shutter to think what happened," Dearing said.

"You've probably got it," Blount said. "Lazarus gave Bart one last warning. He said in a loud voice that got everyone's attention, 'You stick that finger in my way one more time, and I's going to chop it off.' We all turned looking straight at them, saw Lazarus raise the axe, saw Bart stick his finger out still laughing and saw the axe keep coming. It chopped his finger clean off."

"My God!" Dearing said. "I'd have killed the bastard."

"I nearly did," Blount said. "My father grabbed Bart and headed for the house. I just saw red, and forgetting everything except the sight of the axe chopping off Bart's finger, grabbed Lazarus right in front of our guests and nearly beat him to death. George managed to intervene in time to save the poor man. The worst part of it was that Lazarus didn't fight back. He just took his beating like it was his due."

"That's some story, Joe. What happened to Bart?"

"Pa stopped the bleeding, but he'll go through life without his right hand index finger."

"His trigger finger."

"Right. He'll never go to West Point, that's for sure."

"I might have done the same thing," Dearing said.

"It was a costly mistake. Mr. McCone saw my temper in full fury. He'll never forget it."

The two friends continued in silence for a few miles or so, each thinking back on the story. Finally, Dearing said, "I remember a classroom discussion we had at West Point when you said the South ought to free the slaves."

"I never said that," Blount responded. "What I said was that the South would be better off without slaves."

"What's the difference?"

"Plenty. I don't think you can turn four million people, untrained and unable to support themselves, loose on the land, and expect anything but anarchy and chaos. That's why I'm fighting. To get rid of slavery, there has to be a detailed plan that goes far into the future. Let them all loose now, and they'll have no way to eat except by stealing. You wouldn't be able to build enough jails to hold them all. I went into some of the poor houses when we were in New York. The starving Negroes I saw there were some of the most pathetic humans I've ever seen. At least in the south, they are all fed and cared for. They're better off as slaves than they would be in the poor house or in jail. They'll be free eventually though, even if we win this war."

"Why?"

"Because it's happening all over the world. We're late in thinking of the change."

"If we free the slaves, who'll do the field work?"

"The same men who do it now," Blount said. "We'd pay them but only for work actually done - so much for each bale of cotton picked. That would encourage them to work harder. We've bred the laziest group of men on this earth with our slavery. We take all the responsibility of caring for their children and elderly away from them. Their youth and old age are provided for. They live the same way whether they pick one bag of cotton or ten. Why should they work hard?"

"Your views have always been a bit too liberal for me, Joe. Sometimes I wonder why you are fighting for the South."

"Because I love it. It's my home, and I think it's insolent for the damn Yankees to think they can tell me how to run it."

"Let's stop and water the horses at this stream," Dearing said. "We're almost to Cold Harbor."

The men stopped the procession of cavalry, artillery and the infantry following them. They dismounted, took a swig from their canteens and opened up a pack of rations. They seated themselves beside the headwaters of a crystal-clear stream. Their horses were refreshing themselves when Andy Green, the bugler, walked up to them from the marching unit behind.

"Here comes your shadow," Dearing said.

"He's a good fellow," Blount responded.

Upon reaching the officers, Andy gave a sharp salute. The officers responded automatically. "Can I do anything for you, Captain?" he asked.

"How about me?" Colonel Dearing interrupted.

"I meant for either of you," Andy said.

"Matter of fact you can," Captain Blount said. "I was just thinking what a good lookout that tall pine would be. There are no low branches, but Colonel Dearing and I could hoist you up to the lowest limb. Then it should be easy for you to climb the rest."

"All right," Andy said. "The view should be great."

The two officers hoisted Andy up to the first sturdy branch, and he scaled the rest.

"Be sure to test each branch before you put your full weight on it," Captain Blount called out.

"You think I'm stupid or something?" Andy muttered.

Andy got as far as he could safely climb and looked out over the hill and valley below. "Oh God," he yelled. "They're coming. Looks like Grant's whole army. They'll be starting up the other side of this hill in no time. Hey, don't leave me here. How can I get down?"

Before Andy could scramble back down, Captain Blount had summoned his artillery officers and Colonel Dearing was on his horse corralling his cavalry. Blount's battery rushed the guns to the crest of the hill, positioned them with care and loaded them with ammunition. Just as the Bluecoats started marching up the other side of the hill, they were met with a barrage of artillery shells. Their encounter at the battle of Cold Harbor had begun.

The battle raged for thirteen days as the Confederates used all

measures to stop Grant from reaching the James River. Then suddenly Grant's forces disappeared. The Bluecoats had moved out of
their works, leaving the Southerners at first confused. Then, realizing what Grant must be up to, they threw themselves into a mad
rush to beat him to Petersburg. As they raced, on the morning of
June 17th, the Confederate line was attacked again. By late afternoon some of the Federals were crouched in a shallow gully to
escape the artillery shells which sailed above. Captain Blount's gun-
ners were left exposed between the two lines and took refuge
behind a hedgerow. It was visual cover only. From this spot,
Blount's men lay down ricochet fire. He set the elevation of the
guns at a low angle and with a low charge of powder, the shells
skipped across the ground ripping up all along their path. It slowed
the pursuing Yankees and helped the Confederates to win the race.

By the 22nd of June, the Confederate forces were back in the
trenches before Petersburg, but they had not returned to safety.
General Grant crossed the James, and with forces on both sides of
the river was moving up to try to encircle the Confederate city. He
stretched his trenches like a hangman's rope around the head of the
condemned, but he could not make the two ends of the rope meet.

On July 1st from the trenches before Petersburg, Joseph Blount
wrote to his beloved Maggie, "My friends are falling about me
daily. In fact almost every hour some familiar face or name is seen
or mentioned who has paid the soldier's debt. Poor Jamisson
Gardner was shot through the head, lingered for five days in great
pain and died. I would rather have lost any friend than Jamisson.

"Dearest, darling, Maggie, don't be despondent or gloomy. It is
better we should all perish than that the insolent should triumph. I
shall escape, I feel satisfied, but should I fall, don't grieve. I shall act
so that you may be proud of me.

My love for you and the consciousness of being loved in return
make up my chief and only pleasure. In fact, to that can be traced
almost every pleasurable sensation. It colors nature and makes it
wear a brighter look. The battle's fury loses its terror before your
image that I ever keep with me even when the shells and balls are
whistling about me."

Ten days later in mid-July, he wrote to Maggie again. "We have
been fighting constantly since I last wrote. Grant does not seem to
move either to attack Petersburg or to the rear so we may expect a
long tour in the trenches. Already we have been in them longer than

the garrison at Vicksburg. Everything looks favorable for our cause so don't have the 'blues'. I am not despondent, but I fear my fury or rather high temper is growing in strength. I am almost savage at times, when I think how I am neglected and my inferiors promoted over me, men who acknowledge my superiority on the battlefield and ask my advice.

Pshaw, I didn't intend writing about myself.

We are not starving by any means, and I think Mr. Grant is in rather a bad fix. General Lee's army is in good condition, but he seems to have decided to make General Grant attack him behind earthworks for the future. Grant is such a bulldog, he rushes on whatever he meets regardless of circumstances. With McClellan it would not do.

I am sorry to hear that Johnston is still falling back from Sherman's advances on Atlanta. You should be out of harm's way at Talbotton. With a heart full of love, B."

Two more weeks of trench warfare went by before Joseph heard again from Talbotton. He was at his gunnery position in the trenches with his battery when a mail pack was passed through the line for those on duty. The letter came from his mother. He felt particularly close to her. She had often been the ameliorating force between himself and his equally strong-willed father. She had understood him when many others could not. His mother wrote:

"We are becoming more fearful daily. General Sherman is marching toward Atlanta on four roads that run nearly parallel. He has strewn destruction all along the way. General Johnston either can not or will not stop him. General Sherman has vowed to continue in this manner until he reaches the sea at Savannah. We are advised that should he make it through Atlanta, he will continue south, at least as far as Talbotton, before turning east so as to march alongside the rivers flowing east rather than having to cross them. Our little town has virtually no defenses.

Maggie comes to see me frequently, but I can not get her to speak her mind. Are you planning to be married the next time you come home on leave? I feel uneasy over the secrecy in this matter.

Lazarus has run away. I didn't mention it before thinking that he surely would come back. It has been almost two months now so I fear that he has gone for good. The other servants seem content."

Joseph lowered the letter to his lap. He thought back to the dreadful beating he had given Lazarus. Poor devil. When this war is over we will still have the slave problem to deal with. I can't imagine how it will all right itself.

"Captain Blount," said a young man who had crawled through the trench line to reach him. He gave the Captain a jaunty salute then waited for recognition.

"Oh, Andy, it's you. You startled me. Aren't you out of position?" Captain Blount asked.

"No, sir. Colonel Moseley sent me with a message. Handing the captain a folded piece of paper, he continued. "I'm to tell you the latest news about the mining."

"What now? I know the Feds have been digging toward our outer trenches for more than three weeks, and we have been digging toward them from this side. What else?"

"This morning our men, who are digging, started hearing the sounds of the picks and shovels from the other side. The two tunnels have almost met."

"Good God! That means that there is a tunnel almost five hundred feet long between their front trenches and ours. Why hasn't it caved in?"

"They must have shored it up," Andy answered. "Colonel Moseley says the artillery is on all-out alert from now on, night and day."

"His note doesn't say what he thinks they're mining for. Surely they wouldn't be foolish enough to come through the tunnel in a line? We'd pick them off like geese in a corn field."

Andy sat down in the trench as though planning to stay a while.

"Have you gotten any news of your family, Andy?" Captain Blount asked.

"No, sir. No one who has asked about them in Richmond has been able to find out anything. I don't know where they are."

Captain Blount folded and pocketed the letter from his mother. He would wait until he had more privacy to read the rest. Looking up at Andy, he saw that the boy had grown sideburns to match his own and trimmed the rest of his hair to match his own style as well. Both were clean shaven.

"Since I'm here, Captain, there's something else I'd like to tell you about. You know I hear a lot of things people don't know I hear. Often, when I'm doing little chores, they forget I'm in the room."

"That, I've observed."

"Yesterday, I was washing socks in a corner of the officers' tent when your name came up in a conversation about promotions. Seems they have need for Major Read somewhere else. Every one of the officers wanted you promoted to commander of the 38th. That is all but one. I don't want to say who it was, Captain, but he said he felt unsure about your total loyalty to the South. Said you'd always been for freeing the slaves."

Captain Blount gulped. He felt his anger start to rise. Not now. I can't lose my temper now. The danger is too great. Be calm.

Looking away from Andy he tried to force himself to think of a pleasant scene to beguile his fury. Closing his eyes, he saw a cotton field covered with yellow blossoms. In the distance he could hear Andy as he continued, "I wanted to kill him when I heard him say that he doubted your loyalty, Sir. I've seen you fight harder and take more risks than just about anybody in the army. The rest were all for you, but they went on to talk about something else. I just stayed quiet and kept working."

"Thank you, Andy. You better leave the front line now. Tell Colonel Moseley that I received his orders and will act accordingly."

IV

The wait in the trenches grew more tedious every day. There was much shelling of the Union lines, and they were constantly on the lookout for foolish Yankees who raised their heads above the ground. Still there remained long periods when nothing happened. There was nothing to do but talk. Nervous men shared confidences with one another that they would likely not do at any other time.

One afternoon, after they had stopped hearing the pickaxes of the union mining, Captain Blount was seated with Lieutenant Potts in a bunker behind one of their thirty pounders. The mood was somber. They talked in modulated tones with their eyes not on each other but on the Union line ahead.

"Captain, how have you managed to stay alive? You've seen the worst of the war for more than three years, have never been scared and never been wounded. What's your secret?" Lieutenant Potts asked.

"I used to get scared."

"No fooling?"

"It's true."

"What cured you?"

"Something powerful."

"What?"

"I've never told about it."

"Why not?"

"You'd laugh."

"Must be a whopper."

"If I told you you'd think I'd gone berserk."

"I'm scared all the time. Why not take pity on me and share your secret."

"I doubt you'd believe me."

"I'll try."

"Had a strange adventure on my way to Gettysburg. I was riding my mare beside the caisson that was pulling the largest gun when part of the road on a steep, downhill slope gave way under the weight of the gun in front of us. It caused the horse ahead to slip. My horse bolted leaving me on the ground and the gun almost turned over on me. If it had, it would have crushed me to death."

"It didn't?"

"No. It turned up on its left wheel. Then just before reaching the angle of no return, it fell back down, righting itself."

"I don't understand."

"The strange thing about it was that for the few seconds of utmost danger, my person left my body and was perched up on a nearby ledge."

"You what?"

"I knew you wouldn't believe me."

"It needs some explaining."

"The thing was that a total peace came over me. I was perched on a ledge looking down on the scene from above. I saw my body stretched out helplessly on the ground, saw the cannon starting to turn over on me and my only reaction was one of total calm. My thoughts were, 'Oh my, look at that cannon. It's going to crush me to death.' I never thought that it would hurt, and I knew it would-n't matter. I was totally at peace."

"Captain, that story is too much."

"No one could understand it unless it happened to them. As soon as the cannon righted itself, my person was back in my body on the ground. Since then, I've known without question that there is life after death, and that the moment of death involves no suffering. Since then, I've never felt any fear."

"Were you knocked unconscious?"

"No. I just got up and got back on my horse. It was days before I could fathom it all. Then I realized that I'd almost been killed. I had actually started the journey onward, but evidently, I wasn't supposed to die. I was thrust back into my worn and weary old body."

"You've got some imagination, old boy. You ever thought about creative writing for a career?"

"I knew you wouldn't believe me."

A shell whisked over their heads, landed thirty yards behind them and exploded. The earth spit rock and sand. "Those bastards are getting better. Some day they may hit something. What do you think that experience of your means?"

"I think it means there's still something for me to do down here."

"Think it means we're going to win?"

"Of course we'll win. We have to."

V

That night, Joseph read in his bible before darkness overtook him. Then he lay in bed for a long time trying to comprehend what purpose God could have for him that would have caused Him to spare his life back on the road to Gettysburg. He could think of no immediate purpose other than for him to keep fighting the war.

Try as he would to occupy his mind with these serious thoughts, he found that he could not keep Maggie from leaping into his mind and blocking out all else. When sleep finally overcame him, he had just reached out his arms to draw her near. Throughout the night he tossed and turned in his sleep. Just before dawn, he felt Maggie's lips touch his. He was just ready to respond with vigor when he got whiff of a familiar smell and felt a cold, wet object on his lips. Waking suddenly and sitting up with a start, he burst into laughter that woke all his tent mates. The cold, wet object was the nose of a mongrel dog.

"I thought he was Maggie," Joseph said. "I thought Maggie was kissing me."

"You soft head," Potts said, tossing a shoe at him. "You woke us all up before reveille."

"Come here fella," Joseph called. He picked the dog up and held him high. "How could I have thought this mutt was my gorgeous Maggie? He's obviously too virile for a girl's name. What shall I call him?"

The dog wiggled with pleasure, giving out a series of short snappy barks.

"You're a wise mutt for sure," Joe said, "since you chose the best fellow in the tent. I think I'll call you Moses. Maybe you can show me the way."

"Where'd that thing come from?" Folkes asked.

"Doesn't matter. Someone probably abandoned him when they packed up and left town. He's ours now."

"Yours, you mean. He hasn't kissed me yet, and he better not try."

Moses began to bark again in unison with the sharp notes of Andy's bugle as reveille was played.

"A singer to boot," Joe said. "We've come upon a real treasure."

VI

More than a week passed in which little happened. The men were on full alert, and were growing impatient. The sound of the picks from the other side had not been heard for days. The men were tired and extremely edgy. They began to think that the Feds had given up the digging project, but they had no idea what to expect next. Captain Blount called Andy and Jim to his gunnery position. They might be needed to blow an attack or to drum out a forward march. No one knew for sure.

"Keep your heads below ground level at all times," Captain Blount ordered. "Their sharpshooters are on duty full time."

"There's the cemetery over there, ain't it?" Jimmy asked, holding his drum and sticks on his lap. Maybe the Yanks have just been digging some more holes to stash their dead in. Ha! Ha!"

"Funny! Maybe they want to do some grave robbing," Andy said as he tried to turn the collar of his shirt up the way Captain Blount had his. "Union General may need a new pocket watch."

Twelve hours later the sky was beginning to lighten in the east. Captain Blount, who had been on duty throughout the night, could see the thin apricot edge of dawn outlining the objects on the distant horizon. The day would be a scorcher. The back of his neck was damp from sweat and the flies were already swarming. Andy and Jim awakened. "You sleep any last night?" Andy asked.

"No, but I feel like passing out right now," Jimmy answered.

Suddenly a deafening explosion of extraordinary magnitude rent the air and sent earth and rocks hurling into the sky. Eight thousand pounds of Yankee powder tore through Elliott's Salient, on the Confederate front line, leaving a huge crater in its midst and a breach in the Confederate line for the Union soldiers to storm through. On orders, Andy was busy blowing his bugle, first for assembly and then for attack. The hour had not yet come for blowing reveille.

The Union soldiers poured through the line, many into the crater. The Confederates, ready and waiting, fell upon them.

It was not until the air had cleared somewhat from the sulfurous cloud of the explosion that the Confederate soldiers realized that the Union soldiers they were fighting were mostly black men. The Yankees had sent Smith's IX Corps to make the dangerous attack. Although some of the men were free men from the North, much of the Corps was made up of runaway slaves. As the duty-bound men came through the line into the crater, they were mowed down like cattle that had been stampeded into a slaughterhouse.

Before the scorching sun had reached its zenith, the Confederates had regained their line. In only a few hours, they had killed, wounded or captured six thousand union soldiers.

Captain Blount looked with horror at the dead black men in the crater. He couldn't help thinking of Lazarus. Poor devil. Could he be among them? He wanted to rush out to turn over the many corpses in search of the former slave. Fortunately, reason grabbed hold to stop him. Poor devils, every one. How could the Union officers have allowed such a thing? For the first time in three and a half years of fighting true hate of the enemy raced uncontrolled through his body.

A few days after the battle, before Joseph had been able to regain his composure, he received a letter from Maggie telling him of her love for him but warning that her father was dead set against the marriage. The letter touched his emotions deeply, and he took pen in hand to reply.

"Trenches near Petersburg. Aug. 2

.... I believe in duty and one's paying due regard to one's family. Still, I think one's family should have a little regard for one's feelings and wishes. I insist on your letting your father know the relationship in which we stand or let me inform him. For if you love me as well as I believe you do, I wish to make you my wife next winter.

Really, if the flies don't stop troubling me, I feel you will be the sufferer, for I feel my good humor dropping. Imagine me sitting in the open air, a book on my knees, ten thousand flies drinking the ink off my pen and the moisture from my face and hands, and you can form some idea of the difficulties of my position. The flies conspire to make me furious; a good letter from you to make me smile. Another thing, we thrashed the Yankees handsomely on Saturday. I saw their blood run in rivulets and their dead lie in heaps. Two hundred and twenty-five were in a space little larger than your room. Enough of war."

Before sleeping that night, Joseph reread the letter he had received from Maggie. It was the best she had ever written. He thought of her constantly throughout the night as his mind wandered in and out of consciousness. The next morning he began another letter to her.

"Since reading your last letter, I have been dreaming of you while sleeping. I was wandering with you in a beautiful garden filled with everything attractive. Trailing vines screened the ground from the rays of the sun. Clear-running streams cooled the air and made every breeze refreshing. We were children and the happiest pair of the many that were enjoying the pleasant shade and delicious fruits that hung temptingly from every tree and vine. We chased the varicolored butterflies, listened to the many birds that seemed to carol forth their blithe notes, then gathered flowers of which there were every variety and abundance. You led me along making all things seem brighter by your pointing them out. We were perfectly happy, but after a while you seemed sad, because I did not have a flower like one you wore, but which you could not give me for some reason. There was a tree of them in the garden, but I could not get to them as they were too high. At last, though, you thought of my lifting you up so that both of us together might succeed in obtaining what one alone could not reach. After several efforts the flower was obtained. It possessed the combined sweetness of all the flowers in the garden. As you gave it to me, it seemed that everything wore a more lovely appearance, and music softer and sweeter than any I had ever heard filled the air. You remarked that there was nothing else you wished me to have- that you were satisfied. It seemed that the possession of the flower changed my nature, making me more gentle and like yourself. After a while we went to Mother. She kissed you and said she had sought for a long time for the flower for me and my brothers, but had never found it. While she was talking, I awoke. The dream and the beautiful garden vanished. You only remained in my mind's eye, as lovely if not so childlike, as you appeared in the dream. It had the effect of making me very anxious to see you."

VII

In mid-September Joseph received a letter from his mother. She wrote, "General Sherman has occupied Atlanta. The city burned disastrously before he entered it so there will be little left for him to set fire to when he leaves. Oddly enough, he doesn't seem eager to leave. Perhaps he has become addicted to our southern hospitality.

Since you are spending so much time in Petersburg, you may have time to look up some of your Virginia relatives. Your father reminds me to tell you that his family had a plantation on the Blackwater in Southampton County. He thinks it burned years ago. There are, however, two family plantations still in existence. One is called Mt. Pleasant and is one of several Virginia plantations owned by the Cocke family. General Philip St. George Cocke died during the first year of the war. Your father is particularly interested in knowing what happened to his widow, Sally, and their many children.

The other plantation, Four Mile Tree, belonged to the Browne family from which you are descended, actually it belonged to Sally Browne Bowdoin, who married General Cocke, but we don't know who owns it now. If General Lee is able to stop the fighting around Petersburg, you might ride out to see the old places. They both are beautifully situated on the river. If you cannot visit, Mrs. Batt in Petersburg might be able to give you news of the families."

Joseph burst out laughing.

"You've found something to laugh about," said Lieutenant Potts who was sharing the one reading candle with him in the officers' tent.

"My mother suggests that I take a restful afternoon ride out to an old plantation across the river from Jamestown," Joseph said. "Can you believe it?"

"She obviously doesn't understand that the river is full of Yankee gunboats and transports."

"Or that we are almost surrounded by Union troops. Guess it's just as well that she doesn't know."

"Don't tell her."

"They're not in the safest position in Georgia either. She says Sherman is tarrying in Atlanta but may soon be on the road to Talbotton."

"The bastard! Taking the battle to the women and children. Guess he'd be too scared to fight real men."

"Funny thing, my mother says she just found out that Sherman's cavalry commander, General Judson Kilpatrick, is a distant relative of her's, a cousin whom she has never met. This is the strangest war."

"I've heard of him. He's all business. Not a jolly fellow."

"Let's hope she doesn't meet him."

That night after Joseph had stretched out on his camp cot, he spent a long time staring at the canvas ceiling of the tent. He wondered what it was about himself that made so many things go wrong for him. He had fought as hard and as valiantly as any he had seen during the war. He had often been praised yet others less deserving got the promotions. Then he loved Maggie with all his heart and being. He had succeeded in making her love him in return, yet her father disapproved. Would she ever marry him without parental consent? It would take a lot of courage for a young woman to toss away her security that way. If only he could make things right without being untrue to himself. He couldn't help but think of his friend Dearing's success. He was too adventurous to be a crack soldier- too flamboyant and foolhardy. Joseph remembered hearing General Early quoted as saying, "A soldier has begun to wane as soon as he starts thinking of his reputation instead of his opportunities." Yet somehow it all seemed to work out for Dearing. He had climbed straight up the ladder of success despite his recklessness and desire for attention. He was recently made a brigadier general and had just been married to his beautiful Roxanna Birtchett.

Joseph breathed a deep sigh, turned onto his side and closed his eyes. He knew that it would be hours before he could fall asleep.

VIII

In early October, Joe wrote to Maggie from a camp near Drury's Bluff.

"The day after I wrote Mother, I went into the trenches again. The day I came out, I was ordered across the James River to meet Grant's army, the greater part of which has passed over and captured Fort Harrison. My classmate, General James Dearing, was unable to lead his cavalry brigade because of ill health, and his absence cost us dearly. We attempted to retake the fort but were repulsed. Since that time I have been constantly employed and wet as rain could make me. It has poured for the last four days. Grant is giving us all we can do. I feared, three days ago, he would have Richmond by this time, but fortunately we got in front of him in time to arrest his progress. He is again checked, and I hope we will be able to hold him where he is, though it is impossible to tell anything about it from where we are. His army has been greatly increased and ours constantly grows less. Our loss was about two thousand- his about the same."

By the end of October he was again writing, this time from a camp near Petersburg.

"We just had another fight on the lines about Richmond and Petersburg in which the enemy was badly worsted. At night we had Grant, Meade, Hancock, and Joe Hooker- the latter on a visit to the former- cut off with about eleven thousand. If we only knew it, what a grand thing we might have made of the day's fighting. The Yankees moved out and rejoined their main body by a little path that passed within two hundred yards of our line of battle that was waiting 'till daylight to attack them. It seems hard that fortune should have so favored their escape. Anyway, we worsted them badly - forced them to leave their dead and wounded on the field."

Three days into November, Joseph Blount sent a short note to his father. "Was promoted to Major. Now am the official commander of the 38th Artillery Battalion. I hope that General Sherman is not bothering you."

That same day he received a letter from his mother. "General Sherman has left Atlanta after a two month's stay. His army is marching toward Talbotton as we had been advised he would do. Maggie and Mr. McCone have left all their possessions and fled to Columbus. We have decided not to budge. Too much of our life has gone into the building of our home to leave it to chance. We will stay here to protect our things and not leave the premises unless ordered to do so at gun point."

The letter from Talbotton arrived after a day of heavy shelling. The trenches around Petersburg were a soggy mess after a period of daily rains. In the Confederate army, spirits were low and sinking lower. The number of deserters was growing.

Joseph let his thoughts wander back to the handsome home built to house the large Blount family. There had been almost nothing but open land in Talbotton when his father, the youngest of many sons in his generation, had taken his wife and firstborn son along with a wagon full of slaves he had inherited, and left Columbia County, near Augusta, to travel to the newly-opened inland territory to build his own place and raise his family. His mother had named the home Saving Grace.

It was in the halls, in the dormitory rooms of the boys and girls, in the kitchen complex and even the stately parlor that they had all romped, laughed, cried and fought each other as they grew from infancy to adulthood. Now General Sherman, the ill-groomed, never-shaven, always arrogant perpetrator of destruction was headed toward it. Fate had such a way of turning nasty tricks.

Joe again wrote to Maggie. "Isn't things 'blue'? I'm not though. I visit my friends and try to keep their spirits up, though it is a hard task at times. I believe we will gain our independence if we are worthy of it- if not, we should be slaves and will be. Some nations are made to be the draught animals of others, and that they'll be in spite of all that circumstances or natural advantage has done for them. If we are resolved to be free, the Yankee nation, were it twice as strong, could not subdue us. We will triumph in the end. It is only in such times as the present that men prove of what material they are made. I think these reverses are sent upon us in order to make us rely more on the divine arm for our success. Wickedness abounds, more and more, and it seems that our soldiers are becoming more hardened and wicked every day. I find it almost impossible to read a single chapter of the bible attentively."

The trench warfare continued. General Grant's army kept adding men to its force and extending the arc of the trenches further and further to his left as he tried to encircle Petersburg and gain control of the railroads to the south. The shelling became fierce. On the last day of November, Colonel Edgar Moseley was directing the artillery bombardment of the Union line when, before the horrified eyes of his men, an enemy shell blew his head off.

Joseph Blount, who had held the rank of major for less than a month, was promoted to Colonel to take command of Moseley's Artillery. "What a dreadful way to win a promotion," he told his friends. "I will not write about this to my father. I have no pride in the advancement."

"If you did write, it's unlikely that he would get it anyway," answered the officer who had brought him the news. "The Weldon Railroad has been torn up again. This time it's a very long stretch."

IX

Off-duty officers were gathered around a camp fire enjoying the fact that the air had turned cool. The first frost of a fortnight before had caused the leaves to turn the fiery colors of late fall. The pesky flies of summer had diminished to a scant few. Were it not for the deterioration of their position in the war and the death of Colonel Moseley, the evening might have been a pleasant one.

"That mutt sure was lucky when he found you," Captain Stribling said.

"He's known to be bright," Joseph said as he stroked the dog's head and tickled him affectionately behind the ears.

The smoke from the flaming logs gave off a sweet aroma that suggested pine cones had been used as kindling. Some of the men were playing cards. Others were eating when a cavalry scout entered the group. "Where've you been, Major?" Captain Stribling asked. "Your boots are covered with mud and dirt."

"I've been east on the southside," the Major answered. "I rode inland about thirty miles from the James, then turned north to Surry and a place called Scotland Wharf. That's all familiar territory for me. I grew up around there."

"So?"

"Got an eyeful. The river is choking with Union ships."

"How many?"

"I could only see one stretch at a time. Have to estimate. Guess there're more than a thousand counting the barges, transports and small craft as well. Then there're the gunboats."

"God Almighty. We've only got railroads to bring in our supplies. Railroads on lines that the Yankees tear up as fast as we repair them. They've got the whole river, and we can't damage it at all."

Joseph turned away in despair. He had heard nothing from Maggie and didn't even know where she was. He had heard nothing from Talbotton since the letter from his mother telling him that Sherman was on his way. For the first time he had to admit to himself that things were mighty grim.

Each day brought increased anxiety. One thing built on another. Rations were lessened. Ammunition had to be carefully hoarded. Another railroad track was damaged. Another friend was killed. The worst of all came one evening shortly before Christmas. The Confederates heard the Yankee soldiers fire off a salute. They counted the blasts. Each additional shot increased their state of alarm. Eighty-nine, ninety, ninety-one, one hundred shots were fired. Why would they waste so much ammunition? Were their chests full to overflowing? What could it mean? As the men sat quietly mesmerized after the last shot, word spread through the Confederate ranks that the salute was in honor of General Sherman who had burned his way across Georgia and reached the sea. The Yankee ammunition was not wasted. It hit its mark deep in the hearts of all who heard its roar.

On Christmas Eve, Joseph received a hand-delivered note from his mother's friend, Mrs. Batt, who had remained in Petersburg despite the destruction.

She's like Mother. She'll not leave her home without putting up a struggle. He opened the letter and read.

"Dear Colonel Blount,

Some months ago, you asked me for information about two plantations on the south shore of the James River called Mt. Pleasant and Four Mile Tree that had previously belonged to some of your ancestors. Yesterday, a gentleman named Mr. Wilson came into Petersburg and called upon us. He has been renting Four Mile Tree from a Mr. Graves who apparently owns it. Mr. Wilson said that the old home had been shelled by Union gunboats earlier in the year and that one shell had exploded within the house causing a great deal of damage. He also reported that some of the shells had destroyed the ancient cypress tree from which the place took its name.

I am sorry to have to add this sorrowful news to all your woes, but you asked me about the places and I felt compelled to let you know what I had heard."

We're being blasted into oblivion. Will there be anything left? And still, not a word from Talbotton.

Christmas Day arrived with Joe still in the camp near Petersburg. Moses started the day off for him by jumping up on his cot as the first glimmer of light crept through the cracks of the tent.

At least I have you, old fella. Joe thought of the Christmases of his youth back in Talbotton when their home had been full of greens, full of the smell of festive cooking, full of children, full of servants and full of laughter.

About the only thing good about this Christmas is that we'll probably have a day without killing. Even there, one can't be sure.

The other officers in the tent were beginning to stir. Joe threw his legs over the wooden side bars of his cot and gave a vigorous stretch. He rose and was preparing to don his boots and jacket when a familiar voice at the tent's entrance asked for permission to enter.

Permission granted, the visitor burst into the room, rushed to Joe's side, gave a snappy salute and said, "Christmas gift, Colonel Blount."

"Christmas gift, Andy," Colonel Blount said, returning the salute. It had been four years since he'd heard that greeting and the memory of it made him powerfully blue.

"Quartermaster just found this, Sir. It was stuck in the bottom of a mail bag. You should have received it weeks ago. He sends his apologies and asked me to wish you a Merry Christmas." Andy handed over a wrinkled and dirty letter.

"From Talbotton," said Joe. "Thank heavens. I was beginning to think that Talbotton might not exist any more. I hope there was one for you, too, today."

"No, sir. Still not a word."

"I'm sorry."

"I'll take Moses out for you, sir."

"That's a fine idea. He could use some play."

Joe went back to his corner of the tent, sat on the side of his cot and opened the letter carefully. The sight of his mother's familiar hand had given his spirits an uplift since early childhood. This time was no exception. He spread the long letter on his knees and began to read.

"My dearest son, Joe,

I hope this letter finds you in good health and good spirits. General Sherman's troops have come and gone. We survived without injury. Nothing was lost. The tale is a strange one so bear with me as I start at the beginning.

You will remember that your father and I had decided not to leave Talbotton. When we heard that Sherman's troops were approaching the town, we were tempted to change our minds, but then renewed conviction took hold of us. We stayed with our previous decision. We were as scared as anyone could be, but not willing to give in.

My friend, Priscilla White, who came to Talbotton from New York ten years ago to make her living as our schoolteacher, was another who refused to leave. She actually had no place to go as our neighbors have not been gracious to her since the war began. I was the lone exception. She had been a good friend before the war and had had nothing to do with starting it so I continued to stand by her. As she was all alone, I invited her to Saving Grace to stay with us through the Yankee ordeal.

The afternoon the troops arrived, she stood with Papa and me at the front windows, watching as first the cavalry and then the foot soldiers marched into Talbotton. There seemed to be thousands and thousands of them. They bivouacked all over and around the town. We were completely occupied.

As we watched, a Yankee Captain rode up to the front door and knocked. We all went into the hall to meet him. He stated bluntly that the Colonel, commanding the forces in Talbotton, was requisitioning our house to serve as his headquarters. He told us to pack a satchel and leave. The Captain was tough looking and rudely brusque of speech.

Papa said that he wished to meet the Colonel and that we would await his call.

Shortly afterwards, the Colonel rode up to the house with an aide and came in. I shall not mention his name as I rather liked him. He was very young, younger even than you, Joe. He had a fine looking face and a well educated look about him. He quickly but politely repeated that our house was to be used as general head-quarters and that we were to leave.

Papa introduced Priscilla White to him, letting him know that she was an invited guest in our house. He said that we could not leave the premises when guests were dependent upon our staying.

The Colonel seemed agitated and embarrassed upon realizing that Miss White was a northerner from New York. I immediately sensed his insecurity and stepped forward to say. 'Colonel, you are welcome to use our house as your headquarters. I will see to your comfort and privacy. You may use the writing room as your office. You and your officers may sleep in any of the many empty bed-rooms, but we will not leave the premises.'

To my astonishment, he answered, "Yes, ma'am."

I spent the afternoon in the kitchen with cook seeing that we put forth the best dinner possible for the pleasure of the Colonel and his aides. We laid the table with our finest linens and plate. The officers acted in a most proper manner and spent the dinner time entertaining us with innocuous war stories. I studied the young Colonel's face with care, wondering what his parents were like and thinking that he could have been my son had we lived in the North.

When dinner was over we moved into the parlor for our after dinner coffee. All of the officers except the Colonel excused them-selves saying that they had to be up very early in the morning. Priscilla was standing near the Colonel and heard him say to his aides, 'Order the troops out of here at seven in the morning. General Sherman wants us to make quick work of reaching Savannah. I personally will give the order to burn the town. No one else is to do so.'

Priscilla was heartsick on hearing his intentions but continued to be gracious. In the parlor, I asked her to pour the coffee for us all. The Colonel stayed with us, enjoying the fire, the coffee and the conversation. He seemed to be most at ease in our home.

Shortly thereafter we all retired not knowing what to expect the next day. We slept little, if any at all. At daybreak, we heard the men leave and, with their guards who had slept all over our grounds, gallop away. We heard the thud of the horses' hooves, the bugle call to start the march and then the endless racket of the departing troops. We kept vigilant at the windows for any trace of flames or smell of smoke but could sense nothing. Then at nine o'clock, we heard a frantic racket in the front bedroom. We had been unaware that the Colonel had not left with the others. He had overslept. Within minutes, he came tearing down the stairs, ran outside, jumped on his saddled horse and sped away at a mad gallop.

Priscilla burst out laughing. 'It worked,' she called out. 'It worked.' She bent over, slapped her knees and then went off into peels of laughter again.

'Last night, I tied some laudanum into the corner of my handkerchief. As I was pouring the coffee, I untied it and emptied the drug into his cup. He was talking to you at the time and didn't notice. It was just enough to put him into a very deep sleep.'

By the time the Colonel woke up this morning, all of the Yankee troops had left town. He must have had to ride like the devil to catch up to them. Not a thing was burned in Talbotton.

Maggie and Mr. McCone have not returned yet but are expected soon. I have no idea what damage their property may have suffered. There were so many Yankee troops here that it could be in shambles. All of the other towns that Sherman's troops have marched through have been burned. I know of no others to escape.

Thankfully, your home will be here waiting for you should you get your long, overdue winter leave.

Our thoughts are always with you.

Love,

Mother."

Winter leave. I'd need an excuse to get one. If only Maggie would say 'Yes' I could ask for a leave to get married. He was finishing his dressing when Andy came back into the tent with Moses.

"Andy," Colonel Blount said, "That letter was the best Christmas present I could have gotten. If Marse Robert had only had the foresight to make my mother a general, we would have whipped the Yankees months ago."

"You're the one he should have made a general," Andy said with conviction.

X

Joseph waited to write to Maggie. He needed the time to arrange a furlough. When at last it was in the works, and he found a moment of privacy, he wrote,

"Dearest Maggie,

I've sent in my application for a furlough, and if it's approved, I shall be at home about seven or eight days after you get this. Don't you feel badly? Ain't you scared? Are you blushing all to yourself with no one to see you? Well, I only wish my visit could be made under more promising circumstances, but it is willed so to be, and I'll not complain. I intend to be very happy and to forget for a time the troubles of the country.

Have you sent my letter to your father? If you have, you had better ask Mother for his answer. I wrote her to keep it for me. You can get it and see what he has to say. We will continue to hope that the road will not be cut until I get home at least. I hope you will, as soon as I get home, consent to marry me.

The thought of again seeing you makes me very foolish. How many kisses is it that you owe me? I forgot to keep an account. I know that I sent you quite a number, and you didn't send any in return. I don't approve of the credit system, so you will please pay cash in future. I have been questioned very closely by some of my friends as to whether I was to be married soon. I could truthfully say that I did not know. But, trusting in your love and my determination to marry you, I think I may reasonably expect to be a married man in two week's time.

You know I love you dearly, and I have promised not to beat you more than once a week. I wonder if you will have as much influence over me as my wife as you have had as my sweetheart. I know that I have a bad disposition and few things to recommend me. But, I will hope- that is my nature. Goodbye, dear Maggie. I love you with all my heart and strength. You are more to me than all the world besides. Without your love, I care little for the future or for life. I kiss you my own, dear Maggie - my own, dear wife that is to be. I love you. I love you. I love you. B"

XI

Throughout the winter the war raged on. General Grant's army made progress in lengthening the front with which he tried to encircle Petersburg like the hangman's noose in anticipation of an execution. The cold weather and the bad winter roads kept either side from embarking on an all-out campaign, but the sharpshooters on either side of the front trenches, divided only by a few hundred yards, were ever ready to pick off anyone foolish enough to lift his head above ground level.

Joseph went home on furlough the end of January but did not get married. The will of Maggie's father was stronger than her own. The engagement was broken. He stayed in Talbotton for two weeks, saw Maggie each day but did not accomplish his goal.

Once back in the trenches near Petersburg, he found disbelief in the sentiments of many of his friends.

"I didn't think you'd come back," one said. "Boy, if I'd gotten a pass out of this hell hole, they'd have had to chase me all the way to Tierra del Fuego before catching me."

Desertions were running high. Many soldiers' wives were sending letters of desperation. Everyone was sick of war. Joseph Blount's fidelity to Maggie did not change. In mid-March, three weeks before the end of the war, he wrote his last letter to her.

"Trenches near Petersburg, March 19, 1864.

My dearest Maggie,

You see me safely back with my friends. You can't conceive how delighted I am to be once more where duty calls. Although I find it hard to reconcile myself to being so far from you, my own pet, how long, how long will it be before we meet again? God only knows. I think of many things I wished to talk to you about that I did not remember while at home, but I might have suspected that. When the heart is full, the head is empty. When happiness is perfect, words are non-obedient to our call. The tongue silent. So it was with me.

Moses was happy to see me back. He certainly deserves a place in history. He is the wittiest dog that ever lived. He is absolutely splendid. I am lounging on the bed, reading at times, when he will look at me with the most quizzical face imaginable. I can't keep from laughing.

My horse seemed glad to see me. She came as soon as I called her, whinnying, but she stopped as soon as she got to me, putting her muzzle on my shoulder.

Everyone seems glad to see me again."

In less than a week after posting the letter, news reached those in the trenches that further demoralized them all. A scout came in to report that the James River was not only full of Yankee ships and cargo carriers, but that even President Lincoln's ship, the River Queen, was in the river near City Point, with both the President and Mrs. Lincoln aboard. Not only that. Rumor had it that Mrs. Lincoln had entertained by giving a ball aboard ship.

"They're ready to move in for the kill," Colonel Blount declared. "Imagine the President and his wife only a short distance out of cannon range. It's the most ostentatious display of power one could imagine."

Grant moved his headquarters to a spot nearer to the front. Confederate spirits continued to sink. General Lee made an unsuccessful counter move to recapture Fort Stedman. A portion of the Confederate line collapsed. Grant continued to tighten the noose. Then on April 2nd, Lee ordered the Petersburg line abandoned. When night fell, the artillery with all its pieces led the southern forces out of the trenches and out of the city to the west, south of Richmond. The infantry followed. The following morning when the Bluecoats answered their call to reveille, they found the southerners gone. The nine month siege of Petersburg was over. The hangman had not been able to snap tight the noose. The victims had escaped, but not for long.

The men marched day and night on empty stomachs. The horses had nothing to eat but the corn from their feed bags. As the men became more famished, they began eating the horses' corn. Then the horses had nothing. Each hour brought total defeat nearer.

At the Battle of Five Forks, an unexpected Union attack cost Lee's Army of Northern Virginia two of its four corps. Several days later at Saylor's Creek one third of the remaining army was lost. Still, they marched westward, prayed and hoped.

At Appomattox Station, General Lee found his remaining troops hemmed in by the Union forces under Generals Ord, Sheridan, Meade, Gibbons and Griffin. Even the road to the west was blocked by the Union forces of General Smith. The end had come. The four-year war was over. The cause was lost. The remaining soldiers were sick, tired and hungry. The future hung in uncertainty.

The unthinkable occurred. The Army of Northern Virginia surrendered.

Joseph Blount was sitting on the ground at the crest of a hill, looking back east toward the Federal Army. He was in the depth of depression. He, like so many others, had no idea what to expect in defeat. Would he become a prisoner and be marched off to camp? Would he simply starve to death?

He felt light-headed from fatigue. His stomach growled. His horse moved over and lowered her head in sympathy. "Faithful to the end," he said, turning his head sideways and rubbing his nose against the mare's jaw. He was so tired that he felt he would never be able to rise from the ground again.

"Colonel Blount?" he heard from behind. Turning his head he saw a young man, barefoot and jacketless, give him a slow salute.

"Andy, my friend, I'm delighted to see you. Come sit with me. I haven't the energy to rise. I wondered often where you were after we left Petersburg." A choked up feeling gripped his throat. His voice became thick as though just ready to crack. "Seeing that you are safe is the only good thing that has happened. We've lost so many these last few days."

"Yes, sir," Andy said, seating himself next to Colonel Blount.

"You've still got your bugle, I see."

"I carry it like a baby. Without it I'd have no reason for being here. I've played taps for some very fine men since the war started."

"Did you hear about General Dearing?"

"No, sir."

"He was mortally wounded three days ago at High Bridge."

"Oh, no! Where was that?"

"It's the long railroad bridge across the Appomattox. It had to be held at any cost. He did his duty. The bridge was held, but the cost was high."

"He'd just been married, hadn't he?"

"Yes, a few months back. We were classmates at West Point, you know." Tears began to run down the older man's cheeks. "I thought good fortune would always be his. He seemed to live under a golden star. Now the beautiful Roxanna, married less than a year, is a widow."

The two men sat for a long time in silence, each occupied with his own thoughts. Finally Colonel Blount said, "I think I'll lie down and sleep for a while, Andy. Come back to see me if you can. After the formal surrender tomorrow, we'll know better what to expect in the future."

By nightfall, the Confederate soldiers had all received food from the Federal supply trains. Many slept for the first time since leaving Petersburg. The next morning, the artillery battalions led the way in surrendering theirs guns and the carefully hoarded ammunition of the Southland. Colonel Blount's battalion had been so reduced that, at the formal surrender, there were only three officers and twenty-three enlisted men to lay down their arms.

The men learned to their great relief that all were to be given written paroles so that they could return to their homes in safety. The papers had to be printed and the rolls carefully checked, but the Union troops continued to feed the Confederates throughout the time it took to arrange for their departure. Colonel Blount was eager to leave, but stayed until all the soldiers under his command had received their papers. Then he packed his saddle bags with rations, filled up his horse's feed bag and prepared to make the long ride home.

Andy appeared to say goodbye. "I brought you a glass of lemonade, Sir. A Yankee soldier give it to me."

"Lemonade," Joseph said. "That makes me homesick for Talbotton. He thought back to the lemonade served the first time he met Maggie, the day Lazarus had chopped off Bart's finger. "Tastes mighty fine. Thank you."

"I guess you'll be getting married soon." Andy said.

"I hope so. I've fought four long years to get this war over with so that I could marry. Sometimes I didn't know whether I was fighting for my country or fighting for my sweetheart. It all got kind of mixed up in my mind."

"I found out about my family, Sir. They'd gone to Baltimore to live with some relatives who had a farm near there. They were behind enemy lines so they were afraid to write me. I just heard news of them today."

"Thank goodness, Andy. Now I can stop worrying about you."

"I see you've still got Moses with you."

"I didn't have. I thought I'd lost him for good after Saylor's Creek. Then yesterday, he found me. I don't know how."

"You going to take him with you?"

"Long as he can keep up."

"It's sad having to say goodbye," Andy said. "I won't forget you."

"Nor I you, Andy. You've been a fine soldier."

"Don't you want me to clean the mud from your boots before you leave?"

"Heavens, no. The mud is the only thing that's holding them together."

"Goodbyes are hard," Andy said, lowering his head.

"There are not as many to say 'goodbye' to anymore. Dearing's gone. He almost made it but not quite. On the long trip home, I'm going to try to figure out why God spared me."

Colonel Blount mounted his horse. Then he removed his hat, leaned down and kissed Andy on the cheek. "Take care of yourself, Andy," he said as he left.

Colonel Blount knew that Andy was watching as he rode away. He could feel the penetrating look on the back of his neck. He tried not to turn around. He was almost into the woods when he heard called after him in a loud but breaking voice, "I'll never, ever forget you, sir." Turning around he saw that Andy had sat down abruptly where he had stood, buried his face in his hands and burst into sobs.

Colonel Blount hesitated for only a moment, then gave his mare a nudge with the heel of his boot and galloped away - homeward bound.

THE MANIPULATOR
1938-1945

I

Susan Benson ran her fingers through the brown strand of hair on her cheek and placed it behind her ear. So immersed was she in the book she was reading that she was totally oblivious to the action. Tucking the strand behind her ear had become a reflex action for her. She did it at least a dozen times an hour, even more often when she was nervous.

Across from Susan at a desk that was juxtapositioned to hers, creating a work unit reminiscent of an eighteenth century partner's desk, sat her roommate, Dudley Mills, engrossed in writing a long letter. The work year was over. For that matter, four years of study was over. Graduation was less than twenty-four hours away.

"Knock, knock," came a voice from the dormitory hall.

"Who's there?"

"Frank."

"Frank who?"

"Frankly, my dear, I don't give a damn."

The girls burst into giggly laughter.

"Ha. Ha," Susan said. "Come on in Rhett. Scarlett would never recognize that effeminate voice."

Brenda Benson traipsed into the four-girl suite on the second floor of Gray Hall where her cousin Susan roomed at Sweet Briar College, situated on the grounds of a large antebellum plantation twelve miles north of the James River.

"You haven't still got your face buried in a book?" Brenda said. "Shame on you. Finals are over. I'd like to ride into Lynchburg, stand on the bridge and throw the cursed things into the river one by one, then watch them float into the current on their way to a permanent burial ground at sea."

"How dramatic," Susan said. "Have a seat, Brenda. That is if you can sit down in those tight jodhpurs."

"Of course I can sit down. All you do in jodhpurs is sit."

Brenda eased herself into the one empty, straight chair in the suite's living room. Desks and bureaus took up most of the room's space.

Brenda's long, blond hair fell to her shoulders in a perfectly-set, page-boy arrangement that fell across her face in a wave on one side and was pinned back behind her ear on the other. Her blue eyes sparkled. Her complexion was flawless, and her lips were painted a soft shade of pink.

"Susan tells me you've decided on a double wedding ceremony at Laurel Hill," Dudley said. "Lucky for your grandparents. Which one gets to wear the heirloom wedding dress?"

"Gets to," Brenda said. "Has to, you mean. I can fit into it. Susan can't. She lucks out."

"I get to wear Brenda's May Queen dress. The seamstress was told to buy enough material to add sleeves later and to leave extra in the seams so that it could be let out for me. Grandmother's dress would fall into shreds if it were fiddled with. Brenda will wear it. I'll be wearing her dress. That is, if we can get the grass stains out of the hem."

"Grass stains are no problem. Just have the hem turned up an inch."

"But there are twelve yards of organdy around the bottom. Who wants to re-hem that?"

"Someone has to wear Granny's gown or she'd die of disappointment. The wedding date we set in June misses their fiftieth wedding anniversary by only three days."

"Why don't you marry on their anniversary?"

"We couldn't," Brenda said. "It falls on a Saturday. It's Monday for health, Tuesday for wealth, Wednesday the best day of all, Thursday for losses, Friday for crosses, and Saturday no luck at all."

"You Southerners. You've been quite an experience," Dudley said. "I hope you'll remember that you met your future husbands at my debut party in Washington. You owe me one. Make sure he's tall and has lots of money."

"No one has money anymore," Brenda said. "It's true you introduced me to Otto. I'd never have met a handsome Norwegian in Surry County, but Susan and I have known Jordan since we took our hair out of pigtails. He's a country boy from Franklin, Virginia. Grew up not thirty miles from Laurel Hill."

"He's working in Washington now. Susan would've missed him if she hadn't come to visit me. Besides, Otto is rich. His father keeps him on a short tether, financially. The old man owns a major shipbuilding company outside of Oslo. He just doesn't realize how high prices are in Washington. That's why Otto has to be careful with his money."

"Miss Susan?" came another voice from the hall. "I got your blouses done ironed. Can I bring them in?"

"Sure, Naomi. Come on in."

A stout, middle-aged Negress, in a flowered gingham dress with her hair tied in a kerchief, walked into the room carrying four, freshly washed and ironed blouses on wire hangers. It was evident to all who saw her that her bones ached and hurt from standing long hours on crooked feet.

"I hopes they'll do," Naomi said. "I did them the best I can."

"They're beautiful," Susan said. "I couldn't possibly have done them as well."

"Nor would she," Brenda said to Dudley.

Susan opened her change purse and gave Naomi sixty cents. The Negress nodded her thanks and turned to leave the room.

"Naomi. Don't leave yet," Susan said. "I have something else for you. Is it true that you take our things to your house and do them up without an electric iron?"

"Yes M'am."

"How do you do it?"

"I just heats my iron on a metal plate that sits on the stove at my house and irons with that. When it cools down, I rests it back on the plate a bit."

"I see," Susan said. "Well, Naomi, the iron at the end of the hall is one that all the girls on this floor chipped in to buy together. Now that we're leaving, we decided to make a present of it to you. Just leave it until after graduation. Then you may take it home with you."

"Um-m. Um-m," Naomi said.

"What's the matter? Don't you want it?"

"You don't understand. It ain't just that we got no 'lectric iron. We got no 'lectricity."

A deadly quiet fell on the room. It was several seconds before anyone spoke. Susan opened her change purse again. She took out two quarters and gave them to Naomi. "A little extra as a parting thanks," she said.

Naomi smiled, took the coins and left the room.

"Really, Susan," Brenda said, "as hard as it's going to be for Gramps to foot the bill for the weddings. How can you be so loose with your money? Besides, you'll spoil her."

"Oh shush," Susan said.

"Don't get mad. I need your help."

"What now? School work's over."

Brenda opened up a hand towel she had been carrying with a four-needle piece of knitting wrapped inside it.

"I've gotten this darn thing all messed up."

"I'll say you have. It looks like a bird's nest."

"It's one of a pair of argyle socks I've been knitting for Gramps. I got some stitches twisted up funny as I was trying to turn the heel. When I tried to pull it out, back to the mistake, it all knotted-up on me."

"You can't pull out argyle." Susan picked up the knitting and scrutinized it. "You've thrown your yarn every time you've changed color. The only way to undo argyle is to un-knit it stitch by stitch."

"I knew you'd know how to fix it. There's no mistaking where the brains are in our family. I'll just leave it here with you until you can get it in order. I've got to run. I'm due at the stables right this minute."

Brenda dropped the tangled knitting on Susan's desk and darted from the room.

"Fooey," Susan said.

"You going to un-knit that mess?" Dudley asked.

"I don't know. She's such a helpless child."

"My foot."

Susan picked up the book she had been reading before Brenda

came into the room, but her ability to concentrate had been squashed. She read half a page without remembering what was on it.

"Doesn't Brenda realize that Otto's from a wealthy family?" Dudley asked.

"Course, she knows," Susan said. "She's just playing it cool. She told me I was nuts to be marrying Jordan when there were much bigger fish in the sea."

"I'm sure he makes an acceptable salary at the Department of Agriculture. What does his father do?"

"His father's in the lumber business in Southampton County. That's why Jordan went into the forestry department at Agriculture, to learn how things work on the other side. Regulations and all, you know. Unfortunately, lumber's been hit harder than just about anything else in Virginia during the depression. It goes into making durable goods, houses and furniture. People aren't rushing to buy those these days. The business is not turning much profit. Jordan says they are branching out into corrugated board and paper products to try to save the works. It's a big risk. They have to borrow a lot of money for the new equipment and machinery. Meanwhile Jordan lives on his government salary."

"How did you know that he was the one and only for you? It scares me to death to think of picking a husband for life."

"It is scary, but Jordan's a lot like me for one thing. We both love to read, we like fishing and to spend a good deal of time alone, thinking our own thoughts without interruption. That old idea of opposites attracting each other is for the adventuresome, not me."

"Brenda sure picked an opposite. Only thing she and Otto have in common is blond hair," Dudley said.

"He'll find marriage to Brenda a real thriller. Should be fun though."

"Charm will get her everywhere, I'm afraid."

Susan started to pick up her book, but put it down again. She pushed the fallen lock of hair behind her ear and drummed her fingers on the desk top. Finally, she picked up Brenda's knitting and began the tedious job of un-tangling and un-knitting the messed-up argyle sock.

The following day, Judge and Mrs. Benson, driven by their

houseman, Samuel, rode through the brick gates of Sweet Briar College, up the long, meandering road to the campus, around the quadrangle that acted as a hub for the handsome brick, Federal-style buildings, and parked in front of the dining hall.

Brenda and Susan were waiting for them on the arcade between the hall and their dorm. They rushed out to greet their grandparents just as Samuel opened the back door of the shiny, but old, black Packard in which they had come. The car, a 1928 model limousine, was one of the last extravagant expenditures made by the Judge during the previous decade of opulence. Samuel proudly kept it polished and running smoothly.

Judge and Mrs. Benson had been both parents and grandparents to the girls since their four parents had been killed in a motor accident on a winding, two lane, country road near Laurel Hill before the girls had reached their teens. The Benson brothers, with their wives, had been returning to Laurel Hill, from a night of partying, when a milk-truck driver, expecting no other vehicles to be on the road at that hour, took a curve on the inside, collided with the convertible in which the four were riding and killed them all instantly.

Brenda and Susan were asleep in one of the large, square, corner bedrooms at Laurel Hill when the tragedy occurred, and there they continued to live until they left for college.

Judge Benson gave the girls loving hugs. They in turn embraced their grandmother, kissing her on the cheek and then made a gesture of embrace to Samuel, kissing him in the air somewhere around his ear.

"We've been looking forward to this momentous occasion," Judge Benson said. "There've been a good many intelligent women in our family through the years, but you're the first two to become college graduates. That's quite an accomplishment. I'm proud of you."

"Thanks, Gramps," Brenda said. "We've loved it, but I can't tell you how glad I am that the studying is over. Woo eee! It'll be fun to read what I want to read for a change."

Mrs. Benson ran her flattened hand over the black and white, printed, voile dress she was wearing in hopes of eliminating a few lap wrinkles. "Have you got your trunks packed and ready?" she asked. "Samuel can get them stowed in the car while we're at the ceremony."

"He'll have plenty of time," Susan said. "The porters are just now carrying them down. They'll be put in front of Gray. Our names are stenciled on ours in big letters that can't be missed."

"After the ceremony in the gym, we're all invited to lunch in the boxwood gardens at Sweet Briar House," Susan said. "Miss Glass opens the doors to the plantation house as well as the garden for this occasion so you'll get a tour of the beautiful old mansion. You start walking over to the gym. We have to put on our robes and mortarboards to march over with our class."

"We'll meet you on the steps of the gym after graduation," Brenda said. "Look for a red-headed usher. I made her promise to save you good seats."

Hours later, Susan and Brenda were trying to eat chicken salad and biscuits stuffed with Smithfield ham while standing in the boxwood gardens near the entrance to the handsome, yellow, stucco, antebellum mansion. Garden seats had been found for Judge and Mrs. Benson, but all the graduates were balancing plates atop glasses of iced-tea as they stood on the newly mowed and edged garden paths that ran between the rows of elegant English boxwood.

It had been rumored in the dormitory halls that the ancient bushes in front of Sweet Briar House were worth more than the entire endowment of the college, but that was the kind of rumor that never had a foundation. It was, like most gossip, just something someone had heard somewhere.

The college president, Meta Glass, was dutifully making her rounds. "Judge and Mrs. Benson," she said as she strolled into the family group. The diminutive president walked with perfect carriage, like a royal princess, as she greeted her guests. "My brother, Carter, asked that I be on the lookout for you. He says you are a powerful source of support for his policies, on the southside."

"Miss Glass," Judge Benson said, rising from his seat and depositing his plate on the bench where he had been sitting. "This is a great pleasure, indeed. The senator is a dear friend of mine and a great honor to Virginia."

"Thank you. Your granddaughters stole the show in this class, you know," the college president said with a dignified, long-practiced smile. "Susan as president of the Tau Phi honor society and Brenda as May Queen surely held center stage throughout the year."

"We're proud of them."

"Carter tells me you are still deep into politics despite your retirement."

"More so than ever now that he has the time for it," Mrs. Benson said.

"We have to look out for the welfare of this great state," Judge Benson said, "and I can tell you that there is no better way to do it than to see that Carter Glass and Harry Flood Byrd keep getting elected to the United States Senate. They are the two best senators in Washington, and they both belong to us."

"That's very kind of you, Judge."

"It's the simple truth."

"And the girls are each to be married soon, I hear," Miss Glass said turning her attention to Mrs. Benson.

"Yes. We'll have them back at Laurel Hill for little more than a month before the wedding. Then they'll both be moving to Washington. Things will be mighty quiet in Surry County after that."

The conversation followed the usual paths of well-mannered rhetoric.

"Carter asked me to tell you that he is at Montview Farms this week if you would like to stop by on your way back to Laurel Hill," Miss Glass said.

"That's kind of him, but much as I always enjoy a visit with the senator, we must decline his hospitality this time. I have another engagement at Laurel Hill this evening. We'll have to mosey on down the road as soon as Sam can get the girls' things in the old buggy."

"He'll be disappointed, I know," Miss Glass said as she took her leave of them.

"Who's coming for dinner?" Susan asked.

"No one," her grandmother answered. "Gramps doesn't want to miss Amos an' Andy."

"You're kidding."

"Quiet. You'll give me away. I'd much rather spend a half hour with Amos an' Andy than with Carter Glass, much as I admire the man. Amos an' Andy are my best friends."

"But he must have wanted to see you," Susan said.

"Not really. It's just that I've got Surry County in my pocket, and he wants to make sure my pocket is sewed securely to his suit. It is, so why waste his time?"

"I see."

"Better say your farewells, girls. It's time to go."

II

The family arrived at Laurel Hill in plenty of time for Sam to get the girl's trunks and other luggage up the wide, three-level staircase to their rooms on the second floor, to change his uniform from that of a liveried driver to the white jacket of a houseman and to mix and serve the carefully measured bourbon cocktail that the Judge enjoyed before his dinner each evening.

"Susan. Where's Susan?" the Judge called.

"Here, Gramps. What's up?"

"Time for Amos an' Andy. Switch on that box over there. This is the best time of the day. Right, Sam?"

"Right, Judge," Sam said.

"Sam enjoys this as much as I do."

Susan turned on the radio. The dial was already set to the station that Judge Benson listened to with regularity. He had Amos an' Andy to enjoy with cocktails, then the evening news with a new correspondent, a young journalist named Edward R. Murrow, reporting from London. Dinner followed the news. After dinner the set was turned on again to catch Fibber McGee and Molly.

Susan sat on the sofa beside her grandfather. She listened to the Judge laugh heartily as the white entertainers played the parts of upscale Negroes, who had moved north, but not forgotten their poor, southern, black background. Susan found it interesting to watch her grandfather. He slapped his knee with delight when a joke was made, in heavy Negro dialect, that reminded everyone of just where Amos an' Andy had come from. She noticed that Sam gave no hint of displeasure at the entertainers as they made fun of the Negro race.

The evening news that followed kept the family up to the moment on current events. The world news came first.

"President Roosevelt and Secretary of State Cordell Hull met today to discuss the continuing consequences of the German annexation of Austria that took place in April. So far, it is deemed unlikely that Hitler will risk the displeasure of England and France by embarking on further deeds of aggression. The alpine country of Austria, after all, was closely allied with Germany. They enjoyed a joint boundary, a similar language and mutual customs. The small nation was not overrun militarily but conquered from within by the internal victory of the Nazi party over other forces there."

Susan moved the lock of hair that had fallen across her face. The talk about the Nazis and Hitler made her nervous.

The national news came next. "Dust storms again hit the central prairies causing thousands of new farmers to pack up their families, desert the devastated fields, which they had planted with such hope only a few months before, and move on."

"On the local side of the news, Senator Harry Flood Byrd announced today that he is confident of success in getting peanuts added to the basic commodities list so that our local farmers will be eligible for allotments that should guarantee them a higher price for their peanuts."

"Dinner's served, Judge Benson."

"Okay, Sam. Switch it off, Susan."

In the dining room a white damask cloth covered the oval-shaped table. In its center, a large bowl of pale, pink peonies gave off a pleasant aroma.

Sam carried in a large platter of roast capon, partially carved, and placed it in front of Judge Benson. The judge apportioned slices of chicken to each plate, ladled gravy over them and handed the plate back to Sam to serve. Ella, Sam's middle-aged daughter, followed him around the table carrying a tray with the vegetable dishes which she served to each person. Delia, Sam's wife, was the cook and stayed in the kitchen.

After the chicken and the vegetables had been served, Mrs. Benson raised her fork giving permission for all the others to begin eating their dinner.

Ella reentered the room with a bread tray full of biscuits which were kept warm by being wrapped in a linen napkin.

"Take two and butter them while they're hot," their grandmother said.

"I could eat a dozen," Susan said. "At Sweet Briar, they just served sliced bread. It was homemade and fairly tasty but never hot."

"No meal's up to snuff unless the bread is hot," their grandfather said.

"Gramps, what's to be done about all the poor people wandering loose around the country because of the dust storms and the depression?"

"I don't know, Susan. We've never been rid of the poor since the world began. Fortunately, Virginia doesn't have many wandering poor. We're primarily rural, and our farmers can pretty well eke out a living and manage to feed their children from the produce of their land even if they are dirt poor. I just spend my time worrying about the people in Virginia. President Roosevelt will have to solve the problems of the country. That's what we elected him for."

"How about the problems of the world. Who's to solve those?"

"I'll think about it. In the meantime, let's talk about you girls and your futures."

Mrs. Benson began to smile as she ate. A twinkle leapt into her eyes, and the corners of her mouth turned up even though she was still chewing. "Gramps has a surprise for you," she said.

"We have a little gift for you," he said. "It's a joint graduation and wedding present."

"Don't stop telling," Brenda said. "You've got me sitting on the edge of my chair."

"Your grandmother and I are planning to give each of you twenty thousand dollars as a gift but with strings attached to it."

"Twenty thousand," Brenda said. "That's a fortune. Where'd it come from?"

"It's a little nest egg we've been nurturing along for you since the time you first became our responsibility. It's all you will get from us until after your grandmother and I are both gone. That's why I'm putting the strings on it."

"What are they?" Susan asked, her face shining and eyes dancing with delight.

"The money's to be used to buy a home for each of you. A home to be placed in your name and to carry no mortgage. You don't have to spend all the money on a house, of course. You can spend less and invest the remainder. But no matter what you buy, it will have to be bought without a mortgage. If there is one thing that Harry Flood Byrd has taught us, it's that you can weather almost any financial disaster, if you just stay out of debt."

Susan got up from her chair and walked around the table to hug and kiss her grandparents. Brenda followed and made a point of hugging more and laying on more kisses than Susan had done.

"I never dreamt of having any money of my own. I can't wait to tell Jordan."

"Me neither," Brenda said. "But Gramps, couldn't I just spend a bit of it on a good wardrobe? I need a fur coat."

"Go on with you, you tease." Judge Benson said. "The money is for a house."

"Clear the table please, Ella," Mrs. Benson said. "Everyone's finished. Delia has something for you all too. She's been working on it all afternoon."

"I know what it is," Susan said.

"What?"

"Strawberry short cake. What else?"

Ella removed the last of the main-course dishes, and Sam, followed by Delia, carried in a large cake plate piled high with short cake, strawberries and whipped cream. Delia smiled and waited for her compliments after which the servants left the room.

"I'll have a humongous piece," Susan said.

"Just a small piece for me," Brenda said. "I still have to fit into Granny's wedding dress."

After dinner, Susan left the family in the living room listening to Fibber McGee and Molly. She could hear Molly's country voice saying, "Tain't funny McGee," as she walked out into the twilight. She wanted to be by herself a bit, to walk around the farm to see how it was doing and to reflect in solitude upon this new aspect of her life, having the money to buy a house of her own. She wanted to tell Jordan about it but wasn't expecting him to call until the next day. Long distance rates were cheaper on the weekends.

Susan walked around the house, then down the entrance lane to the country road that curved and twisted as it meandered around Gray's Creek. Across the road she saw the entrance to the ancient Four Mile Tree Plantation. The land of Laurel Hill had originally been part of it in olden times. It had been sold off prior to the War Between the States by the Cocke family that owned it then. The Benson family, which had previously lived inland on the Blackwater, had bought the land from the Cockes and built Laurel Hill.

Susan walked down the long, tree-shaded entrance to the old place. It looked quite deserted. She thought that its current owner, a writer named Carter, lived much of the time in Washington seldom coming to the old plantation.

Susan saw a large, brick-walled area to the left that seemed to be placed in the middle of an apple orchard. Curiosity got the best of her, and she walked over to the enclosure. Before reaching the white, wooden gate in the center of one of the side walls , she realized that she was approaching a very old cemetery. The gate creaked as she opened it. Inside, there were numerous old stones, some slanted, some broken and some lying on the ground. There were two large, above-ground sepulchers in the center that dominated all else. "Bowdoin, "she saw chiseled in large letters on the mounted, marble caskets. "Sally Browne Bowdoin 1794-1815."

Susan gasped and nervously placed the lock of hair that had fallen across her face behind her ear.

Why that's only twenty-one years. She was a year younger than I am when she died. I wonder why?

There were other markers to study, some difficult to read, others illegible. Susan was about to leave when she saw a very old, small tablet with markings on it. She knelt down for a better look and realized that the letters were quite readable.

HERE LYETH BURIED THE BODY
OF ALYCE MYLES DAUGHTER
OF JOHN MYLES OF BRANDON
NEAR HERRFORD GENT. AND
LATE WIFE OF M. GEO. JORDAN

Jordan. That could be my Jordan's ancestor. I never asked him where the name came from.

Susan continued reading,

IN VIRGINIA WHO DEPARTED THIS
LIFE THE 7 OF JANUARY 1650

READER HER DUST IS HERE ENCLOSED
WHO WAS OF WITT AND GRACE COMPOSED
HER LIFE WAS VIRTUR DURING BREATH
BUT HIGHLY GLORIOUS IN HER DEATH

That's really an old one, almost three hundred years old. Susan got up from kneeling, walked out into the adjoining field, picked a bunch of tall buttercups and returned to place them on the old grave. "Wherever you are, Alyce Myles Jordan," she said, "I hope you can see me doing this."

Susan stood up. She took a last look around the burial ground and felt a shiver move through her body.

What a fascinating old place. Perhaps the shiver was a caress sent by Alice as a way of saying thank you for the flowers.

Susan kept walking toward the river. She walked around the house to the boxwood garden that overlooked the water. Some of the bushes had become ill-shaped but still looked vigorous. The boxwoods no longer rested in neatly spaded and weeded beds. The grass of the lawn grew up to the drip line of the bushes. A few weeds could be seen inside that.

Susan continued through the garden to the path that descended to the river. She wanted to see if things looked good for fishing. The shad season was over, but there should be bass and oysters, maybe some soft-shelled crabs near the shore.

Twilight was turning to the first long shadows of night. The sky to the west was bathed in an apricot glow. Once down to the river's edge, Susan took off her sandals and walked across the narrow beach to the water's edge. Her toes sank into the wet sand. She was leaning out over the rippling current to peer into the water when she heard a man's voice from behind her say,

"There comes a maiden, tall and fair,

Tiptoeing, barefoot, through the river-cooled air."

Susan turned to the sound and let out a stifled cry. She saw a man, perhaps twice her age, seated on the sand with his back resting on the knee of a cypress tree. "Who are y-you?" she said.

"I'm the owner of this little piece of Eden," he said. "Better I should ask, who are you?"

"I'm sorry," Susan said. "I didn't mean to intrude. I thought that no one was in residence. I'm Susan Benson, Judge Benson's grand-daughter."

"Welcome to my haven," the gentleman said, getting up from his seat on the sand. "I'm Clarence Emory Carter. You may call me Emory."

"Emory," Susan said, realizing as she said it that she had never called a man of his age by his given name before. "Thanks. I apologize. I was investigating the fishing. It's one of my favorite things to do, and Laurel Hill isn't on the water. I must confess that I've fished here many times when the house was unoccupied. I thought the owner lived in Washington and was seldom here."

"That was true. I'm an editor and can work where I please. It pleases me to be here just now rather than anywhere else. There are plenty of fish for everyone. Come with your rod anytime you like."

There was a awkward moment when neither of them spoke.

"It's getting dark. I better be going," Susan said.

"The moon's just ready to make its appearance. Won't you stay for that?"

"No really, I can't. Gramps will be worried. I didn't tell anyone where I was going. Thanks for the offer of fishing. I'll take you up on it. My fiance will be down tomorrow. He loves to fish."

"Your fiance. Drats. I retract the offer."

Susan burst out laughing. "Come now," she said.

"I thought you'd been sent, like manna from the Gods, just for me."

Susan blushed, but it couldn't be seen in the dimming light.

"Good night, Emory," she said. "I'll bring Jordan over for fishing this weekend. He'll enjoy meeting you."

"Goodnight, Susan. Can you make your way back alone?"

"Of course."

"Good. I'm going to stay here for the moon rise. No telling what might show up in this magical spot. Perhaps the next damsel to tiptoe in will not be spoken for."

Susan gave Carter a slow, appreciative smile. She started the climb from the river. What a very nice man. I thought he was married. I wonder where his wife can be?

III

Susan and Brenda were married to Jordan Camp and Otto Meier at Laurel Hill in late June as originally planned. Dudley Mills came down from Washington to be Susan's maid-of-honor, and Brenda's Sweet Briar roommate came over from Richmond to do the same.

The Richmond Times Dispatch carried a handsome picture of

the family on the front page of its Society section. A long article described every aspect of the wedding and included a description of the handsome Norwegian, naval architect, scion of the Meier Shipbuilding Company of Norway, who was in Washington representing his family's business, and one of Jordan, descendent of the well-known Camp family of southside Virginia whose lumbering business had recently been merged with the Union Co. to form the Union Camp Corporation of Franklin, Virginia. The article ended with the statement that, regrettably, both brides would be leaving their family home, Laurel Hill, to reside in Washington, D. C.

Ella begged to go to Washington with Susan as soon as she heard that she and Jordan had found a house to buy there. "She won't know how to do all that needs doing without me to help out," she said to Mrs. Benson. "Besides, there's not enough work for all three of us here at Laurel Hill now that the girls is moved away for good."

Mrs. Benson had to agree with that. Delia and Sam could take care of all their needs quite well, and Ella would be a big help to Susan. Surry County had an overabundance of Negro women looking for domestic work. It was just about the only work available to them other than farming. If Mrs. Benson ever needed more help, she could easily find it.

Even before Susan and Jordan moved out of the apartment they were renting, Ella moved her things into the third floor, maid's room and bath of the Wesley Heights home they had bought. She was on hand when the workmen arrived to paint the interior. Later, she showed the moving van men which pieces of furniture to put in which rooms, and then began unpacking crates of china, kitchen utensils and books.

"Be sure to put some liner paper in the sideboard drawers before you put the table cloths and napkins in, Ella."

"Yessum, I'm cutting it just this minute."

"I got most of our clothes unpacked," Susan said, "but I look a fright. I hope no neighbors decide to pay us a call."

"You go on upstairs and take yourself a nice, hot bath, Miss Susan. I can get the rest of this stuff put away. You got to be looking your best when Mister Jordan gets home."

"Thanks, Ella. I'd like that."

The telephone in the hall rang. "I'll get it. You just keep on working. Hello."

"Susan, you're there. Thank heavens. I can't wait to see the house again now that you've moved in. I have oodles to tell you. I'll be over in ten minutes."

"Not ten, Brenda. I'm just about to get into the tub. Make it half an hour."

"Okay, five-thirty. You won't believe my news. It's stupendous."

"Can't wait."

"See you."

Susan drew the bath water and tested it for temperature with her big toe. There is nothing quite like immersing the entire body in a tub of hot water to soothe every tired muscle and nerve. After her bath, she stepped into a gray, glen-plaid skirt, slipped on a yellow cashmere sweater set and fastened a strand of cultured pearls around her neck.

The doorbell rang.

Just made it. Brenda really must have some news. This is the first time she's been on time in years. She went downstairs and opened the front door.

"The house is gorgeous, honey. I love the color of the living room. What do you call it?"

"I don't know. Oyster with a tint of green, I guess. It had to be specially mixed."

"I recognize quite a bit of the furniture. You must have raided the attic at Laurel Hill."

"What are old houses for if not to store discards instead of throwing them away?"

Brenda took off her gloves and hat and lay them on a crate in the entrance hall.

"Sorry, there's no chair or table for your things. Come on into the solarium or library or whatever you want to call it. It's the only furnished room so far."

"I love it. It's octagonal. How chic."

"Jordan will be home in a few minutes and we'll have a drink."

The women seated themselves. "Susan, I can't wait another minute. I'm about to burst."

"You've found a house."

"No. Thank heavens. I was wild about the one on Indian Lane, as you know, but it was out of our price range. Now, we're moving to Oslo. Otto's father has sent the command. Can you believe it? His father is worried about protecting the business in case of war. He wants Otto to return before Christmas. Otto thinks his father may be planning to make him president of the company.

"Brenda, you're joking. Oslo is thousands of miles away."

"It's not as far it used to be. It's only twenty-eight hours from here to London by flying boat. Oslo is only five more from London. It used to take a week. Mr. Meier wants Otto back as soon as he can get away from Washington. There are some business things that will have to be tied up here though."

"But I might not see you for years."

"We'll be traveling back and forth, and you'll have to start planning a trip to Europe. Think of all the fabulous adventures we're about to have. It's mind-boggling. Otto says I'll be able to buy a mansion in Oslo for twenty thousand dollars."

Ella came into the room.

"Hi, Ella," Brenda said.

"Evening, Miss Brenda. Can I get you anything? The Sherry is unpacked, but I don't know as I can find much else."

"Sherry would be great."

"One for me too," Susan said.

"Otto says he wants to give a party for all our Washington friends before we leave. We were wondering if Jordan could arrange for us to have it at the Chevy Chase Club. There's not enough room in our apartment."

"I guess so. When?"

"Whenever Otto can snag the Ambassador and Mrs. Morgenstierne. They have about the busiest social schedule in town. We'll try to have the party in his honor."

"Why? I mean, isn't it just to see your friends?"

"Well, yes. That's the idea. But we'll have to give it in honor of someone that's a contact for the Meier business. We have to pay U. S. income tax on Otto's earnings. If the party's for the Ambassador, we can deduct it from our taxes. It all adds up. Otto wouldn't have thought of this. I did."

"I see," Susan said. "I'll ask Jordan, but I think they may have rules against business entertaining at the Chevy Chase Club."

"You don't tell them it's for business, silly. Just say that Otto wants to entertain for an old family friend, the Norwegian Ambassador."

Ella brought in a tray with two glasses and a bottle of Sherry.

"You've only heard part of my news. The other part is that we're expecting."

"What?"

"It's true. Not till next May so we can't broadcast it yet. We'll be in Oslo long before that. Otto's already thinking of buying the little fellow a pair of skis."

The intimate news sharing was interrupted by Jordan's arrival home. All had to be told again. Later that evening after Brenda had left and Jordan had absented himself to read the evening paper, Ella said to Susan. "Miss Brenda always has set her hopes high, but how do she know what's on the other side of the ocean?"

"She has to follow her husband," Susan said.

"She didn't have to marry no foreigner. She could of had about anybody she want."

"True," Susan said, "but she's married now."

IV

Brenda and Otto left for Norway before Christmas of 1938 after a series of parties in their honor. The following spring, letters of happiness arrived with pictures to affirm their many blessings. The house Brenda had bought, outside of Oslo, looked spectacular and the pictures of little Ottsy in embroidered cap and gown were endearing. Brenda answered all the concerns of her family over the political situation in Europe with a firm "Pooh! Pooh! Your worries are much ado about nothing."

Hitler continued his course of aggression, taking over Czechoslovakia that summer, and then shocking the world into recognition of the true extent of his ambitions by smashing Poland with steel and fire.

France and England declared war on Germany, and strangely enough, the declaration alone seemed to many to tether Hitler's aggression.

Brenda's letters were still full of optimism. "Looks like the little house-painter turned chicken when he learned that France and England meant to fight back," Brenda wrote. "Of course, France has the Maginot Line and England and Scandinavia have the water to protect them from invasion. We actually feel out of things up here in Oslo. We're really more out of the way than just several hundred miles would suggest.

"Ottsy is thriving. I wish you could see him. He can walk now and speak a few words."

On a rainy evening the following spring, Susan and Jordan were driving to the Chevy Chase Club for dinner. It was Thursday evening and Ella was off that day as were most all the maids and other household help in Washington. The couple made a practice of having dinner at the club on "maid's night out" as did many of their friends.

"You're mighty quiet this evening," Susan said as they drove along.

"Sorry, I didn't mean to be a bore."

"You haven't said a word about the office."

The car maneuvered around Ward Circle and headed out Massachusetts Avenue to 49th Street.

"It was pretty boring," Jordan said. "When the world is in turmoil, forest conservation is not very exciting."

"There's not much you can do about a war that we're not involved in."

"We're plenty involved. Roosevelt just has ways of camouflaging it. He knows the American people are against any active participation by us. In the meantime, he's given the British a hand in utilizing our industrial resources and weapons arsenal. Norfolk is booming from the increase in British orders."

The rain became heavier and pelted the windshield. Jordan turned the car onto Western Avenue and headed east. It was hard to see very far ahead. He leaned forward to get a better view. They reached Chevy Chase Circle.

"That's the most dangerous circle in town," Jordan said. "There are almost always fender marks on that old oak tree. I can't understand how it has survived. Something ought to be done about it."

"You're changing the subject," Susan said. "You're hiding something."

"I have been disturbed by news I heard on the radio this morning. Did you turn on the news?"

"Not today, but I can tell from your disposition that I missed something important. Tell all."

"You know me too well already. Aren't you going to leave me an ounce of privacy?"

"Sorry."

"That's okay. I'll tell you what I've been thinking about later tonight." He turned the car into the club grounds and stopped under the porte cochere. "Find us a cozy spot in the sitting room and order me a dry Martini."

"Yes, sir," Susan said.

Boyd, a distinguished-looking, white-haired Negro opened the car door. "Evening, Mrs. Camp," he said.

Susan noticed that he seemed unusually serious. "Good evening, Boyd," Susan said as she waited for the old man to hold open the door to the clubhouse for her. Inside, she left her raincoat in the cloakroom, found two seats near the large, roaring fire in the sitting room and gave the attending waitress an order for one dry Martini and one red Dubonnet on the rocks.

After some minutes of waiting, Susan checked her watch. It couldn't take that long for Jordan to park the car. What could have happened? Just then, she saw him walking stone-faced toward her. He sat down close on the sofa, put a hand on hers and said, "Boyd just gave me some bad news. Seems he had been waiting for us to arrive. Dr. Blair was in the card room when the news came over the radio. He alerted Boyd to be on the lookout for us. He couldn't stay to tell us himself, because he had an emergency call."

"Out with it, darling. You're stalling"

"Hitler has succeeded in overrunning Denmark and attacking all the major ports in Norway. Fierce fighting is going on in all the attacked areas despite vicious snow storms throughout the country. Oslo has been occupied."

"My God, Brenda and the baby. What does it mean? Are they prisoners?"

"I don't know. It could mean almost anything."

"But why Norway? I can understand their wanting Denmark, it juts out into the sea lanes, but Norway's so out of the way."

"It all has to do with iron ore from Sweden that during the winter months, when Sweden's northern ports are all frozen over, can only be shipped to Germany by way of Norway's northern port, Narvik. Big wars turn on little things."

"Poor Brenda."

"I think we should forget dinner and go home to call your grandparents, but let's not leave these drinks. I can't remember ever needing one more."

Back in the octagonal-shaped library of their home, they sat frustrated over the fact that the line to Laurel Hill was continually busy. Susan made them another round of drinks.

"Who're they talking to?" Jordan asked.

"Who knows? They must have heard by now. Try again."

Jordan re-dialed the number. It rang.

"That you, Judge?"

"Here."

"Have you heard about Norway?"

"Everyone with a radio has heard about Norway," Judge Benson said. "I've been on the phone talking with Carter Glass and Harry Byrd, trying to find out what the situation is and how it pertains to Brenda and the baby. The senators are in a state of shock, same as we are, but they'll look into it all for us. We'll have to be patient. They both promised to call me back no later than tomorrow."

"Is there nothing we can do but wait?"

"Looks that way. I'd like to talk longer, but I think we'd better clear the line. Harry or Carter could be trying to call me back at any time."

Jordan said goodbye and hung up the phone. He went into the butler's pantry and mixed another drink. Susan noticed that he poured a hefty amount of gin into his glass.

"I'll make some sandwiches and bring them into the sitting room." she said.

When she returned, she heard the voice on the radio saying. "For the latest news from Europe, we take you to Edward R. Morrow." There was a pause and some static. Then, she heard the commentator say, "This... is London."

The telephone rang. Susan answered it to hear her grandfather say. "Harry Byrd just called. He talked with the Deputy Secretary of State and with the Attorney-General. They feel confident that American citizens in Norway will be safe. The U. S. is not at war with Germany. Brenda and Ottsy have dual citizenship. Otto's predicament is much more serious. As a Norwegian citizen, he is officially a prisoner of war."

When Susan finished the conversation with her grandfather, the report from Edward R. Murrow was over. "What lousy timing," she said. "I wanted to hear what he had to say."

"He didn't say too much more. Denmark is conquered, and Norway, though fighting fiercely in the northern and central regions, is sure to be outmatched by the Germans." The Germans are bombing the devil out of the countries. They're destroying the factories and securing the ports."

"Harry Byrd told Gramps that we'd have a peck of trouble trying to stay out of this war."

"It's coming."

Susan saw that Jordan's eyes wavered. He couldn't look her straight in the eye. "What is it, darling?" she asked.

There was a moment's pause. Then Jordan, seeming to regain some sort of conviction, looked her straight in the eye and said, "I'm going to volunteer for the service, probably the Army Air Corps."

Susan gasped.

"I'm not doing anything important at Agriculture. War's inevitable. I'd rather be in at the start of things."

That night, Susan lay awake long after Jordan had fallen asleep. She was deeply hurt. She could feel his strong arms around her, but was keenly aware that soon, she might be alone. She could think of no circumstance that would have caused her to leave him. He had become her whole life.

Susan replayed event after event in their relationship, trying to think of anything she might have done to make him uncomfortable, make him want to flee. She had always known that he was somewhat of a loner. Had he found marriage to her suffocating? Tears began to stream down her cheeks. Her whole body gave a convulsive shudder.

"There, there," Jordan said. He drew her closer. "Don't be unhappy. I still love you. This is just something I have to do."

V

Brenda, with Ottsy in tow, arrived in New York before Christmas of 1940. As the U. S. was not at war with Germany her citizens were allowed to leave Norway. Otto had insisted that they leave despite his being unable to accompany them. All travel lines were crushingly full and Ottsy, with no pre-arranged seat, was expected to make the twenty-hour crossing seated on Brenda's lap. In turn Brenda was allowed only one suitcase, to weigh not more than forty-four pounds. With much of the suitcase taken up by the essentials of travel with a child under the age of two, it meant that Brenda had left Europe with little more than the clothes on her back.

Judge and Mrs. Benson motored to Washington to greet Brenda and Ottsy but stayed only long enough to see them settled into Susan's Wesley Heights home.

"You're not leaving already, are you?" Susan asked when the old couple made their move to depart.

"Have to mosey on down the road," the Judge said. "The people in Surry County still need me."

"We can get Amos an' Andy on the radio here too," Susan said.

"Not the same thing," Judge Benson said. "There're too many people up here for my liking."

"We want you all for Christmas same as always," their grandmother said.

"I don't know about that. Jordan doesn't know yet where he'll be at Christmas. If he's at March Field, I'll fly to California."

"We hope he'll still be here," grandmother said. "But remember, if not, we'll expect you at Laurel Hill."

Another year elapsed before they were able to accept the family invitation. Pearl Harbor and the U. S. declaration of war on Germany and Japan came in between.

In late 1941, Judge Benson called to insist that his granddaughters come home for Christmas. "Now that we're officially at war, it might be your last chance," he had said. "In another few weeks, you'll have rationing cards for gasoline. Then you'll barely have enough gas to get to the market once a week. Better come now while it's still obtainable."

On the afternoon of Christmas Eve, Susan headed for Laurel Hill. The car was crowded with Ella and Ottsy on the back seat and

Brenda on the front seat beside her.

Brenda talked incessantly on the trip down. Many of her stories were ones that Susan had heard before during the year that had elapsed since Brenda's return, but she listened to each telling as though she was hearing it for the first time.

"Norway didn't really agree with me," Brenda said. "I couldn't ski and didn't like the taste of smoked fish, so I was a social disaster. I tried some of my southern cooking on Otto's friends, but they didn't appreciate it."

"We thought you loved Norway. Maybe we mistook your love for Otto as love for Norway too."

"The scenery's magnificent. But you can't spend all day every day looking at the fiords and mountains."

Susan noticed that Brenda seldom talked about Otto. She must be afraid of breaking down if she does. She's bound to be having a very hard time of it.

Shortly before dark, Susan turned onto the laurel-bordered lane that led up to the house at Laurel Hill. "Made it in time," she said.

"You don't think they'd eat dinner without us, do you?" Brenda asked.

"No, but I don't want it overcooked either."

Christmas dinner, by tradition at Laurel Hill, was served on Christmas Eve so that the help could be "off" on Christmas Day.

The dining room table was beautifully decorated with a large bowl of polished fruit, red candles in the candelabra and red, gros-grain ribbons festively tying up each table napkin. Mrs. Benson wore a dark green velvet dress that she brought out of her closet each year for this particular occasion. It was as expected as the Christmas turkey. The family tried to find things to talk about other than Jordan Camp's departure for the far east or Otto's internment in Norway. Even so the conversation seemed to continually turn back to the war and the missing husbands.

"There never was a better riches to rags story than mine," Brenda said. "I felt just like Cinderella riding along in a golden carriage and having it turn into a pumpkin at mid-night or rather early dawn in my case."

"What actually happened?" the judge asked.

"It's a spooky tale. We went to bed one night feeling privileged and secure, then awoke the next morning to see German soldiers driving and marching down our streets."

"The havoc must have been dreadful."

"There was nothing much that could be done after they had secured the waterfront. It was all completely unnecessary brutality. The Norwegians had no way to effectively fight back the Germans without a counterattack by the British and French. They held out in the interior and northern area for as long as they could, hoping for an allied counter invasion, but Germany's invasion of Belgium and France put an end to any further hope of that. There was nothing they could do but surrender. Even then the Germans kept bombing everything they could think of. It was useless destruction."

"Where'd you hide?"

"In the cellar. But lots of people didn't have cellars. Our house wasn't hit, but the Meier factories were destroyed."

"You'd think they would try to keep the shipbuilding capacity," Judge Benson said.

"They seemed more set on breaking the Norwegian spirit. They broke mine. I have nothing left except Ottsy."

"We thought you might decide to stay in Norway with Otto."

"With the Meier Company gone, we had no source of income. We thought I might get some compensation for my house since it was in my name and the U. S. was not at war with Germany. Now, that's an impossibility."

"Was it hard, making the decision to leave?"

"No. Otto was adamant that we should. He said he'd get out, but I can't imagine how. The Germans are everywhere and have machine gun nests guarding every possible exit route. I'm afraid I'm on my own, at least till the end of the war, and I have no idea where the money for living will come from."

"You're always welcome here," her grandmother said.

"Thanks Grandmother. I shouldn't be so down. I know we won't go hungry."

"I'm planning to do some kind of volunteer war work, but I don't know what," Susan said. "Things aren't very well organized in Washington yet. Of course, the Congressional wives have been rolling bandages for Britain for some time, and they always want help, but I'd like to do something more useful than that."

"Gramps has some plans," their grandmother said.

"Really? What?"

"The peanut allotment program has been scrapped," Gramps said. "The government wants us to grow as much as we can. It'll take all the peanuts we can harvest to help feed the soldiers. I'm planning to have the old fields re-dug. Come spring, you'll have trouble finding a square inch of untilled soil past the rose garden."

"You better not touch that," their grandmother said.

"Wouldn't dare. Trouble is we're shorthanded. Field hands round these parts, who were lying idle this time last year, have made a bee line for Norfolk where the shipyards are paying obscene wages for the privilege of teaching unskilled workers something useful they can do. Then the lumber business is booming. Demand for packaging and paper are way up. Union Camp's hiring all the time."

Sam brought in some fresh, hot rolls and served them around the table.

"We haven't heard what you all were doing when the Japs started bombing Pearl Harbor," their grandmother said.

"We were at the Redskins game," Susan said. "The tickets are close to impossible to get, but Hiram Mills, Dudley's brother, called to say that he had three tickets and one wife who hated football. He wanted to donate two of his tickets to the war wives left behind."

"We'd hardly gotten seated when we realized that something big was up," Brenda said, "but they never announced what it was. They may have been afraid of a panic."

"The loud speaker kept paging various Admirals and Generals," Susan said. "General So and So, report to the War Department. Admiral what's his name, report to Naval Ordnance. Calls like that kept coming over the speaker system. Everyone was alarmed. Long before the game was over, there were long lines of people trying to get to the telephones or just to get out of the stadium. We didn't know about the bombing until we got to the car radio."

"Then, we were held up coming home. The police had Massachusetts Avenue blocked off in front of the Japanese Embassy. We could see black smoke coming from behind the embassy grounds. Later we learned that it was the Japs burning all their secret papers."

"Telephone for you, Judge Benson," Sam said.

"Ask who it is, Sam, and say that I'll call them back."

"I already done that. It's Senator Byrd, and he say to get you to the phone at once."

"Sorry," the Judge said looking at Mrs. Benson.

"He's at their beck and call at all hours," she said, shaking her head.

Minutes later the Judge rushed back into the dining room calling out, "Christmas gift. Otto has escaped."

"What?" came simultaneously from all the others.

"It's true. Harry just called with the official word."

"But how?" whispered Brenda.

"Otto's in Sweden. He's scheduled to leave today for London. The State Department contacted Harry when they were unable to locate Brenda."

"But how did he get out? The Germans were watching everything."

"We might never know the whole answer to that. The State Department said he traveled north in Norway to the far northern ridges of the Kjolen Mountain Range that separates Norway from Sweden. He climbed one of its mountains in Norway and skied down the other side of it into Sweden. It was extremely dangerous. The Germans are on to the possibilities and have most every pass guarded. The only way to escape now is to don a white sheet and ski down either at night or in a snow storm. Otto's a very brave man. They can't publicize the precise route. Others may need it."

Brenda got up from her chair to grab Ottsy who was playing on the carpet nearby. She raised him squealing high above her head. "Daddy's free, Ottsy. Daddy's coming home."

"Daddy," the child squealed.

The whole group exploded with joy. Delia, Ella and Sam rushed in to show their pleasure too.

"We got the perfect Christmas gift," Brenda said. "I'm so lucky. It's fantastic."

Harry says the Norwegian government in exile is sending Otto to the U. S. to work with our shipbuilders. He could be in

Washington in only a couple of weeks' time."

"Things never are as bad as they seem, are they?" Brenda said.

"Not always," Susan said. "Merry Christmas, Brenda. I'm thrilled that Otto is out."

VI

In Washington, when word came that Otto would arrive from London the following day, Susan packed a couple of suitcases with her most casual clothes and announced that she was going to the country for a while to help Gramps with his victory farm.

"He's too old to be starting out farming again, especially with so many of the hands off in the army or down in Norfolk working in the shipyards. It'll also give you and Otto a bit of privacy for your reunion."

"You're a doll, Susan. Can we keep Ella, too? Ottsy would be heartbroken if she went with you."

"Sure. Ella loves Washington. Besides, I'm only going to help get things started. I'll be back in a couple of weeks."

But a few weeks led to more. Susan found herself content in the country where she was continually busy. She helped Gramps with the hiring and instructing at first, but before long, he was doing less and less while she was doing more and more.

Letters came regularly from Jordan. He was in Burma, flying bombers to hit the Japanese positions in China. He wrote long descriptions of the spectacular scenery and deep evocative evaluations of the all-pervading faith by which the Burmese people lived. He wrote little of himself and never mentioned his fears or the dangers he faced with regularity.

When a letter from Burma arrived, Susan often left the house with it still unopened and sought out a place where she and Jordan had been together to read it. It helped to bring him closer. The small, river beach in front of Four Mile Tree was one such place. They had spent a day fishing there shortly before they were married.

One day Brenda called with the news that the U. S. Navy had asked Otto to work as a regular consultant in Norfolk where he was to help with construction techniques in the shipyards.

"It's too bad that with gasoline rationing it's so difficult to travel between Norfolk and Laurel Hill," she said. It's really easier to get back and forth to Norfolk from Washington. Ottsy and I'll go down as often as we can. There's an overnight ferry from Maine Avenue in D. C. to Portsmouth. Also Otto can probably hitch air rides to Washington on a good many weekends."

"Do you mean that you're not going to move to Norfolk to be with him?" Susan asked.

"Heavens, no." Brenda said. "I couldn't subject Ottsy to that. No one lives in Norfolk. It's just a city for prostitutes and drunken sailors on leave."

"Brenda."

"That's true."

"We even have relatives who live there."

"Well, they're nuts," Brenda said. "You know perfectly well that Aunt Sophie's as dotty as they come."

"She's not dotty, she's just elderly. And she has a lovely house there."

"I hope she stays inside it. I'd rather be in Washington. Did you know that since the war started, there has been a formal dinner-dance at the Chevy Chase Club every Saturday night? During the summer, they have them on Thursday nights too. It's glorious sitting out on the lawn and dancing by moonlight to Sidney's orchestra. You have no idea what you're missing."

"You're not even a member of the club."

"Doesn't matter. Hiram Mills says that as long as I'm a female relative, living in the household of a member, I have the club privileges."

"That's not quite right. You have the privileges only if you're with the member, not on your own."

"Don't worry. The Mills are members and I'm almost always with them. I've only signed Jordan's name to a few luncheon chits. I'll pay you back for them."

"I'm not sure that Jordan would like this."

"Then don't bother him about it."

The summer of 1942 brought in a bumper crop of fresh vegetables. Susan was busy all fall picking over, cooking and canning the produce. She had branched out in a few other directions also. Poultry for their own table had always been raised at Laurel Hill, but as part of the war effort, Susan had nurtured a large flock of turkeys to be ready for the Thanksgiving Day market. When time came for their sale, she was advised that the best way to deliver them to market was to have them packed, live, in open, wire-sided crates, drive them to a commercial wharf at Hampton Roads, where they could be sent by boat to Baltimore and sell them to be slaughtered there. She decided to take the advice, and for the safety of the turkeys and insurance purposes as well, decided to drive the farm truck to the coast herself.

"You shouldn't drive both ways the same day," Gramps said. "It might be dark before you could get home. I don't want you on the road at night."

"You can spend the night at Aunt Sophie's," her grandmother said. "She'd love to see you. She can't get out much any more."

"She might like to see me, but would she like to have a farm truck full of turkey droppings parked in front of her handsome house?"

"I dare say not," Gramps said. "Sophie's quite persnickety. You'll have to find another place for the truck."

"Where?"

"Heaven only knows. No one else in her neighborhood would want it either."

"Why don't you call Otto and ask him to find a place for you to leave it? He can ask around. Things have changed so much in Norfolk since the war that we don't know where," her grandmother said.

"Good idea. Will do," Susan said. "Has anyone got his number?"

"It's in the little red book on the desk in my bedroom."

Susan left to make the call. Upon returning to the living room, she said, "Otto will find a place. He was quite amused to hear that I'd be driving a truckload of live turkeys to town."

"Did he have any news?"

"Not much. He said that Brenda had not gotten down to Norfolk last weekend as planned, and that he missed her terribly."

"I don't understand Brenda," Gramps said.

"He said he was about out of his mind with after-work- hours boredom. Said I could stay at Aunt Sophie's, but that I had to have dinner with him. He's tired of eating in a restaurant by himself. He also said that he knew of only one hotel where you could get a proper meal, and that they served spotted ham. He seemed to find that quite amusing."

"Sounds like he's about as fond of Virginia food as Brenda is of Smorgasbord," Gramps said. "Did you accept?"

"Sure."

"Don't forget to let Sophie know that you won't be eating dinner at her house. Otherwise she'll have her cook spend the day baking you a coconut pie."

A week later, Susan delivered her turkeys to the wharf at Hampton Roads and then drove the truck across the new bridge into Norfolk. As planned, she parked it in the spot Otto had found for her and took a taxi to her Aunt Sophie's house. Otto was to pick her up at seven.

Susan was in the parlor, visiting with her aunt when Otto was shown in. To her surprise Brenda was with him.

"Aha!" Susan said, smiling. "I didn't know you'd be here. This will be fun."

"I can say the same. When Otto told me you were coming to Norfolk, I thought I'd better hurry down to protect my interest," Brenda said, tilting her head and looking slyly sideways.

"You tease," Susan said. "I know you didn't know I'd be here, because you're wearing one of my dresses."

"Girls, Girls," Aunt Sophie said. "No fussing."

"Are you sure you want me intruding on your evening," Susan said. "Two's company and three's a crowd."

"You can't escape dining with me," Otto said. "I insist upon having two beauties to keep me company to make up for all the evenings I've had to dine alone. I think Aunt Sophie should come too. Three beauties is even better than two."

"I don't go out any more," the elderly woman said. "I can't keep up."

"Then two beauties will have to do. Let's hurry. The spotted ham is waiting."

VII

Susan stayed the winter in the country. Somehow she didn't relish the idea of returning to Washington. Jordan got a stateside leave in the spring of 1943, and she flew out to California to be with him. She thought that the reunion had drawn them closer. Even so, when his leave was over, Jordan did not request a stateside assignment as he might have done considering his lengthy time of service. In May, he shipped out again, and Susan returned to Laurel Hill.

One afternoon in early March of the following year, Susan was seated at her farm desk in a small room adjacent to the kitchen when Sam came to tell her, "There's two gentlemen in the parlor who wishes to see you."

She rose to go to the front of the house when Sam added, "They's officers."

Susan froze. She looked questioningly at Sam and saw that he lowered his head so that his eyes would not make contact with hers.

"Oh God," she said, "No.".

Minutes later Susan entered the parlor and with poise listened to the two officers as they tried to cushion the blow of telling her that Jordan was dead. "His plane was hit on February 28th, somewhere over the hump as he was returning from a successful bombing mission of some Japanese warehouses" one of the officers said. "His plane was seen to explode. There is no chance of survival."

Susan heard herself thank the officers for coming so far out into the country to tell her. She heard herself say all the polite, gracious things she had been taught from childhood, but somehow she felt that these things were being said by someone else. As though acting by rote, she led the men to the front door and saw them out. Then, closing the front door behind them, she burst into uncontrollable, but quiet, sobs.

Susan waited until she heard the car leave the entrance path and turn onto the county road. She didn't want to see anyone. Her eyes scanned the doors in the hall. She knew that Sam was behind one of them and Delia behind another. She reached into the hall closet, grabbed her pea coat and fled down the front steps. She could feel a sea of emotions swelling up within her. She was like a balloon being blown up to the bursting point.

Susan began to walk fast. She didn't know where she was going, but something kept taking her toward the water. She raced down the entrance lane to Four Mile Tree with the wind sweeping her hair out behind her. At the top of the path that led down to the river, she stumbled. Her knee hit the ground, but she got up quickly and, moving more slowly, descended to the river.

"He's gone," she said. The tears continued to slip down her cheeks. When she got to the water, she walked out to the end of the short pier and stared deeply into the moving current.

Susan tried to remember the last time she and Jordan had stood in this same place. They had been on this very spot, with fishing rods in their hands and lures in the water, talking about all the things they would do when they were married. The emotion within her continued to grow. She wondered how long she could stand it before she would burst.

She looked into the water. She thought she saw Jordan's face in it. She took off her pea coat. "Oh God," she whispered. She leaned further out over the cold winter water. She slipped off her shoes. The tension within her grew past her level of control. Involuntarily, she gave a painful wail. Her body shook convulsively. She took another step forward trying to see Jordan's face again. Cloud cover made the water dark.

I see something. He's there. He's calling me. He needs me. Jordan. Jordan. She leaned forward at the edge of the pier. Tears streamed down her face. Her body shivered.

A strong arm reached around her waist and pulled her back from the pier's edge. "You don't want to do that," she heard said in a deep masculine voice. Her sobs continued. She felt herself lifted and carried back to the beach.

"Let it all out, Susan," said the voice again. "Get rid of it all."

Susan turned and grabbed frantically for the comforting body beside her as a drowning swimmer might grab for a lifeline. Then she let herself go. Tears continued to stream down her face wetting her chin and her blouse. She felt her jacket being wrapped around her shoulders. She buried herself in the comfort of the strong embrace.

"How'd you ..."

"I saw the army car leave your drive," Emory said. He cuddled and patted her. He stroked her hair and drew her closer to him. Then, propelled by the uncontrollable strength of his own desires, began kissing her tears away.

VIII

Susan ran her fingers through the curl at the side of her face and tucked it behind her ear. "I'd never have been able to get through the last few days without you," she said to Brenda. "I've felt like a jellyfish ever since Sam told me some officers were waiting in the parlor to see me."

"You're doing fine," Brenda said. "We're proud of the way you handled yourself at the service. It's hard. You can't escape that."

"So many people were there, people I'd never seen before. It was a shame they couldn't all get in the church."

"There was a speaker outside. They didn't miss anything."

"Who were they?"

"Practically the whole town of Franklin. Jordan had a lot of friends. I met one of his school teachers, his scout master, a lady who lived next door to him when he was a boy."

It's good you're driving. I could barely get myself dressed this morning. I'd never be able to find Franklin."

"It's only another mile or two. Look at all that new construction. Are those low flat buildings factories or warehouses?"

"Probably both. They've expanded a lot since the war started. Packaging and shipping materials are in heavy demand."

Brenda turned the wheel of the small sedan and looked for the Main Street of the town. "The last time we drove into Franklin was for the rehearsal dinner party before our weddings. We came in the Packard with Sam driving us in style. This sedan is quite a comedown."

"The Packard uses too much gas. It's racked up for the duration."

"This has to be Main Street," Brenda said. "I'd recognize Main Street in any small southern town. Rows of flat-topped, two story buildings on both sides of the street. What's the number of the lawyer's office?"

"Three twenty-one."

"They made those digits up to sound impressive. There can't be three hundred and twenty-one addresses on this street."

"There it is. Park right in front."

Brenda pulled the car to the curb and turned off the engine. They stepped out of the car. Susan looked up and down the street. She knew, instinctively, that Brenda was dressed much too stylishly to go unnoticed in Franklin but shrugged her shoulders in a gesture of "who cares."

When they entered the office, a portly, white-haired man in a gray business suit rushed toward them. "Right this way, Mrs. Camp," he said taking Brenda's arm to steer her.

"No. She's Mrs. Camp," Brenda said. "I'm her cousin, Mrs. Meier."

"I'm sorry," he said turning to Susan. "I wish to express my condolences. I'm Jessy Williams, Major Camp's lawyer. Come into my office ladies. My clerk has gone for the will."

The two women took seats in the chairs opposite Mr. Williams' desk. There was an awkward moment while they waited. Mr. Williams cleared his throat.

"I suppose you ladies have heard about the riot at the naval base last night," he said.

"No," Brenda said. "We've heard no news today. What happened?"

"A group of Negro sailors went on a rampage when they were turned away from a celebrity performance for the service men. Said they were in the Navy too and deserved seats as much as the white boys. It was about the same kind of thing that happened at St. Julian's Creek this time last year. We might have known there'd be trouble when we took darkies into the service. Next thing we know they'll want to go to school with us."

The clerk came in with the will. Mr. Williams took it, cleared his throat again and said, "We might as well begin."

The will was straightforward. Jordan had listed his assets and left them all to Susan in a will he had made before going overseas. It was just about as Susan had expected, a few shares of stock, some insurance, the sailboat he had left with a friend and his shares of the Union Camp Company that had been left to him by his grandfather.

"Unfortunately, the insurance and other cash assets will not be enough to pay the inheritance tax on the estate." Mr. Williams said.

"Why not?" Susan asked. "I wasn't aware that there would be an inheritance tax at all on such a small estate."

"The estate was modest when Major Camp made out his will back in 1940," Mr. Williams said. "He had arranged for his dividends from the Union Camp stock to be reinvested in the company back in the late thirties when the company had need of cash to expand the operations into the paper and packaging business. The company brought in some sharp, Harvard Business School graduates just before the war started. Fellow named Sox Calder has done wonders. The company has expanded tremendously to meet the wartime needs. Major Camp's share now, or I should say your share, is worth well over a million dollars today."

Susan was stunned. She sat quietly for a moment, then asked, "Will I have to sell any of the Union Camp stock to pay the taxes?"

"I think that would be the easiest thing to do," Mr. Williams said. "We can use the cash on hand for a first payment on the tax. Then when the amount due is established, sell off the necessary amount of stock to pay the rest.

Susan sighed. She smiled at Mr. Williams. Extending her hand to him as she stood to leave, she said, "Thank you, Mister Williams. I'd like for you to follow through with whatever else has to be done." Then turning, she was startled to see that Brenda's face had taken on an ugly expression. Her bright, blue eyes appeared to have turned dark. Her mouth was clutched into a narrow, thin line.

"You'll receive all this in written form, Mrs. Camp. Please feel free to call me about anything that you wish to have further explained."

In the car driving back to Laurel Hill, Susan broached the subject of Brenda's displeasure. "What upset you so?"

"Honey, I'm not upset. I'm thrilled to death over how rich you are. Otto and I have lost everything. I lost my house. Otto lost his family company and his country as well. All the while you've grown rich. I'm thrilled for you. You're a very lucky girl."

Susan sat stunned. "Lucky? You seem to forget that I lost Jordan."

IX

"Miss Susan. It's Ella."

"Hi, Ella. Anything wrong?"

"Well, not rightly, but I think you better come back up here. Your house needs some tending to."

"I hope it's not leaking."

"No, ma'am, but the yard looks kind of shabby and there's other things,"

"I should have known Brenda wouldn't do any gardening."

"When you coming?"

"Thursday, I guess, if you really think I should."

"Yessum."

"Count on me for dinner."

"I will."

On Thursday afternoon, Susan parked her sedan in front of her house on Garfield Street. She noticed that the lawns of the adjacent houses had already turned a bright, April green, but her lawn showed little color, and the climbing roses decorating the stone wall near the sidewalk had not been properly cut back leaving last year's shoots looking long and scraggly.

"I'm here as requested," Susan said when Ella opened the front door. She doffed her raincoat and gave it to Ella to hang up.

"I told Miss Brenda you was coming, and she spent all day yesterday moving her things out of your bedroom. I got it fixed up nice and fresh for you."

"I didn't know she had moved into my bedroom."

"She said it was much lighter, bigger too. She always left Mr. Meier's things in the spare bedroom though."

"I can see that the yard has gone to pot," Susan said. "Brenda probably didn't know what needed to be done."

"She asked me to tell you when you got here that she'd be on the porch at the Chevy Chase Club at six o'clock. She wants you to join her there."

"Gosh. I'll have to hurry. The clothes in my suitcase are probably a mass of wrinkles."

"Hand me what you want to wear and I'll press it while you get freshened up."

On the far side of six, Susan walked into the ladies' cloak room at the club. She hung up her raincoat and was turning to leave when Natalie Plunkett, an old friend of Jordan's and a recent acquaintance of hers, walked in.

"Hello there," Susan said. "Long time no see. How've you been?"

Natalie seemed taken aback. She paused for a moment. The corners of her lips tightened into a sour expression and she said,

"Umph." She looked straight into Susan's eyes then turned to leave without saying a word.

Susan almost stumbled backwards. *What a way to treat a friend's widow. Does she think I asked him to go to war?*

Minutes later out on the enclosed porch, Susan found Brenda and Hiram Mills sipping Manhattan cocktails.

"There you are, hon," Brenda said. "We've been worried that you wouldn't make it. Peggy was here with Hiram until a few minutes ago, but had to go home to the children. Said to tell you she was sorry to miss you."

"That's nice. Hi, Hiram. How's my old roommate, Dudley?"

"Sis is fine. Still hasn't found a husband though."

"There aren't many men around to chose from these days." Immediately Susan wanted to take back what she had said. She hadn't meant to draw attention to Hiram's "Four F" status.

"Manhattan?" Hiram asked.

"No. Dubonnet is about all I can handle."

"Red or white?"

"Red, with plenty of ice, please."

"Brenda, what's eating Natalie Plunkett? I just saw her in the cloak room and she cut me very rudely."

"I don't know," Brenda said. "She's always very friendly with me."

"She's a bit of an oddball," Hiram said. "Don't let her bother you."

"I can't remember being cut like that before. It's no fun."

"Otto's coming up tomorrow," Brenda said. "As soon as he heard you were coming to Washington, he said he'd catch a ride somehow and get here too. He's always been especially fond of you."

"That's nice. I'll enjoy seeing him," Susan said. "I'd forgotten how pleasant it could be sitting on this porch. Even in the twilight, it's lovely looking out across the lawn."

"We just heard the bad news that President Roosevelt is ill at Warm Springs," Hiram said. "Brenda was having lunch at the Sulgrave Club today, where Mrs. Roosevelt was speaking. As soon as she finished, the secret service men rushed her out of the ballroom. On the six o'clock news, they said that she had left to join the President in Georgia."

"Let's hope it's not too serious," Susan said. "I can't imagine this country without him. He's been President ever since I've been old enough to care about such things."

"Then there's the Truman problem," Hiram said.

"The what?"

"No one knows what to expect from Truman, and this term of office has three and a half years to go."

"Thank God the war's almost over," Brenda said. "How'd you get the gas to drive up?"

"Farmers get plenty of gas," Susan said. "I could have driven up any time, but I didn't want to misuse the privilege."

"Good girl," Hiram said. He looked at Brenda and they exchanged a slight smirk that suggested a private joke between them.

A few minutes later, Boyd came out on to the porch with a deeply saddened expression on his face. "Mr. Mills, may I have a private word with you?"

"Certainly, Boyd."

Hiram stood up. Although his back was between Susan and Boyd, she could hear the old man say to him, "The President has just passed away, Sir." She heard his voice crack with emotion. "I'd like for you to inform the other guests. I can't do it."

Hiram lay his hand on Boyd's shoulder. "I'll take care of the telling," he said.

"Thank you, Sir." Boyd said. Susan saw the old man's shoulders shake as he left the room.

"I loved him too," Susan said. "But no one loved him more than the Negroes."

X

Saturday morning, shortly before noon, Susan went upstairs to dress for church. Churches all over the country were to hold services at the same time as the President's funeral. Those who could not make it to church were asked to observe several minutes of silence, in his honor, at one o'clock.

When Susan came downstairs, decked out in her best suit with hat to match, she found Brenda in the library still dressed in her negligee.

"You'll make us late," Susan said. "Get a move on it."

"I'm not going," Brenda said. "I've got a frightful headache. Otto is determined to go though. He'll take you."

"Won't aspirin do the trick?"

"I have other troubles too. You two go on. I'll remember to keep my minutes of silence at the appropriate time."

In church, the same Episcopal church that Susan and Jordan had attended before the war, Susan was overcome by the obvious emotions of the parishioners. The bells began to ring and the choir to sing. Several boys in their late teens were seated in the pew in front of her. Susan saw tears streaming down the face of one of the boys.

He can't remember any other president. It must be like losing a father to him.

Susan saw that Otto was deep in prayer. Norway was likely to be free again soon. She felt sure that Otto gave much of the credit for that to President Roosevelt.

The service was not long but was, nevertheless, powerful. Susan thought of the President as dying in the line of duty just as Jordan had done. She felt overwhelmed by sadness.

The service ended. Susan picked up her gloves and purse and turned to leave. She saw two young women, several pews behind, looking at her. One put her hand up to the other's ear and whispered something into it without taking her eyes off Susan. The two snickered.

What a strange time for jokes. I'd have sworn the joke was something about me, but how could it have been. I don't even know them.

Otto put his hand on Susan's elbow and propelled her into the aisle. She noticed that many of the churchgoers were wiping their eyes with handkerchiefs. Everything seemed dark and heavy despite the brilliant sunshine of the day. It was a heart-wrenching occasion.

A line of churchgoers formed at the back of the church waiting to shake hands with the minister. It was unusually long. "Can't we skip this?" Otto asked.

"No," Susan said. "He wrote me a very kind letter when Jordan was killed. I must speak to him."

Some minutes passed before they reached the minister at the front door. He was speaking to others and had not noticed them until Susan had her hand stretched out to shake his. He put out his hand as though by rote, but to Susan's horror, as soon as he saw her with Otto, he pulled it back again. Otto's hand on her elbow steered her firmly. "Let's go," he ordered.

Outside, Susan felt the tears streaming down her face. She had kept control of herself up to the moment when the minister had pulled back his hand. That had been too much for her on top of everything else. The tears changed to sobs and Susan knew that Otto was at a loss to know what had suddenly come over her.

Once back at her house, Susan made a beeline for her room. She closed the door, threw herself onto her bed and burst into uncontrollable tears.

XI

Susan stayed in her room alone all that evening. Ella knocked at the door. "Brought you a bowl of chicken broth, baby."

"I'm not hungry."

"I know but you got to eat something."

"Put it on my desk, Ella. I'll try to eat it in a while."

"It was too much your going to the President's service when you hadn't gotten over your own husband's funeral yet."

"That's it, Ella. Don't worry. I'll be alright,"

"Sure, baby. I'll leave you alone."

The next morning when Susan awoke, the chicken broth was still sitting where Ella had left it on the desk. She reached over to the bedside table for her watch. "Ten-thirty," she exclaimed. "Good Lord. I slept for fourteen hours. How could I?"

Susan tried to get out of bed but found it hard to do. The effort was too much. She crawled back in.

Ella knocked on the door.

"Come in."

"I heard you get up," Ella said. "Brought you some hot coffee and the Sunday paper."

"Thanks, Ella. You do baby me so."

"Everybody needs a little babying now an then. My, my you didn't touch my broth."

"I couldn't, but the coffee smells great. How's Brenda today?"

"She's all right. She went out with Mr. Meier and Ottsy."

"Good. I'll just stay in bed a while longer.

Ella picked up the tray with the cold broth and left the room.

Sipping the delicious coffee, Susan began to feel better, but still found herself in a state of confusion as to what was going on.

Why would anyone be intentionally rude to a new widow? Jordan. Jordan. I need you so. Mustn't do that. Mustn't wallow in my grief. She forced herself to sit up straighter in bed. She took another swallow of the coffee and felt it warm her throat. First there was the snub from Natalie Plunkett, then the two women in church and then the minister. I'd suspect they all knew what happened on the beach at Four Mile Tree the day I heard of Jordan's death, but that's impossible. How could they? I haven't mentioned it to a soul, and no one in Surry has shown me anything but kindness. Could Emory have told anyone in Washington about it? No. No. He'd never have done that. Why do I think of such things?

Another knock came at the door. "Got you some breakfast this time," Ella said.

"Ella," Susan said. "Something funny is going on. What is it?"

"Miss Susan, you know it's not my place to get into some things."

"But you did call me to say that I ought to come back to tend to my house."

"Yessum. I did, and it do need tending to. You can see that."

"I think there's something more, Ella."

"You eat your breakfast, honey. I'll be in the kitchen cleaning things up." She left the room shaking her head and looking very serious.

Susan gobbled down the bacon and eggs as though she hadn't eaten in weeks. She got out of bed and quickly got dressed. She found Ella in the kitchen peeling and slicing tomatoes for the family lunch.

"What's going on around here, Ella? I have to know."

"Yessum," Ella said. "But I don't want to be the one what tells you."

Susan looked at Ella, stunned. "Start talking," she ordered.

Ella picked up a dish towel and began drying her hands.

"You're stalling, you know."

"I know."

"Well?"

"Miss Brenda's not acting good."

"What's she doing?"

"Well, she has that Mister Mills over to the house a lot. It used to be Mister and Missus Mills what came. But for the last month or two, it's just been Mister Mills, usually for cocktails on his way home from work."

"I don't get it. Are you trying to say that Brenda is having an affair?"

"I don't know what they is having," Ella said. "I just know he comes by a lot and calls every day on the phone."

"But why would that make anyone snub me? Why don't they snub Brenda?"

"Miss Brenda's done a lot of talking to a lot of people. I can't help overhearing some of it. I heard Mister Mills say he could ask Mrs. Mills for a divorce, but that he couldn't get a divorce without giving her and their children the house."

"Divorce. I can't believe it. Otto adores her. She has no grounds for divorce."

"It's not him upsets her."

"What is it?"

"It's Norway. She don't want to go back there." Ella became even more distressed. "Then Miss Brenda, she said, 'Don't worry about the house, Hiram. I'll get this house.'"

"This house. But it's not hers. It's mine."

"I know, Miss Susan. That's why I called you to say your house needs tending to. It does."

Susan looked out the kitchen window and saw her sedan pull up to the curb and park. Brenda and Otto, with Ottsy between them, one hand in each of theirs, walked stone-faced up the front path. Ottsy, in his velvet-collared coat, was a handsome child, but today, he walked with his head drooped, looking thoroughly miserable.

They've been fighting.

Susan went into the entrance hall to meet them. "Ella," she called. "Please take Ottsy upstairs and put him into some play clothes. He looks tuckered out from wearing that fancy outfit."

"Yessum," Ella said . She took the child's hand and led him away.

Susan turned to face Brenda with unflinching eyes. There was a long moment of tension-filled silence.

"Brenda wants a divorce," Otto said.

"Of course, I do," Brenda said. "I won't stand for the treatment I've gotten."

"Whatever are you talking about?" Susan asked.

"You know perfectly well," Brenda said.

"I don't."

"Well then, you're the last to know. Everyone else in town knows I caught you and Otto playing footsie in Norfolk the time you came up with that preposterous story about driving live turkeys to market."

"You have to be joking."

"I'm not."

"You can't believe.."

"I believe what I saw. If I hadn't showed up the two of you would have had a jolly time."

"We were only going to.."

"Says you."

"Brenda, Otto loves.."

"I've talked to our Minister. He was very kind. He says that as the innocent victim in a divorce case, I'd not lose my standing in the church."

"So that's why you skipped church, yesterday. You wanted the minister to see Otto and me together. You heathen. Worrying about remarrying in the church when you have no regard for morals."

"Don't try to ease your conscience with that drivel."

"I let you live here in my house, rent free."

"Ottsy is Gramps' descendant as well as we are. He deserves a house to live in. You have precious little interest in this one. If I don't get it in the settlement, I'm going to name you co-respondent in the divorce proceedings."

"That's blackmail."

"It's not fair, your having everything."

"I can't believe what I'm hearing." Susan pushed a strand of hair from her face and put it behind her ear.

The front door slammed. The two women looked up startled.

"What's that?" Brenda screamed. She rushed to the door and opened it. "It's Otto," she screamed. "He's driving away with Ottsy. He's kidnapping my baby."

"Ottsy's his son too," Susan said.

"He can't do this. It's preposterous. Call the police."

"While people are leaving, I want you to go too," Susan said.

"Go where?"

"To hell if you can think of nothing else."

"Be serious."

"I suggest you go out and look for a job."

"Doing what?"

"I don't care what you do as long as you leave this house."

"I'll help you pack, Miss Brenda," Ella said, leaning over the upstairs landing.

"You. You meddler. You let him have Ottsy."

Brenda stomped upstairs. Almost an hour went by before she came down, dressed in her best outfit, followed by Ella who carried her two suitcases. It crossed Susan's mind to wonder if one of the bags contained her yellow, cashmere sweater set. "I'll call a taxi for you," she said.

When the taxi pulled away from the front of her house, Susan gave way completely. Tears streamed down her face. She climbed the stairs to the second floor slowly. Once in her room, she flung herself on her bed and burst into chest-wracking sobs.

"There, there, baby," Ella said. "You just get into bed and go to sleep. You've had a heap of trouble sit down on you. I'll just rub your back a bit. Everything will be better tomorrow."

Susan felt the plump, black hand stroke her forehead and hair. She sniffed and sighed. She gave herself over to the comfort of Ella's touch.

How many black hands had stroked away the troubles of white people down through the ages? How much harder would life have been without them?

XII

Susan stood on the sidewalk outside the stone wall that surrounded her Wesley Heights home. The roses planted at the top had cascaded down the wall and some of the long shoots were actually lying on the sidewalk. She cut a branch and snipped it into pieces before dropping them into a cardboard box at her feet.

These bushes should have been trimmed back in February. May's too late for this. She finished one bush and began to trim another.

Susan enjoyed the solitude of gardening. It provided her with uninterrupted freedom of thought. Working away, her mind retraced the events of the past month.

How could Brenda have stooped to such low behavior? If she couldn't stand the idea of going back to Norway, why didn't she tell Otto that so they could work out a compromise? Funny how my feelings have changed. When I first got the snubs, I was terribly hurt. I thought I might have done something dreadful. I felt guilty of something I couldn't see. But as soon as I knew I was innocent, I felt nothing but disgust for those gullible people who let themselves be used to do the dirty work of others. It's as though they were hungry to judge and grabbed at any morsel of sin they could smell. How pathetic. I'm sorry for them. When they face their mistake, they'll never get over their guilt. I'm the lucky one. Now I know that what other people think of us really doesn't matter much in this world. It's what we think of ourselves that's the key to happiness.

Susan had almost finished trimming the third and last bush when she heard church bells in the distance. She paid no attention at first, but as they continued to ring, she became puzzled.

It's not Sunday. Why are they ringing like that?

"Miss Susan," Ella called from the front door. "You better get in here to hear the news. The radio say the war in Europe is over."

Susan grabbed her box of clipping and rushed into the solarium to turn on the radio. She heard the newscaster say. "All Europe is celebrating. There is, however, still the Pacific conflict to be solved. Our allies have stated their resolve to continue assisting the U. S. until the Japanese forces surrender."

If Jordan were alive, he'd still be fighting. But it's over for Otto and millions of others. I hope he gets his country back soon.

Susan turned off the radio.

"It's over, Ella."

"Yes, ma'am. Guess there'll be a lot of changes coming soon. The mail's on the front table. You was so busy with your roses, you didn't even see the mailman."

"Thanks for calling me in." Susan picked up the mail. There was a letter, addressed in a foreign script, with Canadian stamps on it.

"Otto," she said, ripping the letter open. There was only one small sheet of paper inside.

"To relieve your concerns, I am writing to tell you that Ottsy is safe with me in Little Norway, Canada. As soon as the war is over and the royal family has returned from their exile in London, Ottsy and I will return to Oslo. Please inform Brenda that Ottsy will be able to make his own choice of nationality when he comes of age at twenty-one. My best regards to you and to Judge and Mrs. Benson. Ottsy sends his love. Otto.

Brenda, Brenda. How could you have made such a mess of things? And both Otto and Ottsy loved you so. I can't believe you found Hiram Mills so attractive that you would risk either of them for him. But then, that's the way you are. You never see the consequences of anything before you act.

The phone rang. "I'll get it, Ella. Never mind."

"Hello,"

"Susan?"

"Oh, hi, Dudley. Isn't the news stupendous?"

"Fantastic. I never thought it would end even though we've been waiting all month for it."

"I know. Endings always seem to take forever. Are you going to celebrate?"

"In some way, I will. We'd be having a big family do of some sort, but we did that last night when we said goodbye to Hiram, Peggy and the kids."

"Where're they going?"

"Haven't you heard?"

"No."

"Hiram talked his law firm into opening up a new office in San Francisco. He talked the head of the firm into the idea that the next big business expansion will be in the Pacific perimeter. He wanted to get a jump start and open a law office there before the war with

Japan is over. He doesn't think it will last much longer. The firm bought the idea. Hiram packed up his family and moved to San Francisco in jiffy time. Said he was afraid the powers that be might change their minds."

"You mean they've already gone?"

"Yes. They left this morning."

Susan burst out laughing.

"What's so funny?"

"Nothing, Dudley. I shouldn't be laughing. It's all very serious. I guess I'm slap happy over hearing that the war is over."

"Part of it's over."

"That's right. We'll have to get together soon to cheer. Thanks for calling."

"Goodbye."

"See you soon."

Susan raised her arms. She put her hands at the back of her head and with her elbows held high took a long stretch. She could not help but enjoy hearing that Brenda had gotten her just desserts.

The telephone rang again. She lifted the receiver.

"Hello."

"Susan, It's me, Brenda."

"I recognize the voice."

"Don't be that way, honey. I've called to apologize."

"Really? Where are you?"

"I've been staying at Natalie Plunkett's house in Georgetown."

"Oh, yes. I remember. Natalie, your best friend."

"You know that you've always been my best friend, Susan."

"Really, you are full of gall."

"I would never have named you co-respondent. For that matter, I'd never have divorced Otto. I was just so unbearably hurt when I thought you and Otto..."

"You never thought any such thing."

"Yes, I did. I was terribly jealous of you. You'll never know how it hurt."

"Spare me. What changed your mind?"

"I had a long talk with Gramps and Granny. They told me how silly I'd been. Really, Susan, you know that Otto's the only man for me. Why in the world would I let him go? I'll get it all straightened out somehow."

"That'll take a bit of magic. He's in Canada with Ottsy."

"I know. Just as soon as I can arrange it, I'm planning to follow them. I'm heart-broken about everything. I need some money, but I'll find it somewhere.

"Good."

"There's no way I can get them back from over here. You wouldn't want to see Ottsy grow up without his mother would you?"

"Perhaps Otto will find a pretty, new mother for him in Norway."

"How cruel. Can't you see what a mess I'm in?"

"Yes. I can. You've always known how to make a mess of things, but this time I have no intention of helping you straighten things out."

Susan hung up the phone. "Ella, where are you?"

"Here, Miss Susan. What you want?"

"That was Brenda."

"I know."

"I hung up on her."

"Yessum."

"You know she'll call back again and again until she gets her way."

"She always do get her way."

"Why don't we pack a couple of bags and drive down to Laurel Hill? I don't want to hear the phone ringing itself off the hook."

"You sure do sound better. Did hearing about the war being over do all that for you?"

"Part of the war's over, not all of it. Something's changed my thinking though. Something's telling me to shut the door on my heartaches and start living all over again. I want to go to the country, want to fish again at Four Mile Tree. There's a big fish out there that keeps nibbling at my line. I'd like to see if he's still there."

THE POLITICIANS
1991-1993

I

Angela Blount, with hands behind her head, was leaning back in her desk chair at Reuter's News Agency, looking out at the tall New York skyscrapers etched against a somber, late-fall sky. She had turned her back on a sheaf of computer print-out data concerning the redistricting of Virginia's 3rd Congressional district. It was of national interest only because the re-drawing of the political boundaries would create a black majority amongst its voters, enabling a black man or woman to be elected to the Congress of the United States. Despite the fact that Virginia had as her Governor, Douglas Wilder, the first black man ever to serve as Governor of any of the states, no black person had been elected to Congress from the intrinsically southern state of Virginia during the twentieth century.

The newly drawn political district was of particular interest to Angela, as it encompassed much of the area surrounding the Lower James River from the falls at Richmond to the river's mouth at the Chesapeake Bay, all of Surry county and some of the rural, black-populated countryside that abutted it. It made a strangely shaped district that resembled the area of early colonization about which Angela had been writing for the past several years.

Times are changing fast. First, a black governor living in the yellow mansion and soon a black congressman to go to Washington. No one would have believed that either could happen a generation or so ago when Harry Flood Byrd, Carter Glass and Garland Gray had Virginia politics firmly under their control.

Angela ran her fingers through the wave of hair on her forehead as she tried to get her thoughts into focus.

There has to be a good article hiding in all these facts, but somehow it eludes me.

The phone on her desk rang. She turned her swivel chair back to its working position, away from the view, picked up the receiver and said, "Angela Blount speaking."

"Angie, it's Cary. I stayed up past midnight last night to read your <u>Four Mile Tree</u>. I'm looking at two over-used hankies on my bedside table. The Joseph Gray, Civil War story left me all choked up."

"Great, Cary. I like an emotional reaction."

Cary Walker was Angela's closest friend since childhood, a class-mate at St Catherine's School in Richmond and a roommate in New York when they had first gone to the big city to pursue careers before Cary fell in love with a Richmond lawyer, married and moved back to the southland to live the life of a stay-at-home wife and mother. The geographical distance between them had done nothing to weaken their friendship and they still conferred routinely on matters important to them both.

"When I finished it though, I wanted to know more." Cary's voice sounded wispy and tense as though true concern permeated her reflections. "Did Joe and Maggie get married and live happily ever after?"

"What do you think?"

"If I knew would I ask? You tell me."

"In real life it didn't work out so well, but in your imagination you can make it end any way you want it to."

"I haven't your kind of imagination. Tell me what happened."

"Maggie's father never gave his consent. She married someone else but kept Joe's letters in a secret hiding place all her long life, way past the time of his death. They were found by her sister after she died. Thinking they might be of historical importance, she sent them to my grandfather. He was Bart in the story, the four-year-old who had his trigger finger chopped off by the slave, Lazarus."

"You mean that part of the story was true too."

"It's all true. My grandfather refused to read the letters out of respect for his beloved older brother, but he kept them just the same. I inherited them and have them filed away neatly in my desk."

"Why didn't Maggie elope with him? He loved her so."

"Guess it would have taken more courage than she had. Family was the only safety net women had in those days. There was no social security, no aid for women with dependent children, no Medicaid, no 911 number to call for instant help. Being able to turn to one's family was often crucial for survival."

Cary released a deep sigh. "I've also been thinking about Mingo. It was horrible for them to hang him. He didn't harm anyone. All he wanted to do was to see the world."

"Blacks walked a very narrow path back then."

"It made me think about how much things have changed. We forget so much, but I'll bet that even you with your imagination can't picture Douglas Wilder ever having been a slave."

Angela laughed then stopped to check the time on her wrist-watch before continuing. "I wouldn't want to have been his owner. That's for sure."

"There's been more progress than I had thought. Our racial problems seem really rather mild by comparison."

"Actually, I think our two races get along very well. It may be because most of us practice the same religion. Blacks and whites have been living side by side with only a few big acts of large scale violence between us for almost four hundred years. When violence does flair up these days, it's almost always black against black or white against white."

Angela swiveled her chair around and rechecked her watch before noticing that the sky had darkened appreciably in only a few minutes. It looks like snow. How come? It's not even winter.

"Angie are you still there?"

"Sorry. I got distracted. I'm glad you enjoyed the manuscript, Cary. It means a lot to me. Are you interested in helping with a bit of research? It's not finished. I have to bring it up to date."

"What can I do?"

"I want to know anything and everything about the bridge."

"The bridge?"

"The proposed James River crossing from Jamestown to Surry County. The one the Reverend Young and Lila were talking about the time I went to see Four Mile Tree. Remember? I told you all about it. They said the southern terminal would come in at the foot of their property and leave the old place straddling a bridge access route."

"I'd forgotten that. If it's only proposed, how can I look into it?"

"Start with the Virginia Department of Transportation. The office is there in Richmond. If you can find out the status of the project, I'll take it from there."

"That shouldn't be difficult."

"Ask what it's to cost, who's for it and who's against."

"Will do. Angie when are you coming home again?"

"I put in a request to cover the Fortune Five Hundred Forum to be held in Richmond on November 4-6 and got my request. Then the big boys changed the setting to Charleston. I couldn't be more disappointed."

"Phewy! I was hoping. Oh, well. Another thing is I sat next to a columnist for the Richmond Times Dispatch at a dinner last night. Told him all about your book. He covers the area you're writing about and offered to help you in any way he could. Said Pipsico, the old plantation next to Four Mile Tree on the river front, is now a Boy Scout camp, and he can arrange for us to take a beach-hike along the waterfront. He wants to come too."

"Are you still trying to find a husband for me, Cary?"

"Certainly not. It's a waste of my time. You never cooperate. Besides, I think he's married. I didn't ask."

"Sounds like a great stroke of luck. See if you can arrange the hike for the seventh or eighth. I'll stop by Richmond for a few days on my way back from Charleston. Must be back in New York that Sunday though."

"John will call him to work it out. You'll stay with us this time, I hope."

"Love to."

"Don't forget your waterproof boots and binoculars. The beach front should be great for birding."

"That's what Lila said. Thanks for calling, Cary. I always love calls from home. By the way, what's his name?"

"The columnist's?"

"Of course."

"I was afraid you'd ask that. His name is Will Rivers, but the men call him Muddy."

"Oh, no. I think I'll stick with Will."

"See you when you come down."

"Give my godchild a big kiss from me. The others too, of course."

"Will do."

"Bye now."

Angela hung up the receiver and turned her gaze back to the monochromatic, overcast sky. Muddy Rivers. A quiet giggle escaped from her throat. No, no. Don't think about him. Think about black men taking office in Virginia, and what it means for the country, the world. The day is wasting away.

The sky made a convenient backdrop for creative thinking. She needed something to block out intrusive thoughts and allow her mind to wander freely. If she could let her subconscious mind out of its daytime prison, she knew from experience that it would come to her aid and turn the computer list of facts into a human interest story. She closed her eyes and concentrated on opening the door to her mind's storage closet of old ideas. Slowly, she picked up her pen and began writing. "The days of 'Carry Me Back To Old Virginy' are gone forever. Today, the General Assembly of the Commonwealth of Virginia cast off its cloak of tradition and donned in its place a newly stitched jacket of progress."

II

Angela arrived at Cary and John Benson's red-brick, colonial, Canterbury Road house shortly after ten o'clock. She was already tired from the forum coverage and travel from Charleston. Her day had been spent taking voluminous notes on everything she heard at the Fortune Five Hundred Forum, and she still had to sift through all the material and turn it into a news article before she could go to bed. A half night's work lay ahead. The children were sound asleep when she arrived and fortunately Cary and John looked as though they would like to be also. Angela explained her deadline, then, accepting a cup of hot coffee, she toted her portable computer to the guest room above, blew her hosts a good night kiss and closed the door behind her.

It was after one in the morning, when she had her news article finished. She read it over one last time and could find nothing wrong with it. The Reuter's office in New York was dark and empty at that hour, but it was midday in Hong Kong where another of Reuter's offices should be bustling with activity.

Angela picked up her index finger, kissed the tip of it, and with dramatic precision pressed a single button on her computer. With that simple action all her words, her day's and night's work, would travel, not by magic carpet, but by satellite, to Reuter's office in Hong Kong. There it would be evaluated and, if found worthy, transmitted to the various foreign news markets for evaluation when their personnel arrived for work in the morning still hours before the opening of Reuter's New York office.

Tomorrow, I'll try to move my thoughts back into the past. The world is spinning forward with such speed that it's getting harder and harder to remember the times gone by.

She took a deep breath and could smell the lavender that Cary had placed in sachet bags in the linen closet. Southern hospitality was her last thought. Before she could inhale and smell again, she was fast asleep.

III

"I told the scout leader I was bringing two ornithologists with me," Will Rivers said, "one of whom was writing a book. Don't make a liar out of me now. Pay close attention to all the birds."

"I would anyway," Angela said, picking up the binoculars that hung around her neck to confirm her statement. "I'm a dedicated environmentalist."

The two young women and their tall companion looked, to all who might be watching, like consummate, intellectual nature lovers. They were dressed for the chilly, fall day in blue jeans, heavy sweaters and boots that covered their ankles. Each had a pair of binoculars hanging either from their shoulders or around their necks.

Angela's eyes were sparkling with pleasure as the threesome maneuvered the rocky path that led from the scout quarters to the river beach in front of Pipsico. To Angela's delight, their reporter guide, Will Rivers, turned out to be unusually handsome, in a disarming sort of way, which added both excitement and glamour to the planned outing. Then too, she was eager to see Four Mile Tree from the river side. It gave her a devilish feeling to think of creeping up, uninvited, on the old place by way of the back door, though, of course, the back door had been the front door in colonial times.

Angela became aware that although Will was looking forward he was at the same time scrutinizing her closely with sly glances from the sides of his eyes. She knew that her long, brown curls were being tossed by the breeze in a tantalizing fashion that made varying frames for her face. Suddenly, the wind came in a swirl from a different direction causing long strands of hair to blow forward. She pushed them back and turned her face into the wind to straighten the strands again. The wind felt pleasing as it stroked her face. She laughed spontaneously; she was unusually happy today. The corners of her lips turned up forcing her to turn away so that Will could not see her. She knew she was flirting but seemed unable to stop herself from doing so. Bad girl. He's a married man. She laughed again.

"Be on the lookout for eagles," Will said. "They've made a remarkable comeback. I'll write another article about their increase in numbers since the kepone disaster to justify my spending the day out here."

"Kepone? I thought it was DDT that killed off the eagles," Cary said.

"Both," Will answered.

They reached the bottom of the path and stepped out onto the narrow, stony, sand beach. "Turn east," he said. "Four Mile Tree is less than a mile down river."

"I'd almost forgotten about the kepone. It was from a chemical plant in Hopewell, wasn't it?" Cary asked.

"The plant was making its workers deathly ill and pouring tons of poison into the river right before our very eyes with nobody noticing. That was in the mid-seventies before the country became environmentally aware. I don't think it could happen today. One of the sick workers blew the whistle on the operation. After his complaint was investigated, the plant was closed down, and the Lower James closed to fishing for twelve years. Unfortunately, the eagles couldn't read the 'Closed to Fishing' signs and kept right on eating the kepone- contaminated fish. We almost lost them all."

Angela tried to keep her mind on the day's objective, but instead found herself taking sporadic glances at the tall, very tall man who was guiding them along the shore line. He had a boyish face which came as a surprise for one so tall, one who must be near forty years in age. His hair was neatly trimmed around the sides and back of his head in a manner reminiscent of the style of the fifties, but a thick, unruly lock of sandy-colored hair hung across his forehead.

A grown-up Tom Sawyer. She turned her face away so as to hide her interest and amusement. *All he needs to complete the picture is a straw hat, overalls and bare feet.*

"What happened to the kepone?" Cary asked.

"It sank," Will answered. "It's heavy stuff. With time it sank to the bottom and was covered over by soil runoff from up-river." Now, the water runs over it without becoming polluted. The fish are uncontaminated and the eagles, which eat the fish, are repro-ducing again."

"I love to fish," Angela said. "I wish we had time for that today."

"I wonder if I'd recognize an eagle if I saw one." Cary said.

"You'd know," Will answered, "but you're looking too close. If you see one it's apt to be from more than a hundred yards, much more as a rule. They perch in the top of bare-branched trees, the kind with heavy trunks and not many branches. Look for the tree first and then the eagles." Turning to Angela, he said, "You'll have to focus your glasses for a longer distance. Here, let me do it for you." He walked over to her and reached for the binoculars around her neck.

Angela took a deep breath and stood rigidly still as he removed the glasses. She was acutely aware of his masculinity which perme-ated the air between them. She felt suddenly queasy despite the security of knowing that Cary was standing not ten feet away. Then the old feeling that intruded on all her pleasant associations began creeping through her body. She had felt it dozens and dozens of times. It had always confused her. Recently she had come to know, however, that it was a feeling of pure, unadulterated fear. Fear of what? Fear of loving and becoming hurt? Fear of losing control of her life? No matter, she knew it was fear.

"Something wrong?" Will asked.

"No," Angela said emphatically. "I can do that. You must think me an idiot."

Will handed the binoculars back, but kept his eyes on her face. Her smile was gone. She looked nervous. "No offense meant," he said.

"Of course not," Angela replied.

Cary picked up a flat stone and tried to hop it across the water.

"I never could do that. John can make one skip four or five times."

Quiet came over the group as they walked purposefully toward the jutting piece of shoreline that completed Pipsico Bay. "Four Mile Tree is just about at the tip of the arc's end," Will said. "At least that's where they say the old tree was. It was destroyed by a Yankee cannon ball during the final months of the War Between the States. Every time I walk along this shore I visualize the Yankee gun boats, supply ships and fuel barges that filled up the river during the final months of the war. Even Mrs. Lincoln came down to join the President and gave a ball on the *River Queen*. There were more than fifteen hundred Federal vessels here, daily, near the end of the siege of Petersburg."

"I see one," Cary called out.

"A river boat?"

"No, silly, an eagle. Look over there. Across the water. On the other side of the little inlet. There are two of them. They're looking straight at us."

"They have incredible eyes," Will said. "They can see small things two or three miles away."

"They're much bigger than I'd imagined."

"Almost a yard high."

"Are there always two?" Angela asked.

"Usually," Will answered. "They mate for life. Sometimes they even act as though they care for each other."

"Those ugly things. I don't believe it," Cary said.

"It's true," Will answered. "Let's sit down on the log over there. The chiggers won't be out in this weather. We're just about in front of Four Mile Tree. There's the path up the bank."

"I thought we'd find a pier here," Angela said.

"Used to be one," Will answered. "All the places used to have piers but no more."

"Is this where the bridge is to come in?"

"Almost," Will answered, "just a bit further on towards Mt. Pleasant. That is, if it gets built. There's a vicious battle going on right now between those who want the bridge and those who don't. Elmon Gray, state senator for these parts, has been working to get the bridge approved for years. His father, Garland, who held the same senate seat for more than twenty years before him, got the

Benjamin Harrison bridge built up at Hopewell. Like father, like son, Elmon has made it a big part of his life's work to get one built down here."

"Could a few unhappy property owners stop the building of the bridge?"

"It's not just them anymore. For a long time the bridge seemed like a sure thing. Projects proposed by the Transportation Department are almost always approved. A few years ago the board was all for it, but that was before the environmentalists started working them over. Now a group called the Lower James River Association has pulled together all the fragmented groups that oppose it and formed the James River Crossing Coalition. Their head, Patti Jackson, and her cohorts have lobbied every member of the Commonwealth Transportation Board to keep the bridge from being built. She tells them it will ruin the Jamestown river view, stir up the kepone in the river's floor, cost the commuters more, ruin historic properties, allow our black boys to roam Williamsburg after dark, and maybe even start a war in the Middle East. I don't know. She's been very effective. The board shelved the whole thing for a while, but some Surry county citizens got up a petition for the bridge which convinced the county supervisor to ask for a reconsideration. Now they're all battling again."

"Who's winning?"

"Elmon will win. He's a very powerful man, and the poor people on this side of the river need the bridge. Surry's a very poor county with few opportunities for work. The jobs are on the other side."

"I heard Senator Gray has vast land holdings down in Sussex, estimated by some to be as much as 100,000 acres and that he wants the bridge to increase the value of his land."

"People against the bridge will say anything, but I don't believe it. The Grays have always served their constituents. How else could one family, father and son, have gotten themselves continually elected to fill the senate seat for over fifty years? Governor Wilder's not fond of Elmon, though, despite their both being Democrats. He fought hard to keep Elmon from being elected the first time back in 1972. Elmon won anyway. Then, Elmon was one of only two Democratic state senators who didn't support Wilder in his run for Governor. Most of the Gray's land won't perk. It was bought as timberland for the family's lumber business, and growing timber's about all it's good for."

"Speaking of timber, where do you think the old cypress tree was, the Four Mile Tree?"

"Probably near the point over there."

"Do you think we could find some old roots from it?" Angela asked, getting up and walking toward the water's edge.

"The roots would be under water by now," Will said. "There's not much erosion here, but even so, the river must have widened by at least several feet since the old tree was blown to smithereens."

"Out there," Angela shouted. "Maybe it's that dark spot in the water. It looks like a large dark circle."

Angela began taking off her boots and rolling up the legs of her jeans.

"You can't go in," Cary yelled. "The water's frigid."

"Just for a minute," Angela called back.

"Stop her, Will," shouted Cary.

"Who's there?" called out a strong voice from the top of the bank. This is private property, and we're armed. Get off this land."

All three intruders stopped in their tracks. They looked up to see an elderly black man standing atop the sharp rise with his frame silhouetted against a clear, autumn sky.

"Don't shoot," Will yelled. "We're birders from the Boy Scout camp."

"Don't look like boys to me," came the reply. "Get going. We don't want you here."

"We're going. Sorry."

Cary and Will scrambled to their feet. Angela grabbed her boots, and the three raced back down the shore towards Pipsico.

They ran until they felt safely out of the old man's sight.

"Is this still the U.S.A.?" Angela asked. "I thought all the shorelines were public property?"

"In places like this, it depends on who's holding the gun," Will said.

"Did you see a gun?"

"No, but I wasn't going to wait around till I did. You must be freezing, Angela. Put your boots back on. I should have known we might run into a problem. They don't like outsiders at Four Mile

Tree."

"You're shivering, Angie," Cary said. "We've got to get you warmed up."

"We'll drive into Surry," Will said. "The Surrey House Restaurant serves great hot chocolate."

IV

Will pulled his four-wheel-drive Bronco into a parking space in front of the Surry County Courthouse, quickly got out and rounded the car to help the women descend from the high- bodied vehicle. "This town is a small charmer," he said. "People come from all over the country to look up their ancestors or do other research in the records here. Everything in Jamestown was burned up, you know. This courthouse and one on the eastern shore have the best early records in America."

Across the road, Angela noticed an Episcopal Church. She was studying the architecture of the old building in an attempt to ascertain its age, when she saw two women leave the church by a side door. They were both well dressed, in country woolens, and seemed to be on close terms with one another. One of the two, with a long scarf encircling her neck and trailing down her shoulders, looked exceptionally chic in such a country setting. As they came nearer, Angela noticed to her surprise that she was a black woman whereas her companion was white. She saw the women turn as they reached the sidewalk and walk down toward the Surrey House Restaurant which they entered ahead of the beach walkers. Looking down at her own boots and jeans she murmured, "Hope we're not too casually dressed."

"Are you kidding? All you need here is to be wearing shoes."

They crossed the street, following the women.

"Looky here," Cary said, pointing to chalk writing on the sidewalk before them. In large letters, that showed no trace of a childish hand, they saw scrawled in white chalk, "Ferries Forever." A large, black mark scratched out the word 'Forever' and in its place was written an expletive that should have been deleted. "Tensions are high on the bridge issue, I see."

"It's a war," Will said.

The three went inside and were seated in a large room to the right by a pleasant looking older woman who appeared to be the proprietress.

"What can I have Sally bring you?" she asked.

"What'll it be, Angie," Cary asked.

"Hot chocolate sounds divine."

"Same for me, please."

"All around," Will said, "and some of your world-class peanut butter cookies."

"A man after my own heart," the proprietress said. She left with a smile on her face.

"There's a sign between those windows," Angela said, nodding in its direction. "What does it says?"

"Ferries Forever," Will answered. "The owner must be against the bridge too. I tell you they're all stirred up about it around here."

"Excuse me," Cary said getting up to go to the ladies' room. "You coming, Angie?"

"No. I'm fine."

"I'll just be a moment."

Will was silent until Cary left the room. Then he turned to Angela to say, "I was afraid I wouldn't get a private word with you, but it looks as though I've lucked out."

"With me? About what?" Angela's eyes took on an added sparkle.

"About everything," Will answered. "I hope this afternoon won't be our only meeting."

"Whoa," Angela said. "I thought you were married."

"I was," he said, "but I'm not anymore. My wife left me a little more than a year ago."

"Left you? I thought it was always the other way around. The woman got left, I mean."

"You're wrong."

"But why would she leave you?" Her voice reflected her disbelief.

"She got fed up with me for refusing to wear trousers with a sharp crease down the pants legs."

"Come on, you don't expect me to believe that."

"It's true."

"Why wouldn't you?"

"Cause my mother bugged me for years about the same thing."

Angela looked down, away from his eyes toward the table top. She was groping for something clever to say but found herself mesmerized by his hands instead. They were thumping nervously as he talked, large, graceful hands with long slender fingers and neatly trimmed nails.

"Your wife wasn't your mother," Angela said, looking back up and into his eyes.

His eyes engaged hers. He kept them steady as he said, "She began to seem like she was."

"Mothers," Angela said tossing her head back as she spoke. "Why are they always getting in the way? Mine's been dead for three years now, and yet I find myself worrying all the time about what she might think."

"I kind of thought there was something tying you all up."

Cary returned to the table as the hot drinks arrived. "You won't believe who I saw," she said in a whisper. "The ladies' room is in that other room, and right beside the door to it is a screened off table where those two women we saw outside are seated. The black woman's a real knockout. I thought she might be Lena Horne's sister or something. I looked back at the white woman as I went in and was stunned to see that it was the same woman as the one in that newspaper picture you showed me of Lila. With her hair combed it took me a moment to realize who she was. Could she have heard about our trespassing?"

"Not yet. Do you mean to say that that get-up she wore last fall when I called on her was her way of having fun with me, thumbing her nose at me, as she would say."

"Must have been. She got herself gussied up pretty well for tea with her black friend. When I walked by, I heard her speaking and her voice confirmed it all."

"What did she say?"

"I only heard a little. She said, 'You'll lose control, and you worked so hard to get it.'"

"Don't look around," Will said. "They've gone."

The proprietress walked over to their table. "Is there anything else you'd like?" she asked.

"The check, please," Will answered.

When the owner returned with the check, Angela said to her, "That was a stunning-looking black woman. Is she a movie star or something?"

"That woman? No. She's our county attorney, Gammil Poindexter. Her husband is state's attorney. Blacks have had more opportunity around here since Douglas Wilder became Governor. She does a good job."

"I take it you're not for the bridge," Cary said nodding toward the sign between the two windows.

"We don't need it," the owner said. "I always say, 'If it's not broke, don't fix it.'"

V

Angela awoke the next morning in the queen-size, four- poster bed in Cary's guest room. It took her a few minutes to realize where she was. The dreams she had fallen into during the night left her confused, but as she became aware of her surroundings, she felt relieved.

Strange beds make for strange dreams.

Angela turned over and sat up. She gave a punch to each of the two large pillows on the bed, puffing them up as best she could, and placed them behind her back for support. The sheets felt soft and fresh, the bed warm and cozy.

Angela's mind roamed back over her dreams trying to force them into her consciousness. They had been so vivid, so real, so odd.

From below, she could hear the murmur of children's voices and the clink of tableware being placed upon the kitchen table. One piece dropped noisily to the floor, and she heard a child's voice scream, "Don't." She knew that she should get up to help Cary with the children but had no inclination to do so. Children, like dogs and cats, were always more pleasing to her when they were someone else's responsibility. Motherhood was not a state of being for which she had ever yearned.

I'll stay in bed for awhile so as not to get in the way.

A few minutes later, she heard the doorbell ring and heard the children squeal with delight at the arrival of someone. She remembered Cary saying that a teenager came on Saturdays to take the children out for fresh air and play.

Way to go. She immediately jumped out of bed and started to dress.

"Here she is," John said, getting up from his chair at the breakfast table to pull a chair out for Angela. "She looks as though she's in immediate need of coffee."

"I am," Angela said, "these bags must have told you." She pulled playfully on the skin beneath her eyes.

"Coming PDQ," Cary said. "Did you sleep well last night?"

"I did, but I had the weirdest dreams. I'm trying to remember them all."

"John was showing me an article by Will in this morning's paper. After dropping us off yesterday, he must have headed straight for the office to write an article about..."

"Don't tell me. The eagles."

"No. Not the eagles, the bridge."

"To think that he wrote it last night and we get to read it this morning," John said.

"I work that way most of the time," Angela replied. "May I see it?"

"Here." John handed her a section of the paper that was folded to the article.

Angela took a large gulp of steaming coffee, smacked her lips and began to read.

"His columns are always good," John said. "He has a nice sense of humor."

"Most of it's what we talked about yesterday," Cary said, "so he couldn't have written it ahead of time."

"Here's something new," Angela said. "General Elmon Gray, commander of the traditional forces of the democratic army, is waging all-out war in the interest of serving the poor, rural constituents of his senate district. Elmon, and his deceased father, Garland Gray, have held this senate seat for the past fifty-two years. With banners flying, the state senator got off several volleys for the cause yesterday. He reminded members of the Commonwealth Transportation Board that the bridge has been in the planning stage for over twenty years, that the Virginia Department of Transportation has recommended its building, and that the laboring classes of Surry, Southampton and Sussex need the bridge to ease the burden of getting to jobs on the other side of the river."

"Unfortunately for the bridge proponents, a new figure, Patti Jackson, resembling a slightly more mature Joan of Arc, has entered the battle. She has assembled an oddly disparate force of opposition, environmentalists, historic preservationists, cost awareness groups, land developers and politicians of the counties north of the river, into an effective army."

"Who does he say will win?" Cary asked.

"He doesn't really say here, but I know he's for the bridge. He goes on to say, 'Garland Gray, father of the senator and one of an elite handful of Harry Flood Byrd's most valuable supporters during the days of the Byrd political machine, succeeded in getting the Benjamin Harrison bridge built at Hopewell for his constituents. Now Elmon, like his father, is determined to battle to the finish in order to build his own.'"

"It's good," Angela said. "I'm glad his whole day wasn't wasted on us. At least he got a story out of it."

"Did you like him?" Cary asked.

"I did."

"He's a great guy," John said. "What's on for today?"

"I love the guest room, Cary. I could move in and stay."

"Was the mattress O. K.?"

"It was, but I had the weirdest dreams. I can only remember part of them. Is it unlucky to tell your dreams?"

"Depends on who's listening, but you can trust us. Shoot."

"Well, I kept tumbling around in space with all the characters from my novel. They've become my best friends, you know. Most of them lived and died centuries ago, but they keep popping up in my mind as if they have something they want everyone to know. Last night I was revisited mostly by females. The strange thing was that no matter which character I was dreaming about, I saw Lila Young's' face on her, then I would see that black woman, Gammil, come to her rescue."

"What a riot," Cary said. "They must really have impressed

you." Cary handed Angela a plate of bacon and eggs with something white on the side.

"Who're they?" John asked. "I've missed something."

"Lila's the present mistress of Four Mile Tree and Gammil is the attorney for Surry County," Cary said. "We saw them yesterday, in Surry."

"The dreams went back in chronological order. First there was Joseph Blount's mother not wanting General Sherman's Captain to oust her from her home. She was dressed in a Civil War-era, hoop skirt but had Lila's feature on her face. Her school teacher friend, who gave laudanum to the Captain, was wearing Gammil's face. Later, I dreamt that Margaret was standing at the window-slit of her cabin at Berkeley Hundred at the time of the Indian massacre in 1622. She had Lila's features and along came Gammil to rescue her again."

"That's rich. What could it mean?"

"Who knows? All the characters kept falling through space. What kind of seasoning was in that stew we ate last night?"

"Whatever it was, it didn't make me dream," John said.

"Me either," Cary added. "I hope you slept at least part of the night."

"I'm sure I did," Angela said, "but then I had another dream just before I woke up."

"We should tape this confession," Cary said.

"I was sitting on top of a railroad car that was traveling fast. The wind was about to blow me off so I leaned over flat on the train top to hang on for dear life. The weird thing was that my mother was seated behind me. She was sitting bolt upright with a completely straight face as though nothing was happening. The wind didn't bother her at all. I remember calling out 'Why don't you blow off?' and she just kept sitting there without moving."

"Maybe it's saying that your mother's a burden to you. Is she a heavy responsibility?" John asked.

"My mother has been dead for three years," Angela answered. "I don't understand."

"Perhaps you're not supposed to," Cary said, getting up to refill Angela's coffee cup.

"I'd forgotten about grits for breakfast," Angela said. "They taste great and make me know I'm home. I served them to a fellow I know in New York once and he said, 'How original. I've never eaten hot library paste before.'"

The kitchen door flew open. Lizzie rushed in crying,"Johnny's bad. He kicked me."

"There, there Lizzie. Daddy will kiss it. Where does it hurt?"

Johnny rushed in with a fierce look on his face. "I did not. She's lying. She fell down and landed on my foot."

"Now, now, that's enough." Cary said.

"You asked about today, John," Angela said. "I should go in to the state library to look up a few things. The library's on Capitol Hill. I always enjoy walking around the place."

"Good. I'm going to the office for a few hours so I can drop you off."

"You're both deserting me?"

"Just for a few hours. It's something I need to do."

VI

"This is as close as I can get you to the front door," John said as he stopped the car on Capitol Hill to let Angela out. "You'll have to walk the rest of the way. Cars can't get any closer because of the Governor's Mansion over there."

"This is fine, John. Thanks a heap. You were a dear to bother with me."

"How long will you be? I can pick you up again if you can get your work done in three hours."

"I'm sure I can."

"Then, I'll pick you up right here at 12:30. We'll make it home in time for lunch with Cary."

"Perfect. Thanks again."

Angela climbed out of the car with her brief case in hand and her purse hanging from her shoulder. It was a glorious, late fall day, a bit warmer than the day before, but still crisp and cool. She didn't want to go inside, but automatically began walking the brick path from the paved street to the library door. She was acutely aware of how few people seemed to be about. Then she remembered that it was Saturday. In New York, there was never a day without rushing crowds everywhere; here, apparently, many stayed at home on the weekends.

Angela signed in at the reception desk and asked where she could find microfilms of back copies of the <u>Richmond Times Dispatch</u>. She was directed to a large reading room on the right where she gave her request to a pleasant, soft-spoken woman behind the information desk. Within minutes, the woman handed her three rolls of film covering the dates for which she had asked. She pointed to the microfilm readers and photo copiers in a wing off the main room and asked, "Are you familiar with the operation of the machines?"

"Oh, yes," Angela answered. She was stunned by the speed with which her request had been answered, at how easy it was to do things in this quiet, genteel city of the southland. There was no hassle over anything. Everyone she encountered looked rested. Everyone was smiling and eager to please.

Angela fit the first microfilm roll into the reading machine and began turning the crank slowly in order to find the back news item of her quest. It was tedious work. The rolls carried every page, including the classified ads of both the early edition and the final edition of each day's paper. At eleven-thirty, she finished scanning the second roll but had found nothing. She re-wound the film, placed it neatly into its box and took out the third roll. She had been cranking the lever for only a minute when her eye caught the item for which she had been searching. Her heart beat faster. She could feel a nerve above her left eye that began to twitch. There it was, a small, obscure advertisement in the classified section under the column labeled Personals. She read it slowly, giving out a deep sigh of relief as she did so. Then, she reread it again.

"This is public notice that William Jordan Rivers will not be responsible for any future debts incurred by his wife, Pamela Dodd Rivers."

So he had been telling her the truth. He and his wife had been legally separated over a year ago as he had said. His lawyer must have placed the notice in the paper. These ads drew little attention, but were read religiously by accountants of department stores and ladies' dress boutiques.

Why, oh why, am I so distrustful? But she knew the answer. So many men said so many things when they thought it would be convenient for their own purposes. She had seen too much misery connected with love to leave things to chance.

Angela re-wound the film, re-boxed it and got her possessions together. There was no need to make a photo copy of her find. Just seeing the few words was all she needed.

Out into the clear, sunny day again, Angela realized that she would have to kill at least forty minutes before John returned to pick her up. She decided to spend the time touring the hill. The capitol building, with its magnificent statue of George Washington in the rotunda, was one of the most impressive state capitols in the nation. Then too, she had always loved looking in on the original, small assembly room where early political leaders had sat at the small, handmade desks and stood to give speeches to their fellow members. History always thrilled Angela, and this was truly the seat of it for much of the nation.

Leaving the Capitol, she strolled back in the direction of the library, where she had spent the earlier hours at the viewing machine. She stopped to look at the Governor's Mansion, and realized that she had never really scrutinized it before. The square-shaped, Greek revival building had stucco walls, painted a strong yellow color, with its wide window trim, cornices and columns painted a stark, chalk white, giving the house a fresh, crisp appearance. She thought it an elegant size for comfortable living and entertaining, not too big, not too small.

A uniformed guard stood before a small, square guard house at the end of a brick entrance-path near the roadway in front of the mansion. As Angela was walking toward him, she saw a long, black sedan pull up to the entrance. She looked at her watch, twelve-thirty on the dot she noticed; someone is arriving for lunch. A black couple, dressed in high-style business clothes, stepped out of the car. She was about to rush on for her own meeting with John when instead she stopped abruptly.

The woman turned her face around toward Angela, and at the same moment Angela heard the guard say, "Good afternoon Mr. and Mrs. Poindexter."

I can't believe it. That woman's face has been with me day and night for the last twenty-four hours. It's Gammil. The man, apparently, is her husband.

Angela waited until she saw the couple walk up the steps to the front door of the mansion. The door opened to them without their needing to knock. Obviously, they were a privileged couple in the home of the Governor.

Lila's words of the day before, "You'll lose control and you worked so hard to get it," tumbled forth and seemed to ricochet against the walls of Angela's mind. "You'll lose control and you worked so hard to get it." The redistricting, of course, that's what the conversation was all about. Lila didn't want the bridge to ruin Four Mile Tree so she set out to convince Gammil that the bridge would make Surry County into a bedroom community for whites from the north shore. If the whites moved over in droves, the blacks would lose their plurality in the one district where they held control. Their congressional seat would be in danger. Lila had picked out Gammil to be her messenger to Governor Wilder, and Gammil had not lost a full day in arranging an audience with him. Angela stood dazed by it all.

Worrying about the poor who need to get to jobs, worrying about the environment, historic preservation, the transportation needs of the public, these things carried no more weight than leaves floating in the breeze compared to the weight of political advantage. There won't be a bridge. My dream about Gammil coming to Lila's rescue was prophetic. Deep inside me, I knew the meaning of Lila's words from the moment I heard of them.

The sharp honking of a car's horn brought Angela out of her trance. It was John honking frantically in a state of frustration. "Over here, Angela," he yelled from across the roadway. She turned and walked rapidly toward the car.

"Did you find what you wanted?" he asked, opening the car door to help her.

"Did I," she answered as she climbed into the car. "It was a dream come true."

VII

Angela sat at her desk at Reuter's with sheets of papers and 4x6 inch index cards spread out before her. She was trying to piece together a story from the many notes she had taken while researching a subject, but for some reason, her mind would not stay put on the work to be done. She fidgeted restlessly with several of the cards, trying to get them in order, then dropped them on the desk and turned her chair around so she could look out at the glass walls and rooftops of New York's many skyscrapers.

The sky was dark and cloudy. Within minutes the air outside was flecked with small, lacy, particles of snow blowing in from the northwest. She rose from her chair and stepped to the window to look down at the street and sidewalk below. Umbrellas were being unfurled as heavily cloaked pedestrians rushed down the avenue, some trying frantically to hail taxicabs that seemed never to stop.

Moving back to her chair, Angela found herself thinking about Will. She felt a little thump in her chest and was sure that her thoughts were making her feel light-headed as well. It came as no surprise. She had been strongly attracted to him and felt sure that the draw had been mutual. She liked intelligent men. He was unmistakably that. She tried to bring forward a vision of his face but found herself thinking, instead, about his hands, strong hands with long slender fingers and neatly trimmed nails.

What a stupid wife he must have had to bug him about the kind of trousers he wore. That wasn't the real reason for their troubles though. It was just a story told to make light of things to others. Divorced people almost never tell the true story of their troubles, not to strangers. Do they know the truth themselves? Probably not.

Angela looked over at a smiling picture of her mother taken years before when she had played the part of a French can-can dancer for a Junior League Follies. It was a photo of happier days, before her mother had traveled down the long trail of continual abandonment that had plagued her through three marriages. Relaxing a bit she opened her mind to deeper thoughts.

Funny. I actually liked all three of her husbands. I will never understand how such nice men were able to hurt her so.

Angela reached down, opened the bottom drawer of her desk and pulled out a small folded leather case. Inside was a photo of her father in his Air Force uniform. She had loved her father, but that was long ago. She realized with a start that she had never heard his side of the story. He left one day, shortly after returning from the war in Korea. Just walked out to buy a pack of cigarettes and never returned.

The phone rang. Angela put down the leather case to answer it. "Angela Blount here," she said.

"Angie it's me, Cary. Have you got a moment?"

"Sure, Cary. Glad to hear from you."

"Will Rivers called John last night with the latest news on the

James River Bridge. You'll never guess what happened. The Commonwealth Transportation Board met in Winchester yesterday with the bridge as the chief item on its agenda. Everyone thought that the members were evenly divided as to those for and those against it, a cliff hanger so to speak. Will thought it highly probable that Secretary Milliken would have to step in to cast the deciding vote to break a tie."

"I can guess what happened, Cary."

"What?"

"The bridge was defeated by a large majority."

"You heard. I didn't think this would be of interest to the international press."

"What was the vote?"

"Fourteen against, one for it, and one abstention. The board voted to improve the ferry service instead. The bridge is dead in the water. Four Mile Tree is safe for at least another decade. The environmentalists and north side developers won. What a strange partnership."

"They didn't do it, Cary. It was all politics. The old guard that stood watch down there for generations has seen its power crumble. Senator Elmon Gray may be a powerful man, as they all say, but Governor Wilder is more so. When he decided to pound his fist down on the bridge building, the project was over. Things in Virginia aren't like they used to be."

"I'm not upset to see the bridge defeated, but Will is. He thinks the poor people of the Southside need it. He thought Wilder would be for helping them since most of them are black."

"Wilder had to keep control. It was racism through and through. That's a two-edged sword in politics, to be abhorred when used by the opposition but used at will whenever convenient."

"Another bit of news I heard will really interest you. It seems that Four Mile Tree may have found salvation in more ways than one. Gossip has it that Lila just came into some real money. She and the Reverend are about to embark on a serious renovation of Four Mile Tree. I even heard that Lila had called in a well-known landscape architect to see if the boxwood garden could be put back into its traditional shape. When all is redone, I bet she'll be inviting people in to share her pleasure in the old place."

"Hallelujah. It wouldn't accomplish much to save Four Mile

Tree just to have it fall apart."

"Do you think Lila influenced the outcome?"

"Maybe. Down through the ages women have put up a good fight to defend their homes. You can't fault her for that. I'm glad the bridge was defeated. At least Four Mile Tree will be around a while longer and visitors to Jamestown will look out on a river that looks much as it did in 1607 when the first three ships came sailing in. They won't have a 20th Century bridge cluttering up the view."

"Angie, the other thing I'm calling about is that Will wants to see you again. The bridge news was just an excuse for his phone call. He asked John when he thought you might be coming down to Richmond again."

Angela swallowed. She could feel her head growing fuzzy. A small tear suddenly emerged in the corner of one eye.

"I'd invite you down for Christmas, but we're much too involved with family then even to consider it. John suggested New Year's Eve. How about it? We'll make a reservation at the Country Club for the dinner dance and ask a few others, to make it fun, if you think you can come."

"Count me in, Cary. You're a doll."

"But, I'll only do this if you promise to be nice to Will. He's had his share of hurts too, you know."

"I promise to try, Cary, but you know I've tried unsuccessfully before."

"What could you find wrong with Will?"

"There's nothing wrong with him. The problem is with me. I'm prejudiced. At least, I understand it now, I think."

"You prejudiced?"

"Not racially prejudiced, sexually prejudiced. Men are so powerful and can hurt so badly. Both kinds of prejudice usually go back to our childhoods, you know. My childhood didn't produce happy memories of marriage."

"You'll just have to get an ax and chop up that hurdle that rears up screaming 'hurt' at you every time an eligible male walks near."

"I'll try."

"The party will be Black Tie. Buy yourself a pretty new gown."

"Black Tie? Do you think Will has any tuxedo pants with creases down the pants' legs?"

"Who cares? Will you make an effort, Angie?"

"I will."

"Start saying over and over again like the little engine that could, 'I can. I know I can.' You don't want to spend any more years alone, do you?"

"I'm never alone, Cary. I'm always surrounded by a myriad of friends."

"Really. Who?"

"The ones I've created in my writing. They're a great comfort to me, all my characters."

"They're not flesh and blood."

"Sometimes they seem to be."

"On that note I'll ring off. I'll call again when I get all this lined up. Bye, now."

"Thanks a heap, Cary. You're a great friend."

Angela hung up the phone. She sat quietly for a moment trying to assimilate all that was happening.

I've been devilishly mixed up about a lot of things. My heart doesn't belong up here in this mad, multi-million-man metropolis. Could Will be calling me back to old Virginy? Do I want to go?

A shrill siren cut through the background hum of sound from the street below. Its repeated high-pitched call became increasingly frantic, pleading with the cars and trucks, snarled in traffic, to move out of the way, but pathetically, the sound of the siren failed to move forward.

It's stuck, just like me, all laced up in traffic so that it can't make its way. I've been the same, all bogged down by childhood anxieties so that I can't move forward, can't find what I'm seeking. I'll put an end to all that. I'll start anew.

Oh how I'd love to go out and sit under the old Four Mile Tree, if only it were still there, and tell the age-old landmark of my new resolution. Surely, it would understand and help me to get onto a true course to happiness.

New Year's Eve. That should be a good time to start life anew. I'll ask Will to take me back to the spot in the water in front of Four Mile Tree where we thought the old tree might have stood. Some of the other cypress trees on the beach may have sprung from its roots. Nothing dies completely; it resurrects, sloughing off the evils of the past and reaching out for the good in the future.

The river has covered over all that could remain of the tree now, encompassing all that it once was, all that it once knew. The river keeps shifting with the tides, nourishing all that lives within it, quenching the thirst of the land beside it and caressing the secrets of all who live nearby. Nothing changes, it just keeps moving along. Yes, the river holds all the old secrets now and is waiting to embrace future secrets to come.